THE
RATHMORE
CHAOS

The Tully Harper Series Book Two

ADAM HOLT

D1598105

Text copyright © 2015 Adam Holt
Cover art copyright © 2015 Allen Quigley
ISBN: 1940873029
ISBN-13 9781940873022

All rights reserved. Published by Createspace in the United States of America. Edited by Kristen Ball (twitter @k_ball).

Visit adamholtwrites.com for more information on this novel, the author, and his other works. Visit allenquigley.com for cover art inquiries.

For my parents, friends, and family, who love me,
my editor Kristen and beta readers, who put up with me,
the readers, who read me,
and the universe that exceeds us all.

Thanks to Kickstarter,
where more than one hundred fine folks
pledged support for this work,
especially the Stones, my parents, James Turk,
and the Mike Dunns.
Your generosity inspires me.

ADAM HOLT

THE RATHMORE CHAOS

A TULLY HARPER NOVEL

THE RATHMORE CHAOS: A TULLY HARPER NOVEL

Part One: Ευρώπη   1

Part Two: Preparation   81

Part Three: "When you descend upon the Chaos"   123

Part Four: Icarus   215

Part Five: The Seventh Step   255

Little Bacon's Glossary of Terms   311

Character List   315

Afterword   317

About the Author   319

"Hope" is the thing with feathers -
That perches in the soul -
And sings the tune without the words -
And never stops - at all —
-Emily Dickinson

"Houston, We Have Problems": January 1, 2071

The black canyon stretched in front of me, one hundred yards from one frozen side to the other, a jaw ready to swallow me whole. The old Tully—the one who lived on Earth and tried to avoid homework—would never have dreamed of jumping this divide. The new Tully—the one who sneaks into space—could handle bigger problems, like leaping canyons. Also, the new me only weighed 15 pounds on this alien world. Nothing beats low gravity. As long as I hit my first step, I would leap the canyon with no problem, which I did, and waited on the other side for the rest of our team. The stars above me winked their approval.

If it had not been for the Ascendant, we would never have made it this far. Their lies made the Earth so dangerous that I had to leave. I should probably thank the Ascendant for that. I had never been closer to finding my long lost friend than I was at that moment, watching the others leap the canyon on the way to our destination.

The Rathmore Chaos.

My oxygen levels read 90%—nice—so I took a deep breath and watched several moons and planets bobbing across the horizon. I rubbed the backs of my scarred hands, which were supposedly my greatest weapon, but lately hadn't been reliable. I caught my reflection in my helmet visor—*who is this new me, this boy in a battle with a hostile alien race?*

One jumper then another landed nearby, and as our final team member sailed across the canyon, a tremor knocked us to the ground. In the middle of the canyon a geyser erupted, spewing liquid water hundreds of feet into the air. The water transformed into chunks of ice in the frigid air. Oh, no. Up went the geyser and with it went my friend, her arms flailing wildly – a bird beating its wings against an airless, alien sky. The rest of us jumped to our feet and bounded after her, and I hoped like mad for one thing—that my powers would return before she landed in this place of ice as sharp as knives.

The phrase, Houston, we have a problem, comes to mind. In fact, Houston, we have about a thousand problems, but we're millions of miles from you now. I can't explain this geyser disaster–or anything that came after it–unless I back up a few weeks. You know, when the world still thought I was a teen runaway, not a wanted space criminal.

Let me pick up this story in a news studio, right after my first trip into space, and fill you in from there. We'll work our way back to this canyon eventually, and then we'll travel well beyond it to where I am now, in the Rathmore Chaos.

Happy New Year,

Tully Harper

PART ONE: Ευρώπη

ASSASSIN SIGMA.
YOU HAVE RECEIVED YOUR ASSIGNMENT.
THIS IS OUR BEST CHANCE TO TAKE THE BOY.
ELIMINATE THE OTHERS IF YOU CAN.
PLEASE REPORT WHEN THE MISSION IS COMPLETE.
WE ARE ASCENDANT. WE ALWAYS RISE.
-GT

#FindTabithaTirelli

The bright lights of the news studio and one wild trip into space had clearly fried my brain. Otherwise, I would have noticed the figure who came alongside me on my way back from the news studio bathroom. One second I was alone in the bright hallway, trying to clear my mind. The next moment a man shoved me into a dark storage room full of dust and old cameras. He put something to my throat that glowed purple and felt cold. Then he locked the door and put one finger over his lips.

"Shhhhh," he said. "Do you want to live?"

This was the last in a long line of questions that I had faced that morning. There were a number of people on stage at the news conference, but the press focused on me. Hundreds of reporters fought for my attention. *Tully, in your own words, what happened?* My friends and I stole – er, borrowed – a hovercar. We ended up in the Florida Everglades. That's where Tabitha was abducted. *Why do you think the kidnappers are now after you?* Because Sunjay and I have seen them. Also, we injured one of them. He wants revenge. *Do you have any idea where they took her?* She could be anywhere. It's the one thing I want to find out. *If Tabitha were listening right now, what would you say to her?* That she should have faith. We will find her, no matter where she is.

There was so much of the truth in the lies that it hurt to answer. Tabitha was abducted, we were in danger, but she wasn't within a million miles of the Everglades.

Back to the cramped room and my assailant. His dark eyes gleamed beneath his baseball cap. *Do you want to live?*

"Of course," I said, "I have to find my friend, but I can't do that in here."

He tightened his grip. The edge of the knife felt like dry ice against my skin.

"Then why haven't you left?" he said.

"Uh, because you just locked us in this storage room," I said.

"Save your jokes for another day, Tully," he said. "You have to disappear. *They* are coming."

The way he said the word "they" didn't make me think of the kidnappers that we told everyone about. The fake ones that Sunjay and I escaped. No, "they" made me think of something much larger and darker, a predator with the power to enslave the whole human race. It made me think of the Ascendant. But what did he know about it? He was probably just a crazy fan of my dad and the Harper Device who thought the world was coming to an end. Either way, he could be right.

"Thanks for your concern, Guy with a Knife, but I'm under police protection."

He threw his head back and laughed. He took the knife off my throat, and that's when I got a better look at the blade. It had a familiar purple glow. There was an old television camera next to us, and with one flick of his wrist, he cut the entire thing into two pieces that clattered to the floor.

"Do you take me for a fool? I know the truth. You just returned from space. The Ascendant captured your friend on the far side of the moon. Rumor has it that you managed to steal the Sacred and cut off Gallant Trackman's hand. He wasn't very pleased with the outcome of his conspiracy game. No, Tully, they are coming for you. You delayed them, but you and the Sacred are in danger."

He closed the blade. The light from under the door dimly lit our faces. I was speechless. His words silenced me more than any knife or black staff could have. The Sacred. No one else knew the real name of the Harper Device.

"Who are you?" I asked him.

"I am no longer a friend of the Lord Ascendant," he said. "That makes us friends."

"Friends don't let friends play with alien knives," I said. "If we're friends, then tell me where Tabitha is. Where is the Ascendant home world?"

"Stop your search," he said. "Do not seek this place. It holds great peril. The Earth is dangerous enough. The Ascendant have many eyes here but little power. Still, all it will take is for Gallant Trackman to find the right assassin."

"Which is what you are?"

"What I once was," he said sadly, "and what I will no longer be. There are some orders I cannot follow, no matter what Trackman would pay me. Your death is one of them. Now I believe our time is up. You must go. May the Universe rise up to meet you, my young friend. We will not meet again in this life."

He walked to the corner of the room and flipped open his alien switchblade. Then he traced a perfect circle on the floor, and when that portion of the floor fell away, he disappeared into the hole.

He left me alone in the dark, no closer to finding Tabitha but determined as ever. She went into space because of me. She didn't return because of me. I would bring her home or die trying, and so would my dad and my friends.

I heard a knock at the door.

"It's locked," someone said. "Tully, are you in there?" I quickly covered the hole with a bucket and some dirty towels and opened the door. I found myself back in the bright lights of the hallway. A mob of people, including my dad, Sunjay, and Queen Envy, crowded around me. Cameras clicked and questions commenced. I ignored all but one.

"You okay?" asked Queen Envy. "You look like you've seen a ghost."

"Maybe I did," I said.

My dad grabbed Queen Envy and me by the arm and escorted us outside. The double doors opened and revealed a mob of fans and paparazzi waiting for the three of us – the pop star, the world's most famous astronaut, and his runaway son.

My dad and I hopped into a hovercar. Queen Envy and her entourage headed for a hoverplane nearby. Before she boarded the plane, she yelled back for me and held up her bracelet. "#FindTabithaTirelli," read the bracelet. Millions of her fans wore them. The hashtag was trending worldwide. It was the truth and the lie. She and I both knew the truth. Tabitha was farther away than anyone could guess.

"Don't give up hope," she told me. "Hope is the thing with wings, Baby Bear. You don't forget that."

It was the last time I saw Queen Envy for a long, long time.

AWAY TEAM BETA -
OUR ASSASSIN FAILED US.
PLEASE DEAL WITH HIM.
NO SIGN OF THE BOY.
RETURN TO SHADOW MODE
AND AWAIT FURTHER INSTRUCTION.
WE ARE ASCENDANT.
WE ALWAYS RISE.
-GT

THE CABIN BEYOND THE MIDDLE OF NOWHERE

After that alien knife to the neck encounter, my dad decided to shuttle Sunjay and I to a remote location. We had visions of islands in the Pacific or a rain forest in Peru. Instead he sent us back to the place that I wanted to escape from more than any other in the universe.

"The Middle of Nowhere," he explained. "Well, close to it. Your aunt has a cabin about ten miles from there."

"*Beyond* the Middle of Nowhere?" Sunjay said. "I was hoping for something with more, you know, seafood and coconuts."

"And I am hoping to keep you both hidden and alive," my dad said. "You can still holoclass into school from the cabin, and you can still search for Tabitha." He handed me some rolled up papers – maps of the solar system, the planets and their moons.

My dad ran his hand along his crew cut, which told me this was an order, not a discussion. The commander had spoken, so a few days later Sunjay and I found ourselves being ferried across the United States by hovercar, hyperrail, and plane until at long last my Aunt Selma picked us up in her ancient, gas-powered Jeep. We off-roaded our way through mud and snow to the cabin beyond the Middle of Nowhere.

So Sunjay and I followed orders and waited for it. Second Contact. The day that the Ascendant would come to Earth. In the meantime we holoclassed into Space City Junior High and did very little work on some pointless group projects. We kept a fire going and scoured our minds and the star maps in search of breadcrumbs that would lead to the doorstep of the Ascendant. There might be no way to get there, but at least we would know.

What did we know? Their home world probably had more water than land. The Ascendant were covered head to toe in tattoos, mainly of ocean scenes. Their ship was named after a species of jellyfish, too, as Little Bacon had once pointed out. Their world must also be active, maybe volcanic. The Sacred had used the word "chaos" to describe it. And, last but not least, we hoped that it was in our solar system. If it wasn't, the options were endless. So all that narrowed it down to—"

"—Four gas giants, two dozen moons, maybe some type of hollowed-out asteroid, or some giant alien something that no one has ever seen," explained Sunjay, pointing at the map with a fire poker. "About forty options in all."

"I'm tossing out the asteroids," I said, picturing my vision of Tabitha in a tall purple tower.

I tossed another log in the fire and flexed my hands. The lightning scars hurt in the cold, but I had to stretch them. *Use them and they will heal,* the Space Alliance doctor told me. He meant to do normal stuff and maybe cut some firewood, but I had something bigger on my mind.

"If I used my powers for a split second, I might have another vision," I told Sunjay. "I know what to look for now. I could find them." Sunjay poked the log and flipped his shaggy bangs out of his eyes.

"You put the Device to sleep for a reason," he said. "If you turn it on, won't you put the entire world in danger? It's not worth it. You made a promise to your daddy not to use your powers, so don't."

"I made a promise to save Tabitha," I said, but he was right. The last time the Sacred had been on Earth, it caused earthquakes and created a hurricane that flooded a city. What was next? A tsunami, a volcano, something worse? I didn't want the starring role in a natural disaster movie. I just wanted to find my friend.

"So what about Io?" he asked. "It's a moon with active volcanoes that circles Jupiter. Sounds kinda like a villain's lair. Lots of lava and rumbling volcanoes."

"What good are weapons if you don't use them, Sunjay?" I asked him. "My powers could help us."

"Oh, yeah, nuclear bombs are helpful, too. They're really good at blowing up cities."

My best friend compared me to a nuclear bomb. Awesome.

"If I could only go back and do it over," I said. "It's my fault. I closed the portal. I'm the reason that they captured her."

"You saved us all, Tully," he said. "We would all be dead or captured if it wasn't for you. You know that. Even now your daddy is telling the right people about this. They are preparing us for battle. Look, let's do the best we can with what we have. The commander said that."

Besides eating and Queen Envy, there's nothing Sunjay loved more than quoting my dad, and he's pretty quotable. My dad, who was in Switzerland at Space Alliance Headquarters thousands of miles away. He had told a select group of people about the Ascendant. They jumped into action and were gathering world support to defend against the alien attack. If that was even possible. Either way, it wasn't easy to explain – "Hey, Mr. Russian President, aliens exist. Oh, and they're coming to attack us" – but dad was getting it done. He had to.

Sunjay turned back toward the fire. He kept the fire going, and he kept me in check. These were his duties. If I were alone in the woods, I would have already frozen to death...or used my powers and doomed us all.

At that moment the door to the cabin flew open. Sunjay spun around, armed with the fire poker, prepared to battle aliens. Instead we saw Aunt Selma in her overalls with two axes slung over her shoulder.

"You boys are a little jumpy today," she said. "Looks like you're just messing around on a Saturday morning. You ready for some work?"

AWAY TEAM BETA –
STILL NO SIGN OF THE BOY.
THE DAY GROWS CLOSE.
WATCH AND WAIT.
YOU WILL NEED THIS.
-GT

PROFILE: TULLY HARPER
Height: 5'1" Weight: ~100LBS. Brown hair, brown eyes.
CAPTURE ALIVE
Subject weak compared to you—but he is most dangerous.
Limited skill in combat, but he has come into contact with the Sacred. You know what this means.
Treat him as you would one of the Encountered. We do not know his potential.
Do not give him time to think. His powers are unpredictable.
Do not underestimate him. I did.

Await further updates.
WE ARE ASCENDANT. WE ALWAYS RISE.

THE WHAT?

"Stars, did these logs have babies last night?" Sunjay said, grunting with every swing of his axe.

"What?" I asked.

"I mean, there are lots more little baby logs than I remember from last Saturday. The baby ones are harder to cut. Anyway, do we really need to cut them all?"

"It's either cut firewood or freeze to death," I said, tossing another chunk of wood onto the pile.

"What if we had a laser saw? We could program it to do the whole stack in half an hour. Then we could go inside and do what we should be doing on Saturday morning—playing *Cave-In!*"

Video games. That sounded dire good. I flexed my hands. Even with gloves, the lightning scars were sensitive to the cold. And stiff. Scars never seem to let you forget.

"Every time we chop wood, we get a little stronger," I said.

Sunjay chopped the air a few times with his axe. "Yes, for when the Ascendant attack! Second contact. We've got to keep training. I've been thinking up new moves."

"Right now we need to keep chopping baby logs, dude. My aunt said it's getting cold tonight."

"If it gets any colder, I'll be pooping ice cubes, Tully."

"Happy New Year," I said, grabbing a few logs and hauling them across my aunt's yard. Sunjay was distracted by his own sound effects, so I sneaked around the side of the house for a few moments of peace, watching the sun's first rays on Mt. Denali, a shark tooth gnawing on the Alaskan sky.

It was January 1, 2070. We had been there for two months.

I wondered what my dad was doing at that moment. He promised to inform us of what the Space Alliance had planned. I had kept my promises, but we hadn't heard from him in over a week.

The cold bit at my aching hands, so I rubbed them together and watched the north wind blow snow from the peak of Mt. Denali.

The front door of the cabin swung open, and my aunt called for us. "How's that wood pile treatin' you, Tchochtke?" My aunt had a new name for Sunjay every hour.

"Like it wants to kill me, Auntie."

"Well, you and Tullyboy better get in here."

From the tone of her voice, I picked up something was wrong. I sprinted around the house to her front door. "Is it news from dad?"

"No, it's breakfast, and it's getting cold."

False alarm.

We ate our caribou steak and egg breakfast. "Breakfast of champions," I said, picking at my food.

"And I am the champion of breakfast!" Sunjay said, inhaling his food like it was air.

"You know, caribou is just another word for reindeer," I said. "You're eating Rudolph right now."

He stopped inhaling for a moment. "Stop messing with me."

"No, it's true," I said. "He had a very shiny nose and you're probably eating it." After that, Sunjay slowed down a little and frowned at his food. It was early and I was cranky. *I'm a holstered gun. A weapon that no one can aim.*

We listened to the news on my aunt's ancient flat screen television. Every once in a while public service announcement appeared. It began with #FindTabithaTirelli and ended with a picture of the abducted girl: that dark hair, make-me-nervous perfect smile, and lovely green eyes.

We stopped eating. My aunt noticed. She popped a cassette tape into her stereo.

"What the heck is that?" Sunjay asked.

"It's a mix tape," my aunt explained.

"A what?"

"They were used for recording music back in the day. You've never heard of that?" she asked, turning up the music.

"Oh, I saw one in a museum last year. There's actual tape in that plastic box and the stereo reads it, right?"

"Yes, then you rewind it and flip it over. It holds about a dozen songs."

"That's hilarious," he said. "You'd have to carry a suitcase full of those if you wanted any kind of variety. Oh, and what about playlists?"

"A mix tape is a playlist. My mother always talked about how she met a boy at summer camp. She liked him, and he mailed her a mix tape later that year. It was full of love songs from the 1980's. Matter of fact, that was Tully's grandfather. She married that boy five years later." Aunt Selma showed Sunjay the mix tape, which had a big heart drawn on the front. It reminded me of one of Tabitha's doodles. Sunjay laughed hysterically.

"Stars, people used to do dire cheesy things!" Sunjay said. "But, you know, maybe I should make one for Queen Envy and send it to her. Do you think she would like it? Oh, I miss her."

"Speaking of dire cheesy," I said. For some reason the thought of mix tapes made me feel black inside, like a heavy weight settled into the pit of my stomach. I excused myself and wandered into my aunt's study. I caught a glimpse of myself in the full-length mirror. All feet five, one hundred pounds of me, with brown hair spilling out of my baseball hat. I needed to put on some muscle if I was going to fight the Ascendant. Beside the mirror there was a chest beneath a cot. I opened the chest and pulled out a tattered grey cloth. The moment I touched it, the cloth glowed faintly red. My half of Tabitha's mood scarf.

If I could send a mix tape to anyone in the universe, I would send it to you, but who knows where you are. The Sacred's words came back to me like a response: *You must pass through shadow and flame before you see her again.* I let my thoughts ramble and stared at the scarf in my scarred hands. It seemed to melt into a blur of color and image—from red to blue to purple, and then to a figure standing in a distant tower. Ever since the Sacred touched the scarf, it seemed to have a mind of its own, making images where only colors used to be. I wondered if it was real, if Tabitha really stood there in the purple tower, waiting for us to find her. And I wondered if she could see me kneeling beside the cot with half of her scarf in my hands. *Somebody show me to the nearest shadow and flame and let's get started.* This is why I left the scarf in the cabin. It was too tempting to touch.

"Yes, I have created a monster!" When Sunjay cheered it woke me up. I had nodded off with my head on the cot and the scarf in my hand. I wandered back into the room to find him holding his mix tape overhead in triumph.

"When Queen Envy hears this, she will forget all about Commander Harper," Sunjay beamed.

"Man, I hope so," I said.

"The sooner I get this into her hands, the quicker she will fall in love with me!"

And then it struck me.

"You're absolutely right. The time is now. Let's drive into town and mail Sunjay's tape!"

"Oh, please, Aunt Selma," said Sunjay. "You can't deny true love. I will kill every baby log in the whole forest if you will take us to town."

"Well, that weather will blow in by tonight," she said. My head fell, but she wasn't done. "I guess we'd better make this a quicker trip than usual. Let's take the plane."

"The what?" I asked.

Looking back on it, the fact that Aunt Selma had a plane was the least surprising thing that happened that day.

AWAY TEAM BETA –
THE DAY IS UPON US.
EXPECT UPDATES ON LOCATION SOON.
REMAIN IN SHADOW MODE.
-GT

PROFILE: SUNJAY CHAKRAVORTY
Height: 5'8" Weight: ~150LBS. Black curly hair, brown eyes.
CAPTURE DEAD OR ALIVE
Subject has some training in martial arts.
Immature; easily frightened.
Stronger than Tully but ineffective in battle.
Await further updates.
WE ARE ASCENDANT. WE ALWAYS RISE.

Second Contact

"You have a plane?" I said. "Why do we always take your crappy truck to town?"

"That's no way to talk about your Auntie's Jeep. I just prefer ground transportation is all," she said.

"Stars, I guess we should get some better breakfast food while we're there," I said.

"If you want to," she replied.

"But, but, but..."

"But you never asked politely like your pal Funday," she said. *All that time eating caribou and asparagus and stale biscuits. Stars, all I had to do was ask?*

Sure enough, on the far side of the lake from her house Aunt Selma had a hangar, and in the hangar a plane. "It's called a Piper Cub," she said, churning the old motor. "It's a pontoon plane. Your daddy and mamma used to love to fly this old thing when they visited." My dad flew spaceships. It was hard to picture him in this cramped cockpit. And with my mom? She was only a ghost to me.

We piled into the Piper. It smelled like grease, leather, and rust, but it worked. We taxied onto the lake, and in no time were bouncing through the air just as much as we would have on the road. Aunt Selma let us take turns at the controls. If the mix tape made his day, flying the plane made Sunjay's year. If there's anything he loves more than flying—well, it's Queen Envy and food, but flying is high on the list.

Aunt Selma took control close to town, she docked the plane, and we popped into the general store to mail the tape and pick up breakfast options. I hadn't thought about the Ascendant or Tabitha for hours, not until Sunjay and I sat down at the counter in the general store for a root beer float with a bag of gummy worms beside us.

The store had a LiveWall like the one at my house in Houston. It was huge, dusty, and wedged between two narrow mirrors. The college football championships were playing on the LiveWall. Then the screen went black.

Everyone, probably thirty people, mostly burly bearded men, groaned. Sunjay and I just shrugged and drank our floats. He started giving me advice on how to best fly a plane.

"Did you see how I did it, Tully? You've got to make little adjustments on the stick, even when it's bumpy. That's the key, my friend." I took a sip of my root beer and looked back at the screen in front of me. That's when I stopped him mid-thought.

"What's wrong?" he asked.

"Look at that LiveWall," I said.

There on the screen was a logo I had not seen since we returned from space—a crown with three rubies hovering over the Earth.

"What is that?" he asked. Everyone else murmured the same question. I turned my eyes from the LiveWall and in the dusty mirror saw my reflection—straight brown hair, tired brown eyes, and my face suddenly gone white. *So this is what I look like when the universe changes.* It wasn't any better than looking at the image, so I turned toward it again. That crown, with three sharp points and three blood red jewels, was a symbol of everything evil in the universe and everyone who betrayed me. The last time I had seen it was on a disembodied hand, cut from its owner when I closed the portal.

"Wait, is that?" but I stopped him cold. "Wasn't that on…?"

"—Gallant Trackman's ring," I whispered. "That's the Ascendant symbol."

"Second contact," he whispered.

"Second contact," I repeated.

But when the screen went gray and a face appeared, it was not the beady-eyed Gallant Trackman or the tattooed Ascendant Lord. It was the smiling face of a girl whose green eyes lit up the screen.

No Time for Smooth Landings

S he spoke.

"To the People of Earth, I greet you in the name of the Ascendant. My name is Tabitha Tirelli, and I am one of you. You may recognize me. You probably heard that someone in the Florida Everglades abducted me. This was widely reported; however, it is not true. The real story is more complicated: I boarded the spacecraft *Adversity*, piloted by Commander Mike Harper, along with Tully Harper and Sunjay Chakravorty, my classmates. They all returned from that journey into space, except for me. What I am about to tell you will change the history of the solar system."

Our school pictures appeared in the corner of the screen; our actual faces reflected beside them in the mirror. Sunjay and I froze. We needed to get out of there, but the crowd packed in tightly behind us at the bar.

Tabitha continued. "After we escaped into space, I was abducted by the Ascendant, a superior race of beings. Commander Harper sabotaged their ship while in space. Their ship, with me on board, hardly made it back to their home world, but we survived, and now I have a message to deliver to the world.

"For many centuries, the Ascendant observed us from afar. They admire our desires to better ourselves, to reach for the stars. And so the time has come: the Ascendant have decided to reveal themselves to us. And what's even better, they intend to live among us on the Earth."

All the gruff men at the bar looked confused. "Is this some movie trailer?" I wished that it were. The storeowner flipped the channel, but Tabitha's face appeared on every channel.

"I guess this is the real deal, gentleman."

"Time to stock up on food and ammo."

"Dangit, aliens. I knew it. I always told you they were out there, Bo."

"Shut up, Mark. The girl's still talking."

How is she keeping it together? Half this stuff is the truth and half is a lie—well, sort of. Tabitha seemed so calm and composed. Her acting skills saved us in space, and they only seemed to be getting better.

"The Ascendant asked me to speak on their behalf, and I agreed to speak for one reason: I believe they can help us build a better world."

Build a better world or be better slaves? They've threatened her, made her say this. I almost jumped off my stool. That would have blown our cover for sure, but Sunjay put a hand on my arm, whispering, "We need to hear this."

"The Ascendant know that it will be hard to find a place for them. The Earth is a crowded planet, but they come bearing gifts that will make it easier. Here are some samples." Tabitha described them—gene therapies for cancer, superfoods to end world hunger, all the electricity we would ever need. It was a perfect infomercial for the Ascendant, and like most informercials, it was too good to be true.

"The Ascendant will bring us all these good things, but they need something first—as a show of good faith from the people of Earth." A purple tower in a tall city appeared on the screen. In my visions I had seen this place! Lighting the top of the tower was a glowing red sphere. "You know this object as the Harper Device. By now many of you have already guessed the truth: it belongs to the Ascendant. Commander Harper took it from the surface of Mars, and he planned to hide it forever. The Space Alliance did not want you to know about this, but the Ascendant do. People of Earth, it is dangerous in the wrong hands, and so are the people who have handled it."

Our pictures appeared on the screen again. Everyone leaned forward to look at our photos. I put a hand on my forehead and looked down.

"So please," she continued, "before the Ascendant arrive, they request the Harper Device be returned to them, as well as Commander

Harper and his son. They came into contact with the Device, and it has infected them with an alien virus. They are a danger to themselves and to those around them. If you know their whereabouts, please text or call us at the number on your screen. You will be rewarded beyond your wildest dreams."

It was Sunjay's turn to jump. He bumped the man beside him, and the man elbowed him back. At that moment I actually felt radioactive, like I was contaminating everything around me, making these people guilty of crimes they did not commit, making them sick with an illness that no one understood. But another feeling rose to the surface: fear. I was smashed between fifty hunters in a general store, and now there was a bounty on my head.

"In the name of the Ascendant, I am signing off. To my mom and dad and brothers, and all my friends, I look forward to seeing you when the Ascendant bring me back to our shared home, the Earth. And to Tully, for all our sakes, return the Device. I know that you are mad and confused, but I still have faith...that you will turn yourself over to the Ascendant for help."

I still have faith. Her only pause. In the midst of all those lies, one glimmer of truth. *Those were your last words to me, Tabitha, but not that I would turn myself over. That I would fulfill my promise, and that's what I'm going to do... if I don't get captured first.*

Tabitha faded away: the crown and rubies appeared on the screen again. Then, like nothing ever happened, the football game appeared on the screen. Something had happened though. The people around us turned to their neighbors and began to talk. Sunjay and I huddled together.

"We're trapped," he whispered back.

"I noticed," I said.

"Looks like State scored," someone else said.

"Who gives a rip about State, Richard. Aliens are coming for Alaska."

"And they'll pay a bounty beyond your wildest dreams for that virus boy," said another.

"I dunno. My dreams are pretty wild."

The burly man beside Sunjay tapped him on the shoulder. Sunjay turned toward him, on instinct, and the man frowned. "You aren't from around here, are you?" But before he had time to ask any more questions, I heard several loud booms followed by dozens of high-pitched cracks like gunshots. Everyone in the bar ducked for cover. We looked out the window and in the middle of the street were about ten boxes of fireworks. They were exploding, Roman candles launching in all directions. Some people in the bar hit the floor. Some started laughing. A few ran outside to put them out with an extinguisher.

From behind I felt a strong hand on my shoulder grab me and tug me past the end of the bar and out a side door. In the other hand was Sunjay. We fought for a moment until we realized that Aunt Selma was dragging us down an alley and out to the dock where we landed the plane. Her boots thudded, heavy and quick, on the dock.

"Sorry, boys, but we may have to leave without getting that extra cereal," she said over her shoulder. We hopped into the plane. "And just to be clear, you owe me one hundred dollars for all those fireworks. I hate wasting money, but it seemed like the only way to get you outta there. You can explain about Tabitha and your alien problems on the way home."

On the flight back to her house we did our best to explain. It was a lot for Aunt Selma to take in. She nodded, frowned, but in the end simply said, "Well, that all makes sense. When I saw that video you all made about going camping in Florida, I thought, 'Tully isn't the camping type. Sunjay and Tabitha either.' Your daddy's not much of a liar, either. I knew you were up to something. Stars, you devilish boys, you went to space and your girl Tabitha joined up with some aliens. Now all I need to know is this: are you okay, Tully?"

"Of course not," I said. "The entire world is on a manhunt for me and I need to figure out how to save Tabitha, and I don't think Tabitha really believes—"

"No, not all that. I mean the virus thing. I don't care if you infected me, and I guess Sunjay would be just as bad off, too, but I just want to know if we need to get you some medicine. You drive me crazy sometime, Tully, but you're blood. I'd fly this plane to a proper hospital in Anchorage for you right now if you asked."

She kept looking straight out the window, but I looked at Aunt Selma for a moment, her eyes intent on the horizon, focused on keeping me safe even if it meant danger for herself. After a breath: "No, I'm fine. There is no virus, Auntie. They're just making up things. The aliens—I mean, the Ascendant—just want me back, and they want the Harper Device, too. To them it's a weapon. I know how to use it. Sorry we got you involved."

"What will be will be," she said. "Now go on and tell me the rest."

By the time I finished, we were almost back in Middle of Nowhere.

"Don't the Lord work in mysterious ways?" she said, looking over at me. She grabbed my seatbelt and gave it a tug. "Tully, you might want to tighten that. There's no time for smooth landings anymore." We took off longways on the lake, but we landed shortways. We buzzed the treetops on the far side, hit the choppy water with too much speed, and plowed into the shore in front of her cabin.

She bounded out of the plane and headed toward her woodshed. She kicked open the door, and before Sunjay and I could enter, two shotguns flew out from the darkness. I grabbed one and threw the other to Sunjay.

"You boys have taken gun safety classes in Texas?" she asked, but our reaction told her everything she needed to know. "Good grief! Fighting aliens but don't know how to shoot a shotgun. I'll give you a crash course then. Let's prepare for the worst."

"What's the worst?" Sunjay asked.

"Well, those boys at the general store will put two and two together. Then Goldcap or some prospector comes up here looking for information. He fancies himself a bounty hunter, but he's nothing more than a fur-trapping panhandler and propane salesman from Wisconsin. It probably won't come to violence because he's had a crush on me for years. I'll get you boys good and hidden before him or anyone else arrives."

My heart sank. We needed to find the Ascendant home world and rescue Tabitha. I needed to contact Dad. He would know what to do. Mostly, I didn't want to hide anymore, but we would have started running right then, we would have told Aunt Selma to fly us as far as the fuel would take us, if we knew what was coming.

AWAY TEAM BETA –
THE ANNOUNCEMENT IS MADE.
THOUSANDS OF LEADS ON THE BOY'S LOCATION.
TOO MANY TO EXPLORE.
A RESULT OF PANIC.
FLY TO DESTINATION THREE.
REMAIN IN SHADOW MODE.
- GT

PROFILE: MIKE HARPER, Space Alliance Commander
HEIGHT: 6'2" WEIGHT: 220lbs. Blonde hair with red streak, blue eyes.
Tully's father, finder of the Device, crippler of the Lion's Mane, formidable fighter and leader.
Do not engage him without support.

Worse Than Worst

Aunt Selma hid us in an abandoned mineshaft on the other side of the lake from her cabin. She peeled back several boards and we squeezed in. "Stay put," she told us. "I'll give you a sign when the coast is clear." We sat shivering with our guns in our laps and peeked through the slats at the woods outside—for about five minutes.

"We're too far back from the lake to see anything," I said. "Let's go." Sunjay shook his head. "Look, we can always sneak back here if we need to." I pried off a board and crept into the woods. He reluctantly followed. We retraced our steps through the snow to the far side of the lake in time to see my aunt go inside her cabin and turn out the lights.

"A shotgun is useless from here," said Sunjay. "I wish we had black staffs."

"Or I had my powers," I said.

We tried to stay calm, but I felt like a coiled spring ready to pop. Images of Tabitha on the LiveWall kept coming back to me. An alien virus? A reward for my capture? The Ascendant announcement proved just how brilliant and evil they were. They needed to capture me, but it was easier to turn that job over to the people of Earth with a well-told lie. "They're as clever as they are evil," my dad commented on our way back to Earth, and this proved the point.

At the same time their message gave us some valuable information. We had a few more weeks or months before they would arrive and cure us all of cancer and make us perfectly happy. And, more importantly, Sunjay and I knew more about their location—the purple tower from my dreams, an ocean surrounded by ice.

"Where are they, Sunjay?" I wondered aloud.

"It's a planet or moon with ice and oceans," he said. "That doesn't narrow it down that much."

"We've got to figure it out," I said. "We've got to get there."

"I know, but let's not worry about that now. I'm just glad they aren't here."

But somebody was. We heard the sound of gravel under tires. Just as Aunt Selma expected, the Ascendant's announcement inspired curiosity. Unfortunately, this visitor was only the first of many.

A shadow hopped out of the truck and approached my aunt's dark porch, banging loudly on her door with the butt of his gun. Then he stepped off the porch, pulled out a cigar, and turned toward the lake. He was covered in a mountain of matted furs and wearing buckskin boots. He looked more like a beast than a man, and as he lit his cigar, we saw his teeth glimmer.

"Ah, now I get the whole Goldcap thing," Sunjay said. "It's the teeth!"

Goldcap glanced over his shoulder at my aunt's closed door. Agitated, he called someone on his holophone. An image of another mountain man appeared over the water. They grumbled a few words before the image disappeared. Then Goldcap turned back toward my aunt's house.

"Who's he talking to?" Sunjay asked.

We found out. In the distance we heard the rumble of more trucks, and minutes later an entire posse of men and women stood outside my aunt's cabin.

"That escalated quickly," Sunjay said. We could handle one mountain man, but not an entire mob, nor could we run away from them. They knew the mountains better than we did.

"Selma, get yourself out here," Goldcap boomed. "I seen them boys at the general store and figured this all out. So we've come to collect them boys and our reward." No answer. "We don't want no trouble, Selma. We're just here to do the right thing."

No answer.

"This is all my fault." Sunjay's voice trembled. "If I hadn't been so crazy about sending that tape to Queen Envy, we would never have gone to town. If I hadn't wanted that root beer float so bad, they wouldn't know we were here."

Goldcap stepped toward Aunt Selma's door, but before he could knock again, the porch light flicked on and the door opened. He fell forward trying to knock and then straightened himself, looking a bit embarrassed. In her overalls my aunt leaned against the doorjamb, not that I could see much of her behind the bearskins.

For the next few minutes Goldcap and Aunt Selma spoke. She never changed position while he looked agitated, shifting back and forth and gesturing. The mob in the yard did the same. Tension mounted. Looking at all those men in their hides, a dangerous thought crept into my mind. *These men know how to track animals. They can track us. I might need to use my powers tonight to keep us free. That might cause some natural disaster, but to keep the world safe, I might have to endanger it.*

Still, Aunt Selma looked calm. The wind whipped snowflakes across the lake and muffled Goldcap's words, but tension was rising. We couldn't sit there any longer.

"Sunjay," I said, "this isn't going to end well. We have to strike first. It's time to move."

"But your aunt said to wait for a sign." Sunjay grabbed my arm.

"We survived an attack in space by the Lord Ascendant. We aren't going to let a mob of Alaskans take us down."

Across the lake my aunt examined her fingernails and blankly stared at that mob in her yard, looking unconcerned.

"But the sign..." Sunjay didn't finish his thought. We instinctively ducked as a silent shadow glided above our heads and across the water toward the cabin. Sunjay's eyes were as big as saucers, flying saucers. We both realized that the night had gone from worst to worse than worst.

"Okay, there's our sign. Now here's the plan. You take my holophone and I'll take the hologlasses. Let me know when you get to the other side."

We both took off through the snow around opposite ends of the lake, running flat out with lungs on fire. I lost view of the cabin for a few moments, and during that time I heard Goldcap's voice rise. There were screams, wild gunfire, and the sizzle of loose electricity.

I dove into a ditch as bullets whizzed over my head. They weren't meant for me. A purple glow came from my aunt's yard, and a red tentacle whipped back and forth over her cabin. The tentacle was as thick and long as a fire hose. The mob wasn't in the yard anymore but dangling above the yard in the clutches of the tentacle. They shot wildly at the alien ship, but the tentacle simply shook them until they dropped their guns.

The tentacle was attached to a black sphere covered in purple letters. It was a lesser version of the *Lion's Mane*, which had captured my dad's ship in space. My heart was in my throat. We had no way to fight such a thing.

The tentacle dropped its captives into the lake one by one. They swam for shore, drenched and swearing in fear. Only Goldcap hopped out of the water and screamed at the glowing black and purple spaceship.

"Hey, you alien scumbags, I thought we had a deal. Now where's my reward?" he yelled.

In answer, the ship lowered itself into my aunt's yard. A ramp appeared on the side of the sphere. Down the ramp walked what appeared to be an enormous man, dressed in a tunic and covered in swirling tattoos. An Ascendant warrior. He carried a black staff, and the ends buzzed with power. Goldcap aimed a shotgun at him, but the Ascendant wasn't concerned. He raised the black staff, and from fifty yards away, yanked the gun from Goldcap's hands. It flew toward the Ascendant, and he snagged it with one hand. The alien stood on the ramp weighing both weapons.

"Earther, you desire a reward?" growled the Ascendant warrior. "A reward you will receive. I will show you a better weapon."

The gun flew back toward Goldcap, who stumbled backwards. With another flick of his staff, the Ascendant tossed Goldcap over my aunt's cabin and into the woods. We heard a sickening crunch. There was a reason we called these guys black staffs.

The black staff hopped off the ramp and into my aunt's yard. Surprisingly he stumbled once and struggled to keep his balance.

"Watch your step, hon," my aunt said to him, "we don't want you getting that pretty outfit all dirty."

"The boys," he snarled. He walked toward her, standing eye level with her even though she was on the porch and he was in the yard.

"Sorry, I'm all out of boys. You want some coffee instead?"

Down the ramp came three more black staffs of the same size, shape, and attitude. I knew what was about to happen, and we couldn't allow it.

Temptation surged: *Use your powers. It's time. Wake the Sacred and it all becomes so easy.* I imagined what I could do: blast them with fire; toss them into portals that opened over the lake; sever that red tentacle and chop their ship in two. Finally, I yanked my mind out of it. *I might win this fight, but I might destroy something else. There has to be a better way.*

My hologlasses sprung to life. A text message from Sunjay: "That escalated some more. What now? I'm here." Across the yard I saw him wave and duck back behind the woodpile.

We didn't have much time but we had them surrounded. We couldn't shoot them. They'd see the flash and disarm us in seconds. We needed some luck, a distraction, something unexpected. I scanned my surroundings. Not much around but rocks. I grabbed the biggest rock I could throw. *It worked when David fought Goliath,* I thought. Then I remembered something.

"Sunjay, the Upthruster! It's leaning against the cabin," I texted back. "???"

"Grab my aunt and fly out of here. I'll distract them. 3,2,1. Go!"

I took aim as Sunjay made a run for the Upthruster. Then I chucked the rock at the nearest Ascendant's head. It was an awesome shot. The only thing was, at the same moment, several things happened.

A deafening boom came from the woods. A shotgun blast and a roar to go with it. One Ascendant hit the ground, but it wasn't because of my rock. He spun and fell, and the other Ascendant turned to face Goldcap, who flew out of the woods in a limping rage.

My aunt took advantage of the situation. She reached behind her door, grabbed an axe, and hit one of the Ascendant in the leg. He roared and staggered as the other two took on Goldcap.

Sunjay swooped in and Aunt Selma scrambled onto the Upthruster. They flew toward me. I dropped the gun and grabbed onto the railing of the Upthruster. Sunjay tried to pull me on, looking back at the cabin in fear as we blasted off into the woods. I held on to the rail for dear life. Whoosh! A purple flash sailed over our heads and hit a tree in front of us, sending purple sparks and wood chips everywhere. I looked back and watched as the wounded Ascendant shot at us from his knees. The others were still grappling with Goldcap. We flew over a mound of snow and the scene disappeared.

"To the mineshaft!" Aunt Selma yelled, pointing to a small gap in the trees. Sunjay did his best to steer the board toward the gap, but we were above the suggested weight limit and flying low. We narrowly avoided a dozen trees at every turn. Only four feet off the ground, I half-ran, half-bounced as we sped through the forest. Every bush threatened to knock me off. We flew like this for a minute before my aunt said, "Shut this thing down before you kill us!"

Sunjay pushed the back of the board down and we came to an abrupt halt that sent him and Aunt Selma sprawling. Since I had been holding on to the side of the board, I landed softly with the Upthruster in my hands. I tucked it under my arm and put my index finger to my lips. Shhhh. We were a quarter mile from the cabin now, and with any luck, the Ascendant did not have time to track us.

"Now get your tails in that mineshaft and stay this time," she said. "I'll be right back. Gonna make a track to divert these idiots." She tramped back to our landing point, covered our tracks, and hiked up the ridge behind us, making a new set of tracks. Having a survivalist for an aunt isn't so bad sometimes.

The wind began to die and snow continued to fall. I examined our new hideout more carefully. The mineshaft's entrance was a dusty space the size of our living room back in Houston. Sunjay produced his holophone and put it in flashlight mode so we could see further back. The only point of interest was a tattered American flag covering something in the corner. Sunjay wandered back to inspect it, unveiling several wooden boxes that showed the same word: "DYNAMITE."

"We can blow up the Ascendant, like in cartoons," said Sunjay. He started to open the top of the box, but I jumped up and threw the flag back over the explosives.

"Great, but let's not blow ourselves up for no reason," I said. "Old dynamite is unpredictable." He shined his light deeper into the cave and we saw nothing but rubble.

"Huh, cave in," said Sunjay, "or maybe someone covered the entrance. Hey, it's like the video game! If only we had a portal gun, we could portal ourselves to the other side."

"The point of *Cave-In!* is to escape, not to trap yourself deeper in the cave," I said.

Cave-In! The thought of my favorite video game sent me back to my couch in Mission Control, knee-to-knee with Sunjay and Tabitha. Before we sneaked into space. Before we got split up. When life was simple: friends, a couch, and a video game. That simple life was gone, and in its place was a complicated world full of lies, risks, and dangers—but also hope.

"Hey," Sunjay said, "don't get any crazy ideas, Tully. No powers. You promised."

"You're the one reading my mind," I said, looking at the scars on my hands. "Why not, Sunjay? Just make a portal out of here and back to my aunt's cabin. Then toast those clumsy barbarians and get out of here. Seriously, what good are superpowers that you can't use? If I call on the Sacred, I can get us out of here. I know I can."

He shook his head. We both knew it wasn't that simple. I nodded and shoved my frigid hands in my pockets. We heard snapping twigs outside the mine entrance. I pinned myself against the wall and held my breath, but it was only my aunt. She replaced the boards and joined us.

"Sakes' alive," my aunt said. "You should've told me those aliens had magic purple batons. Big, clumsy, and angry. Like a bunch of possessed cheerleader bodybuilders they are." I had a mental image of the Ascendant twirling batons in cheerleader uniforms, with their fierce tattooed faces. I almost laughed out loud. Danger and adrenaline do weird things to your brain. The frigid temperatures brought me back to reality. We grew silent. Our breathing settled down and teeth chattered.

Man, I would rather fight the Ascendant anywhere else. We could lose a few fingers from frostbite before the battle starts. I tried to picture them again, this time without the cheerleader unis. And something struck me about the Ascendant.

Clumsy. One of them fell off the ramp; another struggled to get his footing against Goldcap. In Earth's gravity they were muscular monsters but not very coordinated.

Aunt Selma had managed to hold onto Sunjay's gun. She found an old pickaxe and handed it to Sunjay, making an attack motion to show him it was a weapon. I was unarmed but still wearing my hologlasses. I turned them on. There was plenty of battery and a signal, so I blinked through my contacts list until I found my dad's number. I blinked again and the call went through, his face flashing in front of my eyes. The call would probably give away our location to the authorities, but it was worth the risk. Unfortunately, the call went straight to voicemail. I thought about calling the police, the FBI, the Space Alliance, a dozen other people, but what would I say? "Hey, it's me, the boy with the alien virus. I'm under attack in the woods. Could you come save me?"

And what would they do when they found me? Whether someone saved us or captured us, we wouldn't be free anymore. And if I weren't free, I couldn't save do the only thing that mattered to me.

No, the Ascendant had isolated us. We would fight them alone.

A Slice of Normal in a Pie of Weird

We shivered in silence, listening for snapping twigs. All the while I kept my dad's number on my hologlass display and called it every few minutes just to hear his voice, deep and full, on the voicemail. "You've reached Commander Mike Harper of the Space Alliance. I'm on assignment in Switzerland currently and will return your calls as soon as possible." I decided to call him one last time, to leave him a final goodbye message before the Ascendant found us, but something went wrong.

As I was blinking my eyes to make that final call, an incoming call appeared on the screen at the last moment. I couldn't stop the blink and accidentally hit "accept" instead of "decline." Dangit.

The caller wasted no time in hologramming me into a room. The mineshaft disappeared, and I found myself transported into an unlikely location: a tidy bedroom with framed artwork on the walls, stuffed animals on the bed, and an Upthruster in the corner. That should have told me everything that I needed to know, but the shift disoriented me. Whose room was this?

"Behind you, Tully." There, Janice Chan, my classmate, leaned against her desk, looking stressed. Or was it angry? She adjusted her black-rimmed glasses, narrowed her eyes, crossed her arms, and tapped her foot. I was speechless.

"Don't just stand there with your mouth open and your teeth chattering," she said. "Sit your hologram butt down." She pointed to a chair and I did as instructed.

"Uhhh, why are you calling me, Janice?"

"Seriously? Tully, you're in huge trouble!"

"The entire Earth knows that," I said.

"I'm not worried about the Earth. I'm worried about our group project! You and Sunjay haven't done a thing yet," she said. She waved her hand and the assignment details popped up on the hologlasses: "Remember the Three for Survival Project? Instructions: Find and research three places in the solar system that can support human life. Then present your plan with your partners in class."

Was I ever in school? It was like a forgotten dream from another life, but it was as real as an Ascendant warrior to Janice. Somehow she didn't know that I was the target of a worldwide manhunt.

"School's not that high on my priority list right now, Janice," I said.

"Bangers!" she said, throwing up her arms. "It's a third of our grade this semester. That trip to Florida toasted your brain!"

"Probably true," I said. "Look, this isn't a good time. I guess you didn't hear the big announcement?"

"What big announcement? Like you and Sunjay are messing around with my uncle's Upthruster, not doing any work?"

"Wait, how did you know that?" I said a bit too loudly. Dr. Chet Chan was Janice's uncle. Their family was full of genius scientists and inventors. Aunt Selma put a hand on my arm to quiet me.

"Ha!" Janice said, proud that she had figured us out. "I knew it. You and Sunjay are in Hawaii, sitting on the beach drinking milkshakes and Upthrusting yourselves to death. My uncle would not approve."

"Of course he wouldn't. But you didn't hear the stuff about—oh, never mind. Go on." I decided to let her vent. It was like a slice of normal in a big pie of weird.

"So, I locked myself in my room after school, just me and a cup of chamomile tea, and did this." She flipped off the lights. In her room a number of planets and moon appeared, bobbing in front of my eyes. "I've found holographic maps of half the moons in the solar system all by myself, and I could do the rest all by myself and get an A for our group. But. But I just won't do it. It's time you and Sunjay do something other than travel around and have fun."

"Believe it or not, Sunjay and I might know something about this project. Maybe not as much as you, but listen, some stuff happened today—"

"Oh, stuff happened! Sorry to hear that. My life is soooo boring and stuff never happens to me."

"I didn't mean it like that," I whispered. "We really want to contribute."

"Listen, I know you are sad about Tabitha. I respect her a lot and hope we find her. Everybody does. But you, Tully, have to keep moving on, and right now 'moving on' is finishing—or starting!—the Three for Survival Project. Tabitha would want you to do that. That's why I chose you and Sunjay as partners. I'm the responsible one in group projects. That's my reputation. And you two guys are as flaky as my stepmom's croissants. That's your reputation. If I have to supervise you guys every step of the way, then that's what I'll do."

Janice finally finished her rant.

"Janice," I said, "I'll see what I can do. I know that's a bad answer, but if you don't hear back from me tomorrow, you'll understand why."

"Oh, you'll hear from me," she said, pulling her hair back in a ponytail.

"Either way," I continued, "you should know that you're a great group partner."

Her expression softened for a second, like the compliment had hit home. It was true, and we both knew it, but she shook her head again.

"You know, Tully Harper, you're smart when you want to be. I know life is a mess for you and Sunjay, and I want to help you out. I want you to impress everyone with this project, but you've got to pull your weight."

Pull my weight, I thought, sitting in Janice's room, but I wasn't really there. I was in a mineshaft beside Sunjay with his pickaxe and Aunt Selma with her shotgun, and me with nothing in my hands to fight the Ascendant—all of us huddled together. I wanted to pull my weight more than anything.

"That's all I ever try to do," I told Janice. "Just send us a to-do list or something. We'll get something done."

"Ciao, then. I'm off to bed," she said.

Click.

Janice, that slice of normal, disappeared. It was nice to feel like the old me for a moment—assignments, grades, stressed out group partners. I wanted to stay in her room longer, not because of the warm fuzzies, but because of her holographic maps. Those might have come in handy. I should have asked something about them. She might have better guesses about the Ascendant's home world than Sunjay and me.

Then the whole weird pie returned. Somewhere nearby a twig snapped in the woods. Snow crunched underfoot. Murmurs in a foreign tongue. I pocketed my hologlasses and flexed my hands.

SHADOW IN THE SNOW

A soft purple glow lit the inside of the mineshaft. We peeked through the slats and saw the source—a black staff on his way up the ridge. Another one appeared a few hundred yards to the right. The hulking figures clomped through the snow in heavy snow boots and tunics. They would have looked silly, but their arms were bare and flexed, holding those "magic batons" in front of them. *Stars, they should be popsicles by now,* I thought.

The Ascendant in front of us moved methodically. When his black staff glowed more brightly on one side, he turned that way. It seemed to be guiding him toward something. Straight toward us? He said something to his partner in a low grumble, and then produced a small globe that floated into the air. Like a Chinese lantern, it lit the forest. He scanned the ground and headed past us, following his lantern…and the track that my aunt had created. Her diversion worked. Finally some good news! I felt relieved, hearing him thump past us in the snow, but Sunjay grabbed my arm. I had taken my eye off the other black staff. He was moving in from the right under cover of darkness.

Lit by his staff, he was a dark phantom against the snow. We backed away from the entrance as he approached, his staff buzzing. Then he stopped a few yards from the mineshaft.

Sunjay tightened the grip on his pickaxe. Aunt Selma raised the gun to her shoulder. And I, well, I thought about the color red. *Red, red, red, red, red.* That sometimes brought on the power. No luck. The only color that filled my mind was gray, the only picture a gray sphere—the sleeping Sacred. How much would it take to awaken it before this Ascendant was upon us? The temptation rippled over my skin like the Ascendant's tattoos, and my hands felt warmer. It seemed that the Sacred started to dimly glow, like a spark still alive in a dying coal. That power still lived in me, too. It was ready to burn its way to the surface and light this forest on fire if it needed to. *And it does!* I thought. *It's time. I won't let them take anything else from me.*

Plink! A sharp noise interrupted the vision. Sunjay had his hand on my shoulder. *Nooooo!* He mouthed to me, like he could read my mind. He was right. I could burn down the forest. Harm was as likely as good. But what had caused the sound? On the ground beside him was his axe.

The Ascendant must have heard it fall. He stepped out of view of the front of the mineshaft and positioned himself directly above us on the ridge. His staff buzzed. Then boards on the front of the shaft began to creak. Words in a strange language. Then one of the boards flew off as if an invisible hand ripped it aside. Then another. Sunjay had revealed our location. Or I had. Either way, another nail pulled away and then a board, but the Ascendant stopped. He yelled again. Something was wrong.

A small avalanche of snow flowed down the mountain from above, and then the Ascendant tumbled down the hill with someone else. The someone else yelled. The Ascendant grunted. A fight began. We heard a thud and another thud as they rolled down the hill.

"Now or never!" Aunt Selma yelled. As quick as a comet, she dove through the opening of the mineshaft and we followed. What we saw amazed us. A cloaked figure grappled with the massive Ascendant. It didn't look like a fair fight, but the Ascendant struggled to stay on his feet, even though he was a foot taller and broader than the shadow figure. Aunt Selma charged toward them. The Ascendant saw her coming and, with a powerful thrust, he tossed the stranger aside, aimed the staff at Aunt Selma, and blasted her into the woods.

The stranger swept the Ascendant's feet and pounced on him. They tussled in the deep snow with the staff between them, the stranger's cloak flying. Finally, the stranger raised his knee to the black staff. It cracked and shot sparks. With nothing between them, the Ascendant grabbed the other man in a bear hug and squeezed. Both of them let out cries.

Now or never is right! I thought, looking at my friend. Sunjay tossed the pickaxe aside and threw a jumping kick at the Ascendant. With the stranger still in a bear hug with one arm, the Ascendant grabbed Sunjay by the face before the kick landed. He laughed. Then he threw Sunjay into the snow. I ducked behind a tree, reached into the deep snow, and found a softball-sized rock. *Why not?*

I was a few feet higher up the mountain, so just like the shadowy figure had done, I leapt from my perch. The rock I held above my head, and with a scream, brought it down upon the Ascendant's head.

"Arrrghaaaahhh," he said, which must be Ascendant for "concussion." He staggered and released the stranger who finished what I started: an uppercut that snapped back the alien's head. The Ascendant crumpled. The stranger stood over the Ascendant for a moment and then wheeled toward me. I threw the rock at his head but he dodged it and took a step toward me.

"Tully, the enemy of your enemy is your friend," he said. With that, he threw back the hood of his cloak. It was then that I could see his profile: a stiff jaw, stern eyes, and a red-streaked crew cut. It wasn't Goldcap. It wasn't a stranger at all.

It was my dad. We heard a birdcall from nearby and moments later Buckshot Lewis appeared, wearing a snow-covered cowboy hat.

"You took down the other one?" my dad asked. Buckshot nodded and produced a package of zip ties.

"Just like calf ropin', cap'n," said Buckshot, tying up the stunned Ascendant and throwing his hands in the air when he finished. "Y'all could've saved some of the action for me here though."

"How the?—" I started, shaking my head in disbelief.

"Sunjay, you okay over there? Selma?" my dad asked. They limped toward us with their weapons. I tackled my dad in a bear hug into the snow.

"Stars, I have missed this face," my dad said, smiling at me. Then he grimaced. "Easy, Tully. I may have a cracked rib. Not sure."

"But, but you're both in Switzerland." I was so confused.

"Apparently not. Sorry that we couldn't call ahead. I'll explain later. So we knocked out two Ascendant. How many remain?"

"One alien ship and one more ugly," said Aunt Selma, grimacing. "I think Goldcap shot the fourth one."

"That's good news," my dad said. "We'll leave him for the Alliance." Then he walked toward the mineshaft.

"Uh, dad, that's the wrong way," I said. "Dad?"

He ignored me and scrambled up the hill into the mineshaft. He emerged with a box of dynamite wrapped in a faded American flag. I jumped back.

"Dad, you trying to kill us? That's dire dangerous," I said.

"More dangerous than you know," he said. "Help your Aunt Selma. She's limping pretty bad."

On the way back to the cabin we made a plan to take out the remaining Ascendant. I would "give myself up" because I was voted "least likely to be killed." Great title, right? Then the others would surround the Ascendant and attack.

"No explosives?" I asked my dad.

"Nope," he said, patting the box of dynamite. *Patting dynamite. That can't be a good idea.*

The whole thing sounded like bad really, but we didn't have to put our terrible plan into action. When we reached my aunt's cabin, her front yard was a battlefield of trucks and trees and holes in the ground, all smoldering and smoking. The alien ship looked undisturbed, but the Ascendant and the mob were nowhere to be seen.

"What happened?" Sunjay asked.

My dad came upon a clue in the wreckage. There were two black staffs strewn beside two piles of dust. No, ashes.

"Someone incinerated our enemy," my dad said. "See, look at the footsteps here. He came from the woods and took them out before they could react."

"So Tully has alien friends, too," said Aunt Selma.

"No way," I said.

"You've got one, as I recall," my dad said. He reached down and picked up a black handle. When he pushed a button on the side, a glowing purple blade appeared in his hand.

Chills went up my spine. Someone did save us. The same someone that cornered me in the newsroom. My guardian alien angel. He had once been a devil. He was paying his dues for all the bad things he had done.

Aunt Selma tried to take a step forward and her leg buckled. She cursed. Now that we were in the light, I could see the burn marks on her leg from the Ascendant blast. My dad took a look. It was worse than we thought. I could smell the burns and remembered how it felt to be burned. I stretched my scarred hands. The Sacred's words came back to me: *You must pass through shadow and flame before you see her again.*

"There's no time to waste," my dad said, looking at Aunt Selma's wounds. "We're getting you to a hospital."

"Too much danger and distance," she grunted. "You and Buck take the plane and the boys and get out of here. Leave me, Mike."

"No," he said.

"There's no other way," she said. "I can tough it out."

"Not a chance," he said.

I looked around: the only transportation we had was a half-burned truck and Aunt Selma's old plane that couldn't hold the five of us. Even if we left her and took the plane, chances were we would be captured upon landing. I felt so hopeless: the best we could do was escape for a few hours before someone recognized alien virus boy and his friends. But I was missing something. It was in the defiant look in my dad's red-flecked eyes—a look that told me this wasn't the end of anything. This was the beginning. The very beginning.

He addressed us all. "You're thinking that we are going into hiding. You're thinking that they will catch us tonight, aren't you? Well, if we get caught, it won't be tonight. It won't be tomorrow. If anyone catches us, it won't be within a million miles of here."

I was confused. My dad doesn't exaggerate. It wasn't until I saw him move that I understood his plan. Carrying the box of dynamite wrapped in the American flag, my dad turned away from us and toward the alien ship. He mounted the ramp and disappeared into the side of the ship. Sunjay scrambled after him. Buckshot and I supported Aunt Selma and we made our way toward the ship. No one hesitated.

Some people you just can't stop following—not because of where they are headed, but because of who they are.

AWAY TEAM BETA –
MOVEMENT NOTED.
PLEASE REPORT ON STATUS OF LOCATION THREE.
- GT

ALIEN CONTROLS AND HOSPITAL VISITS

"Okay, okay. Just slow down, Sunjay. I'll answer your questions," said my dad, "but first we have to learn how to fly this ship."

From what we could see, the Ascendant ship's interior was one dome-shaped room with a flat circular floor, all done in black and purple. It was no larger than a living room and a lot less comfortable. Around the room ran a black ledge that acted as a bench. You had to lean forward to sit. My dad and Buckshot motioned for us to sit down while they felt along the walls above our heads. A purple light lit the whites of their eyes as they inspected.

My dad ran his hands along the smooth walls for clues to the ship's controls. Every so often a symbol would glow at his touch; a compartment would open when he touched the symbol. We fidgeted on the uncomfortable benches watching him open drawers and bins full of weapons, spare parts, and alien doo-dads.

"This isn't a ship. It's a clown car!" said Sunjay. "How do they all fit in here?" It was hard to believe the giant Ascendant flew across the universe in such a small ship. It was a fraction of the size of the *Lion's Mane*.

"Let's just call it the *Mini-Mane*," Sunjay said. That name stuck.

"Hey, Dad," I asked, "while you're walking in circles looking for the steering wheel, could you tell us how you both got from Switzerland to

Middle of Nowhere, Alaska so fast?" I asked. "Did you steal a plane or something?"

"That would have been a bad move," he said, continuing his inspection. "The whole world is on high alert for any suspicious activity now. A stolen plane flying out of Space Alliance Headquarters would have drawn attention. And if they figured out that it was Buckshot and me? The Alliance would have detained us, and I needed to stay free." *Exactly,* I thought. "Everyone at HQ focused on the Ascendant message, so we left while we had the chance. I figured that the Ascendant might find you, and there was only one way to get here quickly—a hypertube."

"No way!" said Sunjay. "I've never ridden a hypertube! What's it like flying underground in a vacuum tube at 800 miles per hour?"

"Hypertubes are terrible," Buckshot said. "No windows, hundreds of feet underground, and it's about the size of a coffin. Heck, it is a coffin!"

"But it's quick," my dad said. "Two hours from Geneva to Moscow and five hours from Moscow to Anchorage. Then we, uh, borrowed a truck and drove the rest of the way here. Just in time, too."

"Ah, we could have taken 'em," Aunt Selma wheezed, stretched out on the bench beside me.

My dad found another symbol on the wall and a black staff appeared above my head. I ducked, half expecting to be thrown sideways.

"That looks familiar," said my aunt.

"But it won't get us out of here," my dad said. He didn't bother with the weapon. He kept searching for an ignition switch. *Just our luck. We're in a perfectly good spaceship with no set of keys. Maybe I can help.*

I closed my eyes and tried to picture the *Lion's Mane,* but we spent so little time on board that ship. I recalled the Ascendant Lord standing in the center of his Command Deck with his hand outstretched. Maybe that would work.

I started looking on the floor, and that was the key. Two gray footpads. I hopped up and stepped on to them, which made them glow. Then I stretched out my hand like the Ascendant Lord.

"Tully?" Dad frowned at me.

Out of nowhere into my hand fell a heavy glass ball the size of a paperweight. It had a mind of its own, pulling my hand forward, and as it did so, a holographic map appeared—a projection of the Mini-Mane and my aunt's cabin. There was a small platform extended from the side of the glass ball. With my index finger I pushed the platform into the glass ball. As I did so, I heard a hissing sound. The *Mini-Mane's* platform retracted and closed. *Crystal controller*, I thought. *Classy!*

"Just kill me now, Tully!" yelled Aunt Selma.

"Easy, son. No sudden moves," my dad said. I released the crystal and it hovered in mid-air, surrounded by the holographic map. Cautiously I took the crystal, cold and heavy, in my hand again. "That's it, son. Why don't you fly us out of here?" It was worth a shot.

"I need a bigger map," I said, turning back to my dad.

"Try to stretch this one," said Sunjay. "I bet that it's intuitive, kind of like your hologlasses. Just use both hands. I can try, if you want."

"I got it, Sunjay." I cradled the crystal in one hand. Then I reached toward the map with the other. The map expanded out and out and out: we could see the Pacific Ocean, the curve of the Earth, then the Moon and several asteroids. The map just kept growing. It was like hearing the ocean in a shell, and then looking in the shell and seeing an actual ocean. My mind wobbled with the enormity of truth. *It's a universe map!* A map bigger than our solar system was resting at my fingertips and filling this small ship, and we, we were floating in front of my aunt's house, but we were also circling a star that was flying through outer space in a dim part of the Milky Way. *Where are you hiding out there, Ascendant? Where are you, Tabitha Tirelli? Just tell me. The universe is in my hands.*

"Tully, we can mess with the map later," said my dad, snapping me back to our tiny chunk of reality. "Find a hospital for your aunt."

"Of course, yeah. Nothing is labeled," I said. "Why would the Ascendant label hospitals on their universe map?"

"Try the hologlasses," said Sunjay. I put them on. The words "CONNECTED TO UNKNOWN DEVICE" flashed in front of my eyes. I blinked a few times. Suddenly the map filled with street names and locations. Even sushi restaurants with helpful reviews. From the Milky Way to sushi. Stars, I was hungry.

"That's it!" I said. "They can play together. Hologlasses, show me hospitals in Anchorage." The map flattened out and gave me an overview of Anchorage with a list of glowing blue crosses above several large buildings. "Here's one."

"Oh, I don't need labels to read a map," said Sunjay. "There's the harbor. There are a bunch of restaurants down there. Here's the medical center. I bet there's a hospital right about here." From his seat, Sunjay pointed to the correct location. I knew that he had a great memory for maps, but stars, this confirmed it!

"Between the two of you, I think things are under control for now. Set a course. Just start slow, keep us low, and stay off the radar. Everyone will be nervous about alien ships passing by."

"Oh, you think?" I said, carefully lifting the crystal, and as I did so, the *Mini-Mane* rose into the sky just above the mountains. With the other hand, I slowly pointed toward Anchorage. Harnesses popped out of the walls and everyone strapped in. With each inch I extended my hand, our speed increased smoothly. There were no windows, so we all watched the hologram. The cabin disappeared. Our eyes turned toward the horizon.

Flying the ship wasn't very tricky. It was just a matter of standing still and concentrating on the flight path. My feet controlled the yaw and pitch. My hand controlled up, down, side to side, sort of like that "mouse" thing that old computers used. After a few minutes my dad decided it was safe to unstrap and explore the rest of the sphere.

"I think it's a scout ship," he said. "Limited weapons, unknown power source and propulsion system. The Ascendant will expect contact soon."

"Then they'll see that we took their ship?" asked Sunjay.

"Possibly. We don't know what they know. We need to get a step ahead of them, so we need to disable any sort of tracking or communication systems they use. Since the Earth isn't their home world, let's hope they can't track us very closely. Even if they can, there will be a delay in communication. That will work in our favor but only for so long."

Our trip from Middle of Nowhere to Anchorage was a blur of forests, roads, rivers, and snow. Sometimes the ship lurched one way or another, and moments later we would skim past a radio tower that I could never have avoided.

Finally we sailed over a ridge and saw the lights of Anchorage. The ship pushed back on my hand to slow us down. Moments later we flew over a few skyscrapers and found ourselves hovering over a rooftop. A cross with the letter "H"—it was easy to spot the hospital's helicopter pad on the roof. I extended my index finger and the ship lowered its platform.

"This must be my stop," Aunt Selma said, pointing down the platform. "Tully, I have something for you." She reached into her overalls pocket and out came an envelope with my name written on it. *A letter? What's that all about?* "Open it later," she said, "when things settle down."

"If that ever happens," I said.

"It will, Tullboy. Just give it time."

I took the envelope; she gave me a hug with one arm around the neck. Then my dad helped Aunt Selma down the platform and onto the rooftop.

There was one nurse in scrubs taking a smoking break and waiting for helicopters to arrive with patients. I looked down and watched as my dad handed off my aunt to him. He looked baffled for a moment.

"How did you guys get on the roof?" he said. Then he looked behind my dad and saw the *Mini-Mane* silently looming above him. The cigarette fell from his mouth.

"That's a nasty habit, son," my aunt told the nurse. "Now make yourself useful and get me downstairs. Got a bum leg that needs treatment." She hugged my dad with tears in her eyes but didn't say a word to him. Then she hobbled toward the roof elevator with the help of the nurse.

"Boys, it's been fun. Go kick some alien butt!" she yelled over her shoulder as my dad jogged up the ramp to the *Mini-Mane*. "Especially you, Sandjack!"

It was the first time in my life that I was sorry to leave my aunt, and I felt a bit ashamed of that. As dire cranky as she could be, she put her life on the line for me at the drop of a hat. Not that we had time to reflect on her or her mystery letter then.

"Where to, Dad?"

"A few pit stops," he said, handing me his holophone. I saw several addresses and punched the first into my hologlasses.

"And then?" I asked.

He tousled my hair. "Then we open up that universe map again and start looking for clues. It's time we paid the Ascendant a visit."

"It's past time," I said, stretching my scarred hands.

"This is our ship now, matey!" Sunjay said. "We need a pirate flag!"

"Yep, add that to the supply list," Buckshot said. We rose into the clouds above Anchorage in darkness. My dad took my aunt's letter from my pocket and placed it on his box of dynamite.

SHIP SHAPE AND THROWING STONES

ocus, Tully. I forgot the letter, the dynamite, and the universe map as I took control of the *Mini-Mane* and flew us low over the Pacific Ocean. If I held up my hand to any wall, we could see the outside through the ship's skin. This allowed us to watch the moon shine on the peaks of the waves below us.

As we accelerated, the shape of the ship changed. It flattened from a sphere to an oval. The awkward bench angled down to the floor, which transformed the bench seating into a 360-degree couch. No cushions, but it was more comfortable than before. My dad was more impressed with the ship itself.

"It's designed to reduce the coefficient of drag," he explained. "It's getting thinner and more aerodynamic so we can go faster. Tully, give it some more throttle. We already passed the sound barrier."

"Pardon me, boys, but I'll be taking a supersonic snooze. Wake me up if things get interesting." Buckshot pulled his Stetson over his eyes and kicked back.

A few minutes later we crossed from water to land again. My holo-glasses indicated Oregon. Sunjay guessed our location correctly on his own. Dad and Buckshot rummaged around the *Mini-Mane*. Behind a black panel they located the Ascendant food supply, which was held in two giant cylinders, both half empty. A hose started in the top of the cylinder and protruded out of the top, like a giant straw. *They must all drink from the same hose,* I thought.

"It's the alien smoothie of death!" Sunjay said. "You think they drink that?"

I took a whiff of the hose and almost barfed. I covered my nose with the mood scarf, which turned a nasty shady of green. "It smells like rotten seaweed. We need our own food."

"We don't know where their home world is yet," said Sunjay. "How do we know how much food to get?"

"Here's my best guess, Sunjay. The Ascendant can breathe our air, they get winded when they fight, and when I fought that last one, he began to sweat. They're biologically a lot like us."

Where have I heard that before? I thought. *Oh, the Sacred told me that. It said, "Fight them, but do not hate. They are more like you than you know."*

"So they made the trip from their home world with this much, uh, alien death smoothie. To make a return trip, we need to match their food supply—especially the way you boys eat. I'd say two weeks' worth."

I was less concerned with our food supply than I was with our destination. *Where in the universe could this ship take us in two weeks? What if it the Ascendant discover our plans and take control of the ship?* No one could have answered those questions yet, so I asked something else. "Dad, the Ascendant are twice our size. Well, three times my size, but why are they so clumsy?"

"Based on our battle in the snow, we learned one thing about their home world today..." He let the statement hang like a question. Sunjay and I thought about it for a minute.

"Oh!" said Sunjay, knocking on the death smoothie container. "Less gravity! They must work out or put steroids in their food to keep their muscles huge—"

"—But they can't handle Earth's gravity," I said. "It's like the olds days with space station astronauts. Being weightless made them clumsy when they returned to Earth. Same with the Ascendant. They can crush you to death or toss you through the air, but they can't balance."

"Very good," my dad said. "If you give them a few months here, I'm sure they will be fine—but not now. When we arrive on their home world, just be prepared for low gravity again, like in the Hamster Wheel."

Perfect. I remembered my battles with Lincoln Sawyer in the Hamster Wheel. I always fought better in low gravity, and we needed all the advantages we could get against these muscle-bound, smoothie-drinking beasts.

My stomach growled. *Stars, when was the last time we ate? Oh, yeah, a root beer float for lunch and it's way past dinnertime.*

"I'VE ALWAYS KNEW THERE WAS ALIENS"

Before we headed into space we made three pit stops. The first was a general store near Yellowstone Park. My dad had known Cooper Splintdown, the owner, for a long time. He texted Cooper our order, which seemed like a bad idea to me, but he said Cooper wouldn't ask questions. He didn't. We landed the *Mini-Mane* and found sacks full of supplies waiting for us on the dusty porch: jugs of water, beef jerky, canned fruit and vegetables.

The owner had tacked a scribbled note to the door:

Harper—after I got your text I saw the nws. Media thinks you boys are dan-grous fugitives, but they r idiots. Half the world thinks this thing's a hoax. Other half going nuts. Me, I've always knew there was aliens. Whatever's going on, I figure you're on the rt side. Pay me back some other time. Goen out fshng before the world comes to an end.—Coop"

We grabbed the bags and re-boarded with Sunjay standing at the controls. He grabbed a piece of beef jerky out of a bag before we could set it down.

Stop two was more familiar—a two-story brick house with a pool in the backyard. Our house in Houston. It was so close to stop three that my dad couldn't say no. I "landed" the *Mini-Mane* directly over our pool in the backyard, the ramp lining up perfectly at our back door. I looked over at my dad and nodded, but he didn't notice my flying skills. It's hard to impress your dad sometimes, especially if he's flown fighter jets and spaceships.

"Okay, gentlemen, two minutes," he said. "Make them count."

Sunjay and I ran upstairs and stuffed bags full of books, headphones, underwear, shoes, my journal and sketchbook, anything that lay within reach. We were halfway packed when someone rang the doorbell. The sound froze us.

"Oh, stars," Sunjay whispered, "more Ascendant?"

"You think the Ascendant ring doorbells?" I asked. Still, my heart jumped, then jumped a bit more. Pop! Pop! Pebbles hit my window. Under cover of darkness a shadow rose from the ground, then floated forward. We were about to forget our luggage and run for the ship when we heard someone call our names.

AWAY TEAM BETA —

WE HAVE YOU NEAR SPACE ALLIANCE HOUSTON.
YOU MUST NOT BE CAPTURED ALIVE.
YOU KNOW THIS.
DO YOUR DUTY.
INITIATE DESTRUCTION SEQUENCE.
- GALLANT TRACKMAN

TEARS

"**B**angers, you would do anything to get out of a group project," the dark figure whisper-yelled as she hovered into the light on her Upthruster. Janice Chan. Her black-rimmed glasses winked in the darkness. It's one thing to be tracked down by aliens, another thing when your overeager group partner does it. I wanted to get on board the ship and leave her hovering outside my window, but somehow, I couldn't do it. I shrugged toward Sunjay, lifted the window, and she hopped off the Upthruster and into the room. She straightened her shoulder-length black hair and punched me in the ribs.

"Sorry. I mean ouch!" I said. *Wait, what was I sorry about?*

"Of all the partners!" she said. "I get Space Freak and Bad Music Boy."

"Queen Envy is cooler than you think," said Sunjay, throwing extra clothes into bags.

"What are you doing here, Janice?" I asked.

"Motion sensor on your window. Hooked it up to my phone and it just beeped so I hopped on my Upthruster and, voila, here we are."

"You're such a stalker!" I said.

"And you've apparently got space rabies," she said. "Yeah, I finally heard. So you left Tabitha in space and are on the run from aliens? That's why you didn't do a thing with the Three for Survival Project. Bangers!

Just bangers! This pretty much kills my chances of getting into my first choice college. I bet the aliens will blow up Stanford anyway."

"Yeah, they might," I said. "Janice, we've got things to do."

"You said you were in Alaska."

"We were," said Sunjay.

"Does space rabies help you teleport between Texas and Alaska and your little vacation island? You ought to be in quarantine. Now I probably have space rabies. I should text the alien hotline like Tabitha said in her message." She wiped her hand on her sleeve and then wiped her sleeve against the wall.

"Go ahead, but we'll be gone before they get here. And anyway, Tabitha lied about us," I said. That was true, but it felt terrible to say. "I mean, they made her lie. But I'm fine. I just—maybe I have some powers. Those aliens, the Ascendant, are worried about me. I am dangerous—but to them, not you. So we are going off to find these aliens and rescue Tabitha. If that screws up your Science grade—well, stars, maybe Stanford will understand, but I don't really care. Think about something besides your grades for a minute!" I was way above a whisper by the time I finished my speech to Janice. My fists were clenched.

Janice paused and caught her breath. We heard my dad whistle for us downstairs. I threw up my hands and gestured downstairs. "Go home, Janice. Forget you ever saw us, okay?"

Janice dropped her head. It felt great to vent, but then I saw teardrops on her glasses. Then on the carpet. Wow, I'm a jerk.

"I—it wasn't all about me," she said. "I *asked* to be your partner. Did you know that? I just wanted to help you guys–like Tabitha always got to. So jealous of her, you guys–never mind–I'm dire stupid...the world is ending anyway."

Until that moment, Janice was just a type of person to me. The know-it-all, Stanford-bound, geniuses-in-the-family type that hold their big brains over your head like a cartoon anvil. Suddenly she was a real person though—the sniffling, stare-at-the-ground, sure-I'll-help-my-classmate-any-way-I-can type. If anyone should understand that by now, it's me.

If it had been any other time, I would have tried to make it right with Janice. I felt terrible—*but like I have any more room for terrible feelings about girls,* I thought. Sunjay took a step toward Janice, who turned her back to us and sniffled, but I pointed to the suitcases. He looked about like I felt—guilty—but we grabbed our suitcases and headed downstairs.

When I returned for the final suitcase, my window was still open. Janice was nowhere to be seen. *One day I will make this right, Janice,* I thought. *I owe you that.* I lugged the final suitcase downstairs, chucked it into the corner of the ship, and pulled up the starmap.

"That was a lot longer than two minutes," my dad said.

✳ ✳ ✳

Our third pit stop was nearby. A few miles and security guards, gates, fences, and cameras stood between us, but we could avoid those if we followed the creek that ran from our house to our destination, Space Alliance Headquarters.

We made the trip undetected and into Dr. Chakravorty's lab. Wearing his white lab coat and flapping his arms like a spastic traffic cop, Dr. C flagged us through an enormous bay door, slammed the door behind us, hopped aboard, and greeted Sunjay and me as he usually did.

"You let *them* fly *this,* after what they did to my brand new hovercar in Florida?" he said to my dad.

I didn't blame him for being skeptical of our driving. We sunk his new car in a swamp. I wanted to remind him that we did so on purpose, but this wasn't the time. Dr. C had an important job to do. He circled the *Mini-Mane* inside and out, taking notes and frowning all the while.

"Mike, here's the communications array. This is the propulsion source. It looks nuclear or plasma, not electroplasma, but not sure how they achieve this hover-effect. I just don't have enough time. Get these bags out of here! And these boys!"

So Sunjay and I plopped down on our luggage while Dr. C scrambled around the inside of the *Mini-Mane,* muttering to himself about advanced propulsion systems.

"Too bad about Janice," Sunjay said. "I guess we made life hard for her. She was just trying to be nice."

I didn't want to think about it and was happy when Buckshot joined us.

"I'm surprised we made it this far," Buckshot said, propping his heels on a bag. "Everyone at Space Alliance Headquarters had their panties in a bunch. You know, Tabitha's message was the worst case scenario."

"What do you mean?" I said. "What would be a better case?"

"That the Ascendant would want to make a deal. Instead, they addressed the entire world. That ain't no good."

We both must have looked confused.

"Boys, it's like this. You negotiate with equals. Like if I wanted to borrow your Upthruster, I'd ask for it or maybe give you something for it. But what if I didn't consider you my equal? What if I didn't think you deserved that Upthruster? Well, then I might just take it. So that's what the Ascendant just told the leaders of the world. *We don't need to negotiate with you. We're coming and we'll take what we want.*"

"But Commander Harper almost destroyed the *Lion's Mane* by himself,*" Sunjay said. "They're not invincible."

"Says who? What if they have a million of those ships? And what other weapons? The Ascendant might be able to destroy us from a thousand miles away."

"That sounds more invincible," said Sunjay.

"We're fixin' to find out," said Buckshot. "If your dad can disable the tracking mechanism on this ship, we can get this thing into space undetected."

The ship hovered in front of us as Dr. C continued his work. We heard a strange whirring sound, and suddenly the red tentacle around the *Mini-Mane* sprang to life. The three of us dove for cover as it swung above our heads. The tentacle grabbed a chair, tossed it over our heads, and then fell to the floor like a limp electric spaghetti noodle—or something. My dad and Dr. C emerged from the *Mini-Mane* and surveyed the damage.

"Careful with that tentacle, Doc," said Buckshot.

"Tentacle? That's a fiber optic laser whip!" exclaimed Dr. C.

"Fiber optic laser whip? That's a way better name," I said.

"It's the right name, Tully! Commander Harper described it, but to see it in action! Give me two weeks to study this craft and we could start building such weapons. A fleet of them! We could fight the Ascendant in space on their own terms."

"We have to know our enemy before we can fight him," my dad said.

Dr. C exited the *Mini-Mane* with a small black box in his hand. A purple light on the box blinked, then began to blink more rapidly. Dr. C frowned at the sensor, like it was a dog about to pee on his favorite rug. He walked across the room and pushed a button on the wall. The blinking increased, and so did my heart rate. The hole in the floor opened, into which Dr. C dropped the box. That muffled the beep, but it became one long tone. The box wasn't happy about going into the hole.

"Hmmmm." Dr. C frowned and went to inspect.

The beep stopped.

Click, click, bang.

"Fire in the hole!" Dr. C yelled suddenly. Before he could turn around, whoosh! A fireball sprung from the hole and hit the ceiling. I managed to scramble behind the luggage but not Sunjay. His shirt caught fire. Buckshot used his cowboy hat to smother the flames.

"Geeeyawww!" yelled Buckshot. "Niles, there's a reason I never drop by to say howdy to you. I dunno how you survive."

Dr. C calmly snuffed out the fire on his lab coat—and his eyebrows. One of them was completely gone.

"Well," Dr. C said calmly, "that was the tracking device. I believe it was also a self-destruct mechanism."

"Oh, you think so?" replied Buckshot.

"Most assuredly." He winked at Buckshot with his no-eyebrow eye. "It's good that I removed it. This will throw the Ascendant 'off your trail' for a while, if I said that correctly."

"They have spies inside the Alliance," my dad said, "so you can expect visitors, Niles. They'll want to know where the ship is."

"And that's why you haven't told me any specifics," said Dr. C. "Fair enough. You were never here. I'll call for added security when you're gone. Now keep yourself safe, my friends."

Dr. C blew the rest of the ashes from his lab coat and threw his arm around Sunjay, who looked worried and uncomfortable. I understood why.

"Uh, Niles," my dad said, "I was hoping to take Sunjay along."

Silence. Dr. C tightened his grip on Sunjay, and for the next ten minutes we debated the situation.

"He's safer in space than on Earth," explained my dad. "There's a manhunt on for all of us now."

"So you believe he is safer with you, wandering off to an unknown world, fighting an alien race?"

"Yes," my dad said. "Consider the other option: staying here and being quarantined by the Space Alliance. That's much worse, Niles. Gallant Trackman infiltrated our organization. They sent an assassin to kill Tully. What's next?"

Dr. C shrugged.

"I'm counting on you to find out," my dad continued. My dad walked over and put his arm around me. I could feel his firm grip on my shoulder. "You know that I have counted the cost of this mission, but whether we like it or not, all our lives are at risk."

Dr. C looked at Sunjay, who nodded toward his dad. "No risk, no reward, Daddy. That's what Commander Harper always says."

"Yes, he does, son," said Niles Chakravorty, shaking his head at my dad. He was used to controlling experiments in his lab, but life doesn't always work like that. He held Sunjay's face in his hands. "You are my only son. Make me proud." –and then to my dad – "I only have one son, Mike. He is my pride and joy."

"As is mine," he told Dr. C. My dad does not throw out compliments often, and that one made me feel like a zillion bitcoins.

After a few final words we repacked the luggage. It felt heavy in my hands, like I hadn't slept or eaten much in the last twenty hours.

"Stars, we should stop at a convenience store before we leave," I said, rubbing my eyes. "I could use a TurboFizz." That's when I felt a tug on my pant leg. Looking down I noticed that a pocket on my bag had unzipped itself, and leaning out of the pocket was a familiar character.

"TurboFizz is a carbonated beverage," said a mechanical voice, "with twice the caffeine of coffee. Simply turn a dial on the can to select the desired temperature. The drink comes out blue if it's cold or brown if it's hot. TurboFizz causes cancer and hair loss in laboratory animals. Try a bottle today."

"Little Bacon!" I said, holding him in the palm of my hand. He straightened his floppy hat and bowed. "I thought we forgot you."

"You did. I was face down in a shoe box in your room for thirty-three days, ten hours, and five minutes," he said. "However, I am sure to be of some use on this journey."

U-F-OH, NO

There was no time for Turbofizz.

"You're going to feel some G-force, boys. Hold on." My dad planted his feet on the control pads and maneuvered us away from Alliance Headquarters and out into the Gulf of Mexico. We heard a whooshing sound that made Sunjay jump.

"It sounds like the air tanks are filling," my dad said. "Niles pointed them out. The ship senses that we are headed into space, so it's taking care of its passengers."

The *lights on board the Mini-Mane* softened to black light. A soft voice began to speak in a foreign language. It felt like that moment before a movie starts in a theater, right before the credits, when all the anticipation builds for something awesome.

Then the starmap flickered on, not as broad as before. A dozen or so glowing spheres circled a monstrous yellow ball. The third sphere glowed brightest. It was our location—Earth. Our entire solar system glowed before us. My eyes danced between Mercury, Venus, Mars, on past Jupiter and Saturn, and all the way to Pluto. I looked across more than three billion miles in an instant. *Yes! Our destination is in our solar system after all.* Goosebumps covered my arms.

But something went wrong. The *Mini-Mane* shuddered. The air intake stopped. The fantastic map disappeared and the soft lights turned red; warning sirens sounded; the ship strapped us to our seats. We were trapped except for my dad.

"I think Dr. C tripped the alien car alarm!" I yelled, struggling with the straps.

"Stay calm," my dad said. "The ship senses danger."

More warning lights popped up. The ship spoke to us in the Ascendant language. Really helpful. But a new map popped up. Six red dots on a gridded map. All were approaching one big purple blip. Us.

"We are under attack," my dad said. "Remain calm."

Then another voice cut in. "Unidentified flying object, you are in United States airspace."

"They think we are a UFO," yelled Sunjay.

"We *are* a UFO!" I yelled back.

"Unidentified object, I repeat, land your craft and prepare to be boarded." My dad shook his head. We couldn't do that, but they repeated the request. We heard another high-pitched alarm.

"Mike, I think they've got missile lock," yelled Buckshot. "They won't hesitate. Not now."

My dad wrapped his hand around the controller, but he couldn't move it. We were stuck.

We watched on the map. Six smaller blips headed toward us. Missiles. That would have been bad news if my dad had been in a fighter jet that he knew how to fly. But it was worse. We were in the *Mini-Mane,* which none of us really understood. *If those missiles make contact, we're toast,* I thought. My dad yanked desperately on the crystal controller, but it would not budge an inch. The missiles buzzed across the water at fantastic speeds, then arced toward us. I could picture them impacting the side of the ship, a slow fall to our deaths in the ocean.

"FOOT BUTTON THING!" Sunjay yelled so loud that I hit my head against the wall. He pointed at the floor. Sure enough, a third footpad had appeared. With the missiles bearing down and nothing left to do, my dad stomped the footpad as hard as he could. The second his foot contacted the pad, the *Mini-Mane* responded. Two stringy, red tentacles—no, fiber optic laser whips—launched out of its shell. They grabbed two of the missiles and somehow slung them back in the direction of the other four missiles, which exploded near the ship, rocking us back and forth.

There was no time to celebrate. We weren't safe. The three jets were bearing down on us.

"Mike, now or never!"

My dad seized the crystal with both hands and pressed upward. This time the ship responded, pushing into the clear night sky. The ascent pinned us to our seats. My spine compressed. The blood rushed out of my head and stars appeared—the fainting kind, not the burning in space kind.

Finally the *Mini-Mane* gave us a clear view of the action outside. The three fighters followed us straight up into the sky. They fired everything they had left—guns, missiles, laser cannons—but instead of dodging or speeding up, the *Mini-Mane* slowed down again. *Okay, now we are going to die.*

"Keep going, dad!" I yelled.

"It's not me, son. Not me. Oh, no." He said it like he was worried about something terrible happening. But not to us.

The *Mini-Mane* came to a full stop on the edge of the atmosphere. We heard the bullets impact the shell of our ship, but they plinked like hail on a tin roof. The laser cannons had no effect at all: the ship didn't heat up or melt in the slightest. *Those weapons don't work*, I thought. *It's almost like the Mini-Mane lured the jets this high.*

Oh, no. I understood.

The *Mini-Mane* launched three tentacles out of its shell this time. One latched onto the first jet as it sped toward us and pulled its wings off like a cruel child would to an angry fly. The fuselage of the jet spun right past us before it plummeted back to earth. The other two jets were still out of reach of the tentacles. They broke off their attack. They understood, too. There would be no victory against this UFO. We were safe, but our thoughts turned to the third jet plummeting back to Earth.

"Come on, come on, kid. Get your head right. Eject, eject," Buckshot said. Then he cursed under his breath.

What's wrong with this world? I thought. *Why didn't they just leave us alone?* I wanted to run and hide from the terrible scene. Where could I go? I closed my eyes, but the image of the falling pilot filled my head—trying not to black out, bitter cold air on my face, spinning in the remains of a jet, struggling to reach the eject button. Was that someone's mom or dad? How many kids would be left behind? When would they find out?

They wouldn't hear about the death immediately. Two officers would pull up to their driveway to tell them in person. *Today you lost a parent, lost a hero, lost a love.* Sometimes people feel that loss before they hear about it. That happened to me when my mom died. I was in daycare at the time. Someone told my father that I started crying suddenly at the moment of her death. I did not stop until I saw my dad.

Watching the plane plummet, I started to cry those same tears.

Then everything went red. *Red, red, red, red, red.* I clenched my fists and felt an old power warming my fingertips. I could not just picture but *see* the pilot in his jet now. Yes, it was a Sacred Vision. I was in the cockpit with him. He flopped back and forth, unconscious but alive. Through the red haze I saw the eject button. He would never be able to reach it, but something told me that I could. As I reached for the button, it disappeared into a red haze. A familiar power tingled in my fingertips, and then the vision ended, the scene disappeared.

I opened my eyes and saw on the map a terrible thing: a plane in its death spiral. Above it I saw something beautiful: a parachute open.

"Thank you, God," my dad said. He shook his head and looked at the glowing footpad on the floor. Pushing it had saved us, but it had turned the *Mini-Mane* into a weapon. My dad's actions had almost killed a fellow human, the ones we were fighting for.

But something much wilder and more dangerous had saved the fighter pilot—the Sacred's power.

The pilot was safe, but I worried. *Is it awake? What if the Ascendant can see it now, wherever my dad has it hidden? What if they can see me? I may have saved one life but put our entire mission at risk.* These thoughts troubled me, but the danger seemed to be fading away. Everything on board looked okay... with one exception. The scars on my hands glowed faintly, so I tucked them under my legs. No one seemed to have noticed or understood what really happened, and nobody needed to at that moment. My dad strapped down the duffel bags and his precious box of dynamite. I watched the parachute drift lazily back to Earth as we continued our ascent into space.

Space. The thought brought peace to my mind. I remembered those first few moments of liftoff on my first journey: trapped in an orangutan spacesuit with only Little Bacon and a sketch pad to keep me company—and the strange red glow of the Harper Device. On that day the *Adversity* lifted off like a plane. The *Mini-Mane* yanked itself out of Earth's gravity, but as soon as we reached the upper atmosphere, a familiar feeling returned: my stomach felt a little queasy; my arms floated up from my sides; my head felt lighter, like my chin was floating up, telling me to look up into the sky. A blanket of stars and a bright full moon. Somewhere out there was our destination.

Finding Chaos

"If it ain't in English or Texan, I can't read it. Just pick one, Mike, and let's get this show on the road."

We had managed to get into an orbit around the Earth before the *Mini-Mane* presented us with another challenge. We gathered around the starmap and shook our heads.

It was a question...in an alien language. At least we thought it sounded like a question. It ended on a high note, like when you ask, "Do you want a pizza?" The 'za part is the highest note. Anyway, after the question, the ship gave us options. Each of the locations on the map glowed as the ship said their names—about thirty in all. Some of the names sounded familiar, but the writing below them was foreign, er, alien.

"Okay, I got this," said Buckshot. He cleared his throat. "Computer, take us on home."

The ship responded: an enormous red "X" appeared in the air. Then the question repeated. Buckshot tried again. "Computer, take us to the Ascendant home world."

Big red X.

"Head to the home base."

Big red X.

"Go home."

Big red X. Buckshot looked flustered.

"This thing's about as helpful as a snorkel in a sandstorm."

Two big red X's.

"Maybe she doesn't like your accent," said Sunjay.

"I'm about as useful as a one-legged man in a butt-kickin' contest," said Buckshot. "Somebody else give it a shot."

We all gave it a shot, as Buckshot said. Lots of red X's followed by the names of all thirty locations repeated.

"Wait, we are idiots," I said. Why are we giving it voice commands? We can probably just push the planet like an elevator button." I reached toward one of the planets and it glowed more brightly.

"Don't touch it," my dad cautioned. "That's probably right. Now the problem here is that we have thirty choices. Which is the right one?"

"Oh," I said, feeling dense. "I guess we need more information."

"No, we don't," said my dad. "We have everything we need right in front of us. We just have to put it together correctly. If we can't figure this out, we should just stay here and wait for the Ascendant to attack—and that's not an option. Now everybody, think. Really focus. That's an order."

The universe map taunted me and my mind spun with the opportunities: Venus, that fiery ball of gases; Mars, the red desert planet of my dreams; Jupiter, king of planets, with its rings and dozens of moons; Pluto, cold and alone; even another small planetoid that we had yet to discover. The Ascendant could be anywhere in that maze of moons and planets.

No, no they can't, I thought. *They visit these other planets. There's only one home world. How to find it?* I thought back to my final vision when I put the Harper Device to sleep. *Chaos awaits you,* it told me, *but do not fear. You will pass through ice and shadow before you see her again, but see her you will.*

"Any ideas?" my dad asked me.

"My guess is an icy moon," I said.

"How do you know?" asked Sunjay.

"I don't, but I saw visions," I said. "Like I told you before it's not that simple. The visions are symbolic. Not like exact pictures of a place. You know this. Go ahead and name the icy moons in the solar system again."

"Okay, let's see. Titan. It's the biggest and circles Saturn. Also, Rhea, Mimas. Ganymede, Europa, around Jupiter. And, uh, Cassandra."

"No, Calisto," my dad said. "These are good guesses, maybe better than planets. We've long thought that some of these moons could sustain life. They have water and oxygen, and if they had the Harper Device, what else would they need?"

"Oh, chaos," I said. "So the Harper Device told me I would descend upon the chaos. Which one might be—I don't know—most chaotic? Crazy."

"Titan is probably the most chaotic moon in the solar system," said my dad.

"My guess, too," said Sunjay. "It's only a billion years old. It has a thick atmosphere. Numerous active volcanoes."

"Well," my dad said, "it's our best bet so far, but our best bet isn't good enough. We need to be sure."

Buckshot sighed loudly. We all felt it. We had a treasure map in our hands, but there was no X to mark the right spot.

"Mnmhhhhmfff….fflfeh...mflfff…flff!" A muffled sound drew our attention to the corner, where a duffel bag started to squirm like a caterpillar. A few seconds of confusion ensued, but then suddenly a hand emerged from the bag. It was attached to an arm, which reached out from the top of the bag and unzipped the zipper. From the bag emerged a head.

"Janice Chan?" I asked, pointing at the duffel bag that turned into a girl. It was worse than being speechless. Only two words would come out of my mouth. "Janice Chan? Janice Chan. Janice Chan! Janice Chan!" I said her name about four million times. Janice floated free from the bag. She wiped her glasses on my shirt and stared right back at me. "Janice Stupid Chan. Stars, are you kidding?"

"If you guys had done *any* research on the Three for Survival Project, you'd know where we need to go," she said, crossing her arms.

"Oh my gosh, Janice!" Sunjay pulled his hair. "I tossed the bag. I sat on the bag. You were the bag!"

"I was right beside Little Bacon," she smiled.

"Pleased to see you again," said Little Bacon, emerging from my pocket.

"And you don't think to mention this to me, Bacon?" I said.

"I'm more suited for definitions than observations," he said. I grabbed him from my pocket and flung him at Janice, who caught him and patted him on the head.

"You've been in there the whole time?" I said. "I can't believe this! You never left my room."

"Not until you dragged me out," she said, picking lint off her black sweater. "I planned to hide out for a few minutes and see if you guys were really going somewhere. Then you came back for me and dragged me into your backyard."

Stars, I literally dragged her along for this journey, I thought. *Of all the people in the universe, why her? Someone had better have some dire good reason. I'm looking at you, Harper Device.*

During this whole exchange my dad and Buckshot said nothing.

"Boy howdy, what's with all these clever girls wanting to be friends with you two swamp donkeys?" asked Buckshot finally. "I just don't get it." Sunjay and I were too dumbfounded to respond. Not my dad. He kept his cool.

"Hi, Janice," my dad said. "Welcome aboard."

"Commander," she addressed him, "my apologies for showing up like this and disturbing your mission."

"*Our* mission," I corrected her. "Why aren't you apologizing to me!"

"You don't even know where you're going, and it's not your ship."

"It's not his either—sorry, dad, but it's not."

"What matters?" my dad said. That brought silence. My dad ran his hand along the red streak in his hair. "Let us focus on the right things. It doesn't matter whose ship or whose mission this is. What matters is that we accomplish the mission. We'll have time for apologies and bickering later."

He was dead right, as usual. Tabitha's face came back to me in a flash, that last moment that we saw each other. The reality hit me: Janice was on board. There was nothing we could do about it.

"Janice," my dad said, "it sounds like you have done some research. What do you know?"

"Okay," she said, floating into the middle of the room. The virtual map flickered as she passed through the heavenly bodies. She pushed herself through the center of the sun, past Mercury, Venus, Earth, and

Mars, through the Oort Cloud. She stopped at Jupiter and started pointing toward moons. "Coolest map evs. Not you. Not you. Bangers! There it is. You're just right. It's this moon. Here's where your chaos is."

"How do you know?" I asked.

"It's easy, Tully. Whoever this Sacred person is, he told you to descend upon the chaos."

"Yeah, that's right, but there's chaos on lots of moons."

"I don't think he meant it quite like that, Tully," she said. "He didn't tell you which chaos, did he?"

Which chaos? My dad nodded, like something made sense, but this was thoroughly confusing, just as bad as any Tabism that Tabitha had ever tabbed. "No, the Device just said that I would have to pass through shadow and ice before I descended upon the chaos and found Tabitha."

"Right," she said, pointing at the moon. "Chaos isn't just some thing or idea. It's the name of a place on this moon. It's a geographical term."

The idea hit me like a solar flare. All this time Sunjay and I had puzzled over maps and star charts, we never considered that the Ascendant told us exactly where they lived. It was hiding in plain sight. We'd probably run our fingers over that moon a hundred times and never looked at the word Chaos scribbled all over its skin.

"A chaos," Little Bacon said, "is a surface feature on several planets and one moon in our solar system. It is thought that lakes exist below such surface features."

"Oh, Stars," said Sunjay. "She's right. It was right there, and, wait, the Lord Ascendant. He said something about chaos, Tully. He said he would take you to stand trial for crimes on some chaos."

"Rathmore," I said, cutting him off. I remembered the Lord Ascendant's piercing gaze. "The Rathmore Chaos is where we must go."

Janice pulled out her holophone. She projected a screen of tidy notes beside the map. "Yep, that's it. That's the Rathmore Chaos, as in the proper noun, as in a location. And on the map, the name is in Greek. Check it out." She held up her phone and it showed an English translation of the Greek words onto the screen. That was why the names looked familiar. They were in a foreign language, not an alien one. She pointed to one of Jupiter's moons.

Ευρώπη.

The word Ευρώπη glowed brighter and lit her hand with a pale blue light. A brilliant red dot appeared over one point on the moon.

"Well done," my dad said. "Of all the moons in the solar system, we've long thought it might support life, but the Alliance lost every drone that we sent near her. All those 'mechanical failures' and 'accidents' now make sense. The Ascendant remained hidden until just now. Congratulations, Janice. You discovered life on another world."

Janice clapped her hands together. If there was one thing she loved, it was being right. "Shall I?" she said. She placed her finger on the dot.

"No, Janice! We can't take you!" my dad yelled.

"If only Stanford could see me now," she said. My dad reached for her hand, but before he could stop her, it was done. The map disappeared. Only a red line ran between the moon and our ship. The ship's chairs strapped us in again and we began to accelerate in our orbit around the Earth, preparing to sail into space toward our destination, which was where exactly? Nobody had said the name.

I expected my dad to stop the ship, to take Janice home. *He won't risk taking her with us,* I thought. *Then again, if we turn around now, more lives were at risk.* He could have unstrapped and throttled us down—he still had his hand on the crystal—but he looked at the girl with her finger on the Ascendant home world. A light flickered in his eyes. I knew what he saw; there was something daring and clever about Janice Chan. *And annoying. Oh, no, he's really going to do it.*

"Buckshot, what do you think?" he asked, looking at Janice.

"Shoot, Mike. Why not? But, stars, this ain't much of a crew. It's you, me, superpower boy, the question asking kid, and duffel bag girl. It feels more like carpool than rescue and recon."

"Mr. Lewis," said Janice, "I admire you as an astronaut, but with all due respect, I get most of my homework done in carpool. It gives me time to do other interesting stuff, like study other languages and research the moons of Jupiter. I've got great notes on our destination. You could use a good researcher on this team."

Buckshot shrugged and looked at Sunjay and me. "Well, Little Miss Stanford gets a thumbs-up from me. And you can call me Buckshot."

"And you *can't* call me Little Miss Stanford or duffel bag girl or anything else ridiculous," she said. "And—oh, it's so small…"

Janice stared at the ceiling. Her mouth widened and she let her head fall backwards. I looked up to see what she was gawking at it—the Earth. That swirly blue and white ball of water and land and air and atmosphere and fish and clouds and religions and gummi worms and music and wars and monkeys and vegetables and paintings and touchdowns and video games and books and people and dreams. The place where humans come from. She had never seen her home world from here. I remembered my first look at the Earth from space on board the *Adversity*. Alone, trapped in a monkey cage, but feeling freer than I had in my entire life. And smaller than an atom. Almost everyone that we knew lived on that one blue dot on the black canvass of space. There were only two other moments in space that felt as peaceful and settling as this one. There was silence on board the *Mini-Mane* as, ever so slightly, the dot shrunk.

"That is why we must go," my dad said, pointing to the blue dot. "We have to protect the things we love, and it may cost us our lives. I do not think that any of you are too young to understand that. If you were I would turn this ship around in a heartbeat."

"Don't," said Janice. "Commander, I would rather die than—"

"Uh, say 'fight,'" said Sunjay. "Fight is a happier word."

Fight, but do not hate, I thought. *That's what the Sacred told me once.*

"Words are overrated," Buckshot said. "We gotta put the world in our rear view and get this show on the road."

Janice turned to Sunjay, said something, and grinned, all kinds of confidence beaming from her bright eyes. Hadn't we felt just like this, before we knew the kind of danger we faced? Was Janice Chan really up for that? Stars, was I? She complicated everything, her arrogance annoyed me, but we really had no choice. Maybe she earned it. After all, she did point us in the right direction.

"To the Ascendant home world, then," my dad said. "To the moon Europa."

Part Two: Preparation

"Awkward and Suction"

Why do we still have gravity?

We were weightless for the first few hours on board the *Mini-Mane*. Then the alien ship slingshotted twice around the Earth and headed toward Europa. Somehow gravity returned as we flew toward our destination. Not quite what I expected. Gravity or not, my mind started to wander. *Seriously, why aren't we floating?*

In zero gravity I'd learned to fight. No, to battle. My instructor was Lincoln Sawyer. I was pretty sure that he was just a hunk of frozen metal floating out of our solar system now, but he'd taught me two rules:

#1. Never let your guard down.

#2. No pain, no gain.

Those rules stuck with me, even when I used them against him.

In zero G I learned to use my powers. If I hadn't, we would never have jumped from the *Adversity* to the *Lion's Mane* to save my dad-not like I did that by myself. Tabitha helped. She forced me into using my powers on our space jump. If she hadn't, we would both be dead. In our last moment together, she pushed me again…into making the right decision. It was also the hard one.

Tabitha, with her curly hair poofing out in all directions in zero G. Both times she sacrificed herself—once for me, and once for the world. How could I let a girl like that go? I asked myself that question every day since we returned from our first mission, and I was asking myself that again when my dad spoke.

"Why don't you three take an inventory of this ship?" he asked, checking our coordinates on the starmap. "Start on the lower deck and work your way up."

Sunjay and Janice looked pumped. She grabbed her holophone, pulled up a holographic screen, and scribbled "Inventory" in mid-air.

Oh, yeah, upper and lower decks! The *Mini-Mane* was full of surprises. The second that Dad punched in our coordinates, the *Mini-Mane* expanded. The interior was made of black panels, and they shifted, rearranged, and expanded with a smooth sliding sound. In minutes the *Mini-Mane* grew from alien clown car to an intergalactic yacht—smaller than the *Lion's Mane*, but for five of us, downright palatial.

The upper deck was unfurnished except for the bench seats. There was a shiny black floor, a fancy star map, and an enormous dome for a ceiling. The walls were dire cool. They shifted from one awesome cover photo to the next: the peak of Mount Everest, the Grand Canyon, the Tower of London all filled one wall. Each scene drifted around the room and occasionally shifted into an ocean scene full of whales, sharks, squid, and coral. Everything looked Earth-like until a saw-billed fish the size of a school bus floated past. It turned toward us, flashed purple, and swam away, followed by a toothy fish with paddles for fins. In the background, classical music played.

"It's like a fish tank, too," I said. Sunjay looked at me. "Oh, sorry, conversation I was having with myself earlier."

"Do you think we'll have to swim on Europa?" he asked.

"There's more water on Europa than on Earth," said Janice. "On the outside it's all ice, but there's an ocean below."

"Let's hope so," said Buckshot, pointing at the creature, "I'd like to mount one of those hellbeasts on my wall when we get home."

Dad and Buckshot stayed upstairs while we inventoried the downstairs, which was shaped like a bowl and served as our living quarters. The room was pitch black until I hopped down from the ladder. Cue the creepy purple lights. Sunjay followed, eating beef jerky and carrying a water bottle, and Janice took notes. Little Bacon poked his head out of the pocket when he heard the word "inventory," but I pushed him right back down.

As we entered, black bunks folded out from the walls with alien-sized beds. Soft music played.

"This ship can read our minds," I said.

"Doubt it," said Janice. "Probably reads our body heat and movements. It can tell we're sleepy."

"Who's sleepy?" I said.

"You are."

She was right, darnit, but we had an inventory to write. Janice flicked on her holophone and took notes. We quickly realized that the Ascendant had the same basic needs, even for hygiene: toothpaste, toothbrush, combs. They also have similar interests.

Souvenirs, knick-knacks, and weapons were sprawled across the room, some behind panels and some in the open. We rummaged through the downstairs together. I held up a box of cologne.

"An alien's got to smell good," said Sunjay. "They probably have wives or whatever. They need things to bring home."

"Classy choice," I said, holding up an "I Love Alaska" coffee mug. "Seriously? Nobody's bringing that home to a wife."

"Maybe he would," said Janice. "Oh, look at these seeds. They're roses and lilies. He's bringing them home for his garden."

"Seven foot tall tattooed mercenary aliens do NOT have gardens!" I said.

"Don't get all defensive about it," she said. "I'm just thinking out loud."

"You haven't seen them," I said. "You don't know what they're like."

"Look, just because they're muscular and tattooed doesn't make them completely evil. My cousin Chris has muscles. He's also got a girlfriend and a mohawk. He's smart, too. Astrophysicist. He would so grow roses for his girlfriend."

I picked up a black staff and turned it on. "Does your sweet cousin carry weapons that can shoot purple fireballs and pin people to the wall?"

"No, but he's got a lacrosse stick."

"Stars, don't touch those, Sunjay," I said.

"Those aren't going to hurt him," said Janice. "Everybody wears them."

"What are they——oooh," he said, tossing them down.

Yes, aliens wear underwear, too.

Janice never accepted anything I said as the truth. Why did she have to turn everything into a debate? She pretended like she knew everything about the Ascendant, even though she had never seen one.

There were, however, plenty of things we had not seen before on the ship. We got a better look at the alien food supply.

"Stars, it smells like tuna and spinach!" Sunjay yelled, throwing down the hose and splattering Janice. She picked up the hose and slapped him with it.

"Guys, easy! That stuff could melt your face off," I said. Probably not, but they stopped. Janice punched Sunjay again anyway. He pretended to pick up the hose and drink it. Were they, could they have been flirting? Weird.

One of the bunks also had a music player—the old ones that made you scroll through all the songs on a screen and shove plastic speakers into your ears. *Nasty earwax issues,* Tabitha would have said. Sunjay saw the player first, but I pounced on it before he did. "Hey, that could melt your ears off," he said. I pocketed the player and laughed.

Finally, there was the box in the corner. Shaped like an old timey telephone booth, it was pitch black with two footpads in the middle and one door. A mirror was on the far wall.

"Ooh, I know what *that* is," said Janice. "The one thing we haven't found on the ship so far. Go for it, Sunjay."

"Huh?" said Sunjay. Then it dawned on us. Like I said, the Ascendant aren't that different than humans. "Oh, no way."

"But we're all going to have to," she told him. "Why don't you be the brave one?"

Sunjay looked perplexed. He didn't like uncertainties, but girl pressure got the best of him. He took another swig of water and handed me his beef jerky. "I'll be right back. Eat my snacks and you die." The door opened like an accordion when he approached, snapping shut behind him. Janice raised an eyebrow at me, like she had won some sort of battle. Moments later, after a few cranking noises, Sunjay's muffled voice said, "All clear so far. Purple lights are on. Ooh, a seat appeared! I'm sitting down on the seat, looking at myself in the mirror. I'm dropping my—"

"Look, we don't need a play-by-play of everything," Janice said.

"Okay, sorry. Just going to take my—wait, what is that?"

A high-pitched whine came from the box. "Ooh, guys, uh, that thing looks grabby. It's coming out of the toilet. Is that a…whaahhh!" Sunjay banged on the door. "Whoa, ho, whoa. No-no-no, AHHH! It's got me. AHHH GAHHH!"

Janice and I ran to the door and yanked, but it didn't budge. Sunjay stopped screaming after a few seconds. "No, don't open it. I'm okay. I'm, AHHHHH! No, I'm good, it's fine. Noo. AHHHH!"

This went on for about a minute. Janice and I didn't know what to do. One thing you don't do. You don't break down the bathroom door when your best friend is in there, even if he's dying. Some things are worse than death.

We waited. The sounds diminished.

"I guess he's not dead?" asked Janice.

I shrugged. Then the whine slowed down. The door creaked open. Sunjay stepped out, looking pale.

"You don't look so good," Janice said. "Wait, is your shirt on backwards?"

Sure enough it was, and his hair was shiny and slicked back with some sort of alien hair product. He tried to shake his hair into his eyes but it was glued backwards. We both started to laugh but he held up his hand.

"Two words—awkward and suction," said Sunjay. "Laugh all you want. It's only a matter of time until *you* have to use it." Good point. After that, we didn't laugh.

Constant Acceleration

So our downstairs inventory, including the mysterious bathroom, continued for another twenty minutes before we climbed upstairs. Janice beamed our notes onto the wall, where a glowing shark was swimming in front of a coral reef.

"Thanks," my dad said. "Useful stuff."

"Two questions, Commander," said Janice. "Question number one: besides being tall, what do the Ascendant look like?"

My dad referred her to Sunjay and me. Janice rolled her eyes and tried question number two. "Commander, why do we still have gravity? We ought to be in zero G in outer space."

My dad nodded. Much better question. "Constant acceleration. You know how in a hovercar, you can feel the acceleration? It pushes you back in your seat as long as you keep pressing the accelerator. Well, the physics are the same on this ship. See this?" A number scrolled up and up and up beside the map. "That's our speed. We have gravity because we are constantly accelerating."

"You mean the ship is still speeding up?" she asked.

"All the time. The constant acceleration keeps us standing up and feeling normal. It's exactly 1G. I think it's how the Ascendant tried to prepare for Earth's gravity. My guess is that we will keep accelerating until the halfway point between Earth and Europa. That's about a week from now."

"So we will be in zero G after that?" I asked, hoping for some gravity-free fun.

"Maybe for a little while, but we have to decelerate, too."

That sounded weird. It seemed like we should just keep going as fast as we could until we arrived at our destination.

"It ain't like slammin' on the brakes at a stoplight," said Buckshot. "If we accelerated all the way to Europa and then hit the brakes, we'd fly right by the planet. If we did manage to stop, we'd feel a lot more G's than our bodies could handle. 8, 10, 100 G's? We'd be plastered to this floor like bugs on a windshield."

"100G's? That would make me like 10,000 pounds," said Janice.

"Okay, lightweight. I'd be 22,000 pounds," he said, "and pretty dead."

"So that's one week acceleration," my dad said, "and one week deceleration. We will plan for some microgravity in the middle. We'll use that time to train for Europa."

I tuned out from their conversation thinking about zero G. Nothing would be more fun than floating around the upper deck. The domed ceiling was forty feet high. We would have an enormous free space to play. I imagined myself running up the walls, spinning through the air, and battling with the black staffs. *Oh, yes, those. Where are those staffs hidden in the wall?* As they kept talking and pointing to our route on the star map, I searched the wall until I found the right storage compartment. I pulled the black staff from its holster. As soon as I did, the starmap shot toward the ceiling and flattened to form a starry night sky.

"Tully, what the stardust!" said Janice. I looked at the staff in my hands. "You made the map disappear, and, whoa…"

Whoa, indeed. The star map was nothing: the entire room transformed. The floor suddenly looked like sand under our feet. I could almost feel its grittiness. A new projection covered the dome. An ancient Roman arena with stone bench seats encircled us. Jupiter, its moon, and its rings filled the sky.

Then from the archways between the seats came an Ascendant crowd, tattooed, rowdy and gesturing at us, some cheering and some booing. The crowd swelled to thousands. Tattooed aliens with long black braided hair filled the stands. They wore tunics of different color and sat in sections according to those colors. It was a rude introduction to their way of life.

"Unreal," I said. "Dad, it's a virtual room like your office."

"Your dad's office ain't nothing compared to this," said Buckshot. "No offense, Mike, but this is a full-blown virtual combat simulator, complete with nutso alien fans. And we're the entertainment."

"Yes!" Sunjay grabbed another staff from the holster. He spun it over his head, did a flying back kick, and faced off against me. The crowd roared with approval. "This is going to rule! En garde, Tully!"

"Uh, what exactly are these?" asked Janice, pointing to our weapons. "I'll add them to our inventory."

"A black staff," said Little Bacon, "is an Ascendant weapon designed to toss, freeze, or fry a foe."

"Pretty good definition, LB," I said.

"Hold on," my dad said. "These look like training staffs, but let's test the equipment before we start freezing or frying each other."

In the stands the crowd booed. They expected a fight, but we tested the staffs instead. Fortunately, they weren't as powerful as the real thing. Sunjay and I showed Janice how to use them:

1.) TOSS. The easiest. All it takes is a twist of the wrist, like turning a key in a door, and you can catch, grab, or toss any small object or person. The only problem is it is hard to lock on to a moving object.

Sunjay tossed me across the room as an example. My dad shook his head.

2.) STUN. Also pretty easy. Rear back and then punch toward your opponent to send a stun shot their way. They'll be frozen for a few minutes or maybe an hour, depending on your accuracy. It's effective but your opponent can block it with another black staff.

I stunned Sunjay's arm and he dropped his staff. Then I stunned Buckshot's leg and he fell on the floor. I couldn't resist.

3.) INCINERATE. The trickiest maneuver. It requires you to spin the staff once above your head. That produces the ball of flame. Then you have to fling the fireball toward your opponent. It's slow but there's no way to block this one. If you don't dodge it, you'll be burned or turned to ashes.

For this one, Sunjay took off his shirt and threw it into the corner. He "incinerated" it, which only made it feel like it came out of the world's hottest clothes dryer.

"Okay, four staffs added to the inventory," said Janice. "Let's move on."

"Enough inventory," said Sunjay. "Let's fight."

"Uh, let's not," said Janice. I gripped my staff and motioned her aside. She rolled her eyes and backed up to let us fight.

"Take it slow," said my dad. "Just spar for a minute and put them away."

Sunjay and I shrugged. We had hoped to toss and stun each other, but this was better than nothing. So Sunjay let out a war cry, circled me, and then unleashed a flurry of kicks and staff attacks, most of which I dodged and the rest I blocked. He spun the staff over his head. The virtual crowd cheered for him and jeered at me. Then Sunjay looked over at Janice and winked.

"Oh, my gosh, did you just really?" she said, laughing. "Tell me there's something in your eye."

"Oh, no, not the wink attack. Janice, you're doomed," I said.

Sunjay frowned and redoubled his attacks. The crowd went roasters, cheering him on as I backed away. I played defense, as usual, and was blocking fine until his staff contacted the back of my scarred hand. The pain shot up my arm, and memories flooded my mind – of fighting Sawyer in the Hamster Wheel, of the last seconds with Tabitha. My anger rose. It was time for offense. Sunjay wasn't ready, and I felt an extra jolt of power and speed. Were my powers kicking in again? I wasn't sure, but in a nanosecond he was in retreat mode. I heard the clack of my staff against his staff, then against his shin and his head, and I was about to strike again when something rattled behind me. Sunjay dropped his staff and pointed over my shoulder. Everyone else backed away from me. I turned around and noticed that it wasn't me they were backing away from. I had bumped the crate of dynamite with my staff.

The word "DANGER!" glowed red for a moment, like the box was angry with me. I placed my staff on the wall and backed away. The dusty floor changed to shiny black, and the arena, with its roaring crowd, disappeared as if it had never been there. The star map and music returned. Fortunately, the crate no longer glowed.

"I said to take it slow," my dad said.

"Are you serious?" I said. "You're the one that brought a box of dynamite on board. Inventory that, Dad!"

Silence. Tension. Whoops.

"Janice," my dad said coolly, "please add box of dynamite to your inventory at Crewmember Tully's request."

My dad gave me his "I'm the commander of this ship" look. It's twice as scary as the "I'm your father" look because it's not a look. It's just him in total command of our situation, and it made me remember why we were there. We promised to find Tabitha, he was the commander, and I was a crewmember. That settled me down.

"Wow, sorry," I said. "It's just...sorry, sir."

"Apology accepted," he said. "I'm glad you found the training simulator. It will give us something important to do for the next two weeks – and fun if we can keep our emotions in check." That stung a little. The royal "we." He should have said, "If Tully won't be so spastic and emotional."

"Stars, two whole weeks?" said Sunjay, rubbing his shin. "I can only fight, sleep, and beef jerky so much. This could get boring."

"People bore themselves, Sunjay," my dad said, running his hands along his streaked hair. "Two weeks is fourteen days. It's 336 hours," my dad said. "It's 20,160 minutes. It's over a million seconds, Sunjay, until we land on a hostile alien world. We need every last second to prepare."

THE BULL AND ITS RIDER

That night Dad and Buckshot stayed on the upper deck and the three of us went below deck to sleep. Exhaustion crept over us like an invisible blanket. The *Mini-Mane* could tell. It dimmed its lights to an eerie, relaxing red glow, like the vampire cave at the Houston Zoo. Three beds much bigger than we needed extended from the wall.

As tired as I was, I could not sleep. Too many images crept through my mind that wanted me to stay awake and keep them company. I kept picturing the Sacred asleep somewhere, like a bear in hibernation. When I opened my eyes, the red sleeping light only reminded me of that fact. I rubbed my eyes and scrolled through songs on the Ascendant's old music player that I had claimed. Who knew the Ascendant would like music? The Beatles, U2, Beethoven, the Daisy Chain Gang, even Queen Envy. Then there was a whole playlist written in Greek, not English. I would have to get Janice to translate.

Thud. My bed shifted. I looked up from the playlist and sitting there was Janice. She wore one of Buckshot's rodeo t-shirts as a nightgown. Janice was our luggage, so she had packed none of her own.

I popped out one of my earbuds and held it out to her. She shrugged, put it in, and then demanded the player. Janice liked to be in control as much as I did, I guess. She flipped through the playlist and we listened to music together.

"How are you?" she asked.

"I'm glad I didn't blow us up today with that stupid crate of dynamite," I said.

"How are *you*?" she asked again. Her dark eyes twinkled in the dim red light.

"Really? Uh, confused, angry, optimistic," I said. "Pretty good for a guy that left his friend in the hands of aliens."

"You're going to save her." She looked back at the music player. "I didn't know your powers would make you so fierce. You terrified me, Tully. You moved so fast."

"Seriously? I wasn't sure they were even working. My powers scare me, too, Janice. I have to be really focused and in control to use them. They are coming in spurts right now, and I don't know when to expect them."

"Why not?"

"Because the Sacred is still asleep."

"The what?"

"That's what the Harper Device calls itself."

"So it talks directly to you?"

"Uh, most of the time it just gives me visions, but we did have some conversations. In the last one, I asked the Sacred to go to sleep. If I hadn't, it might have wrecked the Earth. Not like it wanted to do anything wrong. It's good, but it's dire powerful."

"Bangers."

"Yeah, bangers. So I'm not sure how to wake it up, or even if I should try. If it awakens, I'll have more control. Right now my powers only pop up when things get dire bad."

"Dire. That's such a Tabitha word," she said. I smirked and nodded. She ran her finger along the wheel of the music player, clicking through its content. "I love this old technology," she said. "It reminds me of my grandma. She used to...wait."

"She used to wait?" I asked.

"No, look." The clicks stopped as she pointed at the title of the song. Only it wasn't a song. It was a story. In English. "Check it out, *Zeus and Europa*."

A story about Europa? Something besides the wheel clicked. *Oh, mythology!* Just like I had never thought about the Rathmore Chaos as a place, I had never thought about the name of the moon we were about to visit. Europa was a girl's name, and names mean things. Janice pushed play and the narrator's deep voice filled my mind.

ZEUS AND EUROPA

"Hear, O Ascendant, the stories of old. You were born for greatness. Hear and remember the stories of your people. We are Ascendant. We always rise.

"Since the first epoch of time, the gods have intervened in the lives of men and women. Zeus, great god of thunder and the sky, was foremost among them. One day, while seated upon his throne on cloud-high Mount Olympus, he spied a stunning girl with hair black as the deepest ocean valleys, eyes like young kelp, and skin as soft as a jellyfish's great hood. Zeus was smitten."

The images were bizarre, but I pictured Tabitha's eyes and her dark hair.

"The girl was counting cows in a field. Her father, great king Cadmus, gave her this simple job, and the royal maiden was bored. She combed her hair. Zeus looked down from on high. He wrestled with his feelings. *I cannot visit her in godlike brilliance*, thought the great god to himself. *Surely she would die at my magnificence. And, yet, she is meant for more than counting cattle.* And so, in great Zeus' mind did an idea emerge. *I will visit young Europa, but I will disguise myself so as not to frighten the dear girl. Thus Europa will love me.*"

"Oh, Europa!" Janice hit pause. "Have you heard this story?"

"No, but this is an English-speaking Ascendant telling a Greek story. What in the universe is that all about?"

Janice didn't know, but she produced her holophone notes and called up picture of Europa. We found one of a girl riding a bull.

"Uh, Europa is a female bullrider?" I asked.

"Not exactly," Janice replied, clicking play again.

"Dear Ascendant, Zeus chose his disguise wisely. One day, as black-haired Europa counted her cows, she found a problem—an extra head of cattle in the sun-bright field. She inspected her father's herd and discovered a beautiful newcomer, a bull as white as a comet's tail. The beast knelt upon his front paws before her and offered her his lordly neck, as if to say, *I am most tame among the animals of men. I submit to offer you a ride.* Europa was amazed, and thus she mounted the bull without another thought, gripping its broad horns.

"No sooner had she sat upon his back than the great bull bolted across the seaweed-green grass, leaping and tossing her about. Rather than fear, she felt fascination. She laughed and held on tightly as the bull dashed through town. Her father heard the commotion. When he saw her, he knew that a god was to blame. With fear in his heart, he ran after her on meteor-fast feet. 'No, daughter, it is not as it seems!' he shouted, but it was far too late. Europa heard him not, for her pleasure had turned to terror. The bull made for the beach, bounded through the deep sand, and into the foaming waves. Fear-eyed Europa clung to him as they bolted into the wine-dark sea.

"O Ascendant, she found herself, days later, on new shores, as far from her father's land as the sun is from Pluto, as far as good is from evil. But all was not lost. Great Zeus left her an inheritance. He left her Taurus the Bull, great constellation in the sky, to remind her of how special she was, God-blessed child of a king. What's more, she was with child now, and that child became a great king, and that king is destined to rule the universe. He will be called 'Chosen of the Sacred.' One day he will once again ride the bull. So the myth tells us. So is it written in the stars. We are Ascendant. We always rise."

The story ended. Janice and I stared at the music player, our heads together.

There was something in the back of my mind, a word I couldn't remember, a question that would not take shape. It left me feeling unsatisfied, but there was one thing I understood.

"That story is more than a myth," I said.

"Yeah, something like that," she said. "The Chosen of the Sacred who rules the universe. That sounds pretty clear."

"Right, they deserve to rule us all," I said, "but something else." The itchy feeling stuck with me though. I couldn't shake it.

I flexed my scarred hands and pictured a giant bull rumbling through space, passing us on its way to Earth. Purple fire lit its eyes. It was ferocious, unstoppable, and planned every step it would take on its way to Earth. Once there, it would trample the Earth, all our work and history and people. Janice and I sat pondered the story in silent fear and awe. Not for long.

"Hey, you got any beef jerky?"

Sunjay plopped onto my bed and scared us to death. Janice fell onto the floor. I hit my head on the wall and then threw a punch at Sunjay. He saw the punch coming and flexed.

"I was ready for you that time," he said.

"You breath smells terrible," I said. Janice nodded in agreement. "Sunjay, have you heard the Europa myth?"

"The one about the girl on the bull? Yep. So you don't have any jerky? You want any? I'm going to get food and check on your dad." We watched him go and tried to regain a foothold in our conversation. Maybe we were making too much of the myth. I wasn't sure.

"Tully, the Ascendant don't have every advantage," Janice said. "They don't have the Sacred, so they must need a Plan B."

"Either way, they're planning to trample us," I said. "We have to stop them before they get started."

That night I dreamed of a black-haired girl riding across the universe on a white bull trailing stardust like a comet. They swerved between planets but smashed through asteroids without a thought. I chased them. Then they saw the Earth and jolted toward it. The girl held on for dear life. I was so close but could not catch them, and I had to watch as the bull barreled into the Earth in an explosion of purple sparks. He landed in the ocean. A tsunami rose. A million people screamed. A million people underwater. The bull raised his head in triumph and walked ashore.

The next morning, when I awoke in the dim purple room, I kept my eyes closed, replaying the scene, hoping that I could grab his tail and turn him away from his destination, or I could grab the girl's ponytail and save her from danger, but they were always out of reach.

The Letter

T he next few days there was never a good time to talk about the Europa myth. We spent time planning our landing. We studied geography and learned some helpful facts. We couldn't believe Europa had more water than Earth.

"That's impossible," Sunjay said. "Where is it all?"

"On the surface," explained Janice. "There's a layer of ice and then an ocean beneath it, probably sixty miles deep. Then there's a rocky mantle with lots of underwater volcanoes, in the center is probably molten lava. It's like one of those jawbreaker candies, only it's ice, water, rocks, and lava." Sunjay licked his lips, picturing a piece of candy the size of our Moon. He was hungrier than usual, and we had not brought any candy on board. That was a major oversight.

Europa also had very low gravity. I weighed 115 pounds on Earth, but on Europa I would be 15 pounds.

"That can be disorienting," my dad said. "When there's so little gravity, astronauts sometimes lose their sense of balance. They fall over or can't stand back up. It doesn't last long though. Suffice it to say, there may be a few clumsy moments on Europa. I know I had a few on the moon."

"Oh, right," I remembered, pulling out my holophone. My dad had sent me a video of his first moonwalk. Well, not his, but Buckshot's. I showed everyone the footage of Buckshot in his spacesuit hopping up and down about six feet in the air, then losing his balance and landing on his face, struggling to get up before Dad grabbed him by the arm.

"Not my finest hour," said Buckshot, shaking his head, "but look at that Space Alliance suit! It weighed almost two hundred pounds and made me look like a deranged marshmallow. You put your skinny legs in that and see how you do, Tully Harper."

"I won't have to," I said, pointing at the slick black Ascendant suits in the corner.

"You bet your boots," he said. "You kids have got it easy. These Ascendant suits are much more friendly for athletics maneuvers."

Athletic maneuvers take practice, and practice began. Besides planning for our arrival, we worked out and fought.

The arena itself trained us in the Ascendant ways. Holographic figures walked us through a combination of martial arts and body-weight workouts. It felt strange to take instruction from your enemy. My dad said it was the best way to understand them, even if they spoke Greek.

Each session lasted thirty minutes, and we did four training sessions back to back. The first session focused on cardio, the second on blocking, and the third on attacks. Squats, push-ups, and burpees also got thrown into the mix. By the end of the third session we wanted a break, but my dad encouraged us to do one more. Encouraged, commanded. Same thing. During the fourth session the entire room flashed purple and said something in Greek. The walls opened up and held out a black staff for each of us.

"What did he say?" I asked.

"τέσσερα λεπτά μανία," said Little Bacon. Ah, LB. Always so helpful.

"What? No, in English," I said.

"Of course," he said. "Four Minutes of Fury."

That didn't sound like a good cool-down to me. Holographic Ascendant showed us how to play. Apparently, if you could hold off someone for one minute, a timer went off. You won the first round. Then another opponent would join the attack. Two vs. one. If you defend against both for another minute, a third would jump in. Finally the fourth person would join the attack. If you could hold off all four for the entire four minutes, you won Four Minutes of Fury. Or τέσσερα λεπτά μανία. Call it what you like. It was almost impossible to defense that many attackers.

"I like it," said my dad.

No one could do it though. Two people trying to stun or incinerate you was too much to deflect and dodge. I couldn't imagine trying three or four people. No, that's not true. I could. I just needed to use my powers, and I wasn't about to try that.

Later that night before bed I found Dad on the upper deck looking at the star map. Buckshot napped on the bench beside him.

"We're still gaining speed." He rubbed his hand along his red streak and pointed to the moon. "I never thought I would travel this far away from home again."

"Why not?"

He smiled and pointed at my chest. I nodded.

"Thanks," I said. I was about to apologize for arguing with him. Then I remembered to tell him about the Europa myth, but before I could do anything he asked me a question that nearly knocked me off my feet.

"Do you want to open the letter from your mom now?"

"I don't have a mom to write me a letter," I said.

"That's not true. You do have a mom, and she did write you a letter." He handed me the yellowed envelope from Aunt Selma. It wasn't my aunt's sloppy handwriting. My name was written in cursive, and double-underlined. My mind wobbled.

"What does it say?"

"I haven't opened it," he said.

"Of course, yeah, no, right," I stammered.

"If you want to open it alone—" he started. "No, stay. I want you here."

Here? Where was here? Nothing else existed at that moment. I wasn't traveling through space in a stolen alien ship. My dad wasn't looking at me. Buckshot wasn't snoring. Sunjay and Janice weren't asleep downstairs. It was as if I had entered my own virtual world, an envelope that contained four sheets of white paper full of beautiful script. My mom's handwriting. My mom's words.

Love Beyond Always

I read her letter aloud:

"Dear Tully, my heart, my love, my son,

This is just a short note that I hope you never have to read. If you do, it means two things have happened - something has gone terribly wrong with the world, and I am no longer with you.

These two things may have something to do with a strange incident from my work at the Space Alliance. I began work on a secret space base a few years ago. Only a few Alliance employees knew where it would be placed. During this time a former co-worker of mine approached me. He wasn't on the project, and he wanted to know the location of the base and the equipment on board.

"She's talking about LG Alpha," I said. "You mean she created the space base that we visited? The one that the Ascendant destroyed?"

"Yes, she worked on that project," he said. "She died before she could see it completed. Keep reading though. The letter is about this other employee."

Of course, I could not tell him what he wanted to know about the base. I did not tell him. He smiled but there was fire in his eyes. I could tell he was enraged.

A few days later he came back and offered to pay me for the information. I did not take the bribe. Then he said something bizarre. 'What if I told you I worked for a race of aliens that live in the near solar system? And that this base could inconvenience their plans to take over the Earth? That would be a terrible, crazy story, wouldn't it? Stella, give me the information and all is forgiven.'

His words rattled me. His offers of bribes continued. I worried about him, but I said nothing. Aliens? What could I say? He was either a liar, a lunatic, or something else.

I found out today that he was reassigned to this project. I'll be working with him now, and he seems to be normal again, as if nothing ever happened. Still, I cannot forget his strange request or comments. They are too strange to ignore...or repeat. Hopefully they mean nothing. How could they? But since you are reading this, they meant everything. Son, you should keep your eye on Gallant Trackman.

"Dad?"

He didn't respond, just put a hand on my shoulder and the other over his mouth. I kept reading:

I had a dream once, Tully. You were with your father, and both of you were fighting a monster. The monster had children, and they attacked you. You turned to fight them, but I heard a voice whisper to me: "Tell your son to fight but not to hate." I do not know if this means anything, but it is the best advice I could give you now. Fight but do not hate. Hope. And Love.

Love beyond always,
from your mother,
Stella Harper

I held the letter to my head. I had heard her voice and seen her face in recordings, but this was the only letter she ever wrote me.

She had dreams about me. *I heard this whispered in a dream.* The words haunted me. *I found the monster, Mom, and I'm going to fight him. I know who killed you now, Mom, and I'm going to find him, too.* Her advice cut me though. The Sacred told me the same thing, but he had come to her first.

"Did you know any of this?" I asked my dad. "The Sacred spoke to her like it did to me."

"Trackman," my dad's voice thrummed. "Trackman took her from us. He tried to take you. He…"

My dad could not finish his sentence. He stroked his hair, sat beside me on the bench, and looked down. He sat that way for five full minutes. There were tears of rage and heartbreak in his eyes, revenge on his mind, but he took a deep breath and refocused.

"What really matters? It matters that your mother never caved in to his demands. It matters that she was the bravest person I ever knew. She was fearless when it came to herself and protective of everyone around her. It does not explain everything, but it explains the car accident. No, the car *wreck.* It was no accident. I wish…no, she wouldn't want me to wish. Wishing doesn't matter. She would want me to do exactly what we are doing. She saw the war coming. She had a vision of it. Do you know what that means?"

"Yeah, we weren't the first in our family to know something about the Ascendant."

"True," he said, "but, Tully, there are no accidents. Something guides our steps. Maybe it's the Device or maybe something else, something bigger."

The rest of that day flew by. We all went about our days as usual, black staff training, learning some Greek, and eating together. I couldn't wait to lie down on my bed that night when I could re-read my mom's letter. Which I did. So Trackman must have killed her. He took her from us, but I could get revenge. Revenge wasn't enough though. I wanted to set things right. I wanted to get Tabitha back and destroy the Ascendant. I did not know if I could follow my mom's advice. Fight, but do not hate. How could I not hate? Either way, I now had something that he could not take. My mother's voice. Her words in my heart. It was like discovering a new room in my house after living there my entire life, a room full of power and wisdom. The bull and the girl did not disturb my dreams that night. I felt pretty raw but slept soundly, hoping that something much bigger guided us on to Europa.

.1335G and a Discovery

Over the next several days we trained hard. My dad and I shared looks and he tousled my hair with a determined look in his eyes, but we didn't talk about the letter. That was always our way.

We spent most of our time in the arena surrounded by the Ascendant crowd. Four Minutes of Fury was in full effect. We sweated through our clothes and started to stink, so we resorted to wearing Ascendant uniforms. That was a good move. Not that I like wearing a tunic and sleeveless shirt, but they shrunk to fit each of us perfectly and wicked away moisture like nobody's business. Smart fabrics, said Janice.

There was one downside. The sleeveless shirt gave Sunjay plenty of chances to flex his biceps, which seemed to appear out of nowhere. Just what everyone wants – to watch their friend flex his muscles every five minutes. I was kind of impressed, and totally annoyed. I'm still waiting for my growth spurt. It will probably get here when I'm 35.

"Hey, anybody want to buy tickets to the gun show?" asked Sunjay.

"Is this the same gun show from fifteen minutes ago?" asked Janice.

"Nope, it's a new one. Check it out." He balled his fists and tightened his arms.

"Thanks for the invite," said Janice, "but I've got plans already. I'm going to this really great 'How Not to Impress Your Friends' Seminar.

And it's totally free. Oh, look, it just started! Tully, come join me. Prepare to be totally impressed!"

Janice sat forward and stared intently at Sunjay's arms, pretending to whisper under her breath.

"Hmmph," Sunjay said, "you won't be laughing when I take down an Ascendant with my bare hands." He strutted off and picked up a staff from the wall.

I decided not to tell them about my mom's letter. I've kept the wrong kind of secrets before, but this one felt fine. It was the right kind of secret that felt more like hiding a treasure than hiding a crime. Her words were always in the back of my mind though, and sometimes they crept to the front, like when my dad taught us a series of martial arts moves in the arena. He led us through a few that were designed to break arms or knock out an opponent. He finished with some submission holds that would kill. He showed us a chokehold that would cut off blood flow to the brain. It would make an opponent lose consciousness in seconds. It was the first time we realized that we might have to kill or be killed on Europa. We all practiced the maneuver gently on Buckshot to see if we had the right form. Then we had to attack dad in full speed.

"Don't worry," he said, "I'll tap the ground or pass out. That's the worst that could happen."

Gulp. He wouldn't let us fake it either. If we didn't attack quickly enough, he would flip us over onto our sides and pin us to the ground. "Dead," he would say. "You've got to be stronger and quicker. Slide the hand under my chin faster next time. Again." By the end, Sunjay had it down. Janice and I found ourselves getting flipped most of the time. We didn't have the strength for these chokeholds. That's what I told myself, but I knew it was something else, at least for me. How much could I control my powers? What if they returned just as I was choking him? That thought terrified me. He doubled our pull-ups and pushups routine.

A few days later I woke up, sore as usual, but felt strange in some other way. I couldn't put my finger on it. My stomach felt queasy, like when you take that first drop on a rollercoaster. Sitting up did not change the feeling, so I pushed myself out of bed and was surprised to launch myself into the middle of the room. Then I understood. The *Mini-Mane* had reached the halfway point. Constant acceleration ended. It was almost time for constant deceleration, which would feel exactly the same. But here at the halfway point, dad gave us few hours of heavenly low gravity. Finally!

I double-checked with a jump that sent me to the ceiling. Then I woke up Sunjay and Janice. Until then the *Mini-Mane* was simply a fancy alien townhome. Now we were truly in space! It was like a birthday present from the universe.

Sunjay was already up. He came out of the bathroom again with his hair slicked back, smiling but looking a bit green.

"You okay?" I asked.

"I think I'm low-gravity sick," he said. "Let's get upstairs though. I'll be fine."

Janice joined us. We scrambled effortlessly up the ladder to the upper deck, where my dad stood in front of the star map with his hand on the controller. A large number filled the screen. The number went from .68 to .67 as we entered. He took his hand off the controller and smiled at our sudden appearance. I bobbed up and down on my feet like a boxer with too much energy. He had been looking forward to this moment just as much as I had.

"You noticed," he said. "I'm taking us off auto-pilot and decelerating us to Europa's gravity. .1335G."

"13.35%," said Janice.

"Right," he continued. "If you weigh 100 pounds, you're about to weigh 13.35 pounds. So careful how hard you jump. You'll hit that ceiling like a ton of bricks."

.5G. My weight shifted to the balls of my feet. Just a little push from my calves shot me three feet in the air.

.25G. Now we're getting somewhere. A little push and we floated into the air like Charlie in the chocolate factory. Sunjay stood on his hands and catapulted himself to the ceiling. Buckshot balanced on his index fingers like some sort of carnival acrobat. Janice did a quadruple somersault and stuck the landing. Pretty impressive.

.1335G. I knew what to do. I squatted and thrust myself into the air, did half a cartwheel, and landed with my feet on the ceiling for a moment.

I found a grip for one hand and hung upside down like Spider-Man, then let myself fall slowly back to the ground upside down. On the way down, I grabbed a staff off the wall and stunned Sunjay. Then I used it to toss my dad away from the starmap, which disappeared in an instant. The arena appeared in its place. The Ascendant fans filed in. It was on.

"Stop!" my dad commanded. He leaped across the room, grabbed the staff out of my hand, and then took another one down from the wall.

You've screwed up this time, Crewmember Tully, I thought to myself. *You've finally pushed the commander's patience too far.* Fortunately, I was dead wrong.

"Well, what are you waiting for?" he said, aiming the staffs at us and smiling. "You'd better run!"

My dad shot at us with both staffs.

The ensuing fight in the virtual arena was a crazy maze of flying bodies, incinerator bursts, mid-air collisions, and surprise attacks. We wrestled the staffs away from Dad with Buckshot's help and then the melee started all over again. The virtual crowd went nuts, stomping their feet, chanting and singing in Greek, as we crisscrossed the arena. After about five minutes, with everyone panting, we came back to the floor.

"Okay, tournament time," my dad said. He grabbed an empty burlap sack from Cooper's and then produced five slips of paper. "Put your name on a slip."

"Can we put a nickname?" asked Sunjay because he had to ask something.

"Sure," my dad continued. "The first two names drawn will fight each other. Scoring will work like this: get three hits and you win the round."

Everyone jotted down a nickname on the card.

"Janice," my dad said, "would you help me out with this?" The two of them sat on the black bench, drew the other names, and then typed them into Janice's holophone. *What are they doing?* I wondered. *Oh, making a tournament bracket!* Butterflies filled my stomach. It wasn't just from the low gravity.

They returned moments later. "Okay, everyone ready for this? Okay, Janice, hit it!"

Her holophone projected this into the air:

First Ever All-Star Black Staff Battle Royale

Carpool

Zaxon the Almighty

Tully

White Knight

Shuckbot

* **Three points wins the round.**
* **Points are scored by toss, stun, or incinerator.**
* **Winner receives one handful of candy from the candy bag.**

Everyone had nicknames but I pieced it together in a nanosecond – "White Knight" was my dad's call sign in the Navy, and "Shuckbot" was, well, pretty obvious. So was "Carpool" and "Zaxon the Almighty." The good news was that the three of us were all in the same bracket and the astronauts were on the other side. Maybe White Knight and Shuckbot would tire each other out before fighting one of us. The *really* good news was the prize.

"Dad, you brought *candy* on board?" I asked. "When did you plan to tell us this!"

"The right time," he said, "which is now. I figured a few packs of gummy worms might come in handy. Oh, and this." From behind his back he produced one can of Turbofizz. Sunjay lunged for it. Not even space nausea could kill his appetite. We composed ourselves and examined the bracket.

"Okay, we've got Carpool—oh, ha! That's you!" said Sunjay, pointing to Janice. "Your fight first round is against Zaxon the Almighty! You know who that is?"

"Bangers, who else would pick that name?" she asked, grabbing a staff from the wall. "Sunjay, just promise NOT to take it easy on me."

"Heck, no, not if a Turbofizz is on the line," said Sunjay.

This ought to be quick, I thought. No offense to Janice but she was a rookie and Sunjay was a martial artist. They faced off in the arena. Sunjay bobbed up and down and Janice looked timid and frozen. After clicking staffs and bowing, my dad yelled, "En garde. Fight!"

Sunjay wasted no time...showing off. He spun the staff above his head, a la Lincoln Sawyer, and then performed a quadruple front flip while shooting stun shots her way. She hid behind her staff and blocked them. When he landed, he brought down his staff hard on the arena floor with a flurry of purple sparks, all while flexing his arms. He admired his arms and winked at Janice. To everyone's surprise, she winked back. Then she smirked and casually leaned on her staff. "Sunjay, you look so hot right now," she said. "Look at those arms."

"Really?" Sunjay looked down and flexed his arms again with his staff in front of him. Whoops.

STUN.

"Round one goes to Carpool," said my dad.

"Dangit!" he yelled. "No fair! I'm better than that. Just because you think I'm hot and I think you're hot doesn't mean you can say that in the middle of a fight!"

"You think that I'm hot, too?" She shot him a devious smile.

Until that moment, no human, fish, bird, or cat had ever flirted with Sunjay Chakravorty before. He dropped his staff and then turned three shades of red beyond red. I've never seen him get embarrassed about anything. It was epic.

"Are you kidding me or truthing me?" he asked.

"I'll tell you later," she said.

That almost drove Sunjay crazy.

Round Two began. Sunjay was off balance and out of focus. Well, he was focused on one thing.

"I can't live like this!" he yelled, trying to fend off Janice. "Do you like me or not?"

She didn't say anything but pressed her attack. She eventually knocked him off his feet and earned a second point. Buckshot leaned over to me. "She is playing him like a fiddle. You think you can beat her?"

I nodded yes but was not so sure.

Fortunately, I didn't have to find out. Sunjay pulled himself together after that second point and rolled off the next three points straight. He looked relieved.

He helped Janice to her feet after the final stun. "Okay, you said you would tell me."

"I said later," she said. "Not yet."

Poor Sunjay. He flexed his arm, flipped his hair, and pouted in the corner.

My dad and Buckshot fought the next round. Stars, they were ferocious. Watching grown-ups fight brought back memories of Lincoln Sawyer on board the *Adversity*. Memories and feelings, fear and anger, diving for my life as Lincoln ripped apart the space lab, watching him toss my friends around the room, and finally me tossing him into outer space, watching the light in his cold blue eyes die. Before I knew it, the match ended. My dad won 3-1.

It was time for Zaxon and Tully.

Sunjay spun the staff over his head and whacked the floor with an electric crack.

"You don't think you can handle Zaxon, do you?" he asked.

"Bring it on, Ascendant scum."

We tapped staffs, bowed, and faced off. Sunjay's biceps bulged. *Stars, when did he put on that muscle?* I almost fell victim to his first stun shot. The purple ball of energy struck the wall behind me and dissipated.

"You awake, Tully?" he asked.

"Wide awake," I said, launching a stun of my own, which he dodged easily. We circled one another. I usually hung back and played defense but he knew my style too well. I decided mix it up and throw myself at him. He had the same idea. We surprised each other by charging into the middle of the room, our staffs clashing furiously. Attack, attack, counterattack. We both threw our best combination moves at each other, until he swept my leg and I hit the floor. I kept my staff up before he could whack me in the head. He had taken a big swing, which left me enough time to counterattack. I swept his legs with my staff and used the staff to toss him against the far wall. Ha, Zaxon wasn't so tough.

Bzzzrrrttt. Dangit. I felt my limbs go stiff, like I was encased in ice. Sunjay lay on his back with his staff pointed at me.

"Stun shot," he said, hopping up and holding out his staff while flexing his arms. Janice looked impressed.

"One point for Zaxon," said Janice. "Nice move." Sunjay bowed.

Clearly I forgot Lincoln Sawyer's first rule of combat: *never let your guard down.* The effects of the stun shot disappeared after only a few seconds. I was angry with myself. An Ascendant would have incinerated me by then. I would be a pile of ashes ready to be swept into the gutter. Not the way I planned on ending my life.

Embarrassed and frustrated, I faced off against Sunjay for round two. We met in the middle of the room again. This time I was ready for his foot sweep. I blocked it with my staff, but his staff connected with the back of my hand. Breathtaking pain erupted and shot up my shoulder.

Memories and feelings, anger and pain. Of Trackman digging his thumbs into my hands, taking pleasure in my pain. Of Tabitha disappearing behind the portal. In the midst of those memories, time slowed down. Sunjay kept up his attack, but I had no trouble dodging him. I wasn't all there anymore. Part of me was lost somewhere in the red mist. Clack, clack, clack. Red, red, red, red, red.

He attacked again and again, finally doing a back handspring and landing on the far side of the room. He was about to fire another stun shot, but instead I fired one just to his left. I knew what he would do, so I fired an incinerator shot to his right. He fell into the trap. I watched the purple ball of fire consume him as he jumped right into it. I smiled and pumped my fist. I imagined he wasn't really Sunjay. He was Trackman. *You took my mom.* He was the Lord Ascendant. *You captured my friend.* He was the enemy. *You want my world.* He deserved to burn. I walked forward, fired a stun, then another incinerator and another. Burn, burn, burn. Red, red, red. We would save Tabitha, my powers would return, and I would burn the Ascendant to ashes and scatter them across the universe.

Far away someone screamed. Then the scream was cut short. I could feel their pain in my hands and hear the Sacred's voice inside my head. *Fight, but do not hate.*

Hate. Is that what this is? It doesn't feel so bad. I launched another incinerator shot. There was a metallic taste in my mouth and the air smelled polluted, burned.

Someone ripped the staff out of my hands, returning me to the upper deck of the *Mini-Mane.* A few feet from me Sunjay crumpled to the floor, right next to the box of dynamite. A wave of guilt crashed over me as I realized what I had done.

"I didn't mean to!" I yelled.

Sunjay gasped for breath, surrounded by a purple glow. The incinerator shot did not disappear though. It surrounded Sunjay. He breathed in the hot gaseous fumes. Janice tried to get closer to him but the heat was too much. The incinerator shots had singed his hair and was burning the oxygen around him.

"Tully, what did you do?" she said. "You had him beat! You could have stopped. Commander, help him!"

There was no time to apologize. Sunjay needed something. I pushed her aside and crashed through the purple glow. It burned but I had felt heat before. My hand reached Sunjay's chest. His lips were starting to turn blue. That I could see. His lungs were clamped shut. That I somehow knew. My dad ran forward but I motioned him away.

I need you now, I thought. *I need you.*

Beside us, there was a rumble. The box of dynamite. Everyone else backed toward the other side of the room. *Okay, that's not what we need.* My best friend was dying. We didn't need a box of dynamite shaking uncontrollably beside us. I kept my hand on Sunjay's chest. He gripped my wrist and pleaded with me with tears in his eyes. His lips moved but no sounds came out. *Make it stop. Fix me,* he pleaded. Somehow I could hear his thoughts, but they were getting more desperate and fuzzier by the second. He needed air. His eyes looked glassy, then they closed as he lost consciousness. A silence in his mind, and in my mind one word.

No. No, no, no.

Then things got interesting.

Beside us the box rattled again. The word "FRAGILE" started to glow, and through the cracks in the old wooden box seeped a soft red mist. It gathered around my hand on Sunjay's chest, and I could feel it penetrate my skin. A humming sound filled my ears, red filled my mind. Then the mist, in one pulse, left my hand and hit Sunjay's chest like one of those heart-shocker machines. The purple glow evaporated. Then shockwave rattled the inside of the *Mini-Mane*. The lights went out, and in the darkness I could feel Sunjay's lungs expand. His first breath in a while. The lights snapped on and several things became clear to me.

Sunjay was breathing. I had almost killed him. My dad had saved him by ripping the staff out of my hands. And, of course, there wasn't any dynamite in the box of dynamite. Something more dangerous and explosive was there. The Sacred was on board, and it heard me in a moment of dire need.

THE CHOSEN OF THE SACRED

We didn't finish the tournament. My dad offered me the Turbofizz but it only made me feel guilty. I hadn't earned it. That night Dad and Buckshot stayed on the upper deck and we went below deck to sleep. Exhaustion crept over me like an invisible blanket. Sunjay coughed a bit as he drifted off to sleep, maybe the effects of almost suffocating to death from my attacks.

Between Sunjay's coughing and my guilt, there was no way to sleep. I flipped through the Ascendant's music player again and let my mind wander.

Dad brought the Sacred on board. Why hadn't he told me? Was he worried that I would wake it up again? He must think we need it for something. Maybe I have to be close to it to use its powers. Who knows? I'm not going to make it a big thing though. Follow his lead. Focus on what matters, just like he did after you read the letter. What matters is saving Tabitha, staying focused on the right things.

Thud. My bed shifted. I looked up from the playlist and sitting there was Janice.

"Hey again," I said. "I thought you would be mad at me."

"I am," she said. "That was hard to watch. How are you?"

"I'm worried about him," I said, gesturing toward Sunjay fidgeting in his sleep. He coughed and his body shook.

"I think you healed him with your crazy alien powers. Now how are *you*?" she asked again. Her dark eyes met mine in the dim red light.

"Uh, I feel kind of like a guy that almost killed his best friend," I said. "And doomed his other best friend to live with aliens. And my powers are totally unpredictable – I just wish they would either come back all the way or leave forever. And I'm about to land on Europa and I don't know if we can stop the Ascendant. Stupid bull trampling through space." The itch about the myth came back. Something was in it. "Yeah, that's about how I am, Janice. Sorry I got you into this. You should have gotten into someone else's luggage."

"No, I like your luggage," she said. "No apology needed. If I were back on Earth, I would be stressing about our group project. I'd rather be stressing about, you know, real stuff."

"Europa is about as real as it gets," I said. "We've got a lot to figure out." Europa. That itchy brain feeling returned.

"Huh," Janice said, "I wonder what kind of story they would tell if we had not named their moon Europa. I mean, what if we called it Saturn Moon Number Four? They wouldn't have much of a story to tell. They wouldn't be talking about Zeus or the 'Chosen of the Sacred.'"

The itch intensified. Then it disappeared, like it had never been there. Europa. I propped myself up in bed.

"Wait. Who really named Europa?"

"Galileo did. He named all the Galilean moons." Janice scrunched her nose at me. She didn't understand.

"No, what if the Ascendant chose the name? You know, whispered it in Galileo's ear? How long have they had influence on Earth? They might have planned all of this centuries ago. They've just been waiting, watching and waiting, for the right time to attack. They watched us built the Pyramids, the Great Wall, the Coliseum, the Statue of Liberty, the first rocket, the first space station. Stars, maybe they even helped."

"Bangers," said Janice. "Maybe they did plan this for ages. Why would they wait so long to take our planet though?"

A picture flashed into my mind—the Lord Ascendant. I had only seen him once, but I remembered him perfectly. His cruel gaze, his face swarming with sea creatures, seated on a throne.

"I think I know why, Janice. Maybe they finally found the Chosen of the Sacred."

Final Debrief

The next morning my dad woke us up early and gathered us around the star map for the mission debriefing. Sunjay looked peaked but was alive and eating as usual. I was excited to tell Dad about Europa but would have to wait. My dad took us on a virtual tour of the next few days using the star map.

"We'll do an orbital transfer around Jupiter before we land. We have to decelerate. That gives us a fly-by of our destination. There's Europa."

Stars, it was gorgeous even from a distance. We weren't close enough to see the surface features, but it was a stunning blue-white moon criss-crossed by blood-red lines. Or *linea*, as Little Bacon pointed out.

The moon was cool, but the planet beside it was impressive. Jupiter. King of the planets. Its surface smeared with browns, tans, off-whites, and blue. And red. A great red spot stared at us from the starmap.

"It's a storm," my dad explained. "You could fit 2-3 Earths inside it. That storm has raged for over four centuries, scientists think. Before humans invented airplanes, cars, computers, or androids, that storm was spinning."

"That's seriously bad weather for a long time," I said. "You know what else has been bad and staring at Earth for a long time?" Janice motioned for me to wait. I was dying to tell him about the myth.

"At any rate, Jupiter will fill the sky of Europa from horizon to horizon. It will be Europa's main source of light—reflected from the sun, of course. But enough about astronomy for now. We have a mission to discuss." My dad kept it short and sweet.

Two goals: assess the Ascendant and save Tabitha.

Two methods: Stealth—"We avoid contact with the Ascendant at all cost." Camouflage—"If stealth is impossible, we find ways to blend in among them."

"But they're tattooed all over," said Sunjay, waiting for my dad to answer. "You mean, we might get tattooed? My dad would kill me!"

"Your dad won't kill you, Sunjay, but the Ascendant might," my dad said. "Keep that in mind."

"He'll probably ground your tattooed butt though," Buckshot said.

"Now, our weakness: we have no idea how the Ascendant organize themselves. Researchers have long believed that oceans are under the icy crust of Europa. We will see. The Ascendant must be an ocean-faring people, but what will the Chaos look like. We don't know."

"The death smoothie is full of fish and seaweed," blurted out Sunjay.

"Er, thank you, Sunjay," my dad said. "I was thinking of the Lord Ascendant tattoos—most feature ocean creatures. Monstrous ones."

"Yeah, about him," I said. "Janice and I have something." We popped on the music player and listened to the story of Europa together. Then we explained our theory. My dad and Buckshot nodded in agreement.

"So you think they somehow named Europa and used the myth to explain their existence?" my dad said. "That's possible. And if the Lord Ascendant is the Chosen of the Sacred? That's trouble. That would make him like a god-king. His followers might worship him."

"Sounds like Hitler to me," said Buckshot. "Mike, if that's the case, we need to take him out. We take his life and we may be able to end this whole thing before it starts."

"Let's stick to our goals," my dad said. "This is a recon and rescue mission. Assassinating an alien god-king may not be as easy as it – well, it sounds impossible."

Buckshot shrugged. Hard to argue with that point, I guess. My dad continued.

"Now, one last thing: our advantages."

"We have some?" I asked. "Like what? We're weaker and outnumbered? I have powers that I can't use?"

"Don't think like that, Tully," he said. "We are weaker and outnumbered. This cannot blind us to our greatest strength."

"What strength?" I asked.

My dad pulled up the universe map, then swept it aside with one hand. In the middle of the room appeared a man's face—beady black eyes, high forehead, and a small, tense mouth. A video message from Gallant Trackman. I almost threw a punch at the air in front of me. He sucked air between his teeth and said the following:

AWAY TEAM BETA –
WE HAVE YOU NEAR SPACE ALLIANCE HOUSTON.
INITIATE DESTRUCTION SEQUENCE.
YOU MUST NOT BE CAPTURED ALIVE.

"I found a number of these short messages," my dad said. "They tell of Trackman's plan to kill Tully and recapture the Device, but we all know, Trackman lost communication with this ship. You'll remember that Dr. C destroyed the tracking device, too. Trackman will assume that his men followed orders. Either that or the Space Alliance destroyed the ship."

"Ain't that something?" asked Buckshot.

"Yes, it is. We are unexpected and invisible. We can arrive, blend in, and complete our mission before the Ascendant know that we were ever there."

"Oh, we're like ninjas," Sunjay said.

"We're like ninjas," said my dad.

"We just need swords and throwing stars and all black outfits and maybe—"

Before Sunjay could really get going, a man's voice interrupted him, saying something in Greek. We all froze. Two beeps. Another two beeps.

"What's this all about?" I said.

Then an image flickered into the middle of the room. Before it could take shape, my dad grabbed Sunjay and Janice, Buckshot grabbed me, and the five of us hurled ourselves downstairs. We landed in a pile at the base of the ladder. My dad held a finger to his lips. *Like we didn't get the message,* I thought.

Above us a deep voice spoke in garbled Greek. Janice pulled out her holophone and hit record. *Genius,* I thought. My dad motioned for her to hold it higher in the stairwell to catch every word that scraped across his vocal chords. The voice repeated something over and over, and then finally fell silent. My dad pointed to his eyes, then pointed to Janice to take a look on the Flight Deck. She gave us the okay sign, but my dad kept us quiet. He pointed to the holophone. *Translate,* he whispered to her. Janice pressed play. The volume blared for a split second before Janice turned it down to a whisper.

"Ship of unknown make, this is Europa Command. Please identify. Identify. Ship of unknown make. Please state your identity and location." Then another voice faintly at the end, in the background. "It is just another chunk of the *Lion's Mane* floating in space. She hardly made it back to base after the explosions of the Earther commander. A curse upon him and his son! Do not concern yourself with that space junk." We all took a collective breath. Maybe we were not as invisible as we hoped.

"Ready or not, the space ninjas are coming for you," said Buckshot. He sounded so sure of himself. I felt relieved, but there was a twist in the pit of my stomach.

Part Three: "When you descend upon the Chaos"

LANDING

Two weeks. Four hundred million miles.

It was time to land on Europa, even though I wasn't ready. I was unsure of myself. My powers. Would the Sacred wake up? Would it come back to me when I needed it? Could I even use it correctly? I was used to being unsure, but about the world around me. Not about myself. Against all that self-doubt I had my mom's words, my dad's hopes, and the Sacred's advice. *She knew you were meant for this. Something bigger is guiding us. Fight, but do not hate.*

I repeated these thoughts to myself over and over as we double-checked our spacesuits, gripped our black staffs, and watched Europa grow larger and closer on the universe map. The names of surface features appeared. Delphi Flexus, Conamara Chaos, the Callanish, Thrace Macula. All were written in Greek on the starmap, but they were just as foreign in any language.

No signs of life, but we didn't expect any. As we descended the surface features became clearer. Europa looked like a flawed marble. Large portions shown in pure white, so pure that it looked blue. But then massive veins of red ran across other parts, like fingernail scratches on skin. *Lenticulae,* Janice called them. She had trained us well: I knew the planet's topography and recognized, in the distance, a wide plain as smooth as an ice rink.

"There," I said. We grew silent. On the horizon we saw a flat, a wide plane of white ice crossed by no linea at all. It looked like an endless ice-skating rink. The Rathmore Chaos. It was a weird name. Underneath that jaggy, lumpy mess of ice, scientists believed that there was an ocean, slushing around in a mix of ice and water. My throat tightened and fists clenched. They were close to the truth. Below the surface was a city, and in that city a warlike alien race was plotting our downfall. And holding Tabitha hostage. And they weren't going to get away with it.

Upon seeing the Rathmore Chaos, my dad swiftly dropped the *Mini-Mane* toward the surface and looked for a landing spot. Close enough to walk—or swim or who knows what. Far enough not to be detected, we hoped.

Spacesuits. We put them on hours ago and double checked to make sure that every seal was now airtight. "Final buddy checks," my dad said. "No loose connections." I checked over my landing suit and then Sunjay's: an Ascendant suit, purple and black, form fitted. Then the helmets came on. Purple and black with a gold visor. Sunjay checked Janice's suit three times until she looked annoyed. I didn't blame him. There was only a trace of atmosphere on Europa, and the temperature was cold enough to freeze skin within seconds.

The five of us looked intimidating, just a lot smaller than the Ascendant who usually wore our suits.

The *Mini-Mane* shrunk back to "clown car" mode on our landing approach. We slowed down and touched down on a leveled icy plain. Then the wall became a walkway, and we slowly stepped out into a field of penitentes, spikes of ice that jutted out of the ground, some as small as lampposts and others as tall as the flagpoles in front of our school, most of them white, some shot through with blue, red, and black streaks. In the sky, the light from Jupiter provided a soft white light on the penitentes' jagged edges. The sun was a brilliant pinpoint in the distance.

"To me," my dad said. "Sound off."

We all responded with our codenames: *Spaceboy, Zaxon, Carpool, Shuckbot, White Knight*. Good thinking, Dad. Tully Harper probably isn't the best name to say over an open connection on an alien planet. Actually, it was safest not to talk at all. He signaled us forward. We started our trek toward Rathmore.

Space was fun, but arriving on Europa was spectacular. I couldn't stop smiling. We skipped across the icy plain because skipping is awesome. It's also the most efficient way to move in low gravity. I've never felt so strong in my life. My legs were supercharged, and my arms floated beside me. We bounded along the surface, dodging penitentes, trying to stay close to the ground, but that wasn't easy. I weighed less than twenty pounds. One good push and I was shooting ten feet high and twenty feet forward. When we came to our first obstacle, an icy cliff wall, my dad pointed up. We grasped hands, he gave us a "3-2-1," and we leaped thirty feet into the air. We landed on target in almost perfect unison and kept moving.

Not everything went so smoothly. At one point I fell on my face and could not stand. I wasn't injured or anything. My brain just couldn't make sense of what happened. We come from the Earth, and our brains fully expected us to spend our lives there. They weren't ready for .1335G. I could picture my brain floating around in my head, saying, "Look, Tully, you're the one that wanted to land on this moon. You figure out how to get up!" Thanks, brain voice. My arms and legs didn't have any better ideas. They could not push up with the right amount of direction and force to make me vertical again. It was embarrassing, frustrating, and when Buckshot finally pulled me to my feet, my body instantly remembered what to do. Most of us had a few of these "gravity brain farts." That's what Buckshot called them.

We tried different methods for moving. Running up and down the penitentes was slower because each step needed to be planned on the bumpy parts. Jumping from the peak of one penitente to another worked better. We made those jumps one at a time. Jumping half a football field was difficult to judge. Most of us overshot the first few jumps. My dad usually stuck the landings so we watched his example. If we overshot, he could tackle us to the ground before we slid into an icy canyon.

I realized that all of this fun had a purpose – after an hour, we felt better oriented and more ready for the mission at hand. *Adapt or die*, I heard someone once say. I'll take adaptation any day.

We were having so much fun running and jumping that we hardly took the time to look up. Above us, Jupiter filled almost the entire sky. Europa circles Jupiter every 85 hours, which is blindingly fast compared to most other moons. If you looked up once and then looked up again five minutes later, you could see something new. Jupiter's Great Red Spot came into view—a rust-colored oval eye. That storm began before the car, the plane, or the spaceship. I could have lain down and watched it rage for hours. *If only our mission was as simple as staring at the sky.*

All around us in the thin air, microscopic bits of ice floated toward the surface, twinkling in the cold light. *Where did those come from?* I wondered.

The canyon leaps gave me the biggest rush. We had no idea what was in those black crevasses, and I held my breath every time I jumped across them. This wasn't a routine yet, but my mind began to wander after one of those jumps. I watched the ice crystals accumulate on my glove. All those flecks mesmerized me, shined with the light of Jupiter and the sun. *I never look at snow like this,* I thought. *What's different about this stuff?*

I looked back across the canyon to see if everyone else was on track. My dad and Sunjay stood beside me, and we waited on the other side for Janice and Buckshot. My dad gave me a thumbs-up. All systems go. But then...

Whooosh! It wasn't a sound. It was a feeling beneath my feet. The ground shuddered and knocked me to my knees. It felt like the world's largest toilet flushed and I was standing on the seat.

An enormous geyser of water spouted into the Europan air. Since the air was so cold, it froze into chunks of ice almost immediately, flying into the sky with no sign of slowing down. On the edge of that geyser, a black speck headed into the sky as well.

Janice.

She had jumped at just the wrong time. She didn't catch the full impact, just enough to blow her up and sideways. She spun wildly through the air, halfway frozen in a chunk of ice with her free arm and leg flailing wildly.

"No, no, no!" she yelled into her intercom. "I'm dizzy. Something hurts. What do I do?"

The three of us leaped into action. We had to move, but what could we do for her? My dad grabbed my arm and we followed below her. We heard Buckshot, but he was nowhere to be seen.

"Carpool, listen to me. Five deep breaths," said Buckshot, still on the other side of the geyser. "Long and slow. You're going to be okay. You got this. We got you."

"No, no, no, no…"

"Carpool, get with me here. Slow breaths. Slow."

The no's stopped. I could hear her breaths and almost feel her inhalation.

"Okay, good. Now find a spot on the ground and focus on it. Relax. You're gonna be fine. Breathe, honey. Breathe."

She stopped flailing as she flew overhead, her body twirling, her right arm encased in ice, her gold visor trying to fix on a point on the ground, like an ice skater in the middle of her final spin.

We bounded from penitente to penitente chasing Janice. Whoosh. Another geyser erupted in front of us. Then another. My dad zigzagged his way through the minefield of geysers and penitentes. Sunjay and I followed, our eyes darting between Dad, Janice, exploding ice chunks, and the ground. Buckshot kept talking to her, but he was nowhere to be seen.

Suddenly his shadow appeared on the ground. Buckshot had taken a straight route through the geysers, risking everything to catch up to Janice. The risk paid off. He landed on a towering penitente high above us, planted both feet, and took a monstrous standing broad jump that shot him over our heads.

Janice seemed to have peaked hundreds of feet in the air. She could feel it.

"I'm falling. No, the ground. No!"

"Buck, you've got to catch her. That ice won't break on impact."

"Carpool, get with me," said Buckshot. "Keep breathing. I'm coming."

In front of us, the field of penitentes thinned out into a clearing. More geysers opened behind us, but none in front. Janice falling. Eighty feet. Sixty feet. She would land hard and skid to a stop. What would that do to her arm? If what my dad said was true, her arm would break before the ice would. I held out my hand, trying to summon some of my powers. Nothing. Too many distractions. No way to focus. Buckshot rushing. All of us following. Janice falling, falling still.

"Relax, keep breathing. Good girl," Buckshot said between breaths. He trailed her by only a few skipping leaps.

Finally, as Janice got closer to the ground, Buckshot unleashed his best jump yet. He was on a collision course with our falling friend. Then his staff glowed purple. *Of course!* I thought.

Buckshot flew right past Janice, but as he did, he grabbed her with his black staff and pulled her toward himself. This slowed his ascent and her descent. They balanced each other out about twenty feet from the ground, where he pulled her toward himself. They still had a problem though. Janice's arm was frozen in ice. A hard landing would shatter it, but Buckshot kept his cool though. He swung his staff overhead and blasted fire at the ice below them again and again. The heat created a growing pool of water, and they splashed down into the man-made waterhole. It wouldn't stay warm—or even liquid—for long though. Europa is dire cold. The second they landed Buckshot sprang out of the pool, pulling Janice with him. Moments later the steaming pool froze as hard as rock. Buckshot and Janice lay beside it.

It was the craziest thing I've ever seen, and I've seen crazy.

Buckshot didn't seem phased, just breathless. They struggled to stand, cracking the hard, thin shell of ice that accumulated on their suits.

"Hey, y'all wanna pick up the pace? Me and Carpool were getting bored back there," he said, breathless and bent over.

"You okay?" I asked Janice. She flipped open her gold visor. She was pale. There was blood above her swollen left eye, and she had a busted lip. One arm was still encased in rock-hard ice. Sunjay tackled her to the ground and squeezed her tight.

"Uhhh-ouch," she said. "Timing?"

"I thought we lost you," Sunjay said. "Oh, your poor eye."

"That ain't but a scratch," Buckshot said. "Just a flesh wound. She'll heal up just fine, Zaxon, if you stop strangulatin' her."

"Let's avoid any more extreme sports today," my dad said. "Europa is unstable here. We can hope for better at Rathmore. The quicker we reach our destination, the sooner we can find shelter. Surely the Ascendant don't live with this kind of danger every day."

I wasn't so sure. I wondered if we had something to do with the geysers erupting in our path. After all, my dad had a box strapped to his back that contained the Sacred. If anything was going to mess with the atmosphere of Europa, it was in that box.

Sunjay helped Janice to her feet. Then he whacked her arm with the black staff. Janice shouted at him.

"Not like that," my dad said. He pushed Sunjay aside, turn the staff on, and held it against her arm. The staff vibrated as usual and clinked against the ice, which heated and crumbled.

"Thanks, commander," she said. Janice limped across the ice field, which was a welcome sight, but it's not the sights that mattered. The sounds did. Not a whoosh this time.

A thud.

THUD.

Thud. Behind us, maybe twenty feet. More thuds.

"More geysers?" said Sunjay.

Like trees falling in the forest, shaking the ground beneath our feet. And then shadows above us. *Oh, man. I'd rather have geysers. What goes up must come down.* I remembered all the tiny ice crystals on my gloves. Their bigger brothers were about to rain down on us.

"Run," my dad said. Together we bounded across the open field.

Behind us, above us, coming through the atmosphere like mutant cannonballs, were chunks of ice, projectiles from the ice geysers falling back to Europa.

The thuds shook the ground behind us as we made for the next cluster of penitentes. *Maybe we can hide there if we can make it.* Thud. An iceberg fell beside me and shattered to pieces, knocking me sideways. I looked for shelter ahead and saw little to none. *We're not going to make it,* I thought.

It was my turn to act. I dropped behind the group a few bounds, and the next time I jumped, I did a full twist to look behind us at the ice chunks on our tail and above our heads. And me with no red powers. I did have a black staff.

I hit the first chunk with an incinerator shot—just enough to deflect it. I landed, spun, and tried to toss the next block of ice. Too heavy. Incinerator shot. Much better.

Suddenly my dad was beside me. We incinerated the next projectile together, and again and again. It was like playing that old arcade game *Meteor Blast* that he kept in Mission Control. It was pretty easy with one or two targets, but a dozen were headed our way, of varying size and death potential. *In this game you've only got one life, not three,* I reminded myself.

"Cave ahead," Buckshot yelled between breaths. I turned to look. Sure enough, there was a perfectly circular hole in a penitente straight ahead. He and Janice had not completely recovered from their last dance with death, and they stumbled toward the hole. A shadow loomed above them. Looking up I saw an iceberg the size of a school bus descending on them. I blasted the thing with my staff and so did my dad. It had little effect. Buckshot and Janice would make the cave, but dad and I were too far behind to catch up.

"Tully, incinerate straight back! Now! Now!" My dad launched dozens of incinerator shots behind himself, which launched him forward like a turbo booster. I did the same. We slid at high speed into the cave. The last thing I saw was the iceberg a few feet over my head. Then I felt an enormous thud as it sealed the hole behind us.

Thud. Thud. Thud.

The iceberg storm continued as we slid into a cave with slick walls, a dark cave, a cave that angled down, down, down, and we slid, slid, slid in the darkness. I flicked on my headlamp as we zipped through the perfectly round tube. *This can't be natural,* I thought, and it wasn't. This was it, the first sign of the Ascendant on Europa.

A wide opening loomed in front of me. Beyond it, a darkness that swallowed everyone. Their lights vanished. I dug my staff into the ice but it was too hard to dent. There was no way to stop, so I let myself fall. We landed rather roughly in a heap in the dark with a chorus of grunting and panting. Little Bacon repositioned himself in my shirt pocket inside the suit. I checked to see if any of my body parts were broken or ruptured or missing.

We had been on Europa for an hour.

Our headlamps only went so far, leaving most of the room in shadow. All of us stayed still. Then Sunjay and Janice shouted into their mics.

"Ouch, something's poking me! I'm caught. What the heck is this?"

"It's got me, too," yelled Janice. I could feel her flopping beside me like a trapped animal.

Then overhead lights flicked on. We were surrounded by...

...fishing gear? Sunjay and Janice struggled to free themselves from a huge net, which was shoved inside an enormous trap. Buckshot walked over to help them.

We were in a large ice cave. One side was packed full of fishing tackle and nets. The other side opened into a subglacial ocean, which glowed with a purple light. We worked on untangling ourselves from the equipment.

"Huh, these look like crab traps," I said, pushing aside some netting and pointing to the crab trap that had them trapped. I had seen similar equipment on boats in Dutch Harbor before, only this equipment could have caught enormous crab. "Yeah, look, there's even bait inside this trap. You throw it in the water and wait for something."

"Something the size of a school bus," Sunjay said.

"Why do people always compare stuff in space to school buses?" I asked.

"Because they're about this size."

"Anyway, once the mutant school bus crab is inside, you pull in the pod."

"Glad we slid in on this side of the cave," said Buckshot, pointing to a watery opening on the other side. "That looks mighty deep."

"Miles deep," said Janice. "Below the ice there's probably nothing but water until you get to the core. It's warmer here. You were right, White Knight. They fish for a living. Oh, sick, what is THAT?"

Janice tried to wipe some green goo off the side of her spacesuit. It only stuck to her glove. Then she realized where it was coming from. One of the exterior pockets on Sunjay's suit was open. There was a cracked bottle full of green mess seeping down the side of his suit. I knew what it was in an instant.

"Zaxon, you didn't," I said, pointing to his leg. He cringed and pulled the busted bottle from his pocket. Everyone understood in a heartbeat.

"I drank the death smoothie," he blurted out.

"That's the dumbest—WHY?" said Janice.

"It was too tempting," he said, flexing his arms. "It's how I made all these gains."

"It's also why you were sick," I said.

"No, well, probably, but what was I supposed to do?"

"NOT DRINK THE ALIEN DEATH SMOOTHIE!" said Janice.

"You don't get it," he shot back. Did he have tears in his eyes? He pointed at me and said, "Tully has all these powers. Buckshot and the Commander are big and strong. You're smart like Tabitha. What do I have? How am I going to fight the Ascendant? How am I going to protect Tully? Sure it made me sick, but it will be worth it if I can defend Tully. He's the important one. Not you or me. We all know it's true."

His chest heaved.

"You're important, too," Janice said softly.

"Not like him," he said. "And that's okay. That's why I have to protect him. I had to get stronger."

I wanted to say something but words failed me. Sunjay stood tall, and I could see he was proud of what he did, not ashamed.

"You won't do us any good if you hurt yourself," Janice said. "That would make it worse."

"I know, but – "

"Use codenames," my dad said.

"Oh, sorry," Sunjay said. My dad walked over to him and squared up his shoulder. "Zaxon, I know what you are trying to say, but listen to me. You do not know your own strength. You know what it is?"

"No," he said.

"You are a fierce friend," my dad explained. "Everyone should have a friend like you, but they are hard to find. And you should know something else: your best is what you should ask of yourself. Nothing more. It's all that we would ask of you. It's all that a good commander would ever ask of you."

Sunjay stood face to face with my dad, our commander, his hero. He nodded and tossed the bottle aside. I had no idea until then how much he wanted to protect me. A fierce friend. My dad was right. He patted

Sunjay on the shoulder and was about to say something to get us back on track when the lights went out.

My first thought was, *These must be motion-activated.* I waved my hand in front of my face. Nothing. Then I heard a number of sounds: a loud crunch, Sunjay's scream; heavy breathing; and footsteps coming my way. The last sound I heard was a loud boom. I felt a sharp pain in my neck and everything went black.

ICA-WHO?

My senses returned. I heard a gruff voice echoing off the walls of a room, a room that slowly came into focus as I shook my aching head.

A rough-faced Ascendant stood in front of me, with wrinkles around his dark eyes and tattoos scrolling across his worn face. He had a long braid of black hair, as they all seem to have. He wore a grey tunic, and every inch of him was covered with tattoos and muscle and fish guts. A chunk of ice formed in my stomach. We were captured.

"I heard your English styles," the voice said. "You spoke in your sleep. You called out for that Earther girl, her by name Tabitha. What about that, hey?"

I surveyed my surroundings. My hands were bound behind my back with rope. My helmet was off. I was seated in a small room with walls of ice. The Ascendant grabbed me by the chin and pulled me forward. Monstrous sea creatures swam across his face.

"Hey, what about the English then? You some actors traveled beyond the Rathmore out so far? We all Earth-leaving soon so that don't make the sense."

Stars floated across my vision. My head felt bruised. *Tully, focus. Think. Look around. This is a fisherman. He thinks you're an actor. What are you doing out here? Everyone is about to leave for the Earth.* I needed time to "make the sense."

"My friends," my voice sounded hoarse, "where are they?"

The fisherman slapped me and gripped my face again. The impact rattled my brain. I thought that I might pass out.

"Only speaking to me in English, hey? That's grave. Downstairs is where they are. Tossed aside their staffs when I captured you. You, the weak one. Who are you? Make the sense or I take you to Rathmore, let them make it."

How was I supposed to make sense of the last hour of my life? We went from happily hopping across a moonscape to dodging death icebergs to fisherman interrogations. He raised his hand again, and I recoiled. He waited, but he wouldn't wait long, so I said the first thing that came to mind.

"I am Tully Orion Harper," I said.

The fisherman frowned at me for a moment, turned my face back and forth in his rough hands, then dropped my head and let out a rib-splitting laugh. He slapped his leg and pointed at me. His breath smelled like salt and seaweed.

"Tully Harper is you," he said between laughs and leg slaps. "The Red Thief. Him sitting right here in my house. And who's that down there? Your father?"

"Yes, Commander Mike Harper," I said.

"Oh-ho-ho!" More laughter. A lot. The fisherman beat his hand upon his knee. Behind him, a boy appeared, not much younger than me, with black hair and a braid but no tattoos. He stared at me wide-eyed. The fisherman waved him in.

"Son, look what your father caught. You should be deep fearing. It's not a ketea maximus. No, this is worse. It's the Red Thief, he himself." *Oh, bangers. Word gets around quickly on Europa. I have a nickname already.* "He flown on magic wings from Earth to Europa. And what would the Red Thief with us be wanting?" he said. "Him he already stole the Sacred. What he want now?"

"Nothing," I said, looking at the boy. "I want to go to the Rathmore Chaos."

More laughter. Then the fisherman reared back and backhanded me. His face boiled into seething anger. He pulled out what looked like the handle of a knife. He flicked his wrist and, well, the rest of the knife appeared, a glowing purple blade that he held to my throat. This felt way too familiar.

"I'm not you to Rathmore traveling," he growled. "We make our own punishment here in the Outlands. Don't need the Lord Ascendant for to help me with thieves. Now you think on this one: which hand do you want to keep, thief? I'm one of them taking."

The fisherman grunted toward his son, spoke something more in Greek, and left.

Great, now Trackman and I will have something to talk about. Hey, Tully, I haven't seen you since you chopped off my hand. Oh, who chopped off yours?

The boy knelt beside me and tied my wrists tighter. He bound my feet with shaking hands. He stole a few glances at my face but would not make eye contact with me. Something about his demeanor made me wonder about him.

"Your dad thinks we are thieves," I told the boy, "but we are not. I am Tully Harper."

The boy finished binding my feet and picked up more rope. He could not finish the job though. He could only stare at my hands, which I held in front of me. My hands. Had he heard stories of Tully Harper and his terrible powers? He stared at me with doubt in his eyes. There was no time to waste. I had to prove myself.

"Look, wait. Hey, LB, can you help me with something?" I asked. My pocket began to wriggle as Little Bacon popped his head out and straightened his hat. The boy tossed the rope toward me and scurried away from the strange being that lived in my pocket. "Who am I, Little Bacon?"

"You are Tully Harper," he said. "And I am Little Bacon. Who is this fine young man?"

The boy collected himself. He crept toward me cautiously. "You are the Red Thief?"

"I am Tully Harper."

"Like in my dream?"

That comment got my attention. The boy looked unsure, like there were two ideas in combat in his mind. I had to take a chance.

"Will you free me?" I asked. "I can give you my black staff, this space suit, Little Bacon."

"Yes," said Little Bacon, "I can show you better knots for securing people." *Oh, Bacon. Helpful as usual.* Fortunately the boy ignored him.

"You can't be the Red Thief. Earthers cannot be journeying to Europa. So says the Lord Ascendant."

"So he does," I said, "but here I am."

"And how would my dad catch The Red Thief? Him who would have burned us with fire or sliced us open. He's an Earther, and Earthers are full of hate for us. So says the Lord Ascendant."

Of course. More Ascendant propaganda. He thinks I'm a cold-blooded killer. I probably started this war.

"I don't run around toasting aliens for fun—I mean, I don't want to burn you. Those are lies. That's not who I really am. Was there something about me in your dream?"

He didn't respond.

"If you let me go, I promise I won't harm you or your dad. You can tell your dad that the thief slipped out of his bonds."

"That is highly likely, as these ropes will not hold up under duress," said Little Bacon.

The boy looked at me, confused. Without a word, he ran out of the room.

Well, that went well. Little Bacon burrowed back into my pocket. I struggled with the knot on my feet. It was better than Little Bacon made it sound, and I couldn't budge it. With tied hands I could run. With tied feet? Hopping to freedom did not seem like an option even in low gravity. I sat back on the floor, trying to clear my head. Time passed. *His dreams! I should have asked him more about them. That missed opportunity could have cost me my life. Unless the others can escape and free me. Stars, we never even made it to Rathmore. I'll never see Tabitha again.*

In the distance I heard footsteps echoing off icy walls. *Well, goodbye, right hand. I'm going to miss you. Maybe they will call me the Red Lefty now.* I saw the purple glow of the knife blade coming around the corner, but it wasn't the fisherman. It was the boy. He held the knife in a quivering hand. A backpack of beautiful fur was slung across his shoulder.

He put the knife to my throat.

"You are Tully Harper," he said.

"Yes, I am."

"Swear by the Sacred that you will not hurt us," he said.

Gulp. I was about to swear, but the words stuck in my throat. Even a knife could not make me speak them.

"Sorry, but I can't swear," I said. "The Sacred would not like that. I can give you something else though, but first I need your name. I gave you mine."

"Jason, son of Typhon."

"Jason, son of Typhon, I give you my word. I won't hurt you or your dad. I just need to get to Rathmore to save a friend." He hesitated, then withdrew the blade from my neck and prepared to slice my bonds. "Wait, not yet, Jason. Will you free the others and promise to help us get to Rathmore?" He did not respond, just finished freeing me. He helped me to my feet and backed away with the knife between us.

"Stay in front of me," he said.

He guided me through the enormous hollow rooms of his house. Some rooms were made of ice, others were constructed of some sort of metal, all of them connected by a series of rising and falling tunnels. After several rises and falls we reached a final room, which was clearly his bedroom. He pointed to a circular opening in the far wall. *Hopefully he's not tricking me into something.*

"The tube goes to the waters. You will find your friends and the submarine." *Sure, that makes perfect sense. Just jump into the black hole in the wall and everything will be fine.* I put on my helmet, but he grabbed my arm.

"Before you go, some things for Rathmore."

He rummaged through a small opening that resembled a closet. A cot stood against one wall with clothes shoved beneath it. There was one shelf, and it was lined with figurines, some of them Ascendant and some dressed like human soldiers or cowboys or cops. *He's a kid. He plays with these.* I imagined all the figures arranged on the floor doing battle for control of the universe. The rummaging stopped behind me, and he smiled.

"That one is called a cowboy," he said, grabbing the figurine. "These are his guns. He wishes that he had a horse. Can I tell you my secret?"

"Sure," I said.

"Sometimes the cowboy fights against Commander Akakios, the great warrior of Rathmore, and sometimes, when papa is not watching, I let the cowboy win." He grinned at me with mischief in his eyes, and I smiled back. Something big changed within both of us in that moment in his room. Time stood still. We were just two kids looking at action figures. Then we heard clanking sounds echo from another room. Jason put his finger over his lip and handed me a backpack. It was made out of sealskin or something. I opened it to see what was inside, and when I did, the backpack didn't seem so cool anymore.

"What in the solar system are we supposed to do with these?" I whispered.

"You do not know how to use them?" he asked.

"Of course I do, but why would we wear these?" Travel can get confusing sometimes, even if someone is speaking English.

He explained his plan for our arrival in Rathmore in great detail. By the end, it seemed clever enough to work. Clever, stupid, crazy—there's a fine line between them, but we really were ninjas like Sunjay said, this might work out just fine. What made less sense was how a ten-year-old alien boy developed this plan.

He pointed toward the tube. We could hear Typhon in the other room grumbling, but I was too curious to leave just yet.

"Wait," I said. "Jason, you didn't come up with this whole plan by yourself, did you? Did someone help?"

"Maybe," he said. "He doesn't have a name. I call him the Misty Man."

"Then I think we have a mutual friend," I said. The Sacred took on the same form when he talked to me. My dad was right. Something guided us.

"I did not think he was real," Jason whispered, "but now I do. You are good and real, too, and so I think now, maybe the Lord Ascendant is wrong. Maybe Icarus is good and real like you."

"Ica-who?" I asked, but Jason said no more. He pushed me into the tube, and I slid toward an unknown future with a backpack full of crazy.

Thump.

I slid into the fishing cave again. The lights popped on, almost blinding me. Everyone was asleep. *Stars, how long have we been here?* Sunjay and Janice were huddled together in one corner. My dad stirred first, saw me coming, and roused the others. He pointed toward the far wall where our black staffs hung. They were in my hands in a split second, and I pulled at the cage door with a staff while Buckshot kicked from the inside. Success. They put on their suits as I searched for the first part of Jason's plan.

"What are you looking for?" asked Janice.

"A submarine," I said, frantically scanning the room. "Jason said we should take the submarine."

"Who's Jason?" asked Sunjay.

"Who cares?" said Janice. "Let's check the water."

Stupid Tully. We ran to the other side of the room where ripples pattered against the ice. Beneath it hovered a dark shape. It was either a large shark or a small submarine. I aimed my staff at the water and tried to pull it toward us.

"All together now," my dad said, aiming his staff at the water. The ship ascended, and as it did so, the lights went off again.

"Buck, distraction," said my dad.

Oh, great. Return of Typhon, I thought, turning around in the dark. Buckshot flipped on his headlamp. I heard running in the dark. But before the feet could reach Buckshot, I heard a loud grunt. A scuffle. Someone was fighting. I ran toward the sound, as did Buckshot, who shined his headlamp at the noise. What we saw terrified me. My dad held Typhon in a chokehold. The fisherman was losing consciousness, but my dad held him up. He didn't let go, even as Typhon's legs went limp and his eyes rolled back in his head. I could see the alien's lips working. He was fading into a darkness that would not end.

"No!" I yelled, looking at my dad's grip and the determination in his eyes. He did not plan to leave any witnesses to our arrival. In a few seconds, Typhon wouldn't just be unconscious. This monster that planned to take my hand would be dead. I had no choice.

Whoosh.

I hit them both with a stun shot.

Typhon and my dad crumpled to the floor. The lights came back on, and on the other side of the room stood Jason with his eyes wide. He ran toward his father. Buckshot raised his black staff toward Jason. He reared back to stun the alien boy, but I rushed between them.

"Tully, move," he said to me.

"Just wait, wait!" I yelled. "Jason, wait!"

I met him in the middle of the room and he threw a punch at me. I tossed aside my black staff and caught him in a bear hug. He was smaller than me. That's pretty small.

"Tully…" demanded Buckshot, looking for an open shot.

"Buckshot," I said slowly, "he has an action figure of a cowboy in his bedroom. Sometimes he lets the cowboy beat the alien. You understand. He's a kid." I gave him my dad's commander stare, and to my surprise Buckshot lowered the weapon.

"You promised," Jason said, struggling in my arms. "You are the Red Thief! You're lying Earther scum just like they said. Icarus is a lie! My dreams are a lie!"

I spun Jason around to look in his eyes. Purple eyes full of tears.

"Trust those dreams," I told him. "They told you the truth. So did I. I'm not a liar, Jason. Our dads were fighting. I just stunned them to make them stop. Your dad will be fine. So will mine. But we're *both* going to have some explaining to do."

Our dads sprawled on the ground in front of us. Jason straightened himself and sniffled. I wasn't used to giving people commands, but he listened, just like Buckshot did.

"What do I tell my dad when he wakes up?" he asked.

"Tell him the truth. We stole your submarine, and if he says anything about this, we will return." Then I whispered, "But I do not think the Misty Man will let that happen."

Jason nodded and stepped back. He pointed to the sub with a remote control of some kind. It raised the submarine the rest of the way out of the water. Then he sat down on the floor with his father's head in his lap.

"Remember the plan," he said. "And look for Icarus. If he's real, he can help you."

Ica-who? I wanted to ask him more, but time was up.

Buckshot hauled my dad on board, the rest of us behind him. I took one last look at Jason and his father before I ducked into the sub. With tears in his eyes, cradling his unconscious father, Jason flicked the controls again and lowered us into the mysterious ocean.

THREE FOR SURVIVAL

Stars, I stunned my dad. He's going to kill me.
You can imagine what kind of explaining I had to do, crammed into the small, leaky submarine, with Buckshot piloting us underwater. Just like Jason explained, we found the "waterpath" to the Rathmore Chaos, which ran like a luminescent chalk line through the ocean.

The submarine was thin, about thirty feet long, and smelled like my aunt's old plane. There was no room to stand but there were four seats in the hull, which was transparent and allowed for an amazing view of the ocean. One seat in the back of the sub looked more like a gun turret. There were plenty of buttons for nets and controls for a retractable arm. I could imagine Jason and Typhon hunting sea creatures in this ocean together. They probably had great adventures, but I didn't have time to ponder any of that.

"This hunk of junk makes the *Mini-Mane* look like a hover yacht!" said Sunjay, scrunched beside Janice. "Tully, what the heck was that all about?"

I tried to explain.

My dad worked his jaw back and forth, like he'd been punched. He sloughed off the effects of the stun shot, but he didn't accept my reason so easily. "We need to stay hidden," he said. "We left that boy and his father alive. That could get us captured or killed. You understand that, don't you?"

"Yeah, I do, but we can't just run around assassinating every Ascendant we run into. Especially if I promised not to harm them."

"We may have to do some unpleasant things for the greater good," my dad explained. "Why did he free you in the first place?"

"Because he knew who I was," I said.

"How?" asked Sunjay.

"Uh, he just did—and also I told him."

"Bangers, you're nuts!" said Sunjay. "You blew our cover!"

"No, I didn't. He knew. He helped us escape. They're not all bad, the Ascendant." *I can't believe I just said that.*

Nobody was happy with that explanation, so I changed the subject to our arrival at Rathmore. Not like that calmed everyone down or anything.

"Lemme get this straight," Buckshot said. "You want me to drive this sub to an alien city and just pop up beside it in some sort of lake. Then what did Jason say we should do? Swim ashore?"

There are times when telling someone everything is a bad idea. I've learned this, and I knew that if I told Buckshot the rest, *he* would probably wreck the sub.

"I'll explain the rest later," I said, leaning on the backpack behind me as we piloted slowly through the underwater ocean.

The ocean of Europa. Unbelievable. I forgot all about the crazy plan as we wound our way past an amazing array of plants and animals-fish, squid, sharks, whales, jellyfish all swam past us. They were all "one-offs" of the ocean life on Earth, like celebrity look-alikes. Most of them were bioluminescent. They lit the ocean with a wondrous purple hue—some as small as snowflakes, others as big and bright as stadium lights.

"Stars, it's wonderful," said Sunjay. "I just wish it wasn't so dark."

"It's not that dark," I said.

"Tully, your head," said Janice, reaching over to me. I'd forgotten about the Typhon's backhand. Dried blood crusted my forehead. She scraped it away. Her eye was still swollen from the geyser adventure.

"Sorry you got roped into this, Carpool," I said. "This 'Three for Survival Project' is a bit more than you expected."

"Bangers, that's the first time you've been right in a long time," she said, "but seriously, don't be sorry, Tully. I just hope we don't fail."

"Take some pictures," said Sunjay, "that might earn us some extra credit."

"I have been," Janice said, "but I'm not talking about the project, Sunjay. We can fail that. I just don't want to fail the world...or Tabitha. Hey, Tully, we're almost to Rathmore. When do you think you should use the Harper Device?"

"Uh, soon," I said. *No, actually that's just a prayer.*

"What about sooner rather than later?" she asked. "An Ascendant fisherman and his son just captured us. Jupiter's rings, who are we going to run into in Rathmore? We could use some magical powers."

A Submarine Ride

We didn't run into more fishermen on our way to Rathmore. We bumped into numerous bizarre sea animals that couldn't get out of our way, and one that we should have avoided. No one saw it coming except me.

Buckshot piloted us through the underwater ocean. Thousands of feet of ice formed a ceiling above the ocean, illuminated and sparkling by the bright glow of sea creatures and the path. Bright to me, at least. Buckshot seemed to strain to keep us on course.

"I can't see but one beacon in front of us," he said, steering toward it. I could see row after row lined up in a curving path.

"You don't see the others?" I pointed. "Or *that* thing?"

"What others?" said Sunjay. "What thing?"

The line of beacons glowed brightly as we approached. The creature retreated, but not before I caught a glimpse as it strayed too close. Long neck, paddle-shaped legs, and swooshing tail. *It's like a sea dinosaur*, I thought as it plummeted into the darkness below us. *Europosaurus?* That was a good name for it.

"Boy howdy," Buckshot said. "Why don't you drive, eagle eyes?"

We switched seats and I took the controls of the submarine.

"More like an owl," my dad said. "Maybe it's the effect of the Sacred. It came from Europa, so that may be part of your powers."

After all my insecurity about my powers, it felt great to pilot us through the water. The feeling was right, but I was wrong about one thing.

A 3D map appeared in front of us with our location blinking purple. It was much like the starmap. Other blips emerged as well, but one brighter than the rest—our destination. I recognized the word:

Χάος

Chaos.

We were close.

Bump.

"Stars, what was that?" Sunjay asked. I saw a dark shadow for a second under the submarine, but it disappeared.

"We just plowed into some big alien fish," Buckshot explained. "Get used to it, Sun."

Bump, bump.

The map flickered.

"Seriously, it's nothing," Buckshot said. "Ain't no fish in any ocean that wants to eat a metal submarine."

"What do you know about what fish on Europa like to eat?" said Janice.

"Carpool, you ever been fishing?"

"Have you ever been to Europa?" she asked.

"Dangit, you're missing the point," he said. "I do a lot of surf fishing."

"Nobody surfs and fishes at the same time," Sunjay said. Buckshot threw up his arms. Little Bacon popped out of my pocket and cleared his throat.

"Surf fishing," Little Bacon said, "is a sport wherein the fisherman stands in shallow ocean water and attempts to catch fish that are very close to shore. Many surf fisherman wear rubberized pants to stay dry."

Janice laughed. "I'm picturing you in rubber pants!"

"They ain't tight or anything," said Buckshot. "Just waterproof. Anyway, that's surf fishing. Get it? Things bump your legs, but nothing bites you. Fish eat fish, not people. Definitely not metal. Listen, y'all wake me up if anything takes a bit out of us."

Buckshot kicked back and pulled his cowboy hat down over his eyes. Where did he keep that thing? I would have shown it to Jason if I had the chance. The submarine pumped along happily. Janice chuckled to herself about Buckshot's rubber pants. I rubbed my eyes. My dad scooted forward to talk to me, which seemed to wipe away all the silliness.

"I found a hiding spot for the Device," he told me. He gestured to the back of the submarine. There were small grey buoys toward the back. Some were attached to cages, and all of them looked similar to the Device. "We can hide it in plain sight when we park the submarine. I don't know what will happen if you wake it up, but it won't be close enough to hurt us or draw much attention."

"Sure," I said. I still had this picture in my mind of him choking Typhon to death. I had seen him fight before but never fight to kill.

"Son, you okay?"

"Sure."

"You look a little tired," he said. "Hang in there. So explain Jason's plan to me."

"Oh, you mean Jason, the kid whose dad you almost murdered? What about 'Fight, but do not hate'?"

"Oh, I see," he said. He shook his head. Not in a "I told you so" way, but in a way that told me he understood and was sorry. "Son, the fate of the world rests on our shoulders. We can't get captured. If we fail, many more people will die. I will kill to keep that from happening. I suppose I should have asked you this a long time ago."

"What?"

"Will you?"

"Will I what?"

"Kill, if necessary," he said, stroking the red streak in his hair.

"Before I met Jason, I would have said yes. Now, I'm not so sure."

"Well, you need to know. It may come down to that. We're at war. There's a difference between killing someone in war and killing someone on the street. There's a difference between a soldier shooting his enemy and a murderer shooting his victim. The soldier does what he does for God and country. The murderer takes a life for his own selfish purposes. We are more like soldiers; we are not murderers. Do you see?"

"Yeah, I see the difference. It's just hard to accept. What if you kill a good guy instead of a bad guy? Or the innocent instead of the guilty? I don't want blood on my hands."

"No one does, son, but we may have to make those choices."

He tousled my hair. "We've gotten ourselves into quite a mess, Tully Harper. I hope for everyone's sake we can steer ourselves out of it."

Bump, bump, bump.

At that moment, the submarine lurched sideways and rolled over. I smacked my head against the glass and saw stars, but also saw a massive shadow, shiny white teeth and enormous eye peering into the submarine. The Europasarus was back with a vengeance. It had followed us and now it batted our submarine back and forth between its spiked flippers. We bounced like pinballs inside the submarine, all of us thrown forward into an enormous pile. Someone kicked me in the head. I tried to steer us toward the surface but sent us right toward the creature's mouth. Another lurch sent us backward.

It was the last thing I felt before I blacked out. I could feel my body flopping around inside the submarine. Then the black became red.

When I regained consciousness I wasn't seeing out of my own eyes. I awoke in a rather strange spot—a sea monster's mind. I could taste the salt water in my mouth. At the moment I held a rather hard-scaled fish, the one with no fins and the glowing head, between my fins. My empty stomach demanded food, but this fish felt too hard to be eaten. I was growing weak, no longer quick enough to catch healthy prey anymore. I had to go after the wounded and slow. Hunger was driving me mad, mad enough to eat this terrible fish, and this one had something special buried in its belly. Several pink things that would be soft and warm. I had eaten one before on accident and bit into another and spit it out, but now I must eat them or die. Something else was in the hard-scaled fish—I could sense it—some gray thing that would taste better than anything else. It would fill my stomach forever. I must bite through the sharp skin. I will lose teeth but I must eat this fish with a stinger in the back. I must try.

I understood.

Eat or die. She had watched her children starve. She had to fight to survive. There was meat inside, so she bit into metal. She lost a tooth, but bubbles came from the hole in the hard-scaled fish. She bit again. Another tooth gone. This one stuck in the hide of the fish. Maybe it could be eaten. Watch out for the stinger. No stingers. Then she went for a third bite.

No, stop! I thought. *You'll kill us.* She hesitated. Something confused her, short-circuited her hungry brain for a second. My thoughts were in her head, just like hers were in mine. Then I was sucked out of the dream and back to reality, where my dad held me in his arms while everyone else scrambled about the inside of the flooding cabin.

Icy water poured in through a hole, which Sunjay tried to plug. Buckshot shoved my backpack into the other hole and applied pressure, but Janice shoved him out of the way.

"Oh, they won't eat metal!" she yelled, plugging the hole. "Okay, Mr. Surf Fisherman, kill this fish before it kills us!"

"That's not a fish, that's a monster!" Sunjay said.

"She's starving," I said, shaking myself, trying to clear my mind. "I was in her head. I—"

"Does it flippin' matter?" Janice said.

"Yes," I said, "we need a stinger."

I pushed my dad aside and scrambled to the back of the sub. There were controllers for the nets, the arm, and, yes, a harpoon!

"Buckshot, bring us around," I said. He took the controls at the front. Wrenching the submarine away from the sea serpent, he spun me toward it.

The shadow towered over our submarine. A magnificent beast the size of a blue whale, its belly exposed to us. I could see its luminescent skin, and just under that skin its thumping heart. My target, its heart, the heart of a half-starved, beautiful sea creature, who had raised and lost many young, who wanted nothing more than to survive. I couldn't hesitate any longer.

I fired the harpoon. The dart split the water like a bullet, piercing its thick hide. Its eyes widened, mouth opened gasping for breath. The fins flailed for a moment. Then the beast went limp. Its purple skin glowed no longer. I watched it sink into the darkness below, never to rise.

There was no time to think. I pushed myself back to the front of the submarine. Buckshot returned the controls to me.

"We're pretty deep," he said. "I can't see anything out there and the map isn't working."

I could see just fine.

"Closer to the surface!" yelled Janice, water pouring onto her head. "Less pressure, less water gets in."

Janice was, as usual, correct. I pushed the submarine almost to the surface, where the ice met the water. The gusher became a trickle. Our nerves settled.

"Uh, that one is on me, folks," said Buckshot. "They eat metal. I'm just glad that bad boy didn't eat us."

"Girl," I said, picturing her plummet into the deep waters. "It was a mother." She hadn't been bad. She was innocent and starving. She was desperate, and her desperation was the death of her. No, I was the death of her, and if I had not killed her, we would all be dead now. *Can you kill, if necessary?* I tried to shake off the weight of my dad's question. This creature wasn't human, but it seemed like part of the answer.

We found the waterpath again.

Not like we really needed the path anymore. Up ahead, I saw a break in the ice – a light blue patch of water that meant there was sky, not ice, above our heads. We were thousands of feet below the surface, so someone must have hollowed out the ice up ahead.

Now I could explain the first step in the plan, as crazy as it sounded. *Who cares? If it takes me one step closer to Tabitha, I'll walk on water.* "You'll pass through shadow and flame," the Harper Device once told me. *Well, maybe the shadow was past. On to the flame.* The light brightened ahead.

"There's the Chaos," I said.

ALIEN TRUNKS

Light streamed through the blue waters above the submarine. That didn't mean we were near the surface of Europa though. I pointed the sub upward. We surfaced and found ourselves floating in the tourmaline waters. Peaky waves rippled on the surface.

Around us a few other submarines bobbed. Sailboats drifted by in the distance. Groups of paddle boarders and swimmers flecked the warm waters.

Surrounding us on all sides were icy walls. They stretched toward the sky. They were at least a mile straight up and colored a beautiful blue-gray. Above our heads was a clear ice dome that arced across the entire sky. It was as if something drilled a perfectly round hole into the ice until it reached the ocean, then capped it with a crystal lid. It was beautiful.

Through the dome we could see Jupiter and its multi-colored rings. The gas giant took up most of the sky, but a sliver of space showed us, in the distance, a bright pinprick of light—our sun—and the monstrous planet above lit the ocean, walls, and dome of Rathmore. It was quite a sight, but what lay in front of us was harder to imagine.

An icicle as wide as the Amazon River reached from the ocean to the dome. It was broad at the base and top but thinner in the middle.

"Ain't low gravity something else?" said Buckshot, shaking his head. "The city is built like a spiral staircase. That newel is probably two miles tall and a quarter-mile wide."

"What's a—?"

"A newel," said Little Bacon, "is a central post in a spiral staircase that bears the weight of the stairs."

"See, he's helpful," Janice told me.

Around that newel were what looked like stairs, and each step had its own color. It was still miles away, and as we slowly approached, I observed the seven "steps" of the staircase city-well, the sixth step was nearly gone. Its jagged remains looked like a tooth broken off at the base. *What happened there?* I wondered.

The closer we drifted in the sub, the more Rathmore looked like a city. There were figures the size of ants crawling on the steps. *Those aren't ants, they are Ascendant.* I started to pick out buildings on each step, some of them tall like skyscrapers, others round like sports arenas. From the ocean we could only see the bottom of the highest steps.

"Stars, are those Ascendant up there?" asked Sunjay.

"Those buildings remind me of my visit to Italy last summer," Janice said. "Doesn't that look like a Roman arena? There was a great gelato shop outside one of them..."

"Enough about gelato," I said. "We need to get down to business."

"Okay, what's the plan?" she said. Gulp. I didn't want to tell them. My dad bought me some time.

"Before Tully explains," my dad said, "let's be clear on one thing. If separated, meet here on the submarine in twenty-four hours."

Everyone nodded and looked my way. Showtime. *Oh, man, I don't want to say this out loud. They're going to think I'm crazy.*

There was just no way to say the plan, so I motioned for Buckshot to hand me the backpack. I unzipped it and out fell the contents: four pairs of swim trunks and one women's gray one-piece bathing suit with white polka dots. Janice picked it up. I smiled sheepishly.

"You have a backpack full of retro swimsuits," Janice explained.

"There are bathrobes, too," I said.

"Fantastic," she said. "Now what is the plan?"

"See, uh, that *is* the plan," I said. "Jason told me, 'Put on the swim-suits and swim to shore.' Well, he called them 'bathing costumes' but he meant swimsuits because he doesn't speak the best English—so he said, 'Cover yourselves in the bathrobes because you have not tasted the ink.' He said that because we don't have tattoos. Anyway, then we go into the city and find clothes. Blend in. Get tattoos. Find Tabitha. She'll be in a purple tower."

"What about weapons?" asked Sunjay. "We need to defend ourselves."

"We can't just pop out of the water in bathrobes holding black staffs," I said. "Think about it like back on Earth. What if you saw some-one come out of the ocean with a shotgun?"

"Bangers, this is a bad plan," said Janice, throwing her arms in the air. "I can't wear this swimsuit. It's January. I'm not bathing suit ready."

"She's got a point," said Buckshot. Janice glared at him. "No, no. Not about you, Carpool. Look at these swimsuits, Tully. Me and your dad are gonna look like them European tourists in their tiny Speedos."

"Fine," I said, "then swim ashore naked! It's not perfect, but it's a plan, and Jason knows the city better than we do. Like Dad said, we have to stay hidden, play by their rules. Right, Dad?"

My dad stayed quiet. He surveyed the situation. *Come on, Dad. Get my back here.* Surely he had a backup plan, and when he hesitated I thought he might overrule me with some brilliant idea that would rescue Tabitha and return us to the sub in the simplest way possible, but he pursed his lips and nodded.

"If Tully says swim, we swim," my dad finally said. "If anyone can make a weird plan work, it's Tully."

"Uh, thanks?" I said. My dad grinned.

"Is the air safe out there?" asked Sunjay.

"It's safe," my dad said, "as is the water. The Ascendant are much like us, so let's suit up."

"Won't the water be freezing?" Sunjay asked.

"Sunjay, think," said Janice. "There are paddle boarders and swim-mers out there. And remember that geyser that almost killed me? That was heated water breaking through the crust of Europa. The Ascendant must use hydrothermal power. This place is air and water conditioned. I just wish they had better fashion sense."

No time was wasted. We suited up and stood on the deck of the sub with our robes under our arms.

"In our spacesuits we looked like a five-man wrecking crew, but good golly," Buckshot said. "I signed up for a lot on this trip, but not free swimming in the ocean."

"And you made fun of me for over packing," I said. "If only you had your own swim trunks, right?"

"We're going to look like idiots crawling out of the water in soaking bathrobes," he said.

"We'll see," my dad said. He rubbed the cloth between his fingers. "Remember, if separated, meet at the sub in twenty-four hours."

My dad dove in. I forgot we were in low gravity until he did. Watching him jump fifteen feet in the air, do a quadruple flip, and splash far away from us, all with the city of Rathmore beyond him, took my breath away, made me forget about our insane mission for a moment. *Where are we? What are we doing? My life just can't be real,* I told myself. But then I thought about my Red Visions of Tabitha. I would see her again soon, and it started with a plunge into alien waters.

"Hang on, Bacon," I said.

"It's the only way to hang," he replied, grabbing a handful of my hair and holding on for his dear Handroid life as we plunged into the warm blue water.

SHORE

"It's like Ascendant Cancun!" said Sunjay, swimming beside me.

"Come to Cancun!" shouted Little Bacon. "Just shout 'Cancun me, bro!' into your holophone to see video of the beautiful beaches and festive nightlife."

"Are you serious?" I said. "Enough infomercials, Little Bacon."

"Apologies, sir, but I am not myself right now. My last software update included a number of advertisements. I cannot switch them off once they begin."

Great...I have a talking billboard attached to my head. Why didn't I leave him on the submarine with the Sacred? Oh, that's right. Because he can read Greek.

Swimming was almost as easy as walking on Europa, but we had a long way to go and time to view the city from afar. I'm also not the greatest swimmer. Sunjay freestyled right past us. Janice rolled her eyes but watched him. We stuck with the breaststroke.

There was only one beach in front of the steep city streets. All one stretch of sand but divided into different colors, seven in all.

"Make for the grey beach to the far left," my dad said. "We can blend in." That made sense. It was crowded—fewer chairs, more towels, a throng of Ascendant playing in the water. The far right beach was almost completely deserted. The beach chairs and tables were dull yellow against the purple sand. I pointed them out.

"Those look gold-plated," said Janice. "That's classy, like the French Riviera."

"Cheap flights to the French Riviera! Just say 'Bonjour, mon amour!' into your holophone for a chance to win!" Little Bacon said, before I dunked him under the water.

"Be nice to Bacon," said Janice, "you say weirder things than that all the time."

Halfway to our grey beach we could see the sandy shore bustling with Ascendant beachgoers. The beach was stuffed with beach chairs, volleyball nets, and Frisbees that sailed toward the water, only to be caught thirty feet in the air by a jumping Ascendant. People—no, Ascendant—sat on beach chairs and blankets. Further up the beach they warmed their hands around glowing orange poles.

It was like an Ascendant version of Venice Beach. I visited there a few summer ago, and some of the crazy street performers on Venice Beach would love this place. They would fit in, too. Apparently not every Ascendant was seven feet tall and ready to play professional football.

The Ascendant didn't look like just one ethnicity. That was a relief. I thought Sunjay would blend in best because of his skin tone, but the Ascendant skin tone varied from light to dark. We would be okay. Well, almost okay. We could see all the beachgoers clearly now. Everyone except small children had tattoos scrolling across their skin.

"When we hit the beach, spread out," my dad told us. "Regroup near that statue beyond the beach."

Dad and Buckshot went in front of us. They swam through the peaky waves, threw on their bathrobes, and stepped lightly onto the sand, then Janice, then me, with Bacon shoved tightly into my robe pocket. But where was Sunjay? He swam too far ahead.

Immediately I noticed something about our bathrobes. They repelled water like a duck's feathers.

"I think they're hydrophobic," said Janice. "My uncle worked on material like this before he built the Upthruster. You can hold it underwater for an hour. When you pull it out, there's not a trace of water."

We walked out of the surf and up the steep beach. Alien children, teens, and adults all wandered up and down the gray sand wearing swimsuits or robes like ours. They laughed, talked, and played. Street performers wandered around playing drums and horns. It really wasn't so hard to blend in at first because of the massive crowd and the carnival atmosphere.

I felt Janice's hand grab mine from behind. "Stay close," she whispered. "Keep your head down. No eye contact."

With my head down I walked through the crowd. Swim trunks, legs, and a variety of tattoos. One tattoo appeared on every Ascendant's calf: either "I" or "II." *Were those Roman numerals? Well, Ascendant numerals?* In either case, the number was not in motion like the rest of the tattoos. They were fixed in place.

We waded through the sea of numbered legs—and were almost past most of them—when I saw him: a boy who looked familiar, about seven years old, like the one in the virtual arena on the *Mini-Mane*. A flower tattoo bloomed on his face. He stared up at me with a question in his black eyes. He looked at my calf, and I know what he saw. No number. I tried to pull the robe down farther, but it wouldn't cover my leg.

Keep moving, I willed myself forward, gripping Janice's hand. We passed broken chairs, men selling fried alien octopus on a stick, young Ascendant dancing and having jumping contests-*at least fifty feet in the air*-and found a boardwalk with shops on one side and the beach on the other. The beachgoers filed into a line and we did the same. *Yes, the towel line!* Up ahead, the Ascendant walked up, grabbed a towel from an ancient female Ascendant, and moved on. Janice whispered to me. "Tully, get back to back with me and face the shops. They won't see that we're missing the numeral."

So she noticed it, too? Of course she did. I faced the windows of a shop and tried not to look at the Ascendant girl behind the counter. She was older than me and really cute. Who knows how old she was? 3? 30? 300?

The Ascendant behind me tapped me on the shoulder. He said something in Greek and waved his hand at me. He frowned at me for a moment and then said something to everyone in the rest of the line. Immediately the entire line moved out of the way and ushered us to the front!

We're so dead—or something, I thought, keeping a grip on Janice's hand, but she looked relaxed somehow, like this was all supposed to be happening. We arrived at the front of the line and a heavily-tattooed female with ratty grey hair shoved towels toward us. Her wooden jewelry clattered with each movement. We grabbed the towels and started to leave when she yelled something toward us.

"Keep walking," I said.

But Janice turned around. The old Ascendant woman hobbled toward Janice and threw off the hood to reveal Janice's untattooed face.

Oh, stars.

I tugged Janice's hand and prepared to leap over the building behind us. We were about to be attacked, but Janice held me in place. The old alien, with a clatter of bracelets, slapped my hand away. The Ascendant in line laughed.

"Calm down, Spaceboy," she told me.

Then the old woman took the towel and patted the water off of Janice's face. Then she approached me and, with her wrinkled hands, did the same.

Janice walked back toward the towel stand and dropped some shells in a bowl beside the woman's stand. Where did she get those? She kissed the hand of Janice, who grabbed mine and started walking away with me like some sort of queen.

"Janice, what in the seven planets!" I whisper-yelled.

"I don't know," she said. "They treated us like royalty. We have to act the part."

"Yeah, so wrap that towel tight around you. We're going to stick out like celebrities until we get tattoos."

We walked back to the beach, found a clearing, and kept our hoods down low, kind of like a movie star would put on shades and a hoodie to avoid screaming hordes of fans. We scanned the crowd for Sunjay. An orange lamp above us warmed the sand, but it was also a UV lamp. The light would give us a tan if we sat there long enough.

"I didn't plan on working on my tan in space," Janice said.

"Oh, haha. So shells are money?" I asked.

"I stole some from the guy in front of us," she explained. "No sign of Sunjay, huh?"

We scanned the boardwalk for him. Minutes passed. Tension. Fear. *Breathe, Tully. Just observe them and be ready. Maybe they will treat him like royalty, too.* I tried to calm myself, but it was hard to get used to sitting on our enemy's beach. *They won't look so friendly when they enslave the Earth.*

A couple walked toward us holding hands. They were probably a foot from where we sat—and didn't look like they planned to stop—so Janice and I moved apart. The man frowned at me as they both leaped lightly into the air and landed on the other side of us. Janice looked at me.

"Don't flinch next time," she said. "He noticed."

"Uh, sure," I said. *Okay, notes to self: cover your calves, shells are money, and in low gravity, you can go over, not around, people.* Moments later we saw my dad and Buckshot. They walked past us.

"Zaxon?" my dad asked, hardly slowing down.

"Not yet," I said.

"We'll be back in five minutes. You should hold hands," he said.

Janice and I tried to play the happy teenage couple at the beach, sitting on the gray sand together, waiting for a friend. Holding her hand made me feel comfortable until she rubbed the lightning scar on the back of my hand.

Finally, he appeared. Sunjay, with his brand-new six-pack abs, muscular arms, and floppy black hair cascading from under the hood of his robe. He looked, well, dire cool for the first time in his life. Wrapped around his robe was a towel with gold trim. Also around his waist, the arm of an Ascendant girl.

Sunjay saw us. He pointed toward our lamp and he sat near us in the gray sand, he and this really pretty alien with wet black hair, a gold necklace and earrings, and dark smiling eyes. Probably two years older than us. Or two hundred. Janice nearly cut off the circulation in my hand.

"Pretty boy, your English sends me beyond the Pleiades," she said.

"Oh, thanks."

"Where is your promised one?" she asked with an Ascendant accent. Almost an Italian accent. "Why to the Gray Sand are you coming without her?"

"Uh, I like to eat those things," he said. He pointed toward an alien-octopus-on-a-stick vendor.

"Really? My mother makes the best fire *okto-poos,*" she said in heavily accented English. "Oh, *grilled.* That is the word. Grilled okto-poos." She motioned for the vendor. She gave the vendor a few shells and handed Sunjay the octopus. It was actually deep fried and covered in a white sauce like mayonnaise. He looked toward me. I shrugged. *Hey, it couldn't be as bad as the death smoothie.* He bit into one of the tentacles while another tentacle slapped him in the face. He heaved for a second but swallowed the rubbery food.

"To your liking?" she asked.

"Uh, dire good."

"Dire! You have beautiful words. You speak like a real Earther. Maybe I can still steal you before you marry."

"Marry, me?" he said.

"You are matching your tattoos with your new wife," she said. "Why isn't she here? She could still you be losing."

"Uh, yeah," he said. An octopus tentacle clung to his face, but he forced it into his mouth.

Janice poked me in the rib. "Do you get it? Aliens that are about to get married do not have tattoos. Everyone else does. It's some kind of ritual."

"Oh, that's why they cut us to the front of the line," I said. "The old lady alien thought we were cute together."

"Well, pretty boy with beautiful words, you must see my beauty as well." She pointed to her leg – a "IV" was tattooed there. "Is your girl from such a high step as me?"

"My girl," said Sunjay, slurping okto-poos. "Oh, she's, uh, great. She is the best."

"But she is not here. I come because I like a crowd. My beach is-how is it to say?-so few people. My friends there are boring. They worry about leaving. They say, 'What if Earthers are bad servants?' and 'What if I do not get the best house near the ocean beautiful?' Silly stuff. You do not have these worries. The Lord Ascendant will reward you for your service, yes? You are pretty small for a black staff though, yes?"

"Uh, yeah, but I'm growing," he said.

"Yes, you are. We will have to fight the Earthers, but we will have victory in the new world, dream living."

"Yeah, I guess so."

"Oh, there is no guess. Even the Firsters will have the good life living. Earthers will envy them for their beauty and power. Here, Firsters want to be like us. Their Firsters will be like gods. Still, they will never ascend to me."

"Where do you want to ascend to?" he asked her.

She dipped her head and looked at him as if to say, *You know, don't you?* Then she nodded toward the city.

For the first time I took a good look up the beach toward Rathmore. It took my breath away. The wide steps swirled upward in grey, yellow, blue, jade, crimson, and the last step, a radiant purple and gold. Rathmore, the "City of Seven Steps," spiraled toward the clear ice dome that held in this perfect atmosphere.

Oh, the steps! I thought. *She's a Fourther. She lives on the jade-colored step. She must want to be on the Fifth or Seventh. It's where the rich and powerful must live. Tabitha will be there.* But why wasn't there a Sixth? I didn't care what happened to it. I just knew that we needed it if we were going to reach Tabitha. The Seventh was purple and gold, and though I could not see the top, I imagined the purple tower from my dreams in the middle of it.

The Ascendant beauty was talking to Sunjay again, and he was starting to enjoy his octopus—and maybe all the attention from the alien girl.

"The Fifth Step," said the beautiful girl to Sunjay. "Do you think my dreams are too big? Not many cross from Fourth to Fifth, but I will. Do I not have the beauty and the mind?"

She smiled at Sunjay, who flipped his hair out of his eyes nervously. Janice almost broke my hand. My lightning scars throbbed.

"Uh, yeah, definitely," he said. "The beauty. And mind. You got it. The whole enchilada."

"Enchilada plates 1/2 off this week only at Green Turtle Beach House of Tex-Mex!"

A voice emerged from my pocket. You know who. The girl frowned and looked across Sunjay toward me. I scrambled to silence Little Bacon's latest advertisement. The girl looked curious. Before I could silence Bacon, I felt a slap across my face. Janice looked at me in disgust. *Why did she do that?* It became clear to me immediately as she glared at the Ascendant girl.

The Ascendant beauty sat back and whispered to Sunjay, "Look at the Firster dirt. Her boy looked at me too long. Like animals they are. So, the whole enchilada, a strange phrase," she continued. "You have the gift of language, pretty prince of a boy. I can see why the Lord Ascendant picked you. Are you sure you do not want me for a wife?"

Sunjay's jaw dropped.

"Pretty prince, maybe we will see each other again, but until then..." She kissed him on the cheek and sauntered down the beach.

IN AN ALLEY OFF THE BEACH

We regrouped in an alley behind the stores on the beach. Above us stood an enormous statue.

"Stars, it's not like I was looking for a date with the hottest alien on the beach! I got out of the water and she wrapped that towel around me."

"You needed a towel, not a wife!" Janice said. "She thought you were about to get married."

"I know, I know. She did think I was hot though, right?"

"Oh, sure. Nobody is hotter. Oh, but it might help that she thought you were one of the Lord Ascendant's warriors, too."

"A *pretty* prince," Sunjay corrected her.

"She was flattering you because she wanted power," Janice said.

"It was the muscles...wait, are you jealous?"

"No!" Janice said. "I was terrified! If we were found out because you couldn't stop from flirting with the first alien that bought you an octopus on a stick—"

"That thing did taste pretty good, even with the white sauce," he said.

"Okay, enough," my dad said.

That was too bad. I was enjoying the conversation, and so was Sunjay. Somehow, I think that Janice was, too.

We disrobed and my dad handed us each a blue tunic and sandals—clothing of the Third Step, he explained. We tucked our towels into the back of our tunics to cover our untattooed calves. It looked stupid but did the job.

"We have to make some inferences here," he said. "First, all five of us are engaged to be married. That will draw suspicion. We need tattoos. Second, we are at the foot of Step One. Everything there is gray, including clothing. Look farther. Step Two is yellow."

We looked up the spiral staircase. We could see the next two steps but the fourth and fifth step wound around the other side of the newel. Each step had a slightly larger gap. A mile over our head was the bottom of the Seventh, and final, Step.

"Based on your conversation with the girl, this is a hierarchy," my dad explained. "Each step is a different rank in society, from lowest to highest, from gray to the very top—purple. The Third Step clothing will buy us respect. The Firsters and Seconders won't ask many questions, even if we don't have tattoos."

"The Ascendant babe showed us her IV tattoo," I said. "So we must need the Roman numeral III to be Thirders."

"Don't call her a babe," said Janice. "That's insulting to women."

"She's an alien, Janice! Maybe she likes the word 'babe,'" said Sunjay. "Who cares?"

"I do!" she said.

My dad shook his head. "Janice, Sunjay, listen up. I will not repeat this, and I will not have to. The both of you need to learn to cut each other some slack. You're both trying to score points in an argument. And do you know who loses in that game?"

"Both of us," said Janice.

"No. Tabitha loses," my dad said. Just the mention of her name and I could envision her in the tower. He never had to ask them to knock if off again. "Now it's getting darker. That's good. If we stay away from those lamps, we can make our way to the Third Step without drawing too much attention to ourselves."

I looked toward the ice dome miles above our heads. Jupiter took up less of the sky. It was getting darker. And colder.

We followed my dad out of the alley and onto a street full of Firsters. Their gray tunics and sandals were worn down to nothing. So were they! Firsters had hollow eyes and gray faces to match their clothing. They looked underfed, but they walked with confidence and purpose. I remembered what the girl at the beach had said. They would soon have slaves of their own, so they must be slaves themselves.

Many of the young men, women, and children carried long poles full of giant fish—way too heavy if we were on Earth—up the street toward their destinations.

"Must be the day's catch," Buckshot said. "Somebody's got to feed those folks on the higher steps."

On the beach people jumped over each other to avoid colliding, but the Firsters stepped off the street and bowed as we walked past. They also avoided eye contact, so the blue tunics were the only things they noticed, not our untattooed faces.

The street ran on a serious incline, with steps on the steepest parts, paved with ground-up shells and lined with decrepit gray warehouses. One warehouse smelled like the death smoothie. Sunjay craned his head to peek inside. Another reverberated with construction noises. Above the entrance was the Ascendant symbol, the crown with three red stones. Inside, welders worked with handheld lasers to fuse giant chunks of black metal together. Above the door a 3D image of the Earth rotated slowly, and a slogan was written below it in English: "WORK LIKE IT'S YOUR PLANET—NOT THEIRS!"

It was the first of many warehouses with similar slogans.

"Those look like *Mini-Mane* parts," I said. My dad nodded.

"It reminds me of the shipyards at Annapolis," he said. We heard a rumble and saw a completed *Mini-Mane* float out the back of the warehouse. It sailed over the beach to much applause, and then submerged underwater bound for destinations unknown.

We continued up the steep rough street in the gathering darkness along with other Ascendant. A few Seconders and Thirders were in the crowd, but mainly Firsters. We could just see the edge of the Second Step, made of a dull yellow stone. It looked tidier, more organized even from afar.

"Poor Firsters. It smells like dead fish and dust down here," said Janice. "I wonder if they get to see the other steps."

"I doubt it," I said, "but they've got more motivational signs than a high school counselor's office."

We read them as we walked. Signs with smiling, tattooed Ascendant workers in flowing tunics, standing with their chins held high. All of them encouraging people to prepare for the Earth invasion. Most in English, and a few in Greek and Chinese.

"FIRSTERS, PRACTICE YOUR ENGLISH! PREPARE TO RULE!"

"WORK HARD TODAY! TOMORROW YOU WILL LIVE IN PARADISE!"

"CHILDREN, THE LORD ASCENDANT IS YOUR FATHER! REPORT YOUR PARENTS IF THEY SPEAK AGAINST HIM."

I looked at the picture of an Ascendant boy. He pointed out his parents to a tall Ascendant in a black tunic, who pointed a black staff at them.

"They would betray their own parents?" Sunjay said.

"Bad alien mojo," said Buckshot.

"Propaganda," my dad said.

"Oh, yeah," said Sunjay. "It's like those videos we watched about World War II. Governments used slogans just like this."

"Yes, but lower profile," my dad said quietly. We spread out and stopped talking so much. If they took their propaganda seriously, they would be looking for suspicious activity—like five Ascendant with no tattoos talking about propaganda.

THE SECOND STEP

We crested a hill and suddenly there was nothing but air in front of us. We had reached the gap between First and Second Steps, which was fifty feet across and fifty feet high. It wasn't much farther than the canyon leaps. I desperately wanted to jump the gap, but this wasn't the Ascendant way. Instead, there two options. First was a crowded trolley that ran on glowing purple rails between the steps. Second, several black staffs stood above us on the Second Step. For a few shells, they would ferry you across the gap using their weapons. Their muscles rippled as they lifted two Ascendant at a time across the gap.

Pretty easy choice. We headed for the trolley. On board, the Seconders gave up their seats for us. We sat down, folded our arms, and kept our heads down to avoid stares. The trolley buzzed lightly on electric rails as we crossed the gap. On the ride over I noticed something faintly scratched into the armrest of my seat. Not more propaganda, but graffiti, it was a pair of outstretched wings. I like graffiti so I made a mental note of it. A word was scribbled beneath it:

Ἴκαρος

I reached into my tunic and pulled out Bacon's head just enough to read the word. He translated it for me: Icarus. That name again. I had seen the wings on a wall at the beach as well.

The buzzing trolley lurched to a stop. We made it to the Second Step, leaving the poverty of the Firsters behind.

"Ooh, this looks a little better," whispered Janice. "I like the Second Step."

"That looks like the Alamo," said Sunjay, pointing up the street. "Is that a taco vendor over there?"

"Say 'Buenos Nachos!' to Uncle Antonio's Tacos," said Little Bacon. I clapped a hand over his mouth and we walked toward the alien Alamo.

Propaganda was mixed with advertisements on the Second Step. Billboards lined the streets, floating images of Ascendants involved in various activities:

"HIGH GRAVITY TRAINING: WALK THE EARTH LIKE A KING!"

"EARTH PROPERTY FOR SALE. FIND THE BEACH OF YOUR DREAMS!"

"WE ARE THE ASCENDANT. WE ALWAYS RISE."

Seconders were better off than Firsters. They didn't look so overworked or move off the street as we approached. Instead, the Ascendant at this step leaped over one another. I figured it out pretty quickly: if you were going up the street, you nodded toward the sky. Then you leaped over the alien in your way. If you were going down, you kept walking.

It was "dusk" now, I guess. Not much Jupiter light left in the sky. I placed Bacon in my tunic, hiding him in a fold.

"Hey, buddy, keep whispering the names of the signs?" I said.

"As you wish. THE SALTY SERPENT RESTAURANT. CAESAR'S FINE TUNICS. BRUTUS'S FINER TUNICS, THE BLACK STAFF EMPORIUM..." Little Bacon continued his monologue.

We walked for a few minutes, hopping the Ascendant as we went along, trying not to land awkwardly or on top of someone else. If you had been playing "hop the pedestrian" your entire life, it was probably easy, but we were rookies. I almost landed on a muscle-bound Thirder at one point, who turned around and mumbled something at me in Greek.

"He called you an undersized ripplebacked scalefish," said Little Bacon. "I believe that is an insult."

"You think?" I asked.

BWAAAAAAAMMMMPPP.

The sound knocked Sunjay sideways, and Janice gasped. All of the Ascendant, whether they were going up or down the street, stopped immediately, put their right hands over their hearts, and turned toward the alien Alamo.

"We are the Ascendant," a loudspeaker announced.

The Ascendant took their hands off their hearts. Then they raised their hands in the air with the palm facing up.

"We always rise!" they shouted.

It was the first time we saw the Ascendant Salute.

All of them headed up the dark street toward the Alamo. We stayed near the back of a crowd of Firsters, as far from other Thirders as we could, and avoided potholes in the concrete street. In no time we found ourselves standing in front of a perfect replica of the Alamo. Another loudspeaker boomed an announcement.

"Dear Ascendant, the Great Leaving is almost upon us. Before we leave, we shall celebrate. Tomorrow night, the Lord Ascendant's Royal Theater Academy will perform Shakespeare's *Romeo and Juliet*." No one looked terribly excited about this announcement at first. "The performance will take place in the Fifth Step Theater, and will star our Earther friend, Tabitha Tirelli. Dear Ascendant, for this performance you are all invited."

The crowd went absolutely roasters, cheering at the tops of their lungs, hugging one another, tears streaming down their tattooed faces. It was like they won the lottery. A few Thirders stood near us, and they looked surprised but not "I just peed my pants" excited like the Seconders. High in the air above us we could just see the edge of the Fifth Step spiraling around the other side of the newel. It occurred to me that the Seconders *had* won the lottery. This was Europa's version of a cool Hollywood New Year's Eve party—right before they left to take over our home planet.

I nudged my dad and he nodded. We shared the same thought. In one day's time, we knew exactly where Tabitha would be. The Ascendant crowd dispersed after, of course, the Ascendant Salute. Place hand on heart. Then palm up over the head. Shout "WE ALWAYS RISE!" at the top of your alien lungs.

We continued down a broad yellow street lined with sand colored apartment buildings until we reached the end of the Second Step, but not before I spied, on the low wall surrounding the Alamo, just small enough to make them difficult to see in the fading light, another set of wings carved into the stone.

THE INK SQUAD

The distance between the Second and Third Step was a bit farther. Once again, it was take a trolley or be tossed by a black staff. We stuck with the trolley, full of Thirders happy about returning to their homes and the royal invite to see a play on the Fifth Step. They spoke pretty good English mingled with Greek, so I got the gist of their conversations about *Romeo and Juliet* and the "Earther girl" even without Little Bacon's help.

The Third Step itself was full of the Ascendant enjoying the last light of our solar system's largest planet. Trees, statues, and streetlights lined the wide cobblestone streets, and blue marble fountains were erected at every intersection. The smell of grilled seafood wafted out of open windows in tall blue apartment buildings. In the distance, the newel rose above us, taking on a rainbow of colors in the fading light.

Alien children leapt out of third story balconies and made for the town square, where they played something like lacrosse. They used small black staffs to throw a ball-and sometimes each other-through a soccer goal suspended fifty feet in the air. The game involved all sorts of mid-air acrobatics and combat, including leaping off the sides of buildings. It looked fun.

"It smells like lavender," said Janice. "And all these fountains! Some of these signs are French, not Greek. I think each of these steps has a theme."

In the distance I could make out a triangular skeleton of a building. It was taller than the nearby apartments. Even though I only saw the tip of it, the structure was unmistakable.

"Stars, it's the Eiffel Tower," Janice said. "The Third Step *is* France."

"Then I guess we just left Texas," I told her.

Bacon kept reading signs. "PEARL WHITE DENTISTRY. FANTINE'S FINE FRENCH CUISINE. THE INK SQUAD..." My dad slowed his pace when he heard the last sign.

"Follow me," he said, crossing the blue cobblestone street toward the neon 3D image of an Ascendant flexing his tattooed arms.

We walked through the entrance and found ourselves in a small black box. My dad frowned, then reached his hand forward, and like magic, his hand disappeared. *It's a virtual curtain*, I thought. We stepped through it into a bright room. I expected chairs, like in a barbershop, but there was no furniture, just a white floor, a glowing white ceiling, soft music, and the walls. Wow, the walls. Lined with every tattoo imaginable, all of them in motion. The tattoo parlor swirled with beautiful images, and at the far end stood the tattoo artist.

He was about 6'2", my dad's height, and not as musclebound as many of the other Ascendant. He didn't turn around to greet us, but his tattoos did. His entire body swam with snakes. They curled around his arms, showed their fangs and rattlers, and hissed at us as we approached. I almost forgot why we were there. He finally greeted us in Greek. Janice responded.

"You want to use English," he said with almost no accent. "Well, nice to meet you. I am known as Ekphrasis. My English is almost as good as yours, isn't it? I practice a lot. It is our duty to practice. Few Earthers will not understand our Greek — they do not know our beautiful language. They do not know how to decorate themselves like we do, my friends. Can you imagine their surprise when I open up a shop in Paris and show them all of this?"

"That *would* be a surprise," Buckshot said.

"It *will* be," he said. "I will open the shop, and I cannot wait to pick out my apartment near the Eiffel Tower. Maybe I can offer its owner a free tattoo before he is relocated."

With his back to us he gazed at the wall of tattoos, envisioning his new apartment and tattoo parlor. Not me. I pictured the poor family that would lose their home. Where would they stay? What would they eat? Would they live on the streets or did the Ascendant have some relocation plan? I imagined how the colonists treated Indians in Early America. Yeah, that was our future.

Then he laughed, and his tattoos changed. The sea of writhing snakes melted away momentarily. Beneath them I thought I saw the feathers of a bird. Cold scales replaced the feathers in the blink of an eye. Did he have several layers of tattoos? Stars, I guess that made sense. He was a tattoo artist.

He finally turned around and we saw his face. He was young, probably in his alien thirties, with deep laugh lines below his eyes. He also observed us for the first time. Five strangers in his shop without a single tattoo. He took a step back, then steadied himself, and clucked his tongue.

"In the name of the Galilean moons," Ekphrasis said. "All this naked skin! You cannot all be engaged to a promised one…wait, where are your numerals?"

"We need some," my dad said.

"No one walks the streets unnumbered," he said. "The Lord Ascendant says so."

The Ascendant looked over our shoulders, and so did I, expecting to see black staffs storming into the shop behind us. Had he pushed an alarm? I could see the answer on his serpentine face. No. He was alone, and we had him cornered. Nobody was on the street behind us. Nobody was coming to help him.

Suddenly Little Bacon spoke up. A sign across the street caught his eye—and mine. "SEE THE EARTH BEAUTY TABITHA TIRELLI IN ROMEO AND JULIET. ONE NIGHT ONLY."

"Talking tunics!" yelled the tattoo artist, creeping toward the back of his shop. "What kind of wizardry is this?"

The tattoos scrawled across his lined face—a viper wound itself around his neck. "Leave my shop this minute. I will give you nothing. Give me one reason not to report you all."

"Sure," Buckshot said, leaping forward. In an instant he had the tattoo artist in a headlock and jumped to the ceiling with him, slamming his head into one of the lights. They landed lightly, the Ascendant dazed.

"*That* was not necessary," my dad said.

"Sorry, just wanted to make a point," Buckshot said.

"The point is to keep a low profile," my dad said. He peeked out the window, then flipped a sign that must have said "closed." The entire front of the store turned blue as if it were a wall. After a few minutes, the artist regained his senses.

"What did you do to me?" he said.

"Something unnecessary," said Buckshot. "Now about those tattoos…"

"What did you do with yours? You don't even have numerals. How were they removed?"

"Not important," my dad said.

"If they track these tattoos to me, they will kill me," Ekphrasis said.

"Look, I don't wanna do anything else unnecessary," Buckshot said, cracking his knuckles. "Now they *might* kill you later. Who says we won't kill you now?"

The artist stood, shook the cobwebs out of his mind, and straightened his tunic. He was about Sunjay's size and no match for us in a fight.

"Ekphrasis, we mean you no more harm," my dad said. "Simply do what we ask and we will leave."

Ekphrasis sighed and adjusted a band on his wrist, and then reached into his pocket. He produced a black pill and gestured to the walls.

"Well, let us not waste time. Who's first? Pick your style and then taste the ink," he said, holding out the black pill. None of us moved to grab it. "You don't know how this works? Ah, now this is starting to make sense. You're criminals or fishermen from the Outlands. First time in the Rathmore, and you've decided to conceal yourselves among us. These numerals are your first-class tickets to the Earth."

"It's not your business," my dad said.

"You do not want to wait your turn to get to Earth. I can't blame you. The ocean is dying. It is not fair that they make you leave last."

"Yeah," said Sunjay, "geysers shooting off everywhere and hungry sea monsters."

Ekphrasis eyed Sunjay. His eyes weren't just blue. They were flecked with purple and red, too. He studied Sunjay like he was trying to solve a riddle. I didn't like that look at all.

"If only the Earthers had not stolen the Sacred, we could stay. Ah, but now to your tattoos—every good boy and girl in Rathmore knows that you take this pill. It's called 'tasting the ink.' After that, I program your tattoo. If the boys and girls do not like their tattoos, they return to the store and I change it. For a fee."

"It's not permanent!" said Sunjay. "Good. Dad won't kill me."

"Ah-ah-ah," he said, shaking his finger at Sunjay. "The numeral will be permanent. It burns into the skin. Surely you have heard the saying, 'You never rise above your step.' You might make your way higher someday—if you're lucky—but everyone knows where you started."

My dad had heard enough. He reached for the pill and turned toward Buckshot. "If anything happens to me, you know what to do." Buckshot cracked his knuckles again and looked at Ekphrasis, who didn't want any more trips to the ceiling.

My dad swallowed the pill without a moment's notice. Nothing changed at first. Then the Ascendant adjusted his glowing purple bracelet. Dad winced like something stung him. Then he looked at his right calf. The numeral three appeared there.

"Voilà, you are now a Thirder," the Ascendant said. "Now choose your ink."

My dad pointed to a scene: of a lion and cub with a meteor shower in the background.

"Ah, a wise choice. The artist Phaedrus designed this tattoo before he died. See how the lion turns his head toward the meteor shower, but one of his paws covers his cub's paws? The lion watches the meteor shower, but he still watches over his cub. This is a popular choice among fathers, especially those of the Fifth Step." The Ascendant put his heavily-tattooed hand on my dad's chest. Then he backed away. We saw a black dot appear where his hand had been.

Then my dad fell to the floor, writhing in pain. Buckshot jumped toward the Ascendant, but he held his ground.

"I didn't say it was pleasant," said the Ascendant.

I rushed over to my dad. He held up a hand, as if to say he was fine. Soon he settled down. The black dot swirled, expanded, and morphed into the scene on the wall, scrolling across his arms. Meteors streamed from his temple to his chin.

He regained his feet and stood in front of us as a different man, an alien.

"Wow, Commander, those things really move," Sunjay said.

The Ascendant's eyes darted toward Sunjay again, so I punched Sunjay and whispered, "Stop talking."

"They will settle down soon. You know, Earther tattoos are not like this. They are like stick figures drawn in a cave. Very primitive. At any rate, I have decided that you are definitely not Outlanders. The English is too good. You're from some other Chaos. Conamara maybe? Oh, or from a flexus. I met a slave from the Delphi Flexus once that spoke like you. He had never been to Rathmore before, never seen the City of the Seven Steps or heard of the Purple Tower."

"There are only six steps," Sunjay said.

"The Sixth Step fell," he said with a sad smile. "It's lying at the base of the city. You do not know this? Have you been frozen in geyser ice for the last ten years? Did you know that the Sacred has been stolen? Surely you have heard this."

We all nodded.

"Are there any other employees?" my dad asked him. Ekphrasis shook his head no. "Then we'll be sleeping here tonight. You will tattoo the rest of us in the morning. First, I must ask you some questions about the Fifth Step."

Ekphrasis wanted to object, but he looked at my dad's tattoo again and thought better of it. One of us watched Ekphrasis in the backroom while the rest of us developed a plan to rescue Tabitha the next day.

My dad took the first watch on Ekphrasis while the rest of us slept in a heap on the floor with the tattoos on the walls as our nightlights. It was slightly better than a giant crab cage. No one had energy for small talk. Of course not. Janice had been launched into the sky by a geyser. I had been inside a serpent's mind and then killed it. Sunjay had befriended the most beautiful alien on the beach and survived Janice's wrath. Buckshot cold-cocked a tattoo artist, and my dad now looked every bit like an Ascendant. And we now knew where Tabitha would be tomorrow night.

I laid on the parlor floor, closed my eyes and let sleep, that persistent boulder, crush me. Before it did, I saw Tabitha's face gazing from that purple tower high above me. And saw the image of the wings and heard that name—*Icarus*—as if it should mean something to me.

In the night a deep rumbling jolted us awake. I heard Ascendant yelling outside, the sound of shattering items. Hopping to our feet, we prepared for some sort of attack, but our Ascendant captive just sighed.

"Since the Earthers stole the Sacred, Rathmore shakes like a fish out of water. It's only a matter of time before…never mind. Just go to sleep." We didn't argue with him. We saved all the arguing for the morning.

"No Outlander"

"I would rather die. You may murder me now. Just let the big one do it so it's quick."

This was what Ekphrasis said when my dad told him the next morning that he would guide us to the Fifth Step. It made sense for us. The fewer Ascendant that interacted with us the better. If our tattoo artist could also be our guide, that was best. Also, Ekphrasis knew Rathmore from top to bottom. "The tattoos will disguise you, but there are certain checkpoints where they will scan your voice and eyes. Those are points that you shall not pass. Trust me. I do much of my tattoos on other steps."

Still, there was nothing we could say to convince him to take us, so my dad shrugged his shoulders and asked for the rest of the tattoos. That shrug scared me.

The others tasted the ink first, so I watched as they received their tattoos: Sunjay a beach scene, Buckshot a desert full of scorpions and rattlesnakes. Ekphrasis explained the history behind each tattoo like a docent at a museum would describe a painting. Janice listened to each one and finally picked one with beautiful buildings all lit up at night.

"Oh, this one's lovely," he said, "but let me take a look at this cut. Sometimes the ink can heal, too." Ekphrasis touched her eye. She winced, but after her tattoo was fully in motion, the swelling began to go down. I wasn't paying much attention though. I was watching my dad.

He was deep in thought, probably reviewing our plan to recapture Tabitha. Ekphrasis had described the Fifth Step in perfect detail, so he (and I) was visualizing the route. But something troubled me. If Ekphrasis refused to guide us, he was another loose string, like Jason and Typhon. Only he was much closer, and much cleverer.

"And last but not least," said Ekphrasis, interrupting my thoughts. "It's an old English phrase. It means your turn." He gestured to the wall behind me, and with the sweep of his hand the tattoos shimmered like jewels. I walked over to the wall and stood beside him. There was an ocean scene with a sea serpent swimming in deep waters. It reminded me of the one I had to kill. Sort of a sad moment in Tully history, I realize, but it was a way to make my own memorial to the serpent. I pointed to it, and as I did so, Ekphrasis gasped. He stared at my scarred hands, which I hid behind my back.

"Is there a problem?" my dad said behind us.

"No, no," Ekphrasis said. "This one is modeled after the Lord Ascendant's own royal tattoos. Older men generally like this tattoo, but the Lord Ascendant would be pleased to see a youth wearing it. He likes to be imitated and adored."

Oh, great, not only does the Lord Ascendant love it, it's also a dad tattoo. I'll be telling the same stupid jokes twice a day for the rest of my life now. Like, "Hey, so you're Surprised. It's nice to meet you, Surprised. I'm Tully." Let's get this over with…

Ekphrasis handed me the black pill, which I popped. It tasted like dirt, and I didn't feel anything like the others, but I checked my calf and sure enough, the numeral appeared. No pain, just the tattoo. Then Ekphrasis completed the process. There was no "falling on the floor like I was being attacked by bees" moment either. My tattoo appeared, which was pleasant and all, until I stood in front of the mirror.

What I saw made me dizzy. My tattoos were moving dire fast. The serpent swam laps around my body, devouring five fish every second. My tattoos needed to slow down, so I took a breath and focused on slowing them down. When I looked at myself again, they had disappeared. Whoops. So I closed my eyes again and finally felt it – the ink under my skin. I could picture it. I could control it. This felt like the right pace.

"Cool, you've got speed controls on yours," said Sunjay. Ekphrasis stood beside me, and his face went pale.

Up close he looked younger. His face showed no signs of wrinkles except laugh lines around the eyes. *Those eyes!* Blue eyes, flecked with gold, purple, and red. It felt too much like the Lord Ascendant's gaze. I looked away, trying not to reveal anything to him.

"You're no Outlander," he said.

"What's wrong?" I asked.

"Nothing, and everything." He inspected me like I was a puzzle that he could not solve. His voice was a thin whisper. "These scars are the marks of the Encountered."

"No, they're not," I said, but thought again. "Well, what if they are? What would that meant to you?"

"That you are from the Sixth Step, and that is impossible. They are all gone."

"What happened there?"

"This story is not widely known on Europa, or even in Rathmore. When the Lord Ascendant rose to power, the people of the Sixth Step opposed him. They were known as the Encountered. They were the Masters of the Sacred. They led a rebellion against the Lord Ascendant, but he won. And for their treason, he gathered them and their supporters onto the Sixth Step. Then he broke it. The Encountered fell into the sea."

"So these scars mean—"

"That you are Encountered—or at least look like one. Who are you? What *is* your business here?"

I gave it some thought. This wasn't the right time to say my full name again. My dad glanced over at us, wondering about our discussion.

"I came to see a play," I told Ekphrasis.

He scoured my face, searching for more of the truth. Finally, he sighed.

"This will hurt." Ekphrasis grabbed my hands and squeezed them so tightly that I cried out. My dad sprung to my side, but Ekphrasis flipped away from him. He was quicker and stronger than I guessed.

"What did he do?" my dad asked. I held up my shaking hands. They were now so heavily tattooed that I could hardly see the lightning scars.

"I covered the scars. That is all. And now my answer is yes."

"To what?" asked my dad.

"I will be your guide," he said. Then he pointed at me. "However, the boy must never alter his tattoos. Only the Encountered could do such things. And he, no, he can't be."

An Ascendant from the Sixth Step, I thought. *In a way, I am. They were called the Encountered, and I know exactly where they got that name.*

An image appeared in my mind of the Sixth Step crumbling into the sea. I wanted to know more of the story. I could imagine the Lord Ascendant and his army throwing down the survivors. It must have been thousands of feet. My dad interrupted those thoughts.

"We may ask you more questions," he said, "but we will not divulge anything else about ourselves. There is no way to be safe, but it will keep us all safer. Is this agreed?"

Ekphrasis nodded. We all did.

And so it was that Ekphrasis became our guide, and I had another clue to who I was. I definitely wasn't a Master of the Sacred, but I understood why the Lord Ascendant had wanted me to join him.

CLIMB

"**W**hat did he whisper to you?" asked Sunjay as we exited the Ink Squad in the pale morning light. I explained the situation as best I could.

We followed our guide at a distance, just two Ascendant boys with a girl walking between them, headed nowhere in particular. Dad and Buckshot trailed us.

After a few minutes, we took a break from the heavy talk about falling steps and ascendant lords. Walking in low gravity brightened everyone's mood, I guess. It didn't hurt that the Third Step looked exactly like spring in Paris either. The cobblestones, streetlamps, and bridges made us feel like we were on vacation. Sunjay even bought a chocolate croissant. (Janice gave him some of her stolen shells.)

Ekphrasis loved his hometown, and his enthusiasm was infectious. Throughout our journey he pointed out important landmarks that the Thirders borrowed from France. The Ascendant had a real thing for our planet.

"Notice the architecture here," said Ekphrasis. "That bridge is called the Pont de Neuf. I brought my younger sister here once for her birthday. She tossed a stone into the water and made a wish. I asked her what she wished for, and she said that she wanted to visit the real Pont de Neuf someday."

Then he would tell us to drop back as he bounded ahead with purpose. He told us to walk more slowly. We didn't walk like teenagers. It was hard: all I wanted to do was jump over a streetlamp.

Eventually our conversation turned to the rescue mission.

"Let's call it Operation Grabitha. Get it?" said Sunjay.

"No, let's watch this great new movie called 'How to Lose Friends by Being Punny,'" said Janice. I high-fived her for that. Then I looked across at Sunjay and noticed he was holding her other hand. Oh, stars. He grinned at me sheepishly, then broke into a crazy smile.

You guys picked a weird time to fall in love, I wanted to say, but I held back. We were in alien Paris. I shot Sunjay a look. *Play it cool, man. Wipe that maniac smile off your face.*

Ekphrasis crossed a broad avenue and we snapped back to reality. He glanced over his shoulder to see if we were following. There were black staffs at the corner of every street. He could have turned us in at any time, and I half-expected that he would, but after a few blocks, it seemed like he was true to his word.

"Here is the Eiffel Tower," said Ekphrasis, dropping back again.

"Oh, I know," said Janice.

"How would you know?" he asked her.

"Uh, lucky guess," she said.

"Your sister, does she like this, too?" asked Janice.

"I never got to ask her," Ekphrasis said, his face darkening. "She was taken to the Undercity. The Lord Ascendant builds things in the deep."

Bad stuff below the city. I made a mental note. Ekphrasis pushed ahead of us again, lost in thought.

We passed under the Eiffel Tower, and lights twinkled on the giant structure. Janice looked left and right, reached in her pocket, and took a selfie looking up at the tower. I almost told her not to, but then I had a handroid in my pocket that might spout commercials at any second. Who was I to talk?

My night vision was still superhuman. In the distance on our left I could see the icy newel that supported the Seven Steps. The purple glow of black staffs lit the ice with an unnatural glow. We felt a slight rumble.

The side of the newel opened, like an enormous elevator door. *So it's hollow. That's news.*

In the gloom I could see a group of Firsters loading monstrous objects into the elevator. Some of them looked familiar, like the dozens of fiber optic laser whips. Those tend to stand out in the dark. Yes, there was something dangerous happening below Rathmore.

Finally Jupiter's glow crept through the dome above, down the icy walls around the city, and onto the Third Step. The rest of the group could see clearly. The streets filled with Ascendants, most of them headed, like us, to the performance on the next step. We crested a hill and came to a dead stop.

The Fourth Step. Leaving Paris. Next stop? London.

The bottom of the Fourth Step was an endless, seamless block of jade that hung one hundred feet above our heads.

Ride or float? Ride, of course. Sunjay and Janice peeked out the window toward the beach a thousand feet below us. On one stretch of beach I could see the ruins of the Sixth Step. What history lay there slowly being buried by the sand?

My dad looked like he was in a daze, but his eyes never left the direction of the newel. All the movement there caught his eye as well.

The crowds swelled and security was higher on the Fourth Step. An Ascendant "greeted" us, then walked down the aisles, scanning our Roman numerals with his staff. My heart leaped into my throat, but he didn't blink an eye when he scanned Buckshot's tattoo, then mine, then the rest.

The Fourth Step: wider streets, wealthier Ascendant, lots of green marble statues and fountains, and most of all, England. Big Ben, the Tower of London, all the sights spread out before us.

The broad avenue filled with Ascendant, and soon we found ourselves shoulder to shoulder, struggling to stay together. I held Janice's hand because she was a little taller than I was.

"Can you still see him?"

"No," she said.

"Wait, where's Sunjay?"

Stars, we lost him in the sea of Ascendant. Don't panic, Tully. Ekphrasis put you on the biggest street on this Step. Just stay the course and things should be fine.

We searched for any familiar face, but those faces were now covered in alien tattoos. The crowd stumbled along for another five minutes until it slowed to a standstill. I heard something up ahead. Cheering, a strong buzzing sound. The crowd paused on one side of the street in front of a large black and gold gate. Behind the gate loomed a mansion unlike any we had seen thus far—a black marble building with a wide, grassy lawn in front of it. The Ascendant flag flew at its gate.

It was Buckingham Palace, Ascendant-style.

I saw why the Ascendant had stopped. Several thousand young black staffs mustered in the lawn. Some stood at attention, some lifted massive weights, others made a ring around two warriors locked in combat. It was an Ascendant army training ground. The spectacle awed the crowd, most of whom had never been to this Step. The sea of people came to a dead stop, and Janice and I couldn't push our way through. We were too short to see where we were headed anyway. *We're so toast. We lost our guide, the entire Ascendant army is in front of us, and I'm their worst enemy. What could be worse?*

"It's okay," I said, taking a deep breath. "We can still meet in front of the theater."

"Ekphrasis must have taken a side street," she said. "We're stuck watching this."

In the courtyard the battle intensified. The Ascendant leaped high in the air, blasting each other with incinerator shots with no regard for anyone's safety. A ball of purple flames flew toward us and we dove out of the way. One woman put out flames on her arm while the others around her laughed. There were oooh's and ahhh's. Thirty, forty, fifty feet into the air they flew like acrobats, spinning and twisting, blasting and tossing each other in a combination of martial arts and acrobatics.

The show distracted me until I heard a beeping sound in the distance, like a scanner at a grocery store. Standing on my tiptoes, I saw an Ascendant officer picking his way through the crowd. He was at least seven feet tall and wore a black hat capped with a purple light that blinked like an eye. It darted back and forth, scanning the crowd. Where it stopped, he posted his staff, and nearby Ascendant looked into the eye and spoke a few words. Then the staff beeped and moved on.

"It's a retinal scan," said Janice. "If that thing scans our eyes, we're caught."

We started to pick our through the crowd, but the beeping intensified behind us. I peeked over my shoulder to see the eye staring angrily at us. *This won't end well. The harder we push, the more attention we draw to ourselves.*

We heard a deep voice booming behind us. I stopped. Janice yanked my hand forward, but I shook my head. I took a deep breath and gathered myself. It was time to awaken the Sacred, once and for all. It was time to turn and fight.

With my eyes closed, I imagined the Sacred. It was gray and life, still hidden on the submarine. *You said you would try to wake up. It's about time. I made it this far but can't make it any farther without you.* There was a stirring inside the Sacred. A red mist began to fill the submarine. *Yes, you hear me! Wake up now! I need you.*

I could hear the scanner getting closer and feel my hands getting warmer. Would it happen soon enough? I wasn't sure. We weren't just standing in front of the scanner. A thousand enemies, all armed, stood on the other side of the black gate, ready to blast us to ashes.

All of a sudden something gripped my entire body. It was like someone cast a net over me, a net that tightened like a boa constrictor. My eyes snapped open and the image of the Sacred slipped away. Janice was trapped in the invisible net, too.

No! I never even had a chance to fight them. It can't end like this. I can't!

There was nothing I could do though. I could feel some of the old power coursing through my hands, but they were useless, strapped tightly to my side in the invisible net.

The giant approached. The crowd parted. Finally he stood before us, his breath foul enough to make me choke. He looked right through us with dead eyes as the crowd encircled us. He planted the black staff in the street. It cast sparks all around us, but to my surprise, the sparks bounced right off of us. The eye blinked and scanned back and forth, but it did not scan us. The giant looked confused.

He shouted in Greek. We hopped back a few paces, still trapped in the net, but he made no move to pursue us, just looked through us like we were invisible.

We *were* invisible.

The giant knew something was wrong. He swung his staff in a wide arc, and Janice and I ducked to avoid it, falling to the ground. Then he used the staff to drag an old Firster from the crowd. She cowered before him. He scanned her, and his staff beeped happily. Angered, he shoved her down beside us in the street. No one helped her to her feet. With one last glare, he moved on.

The show was over. The crowd murmured and melted together around us, and once they did so, I felt the invisible net release us.

The old woman still lay on the ground beside us. Janice and I helped her up. She held my face in her hands, placed a small seashell in my hand, then let me go. More scanners worked the main street, so we swam through the stream of people toward a side street. We collected ourselves there.

"Wow, good time to find your powers," she said, sounding upbeat. "I thought you might blast him with your hands, but that was better. Was that an invisibility net?"

"Uh, yeah," I said, "but I haven't ever done that before."

"You closed your eyes," she said. "So you woke up the Sacred and your powers returned?"

"I'm not sure that was me."

"Well, who else would it be? I guess that's our good luck charm," said Janice. I looked down at the seashell the old woman had handed me. It was a gray shell, and on the inside of it were scratched a pair of wings.

"Where have you been?" someone behind us asked. We both jumped and my hand clamped tightly on the shell. Ekphrasis and Sunjay looked down on us. "You're both very short. Stay close enough that you can see me next time. There are more scanners here than any other part of Rathmore. Your numerals will not conceal you completely."

"Super helpful tip," said Janice.

Ekphrasis ushered us down several alleys with Buckshot and Dad behind us, and before long we finally reached the Fifth Step.

THE FIFTH STEP

"**A**lmost there."

Ekphrasis waited with us as the Ascendant crowd poked its way up to the spot where the street ended and the trolley began.

We crossed the wide gap between the Fifth and Sixth Step on a monstrous, double-decker trolley, with five hundred Ascendant on board. The Thirders and Fourthers stood on the roof of the trolley while the Fifthers sat on the lower level. It looked like drinks were being served below. There was no spot for the Firsters or Seconders. They clung to the sides or the bottom of the trolley and held on for dear life. When we hopped down from the trolley, Ekphrasis gathered us together.

"This is as far as I can take you for now," he said. "You can find your way from here."

"Thanks for your help," my dad said. "It's best that we part without any other words."

"It would seem so," said Ekphrasis, "but not all is as it seems."

"What's that supposed to mean?" asked Buckshot. We all tensed up.

"Nothing, and everything," he said. "It's just the kind of thing that a tattoo artist would say."

Ekphrasis's smiled and his eyes darted over each of us and finally rested on me. Blue eyes that shimmered with purple and red. And without another word, our guide melted into the crowd of people behind him. It didn't seem like a proper good-bye, and it was an unsettling way to begin our first moments on the Fifth Step.

The wide avenues swarmed with Ascendant, and on either side of the street were imposing buildings, all of red marble with golden statues in front of them—museums, theaters, arenas, and mansions. Classical music played in the streets and street performers (living statues, dancers, drummers) all played to the enormous crowds, who tossed shells at them. It was an alien carnival.

The Fifthers themselves wore red tunics with gold belts, and there were few of them. Those that we saw had servants to carry them, or they steered hovering chariots as the crowds dispersed in front of them. They scowled and shook their heads at the carnival scenes that were probably taking place in their front yards.

In front of us, I saw the theater. On the red wall of the theater an image of Tabitha, smiling and waving, greeted us.

"Welcome to the Fifth Step," she repeated in several languages. "Please proceed to Red Storm Arena for a special announcement."

All I wanted to do was get into that theater and start our plan, but they always make you sit through something before the show starts.

The Red Storm Arena loomed in the distance. Images of battle scrolled across the stones, Ascendants battling lions and bears—and each other—on the sandy floor inside the arena.

"This *is* Rome," said Janice.

We filed through a massive black gate and saw a large stage on the sandy floor. The Ascendant sorted themselves out. Firsters, Seconders, and Thirders stood in the middle of the arena in front of the stage. Seats were reserved for Fourthers, Fifthers, and Seventhers.

The crowd hushed and turned toward the newel, which we could see through the great entry gate. Then the newel rumbled. A black rectangle appeared on its side.

"That looks like a door," I whispered to my dad.

"Yes," he said. "I think it's an elevator for troop transport, but there's more to it. It has to reach far below the city."

It also held the Seventh Step hundreds of feet in the air. *Could I make that jump even with my red powers?* I wondered. The hair on my arms stood on end just looking at the size of it all.

From the rectangle emerged an army. Thousands of troops marched in formation, chanting in unison, leaping occasionally and shooting purple sparks into the air with their black staffs. We could feel their footsteps. The crowd cheered as the black staffs approached the stadium. My heart thumped against my ribcage, watching them stream toward us, like a slow-moving but unstoppable tsunami. Once they reached the arena, we could see that, in the midst of them, was a hover chariot manned by the Lord Ascendant.

The crowd went absolutely roasters.

He wore black gloves and a purple tunic that left his muscular arms and legs completely bare. A long black cape pinned with a gold medallion cascaded from his neck and shoulders. Across his face scrolled those familiar tattoos, but they did not hide his features – black eyes, powerful jaw line, a long braid of hair. A scar crossed his cheek, more a complement than a flaw. He held a hand over his heart.

"We are the Ascendant," he said.

"WE ALWAYS RISE!" we shouted in unison.

He leaped onto the stage, waited for total silence, and then began to speak in a deep, smooth voice.

"Greetings, children of Rathmore, the blessed of Europa. I speak to you today in English not because I enjoy it, but because it is one of the primary languages of your slaves. With this tongue you will command them. With this tongue you will claim your homes, your lands, your place in the universe.

"Greetings to you all!

"Firsters and Seconders, your hard work has made you strong. You have served us well, and you will soon be served.

"Thirders and Fourthers, you have gathered skills. You will manage the Earth.

"Fifthers, you hold us all together. You ascend and descend with beauty and grace.

"Sixthers, I honor your memory. You were once majestic, but you came to a tragic end."

According to Ekphrasis, you created that tragedy, I thought. *Why don't you tell everyone the truth?*

"And those of you called to the Seventh, my dearest friends, you rule with honor and pride. You will be a blessing to the Earth as you have been to Rathmore."

The Lord Ascendant put his hands behind him and paced across the stage.

"All of you know how hard I have worked, how much I have sacrificed to reclaim the Earth. Because of it, you worked hard for me. We became a family here, each one of us knowing our place upon the Steps. We made this moon our home, so far from the bright sun's rays. Happy we were here for millennia.

"But now we must face the sad truth—after thousands of years in hiding, the Earthers found us. Yes, and I went to meet with them near their Moon. With a brave and generous heart I tried my best to make peace. And what was the result of my generosity? After these many centuries, and with all of their advances, this is how they greeted me."

The Lord Ascendant raised his hand, and an image of the *Lion's Mane* filled the entire arena. I remembered it well: the black sphere with a red tentacle that trapped the *Adversity*. Purple letters covered its exterior. But it was an absolute wreck. My dad was responsible for that. Of course, they had attacked us first. The Lord Ascendant left that out.

"The wicked Commander Harper sent spies on board our ship," he said, "planted a bomb, and stole back the 'Harper Device.' Yes, that's what he called the Sacred. He named it after himself. What arrogance! A shameful man with no heart, and his son twice as bad, a defiler of the Sacred. He has stolen its power for himself."

The Ascendant gasped. I couldn't believe my ears, but the Ascendant believed theirs. My blood boiled. I wanted to shout the truth: *my dad found the Sacred on Mars. The Alliance named the Sacred after my dad! You attacked us! And the Sacred drew me to itself, you lying piece of Ascendant garbage!* Janice reached for my hand. I tried to shrug her off but she held fast. Sunjay looked at me. *Okay, okay, I'm fine, guys.* I took a deep breath.

Then images of Europa scrolled behind the Lord Ascendant. Exploding geysers, giant cracks in the city streets, dying fish in the ocean.

"So the Earthers stole the Sacred. See what they have done to us? Without the Sacred, our oceans, once so full of life, are dying. The geysers burst forth, the ice moves, and our city crumbles. We have only to look to the Grand Newel to know this truth."

He gestured to where small bits of the Sixth Step still clung to the icy column. The propaganda just got thicker and thicker, but it started to make sense. I knew what he was going to say next.

"I know you worry," he continued, "and for good reason! Europa, our mother, can no longer support us. So we must do what children do: we must grow up and strike out on our own path. We must move or die.

"The Earthers will not share the Earth with us. You see, they do not share it with each other! To them we are alien, foreign, evil. No, they would rather destroy us than help us."

"So what can we do, dear children of Rathmore. Run? To where? Another Moon? Without the Sacred, it would be hopeless. No, the time has come at last. As the prophecy foretold, great Zeus brought us to this moon, and now we will return to Earth once more to rule. We will bring with us the Ascendant ways of peace and law. For we are the Ascendant."

"WE ALWAYS RISE!" The crowd erupted and saluted.

The Lord Ascendant held up his hand to still the crowd. Then one young Ascendant, just a few feet from me, leaped into the air. The crowd fell completely silent.

LAWBREAKER

He wore a white tunic, the first that I had seen. He glided easily into the air with his black hair flying wildly. Then, as he reached the peak of his jump, he opened his hands. The image of a golden dove flew high into the air above our heads. It fluttered above the crowd, who stared in awe. Then he spoke: "Do not believe these lies, brothers and sisters. To enslave an Earther is to enslave an Ascendant. We must rise above pride and hate. We are better than this."

He threw his arms out to his sides as he spoke, and he did not fall. I had no idea what I was seeing, this young Ascendant levitating high above us with outstretched arms. *Is he flying? Is this Icarus?* I wasn't sure, but I knew one thing: he was the first I had seen challenge the Lord Ascendant.

He wasn't a magician though. Someone held him aloft. Onstage the Lord Ascendant raised his hands, clad in black gloves that glowed with purple light. *His hands are like black staffs!* A cold fury flowed from his eyes.

"What a lovely image," he said. "My friends, is this who you want to be? You want to arrive on Earth unarmed, like beggars on the beach. And how do you think the Earthers will treat us if we come wearing white tunics and waving the white flag of surrender? Let me demonstrate."

He raised the young Ascendant higher in the air. The crowd cleared a spot in the middle of the arena.

"I am prepared to die," said the young challenger, "but I am not prepared to kill or make anyone else my slave. We are better than this! Icarus will show—"

But before he could finish, the Lord Ascendant brought down his hands. The young Ascendant plummeted to the arena floor. I heard a sickening thud.

A cold knot seized my guts. Janice went pale. Sunjay held her arm to steady her.

The crowd, frozen with fear and surprise, burst into applause and cheers. Some around me had tears in their eyes, but for some reason they cheered the loudest.

"We are Ascendant!" someone yelled.

"We always rise!" everyone responded. They turned back toward the stage where their leader stood, looking untroubled, flexing his gloved hands. The crowd quieted.

"What a waste," he said and gestured toward the body. "You can take Icarus's way. See how high your wings can take you. Or you can take mine, no, our way."

Once again the image of the *Lion's Mane* appeared in the arena. Only now it gleamed in purple and black majesty.

"Beneath Europa, our great ships wait to take us home. In three day's time, we depart. Now, let us enjoy this evening's entertainment."

The entire mob of Ascendant, maybe 200,000 in all, made their way toward the theater. We walked with them.

Around us some of the Ascendant looked upset. They spoke to each other in low whispers about what happened in the Red Storm Arena. Some said that the young alien had not leaped—the Lord Ascendant sensed that he was evil, so he picked him up and made an example of him. Could the Lord Ascendant read someone's mind? It certainly felt that way when he interrogated me in space. Either way, the young Ascendant had spoken against him. That was brave, insane, or both.

"He threw him into the dust," said Janice. "I don't want to die."

"Courage," my dad said, walking beside us. "You three stay together. Make for the theater. Stick to the plan."

FAMILIAR FACES

The theater towered over us, a blood red marble building the size of a football stadium. *How will everyone see the actors on the stage? Fortunately, the Thirders would have the closest view. That worked well for our plan.*

Inside, we found our place in front of a stage raised forty feet above ground level. Just like in the arena, each Step had an assigned section. The Thirders stood in front of the stage, while the Firsters and Seconders stood behind, and the higher Steps all had box seats above us and behind us. We split up and pushed our way as close to the stage as possible. Just as we planned.

A high crimson curtain loomed above us with a spotlight on its center. The first words of *Romeo and Juliet* rotated above our heads in the shape of a globe, and they flipped from language to language....

> *Two households, both alike in dignity,*
> *In fair Verona, where we lay our scene,*
> *From ancient grudge break to new mutiny,*
> *Where civil blood makes civil hands unclean.*

"Neat trick," Sunjay said to Janice, who looked dire pale.

"I don't want to die," said Janice. "I can't do this. I'm going to Stanford."

"Why don't we all go to Stanford?" I told her. "It's a good school."

That didn't help very much. Sunjay whispered to her.

"Queen Envy once told me, 'If you can't be anything else, be brave.' We are going to be fine. Remember when Buckshot caught you before you fell? Well, this is our chance to catch Tabitha. She's counting on us. That's what matters, right?"

Sunjay could empathize with Janice, so he kept talking to her. He should have talked to me. My heart tried to thump its way out of my chest. When that curtain parted, I would see Tabitha again. I had only seen one of her plays at the community theater. About fifty people attended. Now I waited with 200,000 aliens for the Earther to perform.

The words above us disappeared.

The lights dimmed.

The crowd hushed.

I clenched my teeth and squinted at the curtain, waiting for it to rise and show me my long-lost friend, my Tabitha.

Janice tapped my shoulder. She looked composed again. "Tully, remember, Juliet won't show up until Scene III."

My heart sank. I knew this. We discussed her delayed appearance in planning, but I hoped she would appear in front of us nonetheless. Nothing ever goes as planned.

For instance, the red curtain did not part. It dissolved into thin air and revealed a wide stage with no actors. Dark structures rolled in from stage right and stage left. Squares, rectangles, triangles of various sizes populated the stage. The "set" was now in place, but it was a wasteland of obscure objects, a geometry teacher's nightmare.

"This is one of those stripped down sets," said Janice. "No costumes, no set decoration."

She was wrong for once. The stage held secrets. The Ascendant actors came in from either side. They were dressed in plain black, but the stage changed that. With every step they took forward, the stage covered them in long flowing dresses, colorful pants, crowns, and flowing capes. Every step changed the dull space as well. Before long, the entire stage became a Renaissance town real enough to touch. I would have fallen out of my seat, but I was standing.

The actors were magnified, too, seeming to stand twenty feet tall, their every move clear to us and easily seen from the back of the arena.

"Holy holograms," said Sunjay.

The play began. It was ingenious, alien, and pretty well acted. The Montagues were tattooed Ascendants. The Capulets actors looked human, with no tattoos at all. I thought about those opening lines again. *Two households both alike in dignity…from ancient grudge break to new mutiny…*

In the first scene, a Capulet started the "new mutiny." He drew a black staff (instead of sword) against an alien Montague. The crowd booed the "human" Capulet. The two actors fought for a moment, battling much like we had in our training sessions, dodging stuns and fireballs, until an Ascendant actor broke up the fighting. He had my exact tattoos…or he looked like the Ascendant Lord. Same thing, I guess.

Then the stage changed to an oceanfront scene. I could smell the saltwater and hear the waves. There we saw the Ascendant Romeo, writing poems and discussing his girl problems with himself. His friends dragged him to a party, so the scene changed again—this time, a fancy mansion. A second story appeared out of nowhere, and partiers in masks danced and ate and laughed. Still, alien Romeo moped around, leaned against a column and stared at the floor, but not for long. Without warning, he ripped off his mask, looked to the top of the stairs, and said:

"Did my heart love till now? Forswear it, sight!
For I ne'er saw true beauty till this night.

The entire crowd reacted the same way. Maybe they had seen true beauty, but most had never seen an Earther in person. They had never seen Tabitha Tirelli.

There, at the top of the stairs, her curly hair and green eyes glittering in the spotlight, stood Tabitha, looking every bit like the girl that made me stumble over my words more times than I cared to admit. The Ascendant pointed and whispered at Tabitha, who radiated starlight. She gave them a moment to collect themselves before starting the scene. Like I said, she's a good actress.

The stage magnified her in every way. She loomed over us, twenty feet tall and looking twenty years old, in a gleaming white party dress. It was a masquerade, and she came as an angel, apparently. She held a mask in her hand. Wings fluttered on her back. A diamond necklace hung around her neck. Her face was as I remembered it. Not a single tattoo disguised the face of Juliet Capulet. She gazed on her admirers and then focused on young Romeo.

Alien Romeo ascended the stairs, and Tabitha Capulet began her lines. That's where all the Ascendant magic wore off and I came to my senses.

"Oh, this sucks," Janice whispered to me. "Sorry."

Their whole conversation revolved around kissing. First, Romeo kissed her hand. Then he went for the cheek. I knew how this ended and wondered how kissing an alien would work out. Do I need to say how much I hated this idea? When Alien Romeo awkwardly planted one on her, the crowd cheered. Tabitha smiled like she had just found Mr. Alien Right. I could have ripped his lips off his tattooed head.

But there wasn't time to dwell on alien kisses or holy holograms. Our time to take the stage was almost upon us.

I surveyed our surroundings. There wasn't much security. To our left and right were Ascendant guards. Two were posted at the side exits, two at each door in the back, but none near the stage. I looked back to scope out the balcony. The Fourthers sat on the highest level, the Fifthers in the middle, and the Seventhers had box seats, with the Ascendant Lord dead in the center of the theater in a booth that glowed with a soft purple light. And beside him I saw something else that took my breath away. *No, that can't be.*

Countdown at Intermission

That rigid posture, perfectly combed hair, and glowing blue eyes brought back a floor of memories. I never thought I would see him again, in the flesh. Or whatever covered his Android body.

Lincoln Sawyer.

The last time I had seen him was our epic battle in the space lab. He had almost ended me with a black staff before I opened a portal and launched him into space.

He should be halfway to Pluto by now, I thought, *not watching Romeo and Juliet.*

As I stared at him in disbelief, he glanced my way casually. Among all these thousands of Ascendant, did he see me?

Looking toward the ground, I turned back to the stage, my heart in my throat. Tabitha stood before me, twenty feet tall and radiant. Sawyer sat behind me, with his sharp blue eyes piercing my skull. And on all sides Ascendant guards, but not very many. There were too few to stop our plan, but what if we through Sawyer into the mix? The chances of success dropped dramatically.

Janice nudged Sunjay, who nudged me. "It's time," he whispered. We were supposed to move forward, then split up and jump onto the stage just as the lights went down and the curtain reappeared. Most of the crowd wouldn't notice. They would exit for intermission. It all worked out, except now...

I turned around again. As the darkness fell on the scene, Sawyer's blue eyes grew brighter. Did he recognize me? Out of all those thousands of people, he stared directly at me. Yeah, he recognized me. How could he not? He had unlimited memory, and my tattoos could not hide my bone structure or the shape of my irises. He might have been surprised, but he believed his eyes, which were monitoring my blood pressure and heart rate by then. Tully Harper, enemy of the Ascendant, stood just a few hundred meters in front of him. He looked left and right, then right at me and blinked three times. He was sending me a message, loud and clear. *Of course I see you...*

I didn't move, even when Sawyer stood calmly and lifted both of his hands. At the same time Sunjay tugged on my sleeve. I didn't respond. I wasn't frozen. I was coiled like a spring. *Think before you act, Tully. Sawyer knows you are here, but he has not seen the others. The plan must work. Create a diversion. Save the operation. Save your friends.*

I willed myself to action. I turned my back on Sawyer. "Sunjay, the plan starts now," I said. "I'll be right behind you. Take Janice. Go. Now. But promise me. No matter what happens, do not turn around. Do not look back."

"What?"

"Trust me, Sunjay. The plan will fail if you do. Now go!"

The final moment before intermission came. The theater grew darker before the lights came up. I could see just fine, and so could Sawyer. I turned to face him. He still held his hands up towards me, but I noticed he held up only eight fingers. Slowly, another finger dropped. Seven.

"So you want a chase?" I mouthed toward him. He nodded and grinned. *Yes.* "Then let's go." I knelt down for a moment, prayed, and then, the spring uncoiled. The house lights came up in the theater.

Two things moved in opposite direction. Sunjay and the rest made for the stage, and I charged for the back exit. I threw myself into the air and flew over the Firsters and Seconders. Those that saw me gasped and pointed. After what happened in the arena, they could not believe that someone dared to go flying into the air again. They started a mini-stampede, and I jumped right over them…and under the Lord Ascendant's balcony, where Sawyer was counting down my doom.

But there was a commotion behind me, too, as Operation Grabitha went into effect. I glanced over my shoulder and saw Sunjay, Janice, Buckshot, and my dad land on the empty stage. The stage magnified them to an enormous size. They disappeared backstage in their search for Tabitha. With any luck, they would find her and make for the submarine. I would be right behind them.

I couldn't stay airborne for long. The crowd lurched away from me in horror as I landed, but I managed to melt into them. The surprise drove us all the way through the lobby and onto the wide street. If any black staff had seen me, they lost me in the crazed crowd. Only Sawyer, with his steady eyes on me, could find me now.

He must now be at three. Just move, Tully. Move!

Now on the street I leaped again. The Ascendant below me stared and pointed, splitting apart as I landed and then leaped again. I crossed the broad street to a line of fancy mansions. I leaped over one of them and landed in a thicket of purple fruit trees. *Wow, from theater to orchard in six seconds. That has to be some sort of record.*

All this leaping would have been fun, but then I saw one of the fruit trees burst into purple flame. Behind me appeared black staff after black staff leaping into the orchard in hot pursuit. But above them, one hundred feet in the air, I saw a black speck that could outleap us all.

I crashed through the thicket, then stopped dead in my tracks, trying to control my breathing. *Think, Tully, think.* The Fifth Step was too wide; there was nowhere to lose my pursuers. I couldn't hide in the orchard forever.

I heard several thuds nearby. Five of them. Then the tree above me shook. I didn't move an inch.

"Tully Orion Harper," boomed a voice from the treetops. "Here to save Tabitha? You are quite a dreamer."

You have no idea.

The tree shook again. Sawyer leaped to another vantage point. I took a breath.

Shadows crept through the trees around me. The smell of sweet fruit. The crunch of leaves. The telltale buzz of a black staff nearby. Just one.

I needed to be quick and quiet, just like my dad taught me. The Ascendant passed me before I jumped on his back and put him in a chokehold. He dropped his black staff and raked at me with his fingers, but I held on. In seconds he dropped to his knees, unconscious.

I picked up his staff and looked around for my next opponent. The staff felt heavy in my hands. Then I shook my head. *What am I doing? If two black staffs show up, I'm roasted. If I wait any longer, there will be two hundred black staffs in this orchard. Whatever I do, Sawyer will have me.* It was like being on an unbeatable level of *Cave-In!*, where you just can't advance because you don't have the right equipment. *I can't win the Fifth Step. If the Sacred was awake, I could blast my way out of here and take on Sawyer once and for all. It would be better to restart this game and...*that gave me an idea...*yes, move back a Step!*

There was a red marble wall on the far side of the orchard. After that it was a thousand foot drop into the ocean. *Beyond that was the Fourth Step though. It was only a few hundred feet below and full of shops and tiny alleys.*

Mine as well go for another record.

I put down the black staff. Placing my hand and foot against the nearest tree, I looked at the pale light of Jupiter through the canopy. Then I leaned back and launched myself toward the wall. Purple sparks exploded on my right and left as the black staffs picked up my movements and tried to blast me through the canopy of trees. I bounded forward, covering ten feet, twenty feet, fifty feet with every step. I flew past tree after tree until I reached the open space in front of the wall. I left the ground just as a fireball hit. The heat almost overwhelmed me, but I landed on my final mark—the top of the wall. I planted both feet and broad jumped off the wall, Buckshot-style, leaving the Fifth Step behind.

I did not look down. I looked back at the black staffs. A dozen of them stood on the wall watching me fly away. They did not follow. They fired their black staffs toward me but were out of range. That was the good news. And my distraction worked. Even better! Go, Tully, go!

The bad news? My enemy did not pursue me for good reason. I might as well have jumped into the mouth of a shark with a stick of dynamite in my hands. Yeah, then I looked down. There was nothing below me except water. Once I crossed this gap, I would still be hundreds of feet above the Fourth Step and falling, like a hovercar with no fuel. In the low gravity, it was a gentle fall, but it wouldn't be a gentle landing.

"Hey, Bacon," I said, grabbing him from my tunic. "I could use some help here." He held on to his hat as the air began to whiz past us. "Yeah, we're falling, but I'm not sure if we will reach terminal velocity."

"Terminal velocity is the maximum speed an object can achieve while falling," said Little Bacon. "On Earth, it is roughly 130 miles per hour."

That sounded like a death sentence. Flattened like a bug on a windshield.

"Well, what's our terminal velocity here?" I asked.

"Terminal means 'final' or 'closing,'" he said, "but it can also refer to an incurable disease."

"Eh, thanks," I said. Math was not his specialty, and neither was it mine. *Think, Tully. Terminal velocity on Earth = 125 miles per hour. Less gravity on Europa. .1335G. So terminal velocity on Europa = ????. Sounds less terminal,* is all I could come up with at the time.

Looking down, the shops and streets of the Fourth Step looked so small, like a miniature alien world. The wind whistled in my ears. My hair rustled in the wind like that young Ascendant's tunic in the arena. Was I about to meet the same fate?

I had no control over how or where to land, and it looked like I was headed for an open area behind a gate. *Oh, stars. The Ascendant Warrior's Training Ground. Nice aim, Tully. Now you really need a "Restart Mission" button.*

There was worse news though. Worse than falling to your death? Yep.

I heard a voice behind me, inhumanly loud. None of the black staff jumped, but someone did.

"Tully, my secret friend, you never cease to amaze me!"

GREEN TO GRAY TO BLACK

Lincoln Sawyer looked way too comfortable to be falling. I guess if you're an android with a titanium exoskeleton, you don't worry much about landings. You'll hurt the ground more than it hurts you. His arms were spread wide, and in one hand he held his weapon of choice—a black staff. He trailed me by about one hundred feet and closing.

"The last time I fell like this, Tully, was in outer space," he yelled to me. "Remember your little trick?"

"How could I forget?" I yelled back. The picture crystallized in my mind: his flailing arms as he floated through the portal into space, his bright eyes dimming to black. It seemed so final, like someone's dying breath. Apparently not.

"That was no way to treat your mentor," he said.

"You were never my mentor," I shot back.

"Who taught you to fight with a Bo staff? Me. Who offered you a position among the Ascendant? Me. And who did you betray? Me. Me. Me! Oh, the irony. You could have lived on the Fifth Step. Now you are falling to the Fourth."

"*You* betrayed the entire Earth, you metal-headed monster!" I yelled. *Great conversation to have while I'm freefalling to my death. My last words will be "metal-headed monster."*

"Call me names if it makes you feel better, Tully. You thought I was lost, but I am found. The Lord Ascendant himself searched for me. He appreciates my usefulness so much more than the Space Alliance. He finds it terribly helpful to have someone at his side who can memorize a billion faces and read the lips of 10,000 people at one time." I wondered if he could really do that. I thought back on the theater. *At least we had our back to him the entire time. He doesn't know about Operation Grabitha.* "The Ascendant improved me, Tully. Look at this new skin! And they programmed me to feel emotions, Tully! Real emotions."

"You feel pretty good right now," I said, trying to form some kind of plan in my mind. My hair whipped into my eyes. *Don't die yet* was about all my brain could do.

"I feel fantastic!" he shouted, "but soon you will not. At this rate of velocity, you will impact the ground in twenty seconds at about 40 miles per hour."

"Oh, I already figured that out," I said. No reason to give him the satisfaction.

"This will likely break several bones," he continued. "In case of injury, try to remain conscious, please. The Lord Ascendant and Gallant Trackman would prefer it."

Being hauled in front of them could not have sounded worse. I turned toward my landing spot, the warrior training grounds, a tank full of knives and piranhas. At least Sawyer was there to capture me, not kill me. But capture would be as good as death. My only hope was that Operation Grabitha worked.

That's when my arms and legs began to tingle. Then my whole body.

What on Europa? I lurched sideways suddenly, away from the training ground to a new destination. Yes, a narrow street lined with fruit and fish vendors and a large, deep, green fountain at the end. A splashdown would be better than a splatdown.

An angry bellow behind me. Sawyer tried to grapple me back toward himself, but something had pulled me away from his reach. I was almost between the buildings and too far away for him to do much...but the little he did almost ended me. He altered my fall, and as I fell between the jade buildings, past the open windows, despair hit me. *I'm going to miss the fountain after all.*

The Ascendant below pointed and screamed. "Icarus! Icarus!" they yelled, running for cover. Icarus? They mistook me for someone else. I reached into my pocket and clung to my lucky shell, hoping that a pair of wings would sprout from somewhere.

They didn't. I fell through an awning that slowed my fall. Below me was an alien street market. Flowers, food, arts, and crafts. I saw an enormous pile of ice and raw oysters—or something like that. It was all coming at me so fast. Then, splat and crunch. Not exactly a clean tuck and roll.

A moment of blinding pain. The impact made my left arm completely numb. I tried to prop myself up with it but the pain increased. I saw stars and smelled seafood, but there was no time for pain or stars. I pulled myself from a pile of shellfish. My left arm didn't work but I was on my feet (at least those still worked), limping and bounding up the deserted street. Sawyer would be on my slimy trail in no time.

Tug. A force yanked me sideways into a dingy alley full of rotten fruit and fish bones. *I guess that's a sign.* I staggered down the dark, smelly alley.

From the rooftop I heard Sawyer's voice. "Tully, no more. Your friends are caught. Your plan is foiled."

No. No, no, no. He lies. All he ever does. Keep running.

A gray alley. It looked more like the First Step than the Fourth. And it was dark. *No, it's not that dark. It's my vision. Oh, no, not now.* I could feel my head getting lighter, my stomach churned, the stars returned. The pain from my arm suddenly peaked. Was it dislocated?

I should do it now. The pain will only get worse.

I grabbed my dead arm. I shoved it upward. Nothing happened. I pushed it down and forward. Pop. The pain brought me to my knees, but my arm was back in place.

I tried to stand back up, but the pain held me down. I tried again. My vision blurred. My ears rang.

No, hold it together. Keep moving. Don't pass out. Do. Not. Pass. Out.

Two shadows appeared at the end of the gray alley. One of them carried a black staff. *Oh, no, no,* I thought, turning back toward the street, but a shadow blocked my way. I took a swing at the shadow. It grabbed me from behind and hauled me toward the end of the alley. The pain. The exertion. The whole situation overcame me. Captured by the Ascendant at last.

Five minutes ago I had been standing in a theater plotting how to save the most beautiful girl in the universe. Now I was about to die in a dingy gray alley.

No. No, no, no. Not like this.
Do not pass out.
Do. Not. Pass. Out.
Do. Not...

Part Four: ICARUS

LITTLE OUTLANDERS

Black. Black to gray. Gray to red. The first Sacred Dream in many months appeared to me.

I found myself isolated in the middle of the Red Storm Arena. A crowd filled the stands. It seemed angry and scared, threatening to jump into the arena and tear me limb from limb. They jeered so loudly that I didn't notice what was in the arena with me. Flaring its nostrils, lowering its head, and charging in my general direction, was a white bull. I turned to run.

Then a gust of wind hit me. I stumbled on but looking over my shoulder saw an enormous hawk beat the air with outstretched wings. He landed between the bull and me. They fell into battle, one charging with horns and the other slashing with talons. They rolled in the dirt, locked in combat. I tried to summon my powers and they actually worked! I created a portal and prepared to jump in. I would be safely away in an instant. However, I hesitated. As the bull finally hooked its horns through one of the hawk's wings, I sprang toward them wanting to rescue the hawk, to distract the bull. The hawk saw me coming, and he batted me away.

"But I can save you!" I shouted at the hawk. "We can defeat him together."

"Then who would save them?" the hawk replied, looking at the crowd. "They are the ones you must save."

What did it mean? What were the hawk and the bull? Why did the crowd need saving?

Whatever the dream meant, two things occurred to me. Number one, I was still alive. Maybe captured or tortured but alive. And number two, the Sacred had awakened. My visions returned, and so had my powers. As the red mist receded, I came back to my senses.

My shoulder throbbed, my head felt like a corkboard full of thumbtacks. The muscle between two of my ribs made me wince with each breath. But I guess if I felt pain, it meant that I was indeed alive.

Voices. A number of them, all in Greek. I hesitated to open my eyes, expecting the cold blue eyes of Lincoln Sawyer looking into my soul.

I lifted my head slightly. It was on a pillow. A bedspread covered me. I pushed back the bedspread with my right arm. The left was in a sling. While the bedspread had been on top of me, nothing supported me. I opened my eyes and realized I was in some sort of sleeping chamber.

The Ascendant next to me took notice. He held something like an electronic screwdriver in his hands. He twisted it and I floated out of the enclosure into the main room and found myself on my feet.

He dismissed the other Ascendant nearby and then spoke to me in Greek. I said nothing. He repeated himself in English, but I hardly heard the words. His presence left me speechless.

The young Ascendant before me was striking. Red and gold streaked his braided black hair; he wore a dusty Fourther tunic; his face was sincere and youthful. He looked about 25 years old in human years, but something told me that he was older than that.

His sharp, blue eyes, flecked with gold (and purple and red), told me more. They watched me with a combination of care and cunning. They weren't cruel like Sawyer's, but intelligent, empathetic, trying to read between the lines of my story. For some reason I wanted to spill my guts to him right then, just tell him my dreams about the bull and the hawk and maybe my real name.

His tattoos shifted—a covey of doves slowly winged across his arms and neck. That brought me back to my senses. *Keep up your guard and keep your secrets, Tully. So what if he looks friendly and gives you a pillow? You're not among friends.*

He put down the screwdriver thingy and passed me a cup of water before I realized my own thirst. The room was cold and damp, his hand felt warm upon on my shoulder.

"Welcome to the Lost Catacombs," he said. "Do you know this word?" He gestured around the room. It was a dingy, green corridor full of small arched enclosures along the walls. Most of the enclosures contained bones—lots of them—except for the one where I had been laying.

"I know what catacombs are," I said, looking at a tidy stack of skulls. I felt a rustling on the side of my tunic.

"Catacombs," said Little Bacon, "are underground passageways used for burials or religious practices."

I tried to put a hand over his mouth, but my ribs hurt so bad that I had to lie back down.

"Your little friend is right," he said, like it was no big deal that I had a handroid. *Has he seen one of these before?*

"So you captured and gave me a cup of water," I said. "Now you're going to bury me alive?"

"Catacombs aren't just for the dead. You know how the living used them? On Earth, in Rome, the early Christians used catacombs to gather together and worship and escape persecution."

"On Earth," I said.

"Yes, and Christians built these catacombs, too. Later the Hindus used them. Then the First Rebellion. And now us, the Friends of the Encountered, or what's left of us."

When he said the word Encountered, my mind went completely wobble. Was he a friend or an enemy – or something else?

"It's strange, isn't it?" he said. "We seek safety among the dead. These catacombs have saved us many times, and now so few days left for them to be useful."

With each word, his feathery tattoos rustled. They flitted with every word. My hand reached for the lucky shell in my pocket. I thought about the little wings carved upon the walls all over Rathmore. It all began to come together.

"You're Icarus," I said.

"Indeed." His feathers ruffled along his hands and arms. He smiled. "But you have me at a loss. Who might you be?"

"Nobody," I said.

"Well, he's a bad liar," said a gruff voice from the darkness. A short, musclebound Ascendant stepped forward, sneering at me. "He jumped off the Fifth Step with Sawyer on his tail. Nobody does that...unless he is somebody, or he is insane."

Me, insane? You're the ones hanging out in catacombs. You're the ones tattooed from head to toe. You're the ones coming to conquer my world!

"Bernard, you may be right, or maybe Stephen inspired him," said Icarus. "The boy spoke the truth to the Lord Ascendant in front of tens of thousands of listeners."

"Infinite wormholes! Inspired by Stephen's act? That was a good boy that one, and now he's dead."

"Better to die free than to live in fear," Icarus said.

He put a hand on my injured shoulder. I recoiled and expected pain but noticed that it felt better than it had. I could move it again.

"I repaired it as best I could," he told me. "I am one of the Encountered, and healing is in my hands. I can see from your expression that you know what this means."

"Of course," I said. "You fought against the Lord Ascendant, but didn't the he destroy all of the Encountered? How did you escape the fall of the Sixth Step?"

Whoops.

"A spy or a madman," said Bernard, stepping forward with a black staff in his hand. "We cannot reveal ourselves yet, Icarus. We should have left him to his fate. Now tell us your name and what you know, or we will give you to Sawyer."

I should have kept my secrets, I thought. Everyone on Earth thinks I have an alien virus, the Lord Ascendant knows I'm here, and now the Encountered think I know too much.

Icarus turned toward Bernard, who gripped the black staff tightly.

"Lower your weapon," he said. "We won't beat the truth from this young one. I know that you are upset about Stephen, but you are better than this. We are spies and madmen, too, Bernard!"

"Yes, a few of us escaped the fall, young one. We hid, but now we rise. You know why. The Lord Ascendant wants to rule the Earth the same way he rules Rathmore—with fear and power. We must stop him, and our time is short. There is more to say, but do tell us what we can call you in the meantime."

His blue eyes tracked across my face. *I'm Tully Orion Harper. I am like you. I need to save my friend…no, keep your secrets. They're all you have.*

"Spaceboy is my name," I said, taking a deep breath, "and I should tell you. I will only speak English."

Icarus laughed, long and hard. He playfully pushed Bernard, who frowned even more deeply at me.

"What?" I said, almost laughing myself. Suddenly things didn't feel so serious, like Icarus had flipped a switch and decided to make our tragedy into a comedy.

"Nothing," said Icarus, "and everything. Bernard, maybe it is fate. He's named himself after your favorite Earther song. Sing it for us."

Bernard crossed his hairy arms over his chest. "It's not my favorite. I don't even like Earth Pop. I just started humming it that one time and you noticed…"

"You know Queen Envy's music?" I asked.

Icarus started to sing. "I'll turn red, red, red, when you kiss my f-f-f-f-face—"

"Enough, it gets stuck in the cars!" Bernard grumbled. "Okay, yes, this song pleases me."

The tension evaporated in an instant. I was safe among the Encountered for the time being. This alien with feather tattoos could shelter me, and his friend was an Ascendant Queen Envy fan. *This would totally go to her head,* I thought. *The song that she wrote about my dad is popular around the solar system. She has no idea how big she really is.*

It was this weird conversation that stirred something in my mind. It was a thought connected to the Europa myth, catacombs, jokes, and music. *The Sacred said they are more like you than you know. Yeah, but they're almost too much like us — and they're not faking it either.*

Icarus saw me deep in thought and shook his head.

"This one is so much like the little Outlander that we found yesterday," Icarus said. "They seem to be sneaking in from every corner of Rathmore. What did she call herself, Bernard?"

"Carpool," he said. "Whatever that means."

Carpool? No way.

IN THE GRAND CATACOMB

Icarus and Bernard led me through the narrow catacomb that eventually straightened and descended deeper into the Fourth Step. A light glowed off the slick cobblestones ahead of us. Voices echoed off the walls and seemed to come from all directions. Finally our catacomb ended. It fed into a high-ceiled room with eight other identical exits. There was no lighting, only a soft purple glow from the lichen on the walls.

"Welcome to the Grand Catacomb," said Icarus. "You are among friends now, or at least not among enemies."

Icarus halted at the edge of the room filled with a group of fifty Ascendant. Most of them were young – in their early alien twenties, I guess – and they came from many different Steps, all mingling and laughing and talking as if they were long-lost classmates. A group of Firsters joked with a Thirder. A Seconder and a Fourther reviewed a holographic map in the corner. It felt strangely comfortable like snack break at my school, which was the period that I missed the most. I had the sudden urge to eat a bagel.

One of the Ascendant in a white tunic bounded toward Icarus and through her arms around his neck. She was strikingly tall, probably taller than Buckshot. She had long black hair with red highlights that cascaded down her shoulders, and she wore a red ruby around her neck. She looked over Icarus's shoulder and narrowed her eyes at me. Then she pushed him away playfully. They exchanged a few words in Greek.

Everyone settled down when they finally noticed Icarus. His tunic turned from blue to white, as did Bernard's.

Icarus lifted his hands. "Friends of the Encountered," he said. "There's much to say, but may I start with a prayer?"

"May we skip to the important stuff?" said the Ascendant with the ruby. She frowned but her eyes glimmered with laughter.

"Adèle, I'll just pray twice as hard for all of this later."

"At least pray in Greek or French," Adèle replied. "All this English is terrible."

"No, just Bernard's English is terrible," said Icarus. The Ascendant laughed, even Adèle. "Our Outlander friend here prefers English. He calls himself Spaceboy."

Many nodded their heads to greet me, including one young Ascendant in the corner. Carpool.

Everyone bowed their heads for a prayer. I looked at Janice and mouthed some questions. *Buckshot? My dad? Tabitha?* She shrugged her shoulders. *I don't know. We split up.* She pointed at Icarus. *He found me.* I noticed that Adèle had not bowed her head either. She watched Janice and me.

"God beyond all praising," Icarus began, "you created a magnificent Universe. We do not understand Your ways, but You have made it known that we should love our neighbors as ourselves. Help us bring this message to our people. They live in fear. They need peace. This is our common cause, regardless of our beliefs, that none should suffer, that all should be loved, on Earth and Europa as it is in Heaven. Amen."

"Very pretty, as usual," said Adèle.

I wasn't expecting to hear Ascendant praying or joking like old friends. The words of the Sacred returned to me: *They are more like you than you know.* Still, their tattoos and Adèle's fiery looks set me on edge.

Icarus addressed the crowd. "Friends of the Encountered, our message has spread. Many have taken up our cause. We have seen the wings scribbled across all five Steps now, but this will lead to consequences. A young boy confronted the Lord Ascendant in the arena today, and he was not taken to the Undercity this time. No, he was cast down and killed. I saw it firsthand and learned that his name was Stephen. Let us honor his memory in our thoughts and prayers." The crowd shook their heads, saddened but not surprised. "Now, the rumors are confirmed. The Exodus is upon us. Soon the Ascendant of Rathmore – and all the other Chaoses – will depart for Earth, and against the weapons of the Lord Ascendant, no Earther can stand. Therefore, our time is short. Our mission is bold. Our duty is to our people. In these final moments on Europa, in the spirit of Stephen and all Seven Steps, we must show the Ascendant what it *truly* means to rise—not just from Europa, but above pride, hatred, anger, and most of all, fear."

The assembly nodded, some applauded.

"This plan will not work," said Adèle.

"I have yet to tell you the plan," said Icarus.

"But I know you too well. I have heard this plan before."

"Then let me say it again," said Icarus. His tattoos bristled, the feathers seemed to rise off his skin and make him look larger. "Stephen is just a hint of what is to come. It is time to march."

"You believe that the people will follow?" someone asked.

"After today, yes, I do," said Icarus, looking toward me. "Soon we must gather on the First Step. We will call the Firsters to us. They will march with us to the Second Step, where we will gather the Seconders. Then the Thirders, the Fourthers, and finally all of us will march upon the Fifth Step in peace, the same peace that we hope to bring to the Earth. We will unite Rathmore in peace, and the Lord Ascendant will no longer have anyone left to rule in fear."

"Yes, the peace march," said Adèle. "The Lord Ascendant will slaughter us. It will be a waste of time and life."

"A waste of life," Icarus repeated. "I've heard those words from another's mouth—the Lord Ascendant's—when he cast down Stephen in the arena today."

"How could we move the people from one Step to the next?" someone asked. "It would take more than trolleys, Icarus."

Icarus nodded. His feathery tattoos ruffled along the lines of his arms and shoulders. His white tunic shined. Then for a moment the feathers really did rise off his shoulders and extend above him. I could feel the air on my cheek from his fluttering wings. They were tattoos, but they were also real.

Everyone murmured. I remembered what the tattoo artist had told me. *Only the Encountered can alter their tattoos.* This looked more like *using* a tattoo than altering it.

Icarus leaned toward the group. Everyone watched his tattoos, but I watched his feet. The more he leaned in, the more he stood on his tip-toes, until for a split second, he left the ground. He pointed to the white tunics of Adèle and Bernard and whispered, "You are listening but not understanding. Among you are the last of the Encountered, and that is enough. We *can* move you between the Steps."

"But there are too many of us," someone said.

"Not anymore," he repeated. "The Sacred has awoken. I will fly again. You will see and believe."

The Ascendant looked confused, but not Adèle and Bernard. The three of them were the only Encountered. Adèle closed her eyes while shaking her head. So did Bernard. A moment of silence. Then their tattoos glowed faintly, and their faces softened, as if they felt a long-forgotten comfort. Their powers returned.

"You speak the truth," Bernard said. "The Sacred has awakened. We can move the people between the Steps again, as it was before the fall of the Sixth Step."

Of course. They could create portals. I used portals for escape, but they could be used for transportation. With a big enough portal, the Encountered could move their peace marchers from one Step to the next. The idea would work, but only if Icarus could use his wings. Bernard or Adèle could open an entry portal on one step. Then Icarus could fly to the next step and open the exit portal. First to Second, Second to Third, and so on. The entire group could ascend Rathmore as easily as walking through an open door. It was a vision of freedom. *This must have been the way it once was here. A city of magic portals. A city with Seven Steps but no real boundaries to separate them.* The vision was beautiful, but Adèle shook her head.

"The Sacred power returns," Adèle said. "Why waste it on this risky plan. Icarus, they will shoot you down, and for what? There is another way. As they say, cut off the head of the snake and the body will die. We can assassinate the Lord Ascendant, then make for Earth and set down a peaceful agreement with the Earthers. The power of the Sacred makes this even easier than before. Let us make an end to him and we will not have to march at all!"

Icarus had won me over with his idea of the peace march up until that moment, but Adèle was right. The Lord Ascendant had countless black staff at his command. He could shoot Icarus from the air or simply line up his army in front of the portal and blast the marchers to smithereens. But an assassination? The idea seized me in its grip. I could accomplish something like that all by myself, and what if I revealed myself to the Encountered? I rubbed the lightning scars on the backs of my hands. They felt warm. The three of us could take down the Lord Ascendant together. We could send him to the bottom of the ocean with the rest of his victims.

"We cannot bring peace through violence," said Icarus. "It only leads to more death. So we do not want to kill the snake. We want to turn the snake into a dove. This is the path to peace, even if it means our lives."

"And who would be our assassin?" asked Bernard.

I almost raised my hand.

"Right," said Icarus. "We could confront the Lord Ascendant, but none of us could fight him. We are prophets and protectors, not fighters. The Sacred did not give us those gifts."

I really almost said something.

"Some of us would like to try," said Adèle. "I say that we have a vote."

"Uh, excuse me," I finally said. "I am kind of new here, but why don't you ask the Harp – I mean, the Sacred – what to do?"

The Encountered – and everyone else – stared blankly at me. It was like that moment when you ask the same question someone else just asked the teacher. Adèle and Bernard laughed along with everyone except for Icarus.

"You must have heard these tales from your Outlander mother," said Bernard. "The Sacred speaks in dreams and visions, but not in words that we can understand."

"But, but—" But I stopped myself from blurting out anything else. *You are the Encountered. How can you not know this? The Sacred does speak. It spoke to me.*

Something else was wrong. I could sense it. So could Icarus and Adèle. They didn't get to take our vote.

From deep in one of the catacombs, everyone heard a deep rumbling. Then the clash of footsteps on cobblestones and a faint electric buzz.

WICKED MAGICS

We stood breathless in the middle of the Grand Catacomb, listening to the approaching sounds echo off the high ceiling and the walls. There were eight exits, all of them identical and dark. It was impossible to tell where the sounds originated.

"They've found us," said Icarus. "There's no time to use the Sacred powers. Meet me at the beach in two days. We march from there."

Everyone scattered. Icarus grabbed my hand and started down one tunnel. Adèle pulled Janice in the opposite direction, but I wasn't about to let her out of my sight. I yanked away from Icarus and grabbed Janice's hand. The four of us were left in the Grand Catacomb, along with a few Thirders.

"Come on!" Icarus said. "There's no time."

But there was. The crowd rushed into each of the eight smaller catacombs. If they ran into any black staffs, it would delay them on their way to us.

"Give me a second," I said. "Trust me."

Icarus gave my arm another yank but then relented and let me stand in the middle of the Grand Catacomb with my eyes closed. I took a few deep breaths and listened to the sounds around us. There were battles erupting in some of the catacombs now. I could feel the others behind me, ready to burst into a run. I wanted to run, too, but something told me to wait. We could hear the shouts and bursts of black staffs.

See this, see it all. The sounds echoed in the dark, but the Sacred powers changed them into something quite different. I could see the sounds. They made each of the exits glow. Six of the catacombs glowed red, but there were two that glowed with a peaceful blue.

"Take this one or that one," I told Icarus. "They are safe."

Icarus weighed our options and then rushed down the catacomb on the left. Adèle shook her head and ran after him. The rest of us followed him. We dashed over the damp cobblestones, twisting and turning our way up until we reached a series of pipelines. The smell of rotten food and waste replaced the clean smell of stones and lichen. The sewers of the Fourth Step. Behind us, sounds of battle diminished but we bounded on for several minutes until we saw a light.

During the escape, I thought about my encounter with the Sacred. It had appeared to me, not just given me visions. It had also given me powers that the other Encountered did not seem to have. I thought that they would be more powerful.

"It's not far now," Adèle said, leading us toward the exit.

Up ahead we saw the light growing brighter. It looked like a quiet place to exit.

Wait, I though*t. This is Sawyer chasing me. He's always one step ahead. Remember what Trackman said about him. 'I would never play the Android in chess because he would win.'*

"Stop," I whispered to Icarus, closing my eyes again. Adèle stopped, too, but a few of the Thirders kept walking toward the exit. I tried to picture the street. Something seemed wrong about it. It was all quiet, too quiet, except for a low hum. The hum became a color. The color was a faint red.

"It's a trap," I said. One of the Thirders heard me say this and ran forward to warn the others. Two of them were almost to the exit. I could see the sound echoing down the tunnel. *Whoever is outside must be able to hear it.*

"I do not trust this one," she said. "He is hiding something from you. You know this!"

"Adèle, cover us," said Icarus.

"But it's been so long," she said. "The last time I tried—"

"You must," pleaded Icarus.

Up the tunnel the Thirders crept back toward us. Adèle closed her eyes and shook violently. Then it happened. Her spider web of tattoos came to life. They began to rise off her skin. Her hair floated on a breeze that was not there. With her tattoos gone, I could now see what they covered—a lacework of scars on her shoulders. *Lightning flowers, just like on my hands.*

"I get it now," Janice whispered. "They touched the Sacred but it gave them different sorts of powers."

I nodded. Adèle's web stretched across a section of the tunnel and Icarus motioned us to get against the wall. Janice grabbed my hand.

"Her powers return," Icarus said. "As of now we can be neither seen nor heard."

"Yes, but let me focus," she said, holding out her hands, the lighting scars on her shoulders glowing.

We flattened ourselves against the stones. To my eyes the web-covered walls glowed red, and beneath them I could clearly see the others. But how would they look to our enemies?

The Thirders who had run ahead made it back to us and hid beneath the web. Just in time. A wicked buzz filled the tunnel. Black staffs rushed in from both sides, thinking they had captured Tully Harper or the Encountered. Such was their excitement at catching us that they fired their staffs from both sides. Purple fireballs exploded in the sewer. Most of the black staffs dodged the shots, but one of them was caught in the crossfire. He opened his mouth—to scream or to gasp for air—but before he could make a sound, his entire body glowed purple and then froze. When the purple dimmed, only a statue of dust was left in its place.

One of the black staffs walked up to the statue of dust. He was seven feet tall, muscle-bound, sweaty, and angry. He sniffed the air and narrowed his eyes. His deep voice filled the room. I pulled Little Bacon from my pocket and told him to translate.

"You were told to stun, not to burn," said the leader of the black staffs. "The Lord Ascendant will want a boy, not a pile of dust."

"Sorry, Commander Akakios," said one of the black staffs. "We thought that we heard them."

"Wicked magics," said Akakios. "They were here."

Akakios brushed his staff against the statue, and the thing that had been a living, breathing being crumbled to dust.

"At attention!" Akakios demanded. The black staffs fell into line in front of him. A shadowy figure appeared at the entrance to the tunnel. His glowing blue eyes lit his face.

"You probably don't know the phrase *friendly fire*, do you?" said Lincoln Sawyer. "Well, congratulations. You do now."

Sawyer looked around the "empty" tunnel. He surveyed the walls for a moment.

"Fortunately you did not incinerate anyone important, but it appears that our trap failed. The Encountered and the boy have escaped. If only these walls could talk, maybe they could tell us where they went."

Sawyer ran his hands along the wall. "Commander Akakios, come forward."

They both walked directly toward me, Sawyer's blue eyes boring into the wall above my head. I held my breath and Janice death-squeezed my hand. *They can't see us. Icarus promised. Stars, but what if Sawyer can? He took your pulse one time just by looking at you.* I prepared for a fight. Sawyer reached out suddenly, and I dropped to the floor as he placed his hand on the wall where my head had been. His eyes fixed upon the spot inches above me. "Akakios, place your hand on the wall. Tell me what you feel."

"Warmth," said Akakios in a deep voice, "and the fear of the Encountered."

"Usually people smell fear, but I'll allow that. The walls are warm though. There is a faint heat signature here, but why are these walls not burned? An incinerator shot hit this spot, yet it is not hot."

"Encountered have wicked magics," said Akakios, sniffing again. "They spelled this place evil."

"Wicked magics, indeed. Search the streets and wait for further orders, Commander." The black staff left and Commander Akakios reluctantly followed. Sawyer patted the wall above my head. Then his blue eyes shined and he faced the other wall. From his eyes came a projected image of a figure in a dark room.

"Report," said a high raspy voice.

"We lost them for now," Sawyer said.

"I don't care about them. What about the boy? Is it really him?"

I recognized that voice. The shadow figure leaned into the light so we could see his face.

"Yes, it is definitely him," replied Sawyer. "He can't be far. We will gather the Ascendant in this sector and I will find him. He will be brought to you alive, Mr. Trackman."

Trackman. Still on my trail. The name meant nothing to Janice, but Icarus and Adèle looked stunned. The image on the wall disappeared and Sawyer quickly exited the tunnel. Icarus blew out a deep breath. One of the Thirders did, too, and he took a step into the middle of the tunnel. It was too soon. Akakios had returned, still troubled by our escape. The Thirder froze and threw his hands into the air as the black staff advanced on him.

"Icarus, do something," I said.

"He will be captured," said Icarus. "We will free him after the march."

The Thirder had other ideas. He threw down his hands and ran. Akakios shouted a warning and then stunned him. The commander looked over the Thirder carefully. He took a few steps more and then, without warning, reared back his staff for an incinerator shot. Boom. Where there had been a young Ascendant there now stood another gray statue. Akakios laughed. He was about to crumble the Thirder to dust, but I could stand it no longer.

"No!" I stepped into the tunnel. My left arm was still in a sling, but I balled my right fist. What was I thinking?

He whirled around to face me. Akakios raised himself to his full height. He blotted out the light at the end of the tunnel. He flexed his massive arms and shoulders, grinning wickedly.

"You choose a brave death," he told me. Then he threw down his black staff and advanced toward me.

I tried to remember the fights we had on the *Mini-Mane. Will you be able to kill?* my dad asked me. I wasn't sure, but I knew I had no choice but to fight.

Akakios ran toward me and tried to throw his arms around me. I slid to the side and scaled him – he was like a mountain – until I had my arms around his massive neck. I put him in a chokehold. He grabbed for my hair but couldn't reach me. He stumbled like a drunk, starting to lose consciousness. I thought he was done, but then he suddenly lurched forward and threw me over his shoulder. I landed with a thud in the sewer. His roared and tried to stomp me, but my sacred powers were with me. I rolled out of the way. He threw another punch. I ducked and dove between his legs toward the exit of the tunnel. I wasn't planning to leave though.

Akakios charged after me but stopped abruptuly. He stared in disbelief. I had his staff in my hands and spun it once overhead with my good arm.

He grinned, said something in Greek, and spit at my feet. I locked eyes with him. *He has no mercy, he showed no mercy. There is only one way to end some fights.* Before he could move, I fired at point blank range. A purple blast of fire sprung from the black staff, and a second later a monstrous statue stood in the middle of the tunnel. I dropped the staff, and the statue crumbled to ashes.

On the far wall, everyone looked to Icarus for the "all clear." He signaled to Adèle. *Enough.* The red web withdrew and shrunk, becoming a spider web of tattoos on her back again. She crumpled to the ground, exhausted from the Sacred powers. I felt the same way.

Icarus helped Adèle to her feet. He moved to the middle of the tunnel, his eyes glowing with emotion. He scooped up a handful of ashes and they sifted through his fingers.

"It should not be so easy to erase a life." He shook his head at the scene before him, then turned his attention to me. His eyes shot through me again. "Are you okay, Spaceboy?"

I nodded as Janice helped me to my feet.

"Who is this boy that Sawyer and Trackman hunt, who can defeat a black staff?" Adéle gasped.

"We must move," Icarus said to me. "Sawyer still hunts you, and now we see why."

"She Ran"

All the way through the Catacombs I wanted to ask Janice a thousand questions, but the Encountered would have heard our conversations. We had to act like strangers just meeting for the first time as they debated the peace march.

Finally we reached Adeéle´s apartment. It was a three-bedroom with very little furnishings. On Earth *we take a lot of things for granted. On Europa there aren't vast forests or tons of room for animals. That means they don't have basic things like feathers for a pillow or wood for furniture.* At Adéle's we found a few pillows stuffed with crunchy stuff–dried seaweed?—and sealskins lined the walls and floors. She did have one couch. Janice scanned the apartment and pointed at a row of books, the first we had seen on Rathmore. Adéle frowned at us, as if we were planning to steal them. Janice probably wanted to. She wanted to understand the Ascendant as much as I did.

BWAAAAMP. A loud siren cut through the air. It meant roll call.

Icarus and the rest had to leave. Adèle eyed us and said, "Outlanders, there is food in the kitchen. Stay away from the windows. Touch none of my books. They are precious things."

"When will you return?" Janiced asked.

"It is hard to say. There will be roll calls across Rathmore after the events of today," Icarus told us. "Sawyer will undoubtedly be at our roll call, and his eyes miss nothing." With the Encountered gone, Janice and I hugged like long-lost soldiers coming back from a war. I was the wounded one with an arm in a sling. She was the healthy one. We were happy to be alive, and it felt dire good to be ourselves again and not the fake us. She put on her glasses, and I gave Little Bacon some air.

"Are you okay?" she asked, looking at my arm. I gave her the short version, but that wasn't important right then.

"Did Operation Grabitha work?" I asked Janice. "Tell me everything."

"Part of it. Your distraction worked. The black staffs followed you, but you should have told us."

"Sawyer didn't give me any time."

"Oh, I think I see. So we jumped on stage and made it backstage – all of us – and found Tabitha and..." she slowed down and took a breath.

"What?"

"She, uh..."

"She what?"

"She ran from us."

"Why would she do that?" I asked. "Did she recognize you?"

"I don't know. We look like Ascendant now, so maybe not. There were lots of actors backstage. They panicked. She bolted. Alarms sounded. I grabbed a costume off a rack and ran for an exit. There were lots of Ascendant in the streets, and I saw Tabitha for a second. She was with alien Romeo. Then some weasel-y looking guy grabbed her hand and they disappeared into the crowd."

"What about the guys?"

"I don't know," she said. "Your dad was in the street. Maybe he was able to save her, but I don't think so. And Sunjay...I don't know if he's safe." Tears welled in her eyes. "I'm sorry, Tully. I think we failed."

"No, we didn't," I said. "This isn't over. My powers are back. We just need a new plan. What time is it?"

She pulled out her holophone and checked the timer. "We only have twelve hours to get back to the sub."

Stars, the others might be waiting at the submarine with Tabitha already. We should go! My mind jumped into high gear, but I knew it was misleading me. *Things didn't go as planned. Be patient. Don't rush into a trap.*

A chime sounded. Outside, two black staffs appeared before the crowd, flexing their muscles. The crowd lined up in front of the fountain where I had landed just a few hours earlier. They began their drills, similar to what we did on the *Mini-Mane*, except there were five thousand Ascendant all lunging, thrusting, and shouting in unison. *We are Ascendant. We always rise.* I imagined this same scene happening on every Step.

"Do you see Icarus or Adéle?" I asked.

"You won't recognize them," said Janice. "They can change their tattoos. Remember how you did that in the Ink Squad? It's nice to have so many disguises."

"I guess so," I said.

"We should get away from the window. Now, how much longer should we stay hidden? Do we need to protect our identities? Should we march? How do we find your dad and the rest?"

So many questions and so little time. In the end we decided to "join the peace march," then split off and regroup at the submarine and come up with a Plan B.

At least that's what I explained to Janice.

IN THE NIGHT

That night I had a vision. In my vision I stood on a narrow ridge at the base of a mountain peak. Fog obscured my view. The wind whipped my hair and threatened to blow me off the rocky cliff. I had to move, but which way? There was a path down the mountain behind me. It would be easiest to turn back, but no. *I want to make it to the peak.* Up ahead the peak loomed, and on top of it, a purple tower. There was no straight way to my goal.

Two paths stretched around the mountain on different directions. There was no way to see their ends. To the right was a rickety bridge that looked like a piano with missing keys. On the left was a frayed guide rope strung between rusty poles. *It's either trust the bridge or trust the rope.*

Something brushed against my shoulder. Standing next to me was a creature with a face like a man's and wings of a dove. His red and gold eyes shined. He nudged me toward the rope, then began to climb. *It's too windy for him to fly. Should I go that way? Maybe he knows the mountain. At least I will have a guide.*

Following him were other creatures, some with wings, others with antlers or claws. They trudged along the rope, but a strong gust of wind nearly blew them off the ridge. They stopped in their tracks, unable to move forward. *They're not going to make it to the top like that,* I thought.

"The wind isn't going to die down," I shouted. "You have to press on. Why are you waiting?"

"For you," the dove man said.

"You want me to follow you?"

"No," he said, "we want you to lead."

I looked down the two paths. The rope path seemed long and safe. The bridge looked weathered and dangerous.

"Why would you want me to lead? I don't know this mountain," I said.

"But I know you," he said. Then the fog covered the scene again.

There are times where waking up takes twenty minutes, like my brain is some ancient laptop trying to boot up. Other times my brain snaps on so fast it makes me move before I know what I'm doing. After this mountain dream I found myself standing in Adele's apartment beside the sleeping Janice and looking out the window. There was a picture in my mind of a purple tower, and only one thought.

Go.

I stepped lightly over Janice and made it down the hallway to a sitting room before pausing to think. *What am I about to do?* It was just long enough to feel someone else in the room with me, peering into the lonely street. Icarus.

"Sorry if I startled you," he said. "Adéle has a perfect sitting room. I come here sometimes when I can't sleep. Or when dreams awaken me. Maybe you were the same way tonight."

I rocked my weight back and forth but didn't move. I needed to keep my secrets. *I am Spaceboy the Outlander. Just a scared kid running away, maybe headed back to my family, too scared to march with you.*

"What *did* wake you?" he asked, standing slowly and looking out the window. I saw his tattooed wings unfold. They stretched across his shoulders and glowed red in the near darkness. Beautiful.

But I did not answer. More rocking back and forth, feeling ready to run, jump, sneak, and attack.

"You want to leave," he said, "but not because you are afraid. This much I know. I have many and more questions about you, my young friend, but I will promise to ask only one, if you will promise to answer it."

He looked at me over his shoulder, his purple eyes flecked with red and gold.

"Go ahead," I nodded.

"Tully?" he said.

"Yes?" I said, waiting for his question. He didn't say anything more though, just looked out the window at the square. His wings stretched down to his fingertips, then bristled as before. What was he waiting for? Was he stalling?

The time for waiting was over. The guys could be waiting at the submarine. My powers had returned. I could rescue Tabitha and be on my way...and hopefully get Janice on the way back. Still, Icarus might be able to stop me. I did not know all of his powers. He was Encountered like me, and he was staring out the window at the light from the distant stars.

"Icarus, what is your question?"

He turned toward me.

"I was going to ask you who you really are," he said, "but I do not need to ask that anymore."

The red and purple light of his eyes shined in the darkness.

"You didn't ask me anything," I said.

"I asked you nothing...and everything," he replied.

"But all you did was say my..." but I could not finish my sentence. He finished it for me.

"Your name," he said. "Tully. Tully Harper. On Europa known as the Red Thief." Icarus took a step forward, reaching for my shoulder. "I've known for longer than you think."

"No," I said, backing away. It wasn't "no" to him, more to the idiot bomb that I had detonated in my own face. *I blew my cover with one word. All that sneaking around—just like last time and all for nothing. Sawyer knew it was me in that orangutan suit, and he toyed with me. Icarus did the exact same thing. Might as well just wear a nametag next time.*

Icarus waited patiently, my mind in tornado mode.

I should have left earlier. He would never have known. He would go on with his peace march. Tabitha and I would be on our way back to the submarine. Maybe I could assassinate the Lord Ascendant somewhere in there.

My heart leaped into my throat. A cold lump formed inside my stomach, and my lightning scars felt hot, ready to burn something.

"Let me go," I said. "I'm on a mission, Icarus."

"I know. So am I—to make my people good again."

"I don't care about that," I said. My hands sent a warm red glow onto our faces.

"Yes, you do," he said.

"You don't know me."

"Better than you think," he said.

"I am here to save a friend. I owe her."

"I know that, too."

"You know nothing," I said.

"Nothing, and everything," he said. "Think about it, Tully. Who are the Ascendant? Where did we originate? What is the Sacred? You came for Tabitha, but you also came for answers." It wasn't a challenge, just a simple statement of fact. Before I could respond, he stepped in front of me. Both my hands glowed red in front of my body. *River of fire,* I thought, *river of fire.*

"I don't want to hurt you."

"Can you?" he asked. "Can your hands burn right through me?"

"Of course they can," I said. "At least I think they can."

"I did not understand this when we first met."

"You mean a few hours ago."

"No," he said. Icarus dropped his arms to his sides. "Tully, look at me."

His feathered tattoos bristled. Red and gold flecks danced in his blue eyes, which he closed. He breathed deeply, and his lips began to move. He whispered something in Greek. His tattoos glowed dimly in the dark room. *He's about to use sacred powers.* I thought about creating a portal and launching myself out of the apartment, but I held my ground, ready for anything.

Then his tattoos shifted. His feathers stretched and wriggled on his arms and shoulders. In place of feathers there were scales. In place of wings there were rattler and fangs. A thousand serpents danced on his skin. The tunic turned blue like a Fourther's. Suddenly, Icarus did not look like Icarus. He looked like someone I had known.

"You can't be," I stammered.

Icarus opened his eyes again. They were his eyes, but combined with these tattoos they transformed him into someone else. Ekphrasis the tattoo artist, our guide on Rathmore, stood before me, but now I knew him by his proper name. Icarus.

"You—"

"You know me," he said. "And I know you. I feel like I have known you my whole life, Tully. I dreamed that we would cross paths. You are a vision in the flesh."

"How did you find me?"

"The Sacred brought you to me. When you appeared in my shop, it was the fulfillment of my very first vision: that I would meet a boy with wounded hands, and I would guide him through a steep mountain pass. The visions hinted at the truth, but I did not expect the boy would be an Earther. I still do not know how you arrived here, but you could be none other than Tully Harper. So I am done guiding you. Now what do I do? I have a choice. I can wake up Adèle. Tell her about you. She will realize you are a valuable asset. She will have many ideas for what to do next."

The snakes writhed upon his skin. They coiled, hissed, rattled. They sent chills down my spine. Great, Adéle. She wasn"t my biggest fan. *He's right. He could trap me here. He could turn me in. I would have to help him. Now he knows my hands are weapons. He might change his mind about the peace march. He might attempt an assassination. That wouldn't be so bad, I guess, but what if he doesn't care about Tabitha's safety as much as I do?*

"Is that a threat?" I asked, my pulse rising. "I thought you were good."

His tattoos transformed from scales to feathers again. He seemed himself.

"Alas," he said. "I am, and I am still your guide. I cannot block your path. But before you venture off alone, why don't we take a brief trip together?"

"Where?" I asked.

"Tabitha is safe in her tower," he said, "but I fear that another is not so fortunate."

"Who?"

"Sunjay."

Two Tales and a Wall

I abandoned my plan and went with Icarus. What else could I do? He was right about Tabitha, and he might be right about Sunjay. So under a starry night sky, we slipped out of the apartment together. The wet night air clung to my tunic and slowed me down. I struggled to keep up with Icarus. We weaved our way down the side streets and alleyways of the Fourth Step. We hopped fences, watched for guard cats and guard foxes (Who knew they could do that?), and finally traversed a beautiful garden. On one end was a dreadfully high wall. There were tall stone spires in the distance above it.

66 Can you portal us through the wall?" he asked.

"Not if I haven't seen the other side."

Icarus didn't look concerned. He kept walking and I stayed beside him until we reached its base.

"It is quite a wall," he said, his eyes flickering in the starlight. He turned toward me and put a hand on my injured shoulder. I flinched, but didn't feel pain. We were now face to face. *What the heck is this? Alien dance lessons?* It was awkward for a split second. Then I felt a rush of power, a kick of energy and enthusiasm. Not only that but my shoulder felt better. My lightning flowers didn't ache. Looking up at the wall, it didn't look so high anymore. The top looked closer than I expected, and the shapes beyond the wall came into focus. *This wall's nothing,* I wanted to say. *And there's a river on the other side. We can jump the wall and the river. Stars, let's jump to the Seventh Step and save Tabitha while we're at it.*

"Okay, we got this," I said, feeling like a million bitcoins. "It's not that high after all."

"Maybe not," he said. "Or maybe the ground has just become that low."

It was a weird comment. Alien dance party weird. Still, I felt great. Then I looked up. To my surprise, there was no longer a wall above me. Instead, I saw wings.

I checked below my feet and what I saw took my breath away. The ground was a hundred feet below us. Somehow we were now perched on the top of the wall.

Big Ben, the Tower Bridge, and a bunch of other familiar landmarks rose in the distance. Icarus took his hand off my shoulder, and the glorious feeling faded. The height of the wall left me dizzy and tingling. I rubbed my injured shoulder.

"How did you—"

"This never gets old," he said. "The first time someone flies, the mind cannot make sense of what's happening."

"You mean we just—"

"Flew," he said, looking down at the street below. "Either that, or you're dreaming. Now let's keep moving. Guard cats on a high wall are common. We, however, will draw some attention."

Good point. I created an entry portal on the top of the wall and an exit on the street below. We dove headfirst into the portal and popped up on the street.

"You're quick, Tully. I can't portal like that."

We crossed the street and stopped in the middle of the cobblestone bridge. Above us the stone arches cast shadows on the rippling water, which reflected two of London's greatest landmarks.

"Big Ben," I said, pointing to the water, "and the Eye. This isn't what I expected to find on Europa."

"Yes, the Eye is new. Only the rich can afford it. I've heard that it's exactly one meter taller than the real one in London."

"Well, why did we stop here? To talk about buildings? We need to save Sunjay."

"I agree," he said, "but I need answers first. We need to trade stories, Tully."

"Maybe later," I said, "because Sunjay—"

"—needs our help, but I need to know some things, too." His eyes gleamed with understanding, curiosity, and most of all, power. "I promise you, Tully, this is the only demand I will ever make of you."

A demand and a promise. I'm not a fan of either, but what choice did I have? I nodded.

"Okay," I said. "You probably know that my dad discovered the Sacred on Mars. It actually almost killed him. It landed in front of him, blew a hole in his helmet, and knocked him out. When he woke up, he found that it was producing some kind of atmosphere and keeping him alive."

"He had no idea what the Sacred was though," said Icarus. "That must have been such a shock. To him, to the whole world. And a shock to you, too."

"Yeah, I full on freaked out. So he returned, got super famous, and no sooner did he get home than the Sacred started messing with our atmosphere. So the Space Alliance decided that they needed to take it back into space."

Icarus's feathers trembled. "Ah, that was no accident," he said. "Someone must have been manipulating it. The Sacred can do great harm in the wrong hands. We both knew whose hands..."

Well, only one hand now. Trackman, of course. Icarus didn't have to explain that any further. Trackman had access to it and used something to make the Sacred go crazy. He put the entire world at risk. He set up the whole thing. Not like I needed more reason to hate the guy.

"Continue," he said.

"Well, my dad agreed to take the Sacred back into space, and I was sick of Alaska so I got on board his ship – with Sunjay and Tabitha's help. I wore the orangutan spacesuit. We hung out with Queen Envy..." Icarus looked a little lost, and I didn't blame him. "Anyway, long story short, I touched the Sacred. It sort of drew me to itself, then it gave me dreams, powers, and then I talked to it at the end of the trip before I put it to sleep."

Icarus feathers pulsed with a brilliant red glow that made me shield my eyes. A few other people walked the bridge, but fortunately nobody saw it happen.

"Talked?" he gasped.

"Yeah, we chatted. You know, the Misty Man in the garden?"

"No, I do not know the Misty Man. The Sacred gives dreams, but it does not speak."

"Oh, well, he spoke to me." The idea almost knocked Icarus off his feet, and it suddenly dawned on me. The Sacred only spoke to me. What did that mean? I had glimpsed something special, like a shooting star that trailed out of sight before anyone else saw it. Or those people that come back from the dead and say that they visited Heaven. Icarus gripped the rail and shook his head.

"The universe is so full of mystery," he said. "I know so little of its designs."

"Yeah, I feel you there," I said. "But you think you know nothing? Icarus, I'm an idiot about all of this compared to you."

He shook his head. "No, you are not. You've met the Sacred. That is special. You may know little, but you acted upon it. There is greater truth in one honest act than in a thousand proverbs. Have you never heard this?"

"No, that's a new one," I said. "I just wanted to help my dad."

"You sought the truth, Tully. Maybe that is why the Sacred chose you." Icarus grinned. He tousled my hair like my dad does, and that feeling of excitement returned.

"So tell me who you are," I said.

"That, too, is a long story. I grew up on the Sixth Step. My father was Encountered, like me – like us. He was offered as a sacrifice to the Sacred, and he offered me in the same way. You've never heard of this, have you?"

"No."

"In Rathmore, it was a great honor, but also a danger. Both parents must agree. You see, only the first child of a household can be presented to the Sacred."

"Presented?"

"Yes, the child would be placed alone in the room of the Sacred. The parents would then leave. This is when the child would choose. If courageous, he or she could touch the Sacred. Then the child would become Encountered, if the child survived."

His words sank in. "You mean, not everyone survives."

Icarus shook his head. "Very few, but it was the price that we had to pay. The only way we could control the Sacred was through the Encountered. If we could not control the Sacred, Europa would fall into ruin. So, you see, the Encountered risked everything to help their people. My father survived, and so did I. We helped our people for many years, but the Lord Ascendant ended all of that."

I looked up at the broken Sixth Step. The jagged edges were all that remained. I imagined the scene. The step cracked. The Encountered fell. A terrible moment. The Lord Ascendant wielded more power than I imagined. Now he wanted the Earth. I wanted to ask Icarus more about this, but I remembered my dad's saying. *What really matters?* Not the past. Stick to the present. Right now.

"How many lived?" I said.

"Seven of us did," he said, "but now only Bernard, Adèle, and I are left. Ah, and you, my young friend. We are the last of the Encountered."

"The Lord Ascendant did all this horrible stuff," I said, "so why haven't you tried to assassinate him?"

"Oh, I have tried. And I have failed. I have discovered that death—"

BWAAAAAMP.

The sharp sound of a horn rattled my nerves. Marching feet shook the bridge, and from the far end I saw hundreds of black staffs marching toward us.

"Relax." Icarus put his hand on my shoulder. Then he grabbed some rocks from his pocket and handed me one. The black staff marched past us as we tossed rocks into the flowing water. Their eyes bored into the back of my head. Their staff buzzed and made all the hair on my arms stand up. I prepared to make a portal, but the warriors passed us and their sounds receded. We were just a father and son chucking rocks off a bridge.

"Right on time," he said. "You see, there were many reasons to slow down. The Ascendant guard is light at this time of night. The coast is now clear, as your people like to say."

He's so smart, and he has this all planned out, I thought. *But he's not going to get me off topic though.*

"Why not try again? This time you'll have me. We can stop him before he hurts anyone else. Before he takes down my world like he took down your Step."

"I have discovered that death leads to death," he told me. "How could we have peace if it starts with a death? Even one is too many. No, only peace can bring peace."

"Even if that means your death?" I asked him.

"Then that is how it shall be," he said. "It is a risk, but only peace flows from peace. This is a hard lesson. So I will ask you to march with me, but I cannot demand it. That is not the way to peace either. It is like touching the Sacred. You must choose it for yourself."

We watched the water flow under the bridge for a moment. It behaved differently on Europa, making tall peaks instead of flat ripples. He expected an either, but I had none for him.

"I suppose it's time we do something about Sunjay," he said finally. "Follow me."

The Weeping Door

More alleys. More sneaking. Another flight up a tall wall. I wished that Icarus would just keep flying up and up, until we could see all Seven Steps far below us, but that wasn't our mission. The last wall put us right where I would have ended up the day before if he had not interfered. The Ascendant Training Grounds.

A dark mansion sat in the middle of the empty training grounds. They would have been dangerous to cross, but we didn't have to. Icarus pointed to a cellar door on one side of the mansion, and I portaled us to it. We entered through a deserted kitchen and crept through a few hallways until we reached a long corridor. At the end was a large purple door.

"That is the Weeping Door," he said. That did not sound promising.

"How do you know this place so well?" I asked.

"I trained here," he whispered.

"You were a black staff?"

"Yes, it was a useful disguise once. I learned this much. They hold captives beyond the Weeping Door. Mostly Outlanders. From there, they take them to the Undercity. They become slaves. They must have brought Sunjay here. Now can you portal us in?"

"No," I told him. "It's not like I've been here. I can't see through that door. Can you?"

"No, but I have an idea. How far away can you portal?"

I closed my eyes. I could picture the entire city of Rathmore in my mind. When I tried to focus on creating a portal, I couldn't see very far. My field of vision grew smaller and smaller until I could see just outside the training grounds. I told Icarus.

"Then that will have to do," he said. "This will happen quickly. Follow my instructions."

We crept down the quiet hallway and stood before the door. It wept with condensation, like old glass does when it gets cold on one side. Icarus motioned to me. *One guard*, he said. *One portal.* His plan became clear. I created an entry portal in front of the Weeping Door and opened an exit outside the training grounds. Then Icarus raised his hand and knocked hard. The knock did nothing. The door must have been made of solid steel. Seconds later, we heard a faint click on the other side.

An Ascendant guard appeared, shivering and groggy. He rubbed the sleep out of his eyes and caught a glimpse of Icarus. That woke him up. He lunged toward Icarus—for a second—before he fell into the portal and disappeared out of sight. I closed the portal.

"Now," he said, bounding into the dank, dark room, a room full of cages. In the cages, skinny Ascendant children huddled together in rags. Dozens, maybe a hundred of them. They staggered to their feet in a daze.

"Portals for them all," Icarus told me. "Gather them here."

"All of them?" I asked. "I can only do one portal at a time."

"Then hurry," he said. "That guard will return with friends."

I had no idea of the rest of Icarus's plan, but he had not led me astray yet. So many cages, so little time. Portal after portal I closed and opened. The children caught on and scrambled into the portals. Icarus shepherded them to the middle of the room and kept them calm. Outside we heard commotion. Shuffling feet.

"Hurry, Tully," he said.

"Done," I said, out of breath.

"Now, one big portal to the same place you sent the guard."

"How big?" I asked.

"How big do you think?" he said, looking at the children. Outside the hallway filled with a deep buzzing sound.

Portal, portal, portal.

A thud on the door. It was thick. Was it thick enough?

Portal, portal.

Wait.

"Where's Sunjay?" I asked, but the children were starting to cry. The door made strange creaking noises. "SUNJAY!"

A little child tugged on my tunic. He pointed at the floor, where a small latch stuck up. I ripped up on the latch and saw, deep in the dark hole, several sets of wide eyes.

Just then the Weeping Door flew off its hinges. It nearly took my head off. Without a second thought, I faced the five black staffs at the door. They lit the ends of their staffs, planning to incinerate us. Icarus, Sunjay, me. All of these alien children. Forget that.

My hands burned white hot and the children took a step away from me.

Someone roared in a deep powerful voice. Then flames burst from my hand and launched those black staffs back into the corridor. The flame died. The enemy was gone. And the roar had come from deep within my throat.

A hand gripped my shoulder and reminded me of my injury. I spun around and looked into Sunjay's bruised face.

"Big fast portal!" he yelled, reaching out to me for support.

Right.

In a flash we had what we needed. The kids filed into the entry portal with Icarus taking up the rear.

Safe houses. That's what Icarus called them. This is when I knew that he was a genius. Leading the Outlander children, we portaled our way across the Fourth Step. We took exactly the same route back to Adele's house, so I could portal us to every stop, and every stop was a safe house.

We dropped off the kids in groups of three or four, sometimes in back yards, sometimes on street corners, often at houses. It was tiring work, but within an hour we dropped off every captured child with one of the Friends of the Encountered. That left the three of us.

"What happened?" I asked Sunjay, when Icarus finally let us take a break.

"A scanner," he said, "outside the theater. After Operation Grabitha went bad. The scanner caught me and these other Outlanders. He started kicking them. They were little kids, Tully. And I tried to fight him. A few of them got away, but I don't remember after that. Just being cold and in that hole."

Sunjay grabbed hold of me and buried his head in my chest. I could only imagine what he saw. After he composed himself we managed the last few portals to Adèle's apartment. She was waiting for us. It was near morning.

"Merde!" she whispered, when Icarus and I stumbled in with Sunjay. "Irresponsible. Always at the wrong time. Where have you been? Oh, out with this little idiot. And you found another one!"

"Yes, just this one," Icarus said, looking at me knowingly. "Spaceboy couldn't sleep and I took him to the bridge. We ran across this young Outlander and saved him from a scanner."

"Fine, our powers return, you convince me to march," she said, "and then go wandering off into the night – I almost said a prayer for you. You almost made me pray!"

"Ah, then you are welcome," he said. "Now let me put this one on the couch. He will need my care."

"Boy on the couch – blood on the couch," she said. "And if I find—"

Adèle stopped abruptly. Janice knocked her out of the way. She smashed Sunjay against the couch with a hug. And I thought Janice was excited to see me. Not even close. Adèle dropped her shoulders. She put a hand on her head looking at Janice and Sunjay whispering to each other.

"Uh, pain. Hug. Not okay," Sunjay said.

"Now you know how I felt," she said.

All the tension melted from Adèle's face. She looked at Icarus and shook her head.

"Carpool," said Adèle. "You did not tell me you had a boy."

"His name is Zaxon the Almighty," said Janice, laughing through tears. "He's an idiot and – we're friends."

"Ah, I have an idiot like this, too," she said, pushing Icarus, who smiled. She held up her hand, and her ring finger shined. No, it was a tattoo of a golden ring. She shook her hand and the ring vanished like magic. *These two are married? No way!* Adèle smiled her fierce smile, but still, she never looked at me. I was glad. She didn't trust me, and I thought she might read something on my face. Icarus didn't explain our whole adventure.

I backed away and looked at the four of them. Two humans. Two aliens. Two...couples...back together. All of us were safe for the moment. I should have felt good about that, but there was that itch in that back of my mind. What about my dad and Buckshot? I hoped they were together. That wasn't the itch though.

A thought gripped my mind and would not release it. A few portals, a little fire, and we saved all of those children. *How hard could it be....*

I stewed on an idea for the rest of the night. It took shape. It snow-balled. *How much help would I need...* Even as Icarus shared his plans for the march, the idea gripped me. *It wouldn't be that hard for me to...* Even as Sunjay stopped shivering and looked healthier under Icarus's care... *portals can keep me safe, and the river of fire can do the rest...* And as I lay down before the rest of them, needing sleep, the idea kept me awake. It told me something else... *take it into your hands...do what you came to do...time for a rescue of your own...*

I spent a lonely day in Adèle's apartment. Sunjay improved quickly, but the last two days exhausted both of us. He slept, and I tried to. Adèle took Janice out for food and supplies – it was weird, watching them leave together to run errands – and Icarus and Bernard planned. All the while I kept my eyes shut and did some planning of my own.

Sunjay and I finally rose around noon. Or "quarter of Jupiter," Icarus told us. We ate and they shared their plan. "The march will begin at Christ the Redeemer," Icarus told us. "You may go with us, if you like." I remembered the giant statue on the beach. I had seen the real thing in movies before – a big concrete Jesus that stood on a mountain above a beach. Icarus glanced toward me. He still wanted an answer.

All I wanted was the night to come. Finally, it did.

That night there were no visions. And no sleep. Jupiter set, and in the dark night I rose from my place on the floor. The apartment seemed perfectly still. This time, when I passed the sitting room, Icarus was not waiting to stop me. Part of me wanted him to be there, to give me some scrap of advice or convince me to do something one way or another. That was not his way though.

I wrapped Tabitha's mood scarf around my hand, tucked Little Bacon into the belt of my tunic, and left the apartment for the last time.

PART FIVE: THE SEVENTH STEP

ROOFTOP RUN

As I bounded toward the Fifth Step, the cold air made me alert and excited. The last few days – of walls and wild histories and The Weeping Door – faded to gray. Back to the real mission. Time was short. Save her and leave.

I took an account of my resources: one half of a mood scarf, one whole Handroid, a vision of a girl in a purple tower, and my Sacred Powers. *What does the Lord Ascendant have at his disposal? Hundreds of thousands of black staffs and one deadly Android.*

Not exactly a fair fight. As I hopped from rooftop to rooftop, the space between the steps came into view. Occasionally I saw black staffs on the streets below me. If any one them looked up, they would blast me into space dust, but I was quiet as a cat. So was, for once, Little Bacon.

My conversation with Icarus kept coming back to me in snippets... *Who are the Ascendant? Where did we originate? What is the Sacred? You can't save anyone without answers to those questions...five times I plotted to kill the Lord Ascendant, and five times I escaped while others died.* I thought about how much history was here. Thousands of years, many generations. *I haven't even scratched the surface. History, yes.* Janice's words echoed in my mind, too...*Europa, Tully. It all makes sense now. They aren't just on Europa. They are Europa.* How were they connected to the myth? I still had no clue what she meant...I just wanted to reach the Seventh Step.

I reached the edge of the Fourth Step. On the streets below Ascendant guards stood watch with black staffs glowing purple. But in front of me, the coast was clear, mainly because there was no entry to the Fifth Step. *Or so they think.* I looked across at an imposing wall made of solid jade. Impenetrable. Just the day before I had leaped off that wall, and now I was headed back. I remembered the distance well—probably two hundred meters across the divide. Two hundred meters to the bottom of the wall. Another hundred meters to the top of the wall. Reality sank in. *Stars, that's a long jump! I can make the bottom of the step, but not the top of the wall.*

Not that I needed to make the top. It would have been more convenient though. I had been on the other side of the wall, so I knew what to do.

I walked to the edge of the rooftop and looked down. One thousand feet below were a Ferris wheel and the foaming waves of the beach. That would be a long, slow plummet to death. Backing away from the edge, I walked to the other end of the roof, probably one hundred meters from edge to edge. *That will have to do.* There was a clock building beside me. Its hour hand hung just before 2 a.m. *When that clocks strikes, you go.* I positioned myself in a track stance and pretended that there was a tape stretched across a finish line at the other end of the building. *Quick start, Tully. When you hear that sound, become a bullet. Run for your life. No, fly.*

I closed my eyes and pictured the hour hand behind my feet. *Fly.* When it sounded, it would launch me toward the other end of the building. *Fly, fly, fly.* Time passed, I heard muffled talk in the street below. Doors opened and closed. A dog barked. Another. A cat meowed. The hand of the clock pressed hard against my heels.

There it was.

I bounded off the line, using every ounce of my legs, trying to stay low and gain speed. Step. Step. Step. My arms pumped. My shoulder burned with pain but that didn't matter. I got in ten steps before the edge of the building loomed. One more step. And then.

Explode.

I catapulted myself into the air, the wind in my hair again. I was flying, gaining altitude, but the Fifth Step was still so far away. *I will not fail, I will fly.*

Halfway across it was clear that I wouldn't make the top of the wall. Everything in me wanted to panic. My body told me that was the right thing to do. So did my brain. But not my will. My will was stronger than either of them. I took a deep breath and focused, even as the height of my jump peaked. I was started to descend in small measures.

I pictured the wall, three feet of solid marble. I could see each molecule in the marble. My will forced its way through the solid rock and out the other side into an open, grassy field. *Portal, portal, portal.*

Opening my eyes, I saw a glowing red circle on the jade wall. *Portal, portal, portal.* It grew, inch by inch, until it was almost my height. *Perfect.*

The only thing that wasn't perfect was my aim. Maybe it was the wind, but I was about four feet too low.

I smashed against the wall just below the portal. A little faster and I would have knocked myself out. An inch lower, and I would not have gained a handhold with my good arm. Which I did. Low gravity comes in handy sometime.

I crawled into the portal and found myself magically transported into the garden on the other side. Well, *magically transported* might be an exaggeration. More like *luckily mangled,* or *breathlessly butt-kicked.* The portal was about four feet off the ground so I fell a few feet into a rose bush.

Stars, I'm out of practice, I thought, finding my footing. Fortunately there were no guards guarding the garden, or they would have seen a boy covered in thorns limping into the woods.

"Uh, sir, if you have a moment," said Little Bacon. I looked down at my traveling companion. His head poked through a hole in his hat, which was full of thorns.

"You're a mess right now, LB," I said.

"I would prefer to be a little mess than a big one," he said, plucking a thorn out of my hand. He straightened his hat and gave it a tip in my direction...before I shoved him back into the fold of my tunic.

Once undercover, I weighed my options. Sorry, *our* options.

We could attempt to run and portal our way across the Fifth Step just like we had on the Fourth. That was my original plan, but the streets were wider. I could not jump between buildings, and the black staffs would see me if I ended up in a street. In the distance I could see the Seventh Step, but there was no place to hide if I took that path.

Also, the gap between the Fifth and Seventh Steps was impossibly far. I could not make the jump, and I could not portal to the other side because I could not see my landing. Dangit, Icarus gave me good advice. We turned up a street and headed toward the Grand Newel, which stretched miles into the empty sky above. The street wasn't the safest bet though. I crossed a streets, sneaked into someone's backyard, and leaped onto their wall. Once there, I saw row after row of gardens separated by walls. Little Bacon cleared his throat. "The French formal garden, also called the jardin à la française (literally, "garden in the French manner" in French), is a style of gardenbased on symmetry and the principle of imposing order on nature."

I crept across the garden and found myself on top of another wall peering into a similar garden.

"...zen gardens are composed of water features, rocks, and raked sand to represent waves..."

"Are you going to do this the whole way?" I asked him.

"Lancelot 'Capability' Brown is known as England's last great gardener," replied Little Bacon.

Bacon and I made quick work of the maze of gardens. Actually, I made a game of it, landing in some powerful Ascendant's backyard and then seeing how few steps I could take before launching myself over his wall.

Finally, at the last wall the Grand Newel loomed above us. The jagged remains of the Sixth Step hung on the side of the newel, but otherwise it was a tower of smooth, impenetrable ice. Occasionally ice sheets fell from its sides.

"Stars, it must be a mile around," I whispered to Bacon.

"By my calculation, 1.24 miles," said Bacon.

In the darkness, the newel took on the colors of its surroundings, so it glowed red in front of the red wall.

I laid flat on top of the final wall and peered down at the street below. From there we could see the texture more clearly. Rectangles of different sizes were carved into the ice.

Two black staffs stood in front of the smallest rectangle, and it occasionally slid open to allow a small company of black staffs to enter or exit. I caught a glimpse of the interior, and that meant one thing.

"I can portal us in," I told Bacon.

We waited until a group of Ascendant left. The door slid open and then slid shut. *Now or never*, I thought. I took a deep breath and created a portal on the ground below us, and one inside the wall. I stood up on the wall.

I waved my hands at the guards. They spotted me, which is when I jumped off the wall and into the portal I had created. The next thing they saw was a scrawny Fourther vanishing before their eyes.

The portal landed me in a dimly lit corridor that cut through the newel. I was exposed there and needed to move quickly, so I darted down the corridor toward the center of the newel. That was almost a fatal mistake. A giant black gap loomed in front of me. I teetered for a moment on a thin ledge, but my momentum sent me over the edge. I reached back and gripped the ledge with my good arm. My feet dangled in the darkness before I pulled myself up. Doing a one-armed pull-up is no problem when you weigh fifteen pounds. I found an indentation in the wall and backed against it.

The interior of the newel was hot and humid. The clanks and grinds of machinery rose from the deep. *The Undercity,* I thought. I peered into the blackness below my feet. Along the walls ran a series of ledges, stairs, ladders, and elevators, but from the deep there rose a hot wind. I was relatively hidden so I closed my eyes and tried to picture the Undercity. Through the red mist I pictured myself jumping off the ledge and into the deep. Down, down, down I went past the exits for the lower Steps and into a cavernous room. There I caught a glimpse of the Undercity.

What I saw horrified me.

Thousands of ships sat side by side. Some looked like *the Lion's Mane* and others looked more like passenger ships. Skinny Ascendant with sad greasy faces labored on the ships, snapping on red tentacles and other unfamiliar weapons while black staffs directed their steps and yelled at those that stumbled. Forced labor. Slave labor.

These ships will leave, I thought, staring at the slave's faces, *but I don't know if the Lord Ascendant will need these slaves soon. He'll make more on Earth.*

I heard the clank of boots on the ledge. A small group of black staffs marched past my hiding spot and disappeared down a corridor. I stepped onto the ledge and looked up into the distance. I could see fairly high. *Just a few portals and I'm on the Seventh Step,* I thought. It was that simple. I portaled my way up the newel, and moments later I found myself walking toward a door that led to the Seventh Step. On it was the crown with three rubies above the Earth. This led to the Seventh Step, but I had not seen the other side. I would have to open it to enter. I would have to fight my way out.

There were two guards on the Fifth Step. Let's hope for those odds on the other side.

The two guards beside the door never saw it coming. When the door to the Seventh Step slid open, they expected to see a black staff or some high-ranking Ascendant. What they saw instead was the scrawny Fourther with no weapons in his hands. I stepped out casually and took in the surroundings. Yep, two guards, another empty courtyard, and in the distance a purple tower. My arrival completely caught them off guard, which gave me enough time to put one of them in a chokehold. *Yes, the sacred powers are definitely in full effect!* He dropped his staff and tried to grab me from behind but I held on tight like my dad taught me. The other black staff realized what was happening, but he could not believe it.

"The Red Thief," he whispered.

"You thought I would be bigger," I said. "Sorry to disappoint you."

One black staff crumpled to the ground, and the other was about to shout for help, so I created a portal beneath him and his shout became a cry of surprise. He disappeared from view, but he wouldn't be gone for long. The portal I created was close by.

I dragged the first guard in front of the door and then grabbed his black staff. I threw myself against the wall beside the door and waited. Moments later the door hissed open and the second guard charged out furiously. He tripped over the first guard and fell flat on his face. I blasted both of the guards with a stun shot and lugged them both into a dark spot on the side of the street.

This might be a good time to pick up a better disguise, I thought. I took off one of their tunics and put it on over mine. It was enormous but made me looked more like a short, fat black staff than the Red Thief. I threw on the other guard's tunic as well. They were both awake and in their underwear at this point, stunned and frozen, thinking that this was their end. I laughed at the situation. I stood there in their oversized tunics with a black staff in my hand.

"I'm a thief, not a killer," I told them.

"However, he has killed a man," explained Little Bacon.

The guards waited to see their fate. I wound up and stunned them as hard as I possibly could and headed on my way. That would buy me at least an hour, and that was all I needed if I moved quickly.

Ear - Heart - Mind

Why did *this* of all things make me stop?

After I knocked out the guards, I hopped from portal to portal to hurry my trip. There was only one street on the Seventh Step, a kilometer wide and paved with massive purple stones. It was flanked by high walls on both sides at first, but eventually the walls gave way to gates. On one side of the street sat an enormous palace behind a gold and black gate. It nearly stretched across the length of the entire Step. The Lord Ascendant's palace.

On the other side were hundreds of futuristic apartment buildings. It was the dead of night, but a few Ascendant still crossed between the palace and the apartments on hovering chariots. It would have been impossible to pass them, but it was easy using portals. I created one in front of me, then dove into it and popped up fifty feet down the street in a dark spot. I portaled my way across the step until I reached the thing that made me stop.

It was a statue of a white bull, probably one hundred feet high. On top of the bull was a girl. *The story of Europa and Zeus again,* I thought to myself, but as I glanced at the statue, I noticed that the bull reared its head in fear. Europa, on the other hand, looked triumphant. She dug her hands into his hide and smiled wickedly. *Isn't she supposed to be scared and not the other way around? Janice would be fascinated.* I felt that itch in the back of my mind about the myth. The Ascendant had changed the end of the myth, and this was yet another twist that she would enjoy.

The first rays of Jupiter streamed across the Step. Dawn. My destination was close. In the center of the street in the middle of the Seventh Step was the purple tower. A field of dry grass surrounded it. Tree stumps, too. The Lord Ascendant once kept the Sacred there, and now that it was gone, the life around it had dried up. I imagined Tabitha trapped in that tower, drying up and blowing away, too. *That all ends this morning.*

A door on the side of the purple tower was cracked open. Finally an easy entrance and exit. I portaled in front of the door and slid through the opening. Inside there was a spiral staircase that led upward through the ceiling. From one room to the next in the tower I advanced cautiously. A yellow room, a green room, then a blue, all the colors of Rathmore. *It won't be long until I reach the top.* I tried to picture it, but my sacred vision didn't work. Maybe I was just too distracted.

Finally I saw the dim purple above me. Up the last few steps I crept and found myself standing in the ruins of a beautiful room. A bed, a desk, several couches and chairs surrounded it. They looked fit for the Queen of England, but the ceiling was cracked. It let in the faint light of Jupiter.

On the far end of the room was a balcony. On the balcony stood a girl. And the girl was my friend. She wore a purple tunic and gazed into the distance just as she had in my vision.

I took in the scene for a moment. *This is the end of sneaking around in the dark by myself,* I thought. It reminded me of something that the Sacred once asked me. *Is this the beginning again? Sometimes I forget if you are young or old, my friend.* After traveling a billion miles to see her, I could now understand. Seeing her made me feel both young and old.

I cleared my throat. She didn't notice. That was probably for the best. I stripped off the two tunics and remembered what Icarus said about the tattoos. The Encountered can alter them, so I made mine disappear. I looked at myself in a mirror on the wall. I looked like me.

I knocked on a wooden table beside me. Tabitha then turned around.

"You came," she said. "I had faith that you would."

She ran toward me. We embraced, and the universe held its breath. This was the perfect moment that I had hoped for, better than any vision I had seen. We were in the tower, and we were as one.

"I kept my promise," I told her. "You knew that I would."

"Always," she said. "Now I wish that you had not." She backed away from me and gathered me in with her beautiful green eyes.

"Well come on, we've got to move," I said, "I knocked out two guards and they'll be unstunned soon. If we get to the submarine soon enough we'll—what did you say?

It took that long for her words to travel from my ears to my mind.

"I wish you had stayed on Earth," she said, stepping back toward the balcony. Her words didn't register.

"We've got to run. Now. My powers have returned. I came to save you."

"No," she said, her hands trembling. "Things are not the same. There's so much you don't know. The Ascendant are not who you think they are. I'm not who I used to be."

Her words ripped their way through the air between us, from my mind to my heart. *How could any of that be true?* She looked back to the balcony. A curtain hung on each side. The head of a black staff appeared behind one of the curtains, held by a golden hand.

"Trackman," I gasped.

He walked into view. Wearing a purple robe and a crown with three rubies, like a king with a scepter. I shook my arm free from its sling and felt the fire in my hands.

"You are a clever little fox, Tully. You had us fooled for a while, but the fox can only stay hidden so long. The hounds always win in the end. Now keep those hands at your side. I do love dear Tabitha and so do you. She has been so cooperative, and I would hate to lose her after all she has done for both of us."

An icicle cut its way through my insides and left a trail of questions in its path. *This was not how the vision went. I saw her in this tower. I passed through shadow to get here, like the Sacred said. I did everything right, and now everything is wrong.*

"Tully, listen to him," she said. "Or at least listen to me. I can explain."

I threw up my hands. *River of fire. River of fire.*

"What's to explain? Trackman, if you let us go I will let you live."

The end of Trackman's staff buzzed. My hands glowed brighter.

"No! The Ascendant are us," she blurted out. "We are them."

It was weird enough to make me listen.

"Is that a Tabism?" I said. She shook her head.

"Better to listen than die," he said. "If you're looking for a fight, you will lose her, here and now. There is only one way to win now, Tully. To understand, and then to join us. Even after all of this, the Ascendant could forgive you. You could be of some value to us when we reclaim the world."

"The world that you lied to?"

"We did not lie," he said. "You *do* have a disease, Tully. You think that you can save the Earth from aliens. You're wrong. We are going to save the Earth from you."

"Tabitha, we're going," I said, creating a portal between us. "Jump in and we're gone."

"No, Tully, I'm staying. I want to stay."

My heart crumpled like paper to ashes in a fire. "No, you don't."

"I am where I want to be," she said.

I rummaged through my tunic and found a crumple piece of gray cloth. The cloth glowed bright red.

"Take hold of this scarf and say that again," I said, tears trickling down my face.

She shook her head.

"Shall I tell him, child? Or would you like to explain?"

"Explain what?"

I was starting to see where they were headed, and I didn't like it at all. I liked it more when I was fighting aliens, but what if...

"Have you not put the puzzle pieces together? Not with all your Sacred Visions? You are Encountered. Certainly you have had visions."

"What about my visions?"

"Europa, Tully. The Ascendant have lived here for centuries. Before that, we traveled the universe, but one can only travel so long before wanting to return home. And Earth is home."

Earth is home? I shook my head. *What was he saying?*

"Foolish boy, remember the myth of Europa and Zeus," he said. "Europa is carried away by the bull. He whisks her away and later reveals himself to her as a god. And so it was with us, Tully. There is truth in the myth, but it's not about a girl. It's about a race of people. Do you not see this, Tully?"

The myth collided with reality. My mind fell through the floor. Someone took them into space like Zeus took Europa. A girl on a bull. A girl, not an alien. I could see her for what she truly was, just like Adèle with her tattoos. It was too much to take in, but Trackman kept speaking.

"We are Europa," he said. "We left the Earth thousands of years ago. The truth is in our name. We are the Ascendant. We *ascended,* Tully, captured by an alien race. Now we return to claim what was ours."

The icicle melted, and it felt like frozen poison in my veins.

"No, that can't be true," I said, but something down deep told me this was not Ascendant propaganda.

"You're not aliens."

"We are human," he said, "but we are not Earthers. Our culture excelled all others on Earth in its day. That is why we were chosen to leave."

"Then who is the white bull? Who brought you into space?"

"We erased their names long ago," he said. "They promised us riches and wisdom and tricked us into leaving Earth. Then they treated us like slaves. In time we overthrew them. We claimed their empire, just as we will reclaim the Earth."

The icicle in my stomach became a frozen poison in my veins.

"We are the Ascendant," he said. "We always rise. We rose from the Earth, rose up against the Nameless Ones, and now we rise to rule the Earth."

"You think you are some kind of chosen race," I said.

"We were born to rule, Tully. The Earthers will see this, and they will be wise to welcome us back with open arms. This would have happened months ago. We would have taken Earth by surprise, but you delayed our plan."

"I wrecked your plan," I said. "You still don't have the Sacred."

"Wrecked is too strong a word, Tully. Operation Close Encounter was not a complete failure. We are resourceful. We found something just as valuable as the Sacred."

He walked toward Tabitha. Trackman placed his hands on her shoulder, like a father would to a daughter. This sight sickened me. My head started to spin.

"So you captured Tabitha. Used her. You made us look like bad guys and you looked like the good guys."

"Yes, you've made this much easier," he said. "As for Tabitha, we didn't have to use her, as you say. She joined us."

"It's true, Tully," she said.

It hurt doubly bad coming from both of them. When a liar and your best friend both say the same thing, it must be true. Still, I could not stomach it. I held out Tabitha's mood scarf. It glowed red in my hand as I looked into her eyes, which welled with tears.

"Touch the scarf," I said. "Prove to me that you feel this way."

"Tully, please," she said. "Join them. They are too strong, and they will treat us fairly. You'll see."

"I have seen plenty," I said. "Their Undercity is full of slaves and warships, and Rathmore is just as bad. The people live in fear of the Lord Ascendant. The answer is no. Now take the scarf."

She shook her head and turned her back on me. Tabitha abandoned me. She walked to the balcony and left me standing in front of Trackman. I looked at the portal on the floor. It reminded me of the words from an old vision: *The hand that opened the door/ Will have to let it close.* The portal flickered, and I lost my train of thought staring at the floor with tears rolling down my cheeks.

Trackman inched forward and clucked his tongue. Then he held up his golden hand and flexed his fingers.

He raised my chin with his golden hand. "If you had joined us, I would have been merciful. You took this hand. I would have taken only one of yours, but now I want *all* of you. But I can't help thinking— what a shame! All this travel and planning and fighting, and for what? Nothing."

Everything within me turned to ice and dust.

NOTHING. NEVERMORE.

Nothing, and everything. It was Icarus's favorite response, and I repeated it over and over in my mind. *Nothing, and everything.*

I remember every detail about that encounter in the purple tower, but then everything gave way to nothing. Life became a blur of noise and tumbling. Someone tackled me from behind. My hands were shackled and something covered my eyes. Strong hands dragged me down the staircase and deep under the purple tower to a damp, dark cell. A needle bit into my arm, then there was a burning in my veins. Seconds later, my pulse felt faint. Whatever they did, I allowed. I was so deep down within myself that nothing seemed real for a while—a minute, an hour, a day? I don't know. I was not asleep but neither was I awake. I was there but I was not. *Nothing, and everything.*

The color of my world was a faint purple. The feeling of my world was cold stone.

Nothing. Nothing happened like it should. My visions of purple towers meant nothing. Tabitha did not want to be saved. Tabitha the tall. Tabitha the beautiful. Tabitha the changed and wrong and cold.

Trackman was still one step ahead of me. *He did not need lies anymore. The Ascendant would not fail. They beat me and now they will punish me. I will let them end this, and nothing can change my mind. Everyone kept telling me 'Fight, but do not hate.' The fight is over. What's left to fight for? Nothing.*

Nothing happened like it should. If I could have arrived earlier, I could have saved her. She would have listened. Trackman would not have been ready. If Icarus had not helped us, I could have found a better way. He slowed me down and made me weak. This was a mistake. I can't take it back. I should have stayed in Alaska, forever cold and alone. Now I'll never see the Earth again or feel the sun on my face...

One clear thought rose above the rest: *There was a time when I knew nothing but thought I could fix everything. Now I know everything and there's nothing I can fix.*

...I'll never play Cave-in! again, never get yelled at by a teacher...never eat fajitas, never go to prom...never, never, nevermore.

Maybe it was the Ascendant drugs or the fatigue, but I started chuckling to myself. *Nevermore! Nevermore!* We read this Edgar Allen Poe poem called "The Raven" last year in English class at Halloween. In the poem, there's this raven that sits over this crazy guy's door and repeats *Nevermore!* about three thousand times. *Quoth the raven, Nevermore!* It drives him totally insane. Sunjay and I even made up a game called Nevermore. He would sneak into my house, hide in my closet, and shout *Nevermore!* when I least expected. I did the same to him. Then we started doing it to our parents. We even *nevermored* my dad a few times, which is hard to do.

Before I knew it, I was curled up in a ball on the chamber floor, laughing my head off thinking about nevermore. There was a raven sitting above the door of my cell. He looked at me with his beady black eyes, eyes like Trackman's. I was about to get nevermored.

"Tully will eat fajitas—nevermore!"

"Tully will make it home—nevermore!"

The Raven sat above my chamber door and croaked back at me, nevermoring it up. That made me laugh harder.

"Tully will kiss Tabitha—nevemore!"

The black raven shook his feathers. "Nevermore! Nevermore!"

Tears, snot, crazy laughter. Nothing. Nothing. Ice. Dust. Nothing. Nevermore.

After a while the raven transformed into something else. He shapeshifted, like an Ascendant's tattoos. Of all things, the raven became a cow.

It was that craziest of hallucinations that made me come to my senses...sort of. I stopped laughing and nevermoring. The cow hopped down from his perch and started licking me. A white cow with an Ascendant girl on its back looked at me with big, innocent eyes.

"Stop licking my face," I said. "You aren't even real."

What was real? The Ascendant were real.

Ignore the face-licking cow. Think straight, Tully. Why didn't you see the connection? Janice was on the right track. Stars, it was in their name all along! They ascended *from the Earth.*

And what about the "white bull"? There were real aliens here at some point. Aliens that abducted the Ascendant. Where does the Sacred fit into all of this?

All I know is that death is coming for me. The Lord Ascendant will make it a spectacle, like some Roman emperor teaching his subjects how to behave. "Remember what happened to Tully Harper. Don't get out of line, children."

Children.

The cow mooed once and then disappeared.

There are children in the Undercity. The Lord Ascendant will leave them there to die. There are children on Earth. The Lord Ascendant will make them slaves. There are fathers that want to help them.

I saw my dad then. His stern blue eyes with that strange red sparkle, stroking the red streak in his hair. My father. Maybe he was still free. Did that even matter anymore?

The ideas crept through my mind as I lay in the cold, black-lighted cell, hearing the buzz of two black staffs right outside my door. Finally, sleep overtook me.

Red, red, red, red, red.

I faded into a familiar dreamscape. It was a bright sunny day. The grass rustled, a stream trickled past a large oak tree. The purple tower loomed in the distance.

"Shhh," a voice said, "save your strength."

I knew the voice. It lived inside me now. A hand stroked my hair.

"I wanted to save her. I wanted to avenge you," I told her.

"I don't need an avenger, Tully. I need a son, and Tabitha needs your help. They all do."

"I missed my chance, Mom. I've got nothing left to give."

"Yes, you do have something left. I know you like I know myself."

"I know myself, too. I've got nothing."

"Nothing," she said, stroking my hair. "That is what you keep saying, but what about the everything? That is the other side of things. The dark side of a planet means there is light on the other side. Everything can be summed up in one word. One small word can stand against all of your nothings."

"What word?" I asked her. She smiled.

"Choose one," she said, stroking my hair. "It is your word to choose, not mine."

What word could stand up to nothing? There was no word in my mind with that much power. It was a riddle with no solution.

"You will find it in time," she said.

"How much time do I have left?" I asked.

"No one knows this," she said. "Each day has enough trouble of its own. I told you this before."

"So did Dad," I said. "Mom, I thought that I could save her. I—"

"—One word," she said. "One word."

She stroked my hair until the red haze turned purple.

In the Cell

When my senses finally returned, I could feel a presence in the room. The hairs on my arms stood on end. Across from me sat the Lord Ascendant. He picked up my head in his hands.

"What now?" I asked.

"The Red Storm Arena," he said. His voice rumbled like distant thunder off canyon walls. "A fitting end to Operation Close Encounter. Trackman is so pleased. He sacrificed much to see this day, Tully Harper."

His face scrolled with ocean tattoos the same as mine.

"You are human," I said.

"We are many things," he said. "We left so many centuries ago. Our history is written into your mythology. Search and you will find us. Europa is only one name."

"Atlantis?" I asked.

"Yes, Atlantis. They called us this most of all. The Nameless Ones destroyed our beautiful island to hide our leaving. That had some strange side effects. It made us into a myth while they became a rumor. Now I use these myths to inspire our people. I use the rumors to instill fear in yours."

"Propaganda," I said. "Twisting the truth."

"It works. It is better to be aliens. Aliens inspire fear. Fear gives me power."

"You already have power," I said. "Why can't you return to the Earth in peace?"

"Earthers would never allow this," he laughed. "Imagine it. One hundred million refugees return from the stars. Would any government open its borders? Where would we live? Would the United States let us in?"

"No, maybe not, but—"

"There is only 'no.' They would not. They would not sacrifice enough to help. If we do not take what we want, it will not be given. Human nature, Tully. We are a greedy race."

"But we can be generous, too. Maybe you could come one group at a time —"

"We will not beg for what we deserve! The Nameless Ones chose us because we were the best among humanity. And we still are."

His gloved hands glowed purple. The hair on my arms stood up. Then he walked to a round window at the end of the cell.

"Tabitha accepted these things."

"That means nothing to me anymore," I said.

"Clearly, and that is why you must be crushed. Now my people will understand that I am their hope – not you, not the Encountered. Those scribblers of wings upon the walls. They filled your head with ideas of peace and love. They are the last of that polluted blood. I will clip their wings in time. Who knows? Maybe today. Until then – guards, prepare him."

INSIDE THE RED STORM ARENA

"**A**scendant! In a few weeks we will arrive upon the Earth. We will reclaim what is ours, but today our great conquest begins. Before you stands Tully Harper. He is accused of treason against the Lord Ascendant and murder of Commander Akakios. He should die for these things, but since we believe in the rule of law, Tully will receive justice. Trial by combat."

I was in the Red Storm Arena kneeling before 250,000 Ascendant. It took two parades to get there.

First they brought me out of the purple tower. Guards encased my hands in heavy iron. Then they chained me to the Lord Ascendant's chariot. *No hands, no powers. No power, no portals. No portals, no escape.* We took the long street toward the newel. On either side were all of the Lord Ascendant's men. A war cry erupted, angry and triumphant. Countless black staffs jeered at me on the way. They shot purple sparks toward the dome above Rathmore. "You will not see the end of Tully Harper," he told them. "You will be in the Undercity preparing to leave, but you will hear about it soon enough."

They're ready to leave. Nothing can stop them. How much time, Mother? I still don't have my word.

We made for the newel—me, the Lord Ascendant, and one hundred black staffs. Inside, the only light came from the black staffs, buzzing like angry hornets. We descended from the Seventh to the Fifth Step.

What's my one word, Mom? Will you whisper it in my ear? I'm alone in the dark and my enemies outnumber me.

The elevator lurched to a halt. The great door to the Fifth Step opened like a curtain on a stage. The second parade began.

The Lord Ascendant floated forward into the light with me behind him. He led me toward the arena. Hundred of thousands of Ascendant lined the wide boulevard. Balloons floated into the air. Purple sparks rained down upon the marble street. The crowd roared its approval. Days before I stood amid these people thinking they were aliens, watching their evil leader throw a boy into the dust. He would throw down another boy today.

Where is hope in the face of so many enemies? Where is hope when you stumble along in chains? When your plans crumble like sand castles? When your friends are nowhere to be seen and your enemy is spitting in your face? I scanned the street, looking for hope, for a glimmer of light.

My mom's voice came to me finally. *It's close now. It's in your heart. Hold on to it. Hold on. Find your strength. Hold on.*

To what? I can't hold anything with my hands in irons, Mom. I can't hold anything anymore.

We arrived at the arena. The black staffs split into two groups and bounded ahead. They bounded up the arena stairs ten steps at a time and found places around the top level. A purple ring of death.

The Lord Ascendant looked back at me with his tattoos swirling, and he smiled for the first time. We walked under the Ascendant banner. Written in Greek, I knew what it said: *We always rise.*

The inside of the arena looked much different than before. No longer was there a stage for the Lord Ascendant's speech. Just a dirt floor. He lifted his arms.

The noise. The Ascendant cheered the Lord Ascendant and booed me. There was violence and fear in their voices and faces. I noticed that they were all Firsters, from the bottom to the top row. *All the other Steps have boarded the ships.* I looked around at their faces. *This all feels so familiar.* And then he caught my eye.

A young boy in the front row. He was older than the last time I had seen him—on board the *Mini-Mane,* in our training sessions. A virtual version of this boy once jeered at me: now he did so in real life, shaking his clenched fists beside his Ascendant father. They had nothing but hatred for me, and I for them—hatred for their twisted society, the Lord Ascendant, my situation, and especially this little boy who was now hoping to see me die. I could taste iron in my mouth. I realized that I was grinding my teeth, but I looked at the small boy's face and felt something shake inside me. The poison in my veins finally ran its course. I felt warm again suddenly. I wanted to turn away but I kept my eyes fixed on the Firster boy, and the child changed me.

Do not give in to hate. Fight them, but do not hate. It was a command that came from deep down in my soul, one that made me breathe again. I threw the hair out of my eyes and watched him, shouting beside his dad, who was smiling at his son for raging at me like they were at a baseball game singing some twisted national anthem. *He has been trained to think this way, Tully. Don't hate him. He is a Firster. He spends his whole life bowing to everyone else. No one has shown him any love or mercy. You have to hope that he can change.*

Yes, that was it.

Hope. Mother, now I know my word.

The Lord Ascendant stopped his chariot. He reached down and, with a gloved hand, crushed the metal chain that held me to the chariot. Then he kicked me in the chest and sent me flying through the air and into the arena dust. It didn't hurt that bad, but in low gravity, it must have looked impressive. The Firsters erupted. Tattoos scrawled across the Lord Ascendant's cruel, brilliant face as he circled me in his chariot. Then he made his way toward his viewing box on the far side, and in his box sat Tabitha. Tabitha the spokesperson for the Ascendant. Tabitha the changed.

Hope. Hope does not fail, Mom. I know it. It doesn't mean that I will win, but that doesn't matter. I will fight. I will not hate. That is all I am asked to do.

Trackman was giving a speech: "...he is guilty, but since we believe in the rule of law..."

I picked one new word out of Trackman's speech.

Goliath.

I was alone in the arena to face the crowd, but I wasn't alone for long. I could sense another presence before I saw him, like a hover-truck that was about to sideswipe you at a red light. The hovertruck was a man, and he stood at the far end of the arena, all eight feet of him.

He wielded a black staff that was twice my height and buzzing like a thousand bees. It didn't look like your "standard issue" black staff, glowing brighter and more intensely than smaller versions, with several extra buttons. I could hear it from the other side of the arena. He shouted something in Greek and gestured toward me. Who knows what he said? "Prepare to meet your doom, Tully." "Hey, everybody, you want to see me crush this fly with my bare hands?"

The Lord Ascendant had broken my chains, but my hands were encased in a block of iron. They were useless. *Can I just jump out of the arena? Uh, no. There are one hundred black staffs along the parapet. Any one of them could grab, stun, or incinerate me. Jumping isn't the answer, not by a long shot. It won't work against even one Ascendant. Without my powers, I'm just target practice for black staffs.*

He began a slow walk toward me with just a few steps, and then built up to a slow jog. I wouldn't have much time to react.

Reaction. That's it! The one Sacred Power that might still work. I could not jump, but I could dodge. It had worked with Sawyer on the *Adversity*. It might work here.

I closed my eyes and focused. *Speed, speed. Know when to go*, I thought to myself. Over the din of the crowd, I heard nothing but felt his heavy footsteps beat a cadence on the dusty arena floor. *Thud, thud, thud. THUD.* I could picture him now. He wasn't running anymore but flying through the air toward me, bearing down on me, four hundred pounds of black staff-swinging muscle and mayhem.

Wait, hold, wait, then roll.

I kept my eyes closed until the buzz in my ears grew to a deafening roar that I could hear over the crowd, until his war cry filled my ears.

And then I rolled. I opened my eyes.

Goliath's staff crashed into the dust and, in its place, a crater. The electricity from the blast knocked me toward the wall. The crowd let out an "Ooooh!" They expected Tully jelly, but got the Tully roll instead.

Hope.

Goliath did one of those veins-exploding-in-your-neck roars and let loose a series of incinerator blasts in my direction. Anger screwed up his aim. The purple fireballs whooshed past me. Instead of jumping, I stayed low and ducked them, then scrambled out of the way of more blasts. Behind me the Firsters dove for cover as the fireballs went smoking into their vacated seats. This was a dangerous spectator sport. You didn't have to be trapped in the arena with Goliath to lose your life or at least your eyebrows.

After several blasts he screamed in English at me, "Enough dive. No more crawl. Stand and like a warrior be fighting!"

"Untie my hands then." He narrowed his eyes. "I'll stand and fight. No more dive. Uh, is that a no?"

As an answer, Goliath an extra button on his staff, and the weapon emitted a low buzz. He pointed one end toward me and spun the staff in slow circles. A purple cone appeared around its glowing head, expanding a few inches at a time. The crowd grew silent. Behind Goliath, the young boy from the virtual room moved to the edge of his seat. Behind me, people seemed to be shuffling in their seats, too. He swirled the staff in larger circles, and the cone grew large enough to swallow me. Or a school bus for that matter.

My feet slid forward, my hair ruffled in the wind. The cone drew me toward itself. I turned to run as the Ascendant spectators in the stands behind me scattered. *Uh, this is really bad. Death bad. Dorothy in the Wizard of Oz bad.*

Goliath was a lion playing with his food. The crowd burst into cheers as they saw my doom unfolding. The cone was twenty feet tall, popping with electricity. I lost my footing and slid toward him in the dirt. Goliath shouted in triumph, but it's not polite to play with food.

My hands heated up as I slid backwards. The metal softened with the heat, but it would not melt before Goliath electrocuted me in his purple torrent. I had to break that spell. There was really only one thing to do.

I looked over my shoulder and waited until Goliath turned his head to admire the crowd admiring him. When he did, I let go of the ground and dove headfirst into the center of his electric tornado. It was like diving into an electric socket: my skin pricked with pain and muscles spasmed, but I knew that would happen. The electricity melted my bonds the rest of the way, and my hands did the rest. Goliath dropped the staff as it melted in my hands. My shackles dripped into a puddle in the sandy arena. I was free.

Free and momentarily fried. I felt like someone had just defibrillated my heart—well, someone had. Goliath gathered himself before I did. He leapt toward me, enraged that his victory would not be picture perfect. He reared back, intending to light me up with a devastating punch, but I shook my own dizziness just in time.

I blasted him with a red fireball that threw him toward the edge of the arena. Before he hit the edge, I opened a portal behind him and another one in front of him. He fell into one portal and popped up in the other one, then fell back through the first. It was a perfect loop: Goliath falling through one portal and into the next in sequence, screaming in anger and confusion. The crowd didn't know what to make of it, watching their greatest warrior squirming, trying to stop himself from an embarrassing defeat at the hands of shrimp man.

The Lord Ascendant's expression didn't change much—maybe went from sneer of triumph to sneer of anger. Trackman ended the comedy though.

"Enough!" yelled Trackman, pointing toward me. One hundred black staffs aimed at me but did not shoot. In response, I drew a portal on the arena floor and pictured somewhere safe outside the arena to land.

The Lord Ascendant held up his hand. Tabitha remained violently still at his side. Then he leaned forward, speaking to me from his golden throne at the far end of the Red Storm Arena.

"You've come halfway across the solar system to find this girl, and now you're going to abandon her again? See, dear Ascendant, the Earthers have no honor. They try to win with tricks and give up when their honor is on the line. Go ahead, boy. Jump in that portal. Run back home and tell the Earth how you tricked our great champion and could not save your friend. And, by all means, tell them that we are coming for them all."

I stood my ground and looked around the stands at the angry, frightened spectators. I had nothing to say to the Lord Ascendant, but something for them.

"You won't live in fear of him forever. I choose to stay and fight. Not for me. For you."

In an instant one hundred black staffs unloaded on the center of the arena where I stood next to the portal. I knew what must be done. *Focus.* The incinerator blasts slowed down to nothing. I dropped into the portal, created another portal on the wall of the arena, rolled out of the way of what was behind me—a forest-fire sized fireball. It roared out of the portal and into the stands, setting them ablaze. The spectators dove out of the way.

They won't try that again, I thought. The black staffs leaped down from the parapet and began to attack me five at a time. I could sense their movements around me. The arena became a blur of entry and exit portals. The black staffs tried to stun and incinerate me but I turned their shots back on them and remained untouched. I made quick work of the first five and quicker work of the next five. And the five after that. Victory after victory. All the training on the *Mini-Mane* paid off. It felt like a video game. Player One was doing well against the enemy horde, as long as he did not exhaust all his energy. The Lord Ascendant realized this all too soon. The attacks stopped. My sweaty bangs fell into my eyes and I pushed them back.

So the Lord Ascendant called for another champion, who showed up without warning. His eyes gleamed blue and unscrupulous. I would have feared him, but I knew this moment must come. I must face him again. Lincoln Sawyer, Version 2.0.

"My secret friend, your skills and speed have grown," he said, spinning the black staff overhead like a helicopter blade, as he did on board the *Adversity*. "Fortunately, I can say the same thing. You won't catch me off guard this time."

"I won't need to," I said. Sawyer advanced on me. A few Ascendant crept toward me from behind. I could sense them. Never taking my eyes off Sawyer, I reached behind with one hand, opened a portal, and blasted the Ascendant into it. I opened the portal in front of Sawyer. The Ascendant popped up in front of him. *Surprise!* I thought, but in a flash, he grabbed two of them by their arms and flung them toward me. They came in like angry bowling pins, spinning and firing their black staffs in all directions. I ducked into another portal and popped up behind Sawyer, but he was ready with an incinerator shot. I caught the shot in my hands but it partly blasted through and singed my tunic. Another incinerator shot went toward my feet, and I made my first mistake of the battle—I leaped high into the air.

"Never let your guard down, Tully. I taught you better," he said.

The Ascendant Lord could have grabbed me at that moment and thrown me into the dust, but he left the game to Sawyer, who seemed up for the challenge. I panicked for a moment, a floating target for everyone to see. Then I opened another portal in mid-air and popped out on the arena floor again.

Whoah, midair portal. That's new, I thought, but didn't have long to think about it.

Sawyer said something in Greek. More attacks from all directions—incinerators, tosses, stuns. I dodged or deflected everything I could. I caught a glimpse of Tabitha: for the first time she showed emotion. She looked nervous, doubt in her green eyes. Was she worried about me? Not that I had time to care. The stuns became almost impossible to defend. Sawyer was coordinating the attack, and he had his troops firing at me in rhythm. Shot after shot, every second they came with no time for me to open an escape portal. I couldn't catch my breath.

"All defense as usual," said Sawyer. "You can only play this game for so long."

He was right. My focus slipped. A stun hit my wounded arm and knocked me to my knees. Just as I thought it was over, a solitary voice shouted someone's name. And again and again. I turned to see the young boy from the virtual room pointing at the sky. It took me a second to process the name though he yelled it clearly.

"Icarus!" he yelled. "Icarus! Icarus!"

Hope.

UNEXPECTED EQUAL

Over the parapet of the arena wall floated a globe of red light. In the center were Icarus, Sunjay, and my dad. Adèle provided the web of protection. Icarus provided flight. His transparent wings extended through the web around them, his glowing hands above his head like he was praying, while my dad and Sunjay gripped their black staffs, ready for battle.

The enemy focused their firepower on this wonder, but their shots deflected in all directions. The arena exploded in purple fire. Doubt crept into the black staffs around me. Icarus directed the globe to the middle of the arena. He put his hands to his sides and landed beside me in the arena, the globe now shielding us all.

"You stand alone no longer," he said.

"But you left the peace march," I said.

"I swore to guide you, and I stand by that oath even now." With that, he lifted us all back into the air, but before we flew more than a few feet off the ground, the globe lurched to a halt.

"Keep moving!" my dad said.

"No, we can't leave without Tabitha," I yelled.

"I can't move us anyway," said Icarus. "Something has stopped us. Not black staffs. They don't have the power."

"And what do you know about power?" the Lord Ascendant said. In the stands in front of us, he had risen to his feet for the first time. His hands extended toward us with his black gloves glowing purple, a look of dire intensity in his eyes.

"This went much better than planned," he said, "but I should have guessed. You Encountered were always so sentimental. You work so hard to save the weak, but your actions are futile. You destroy yourselves." The Lord Ascendant pressed his hands down and we descended to the floor of the arena. He turned to the rest of the black staffs. "Leave us! Prepare the ships. We launch soon. I will handle this with Sawyer's help."

Confused, his men waited for him to repeat the command. The Lord Ascendant does not repeat commands. Instead, he tossed the nearest black staff out of the stadium. The rest of his men took the hint and bounded over the walls or toward the exits. Sawyer stood on the far side of the arena facing the Lord Ascendant.

The Lord Ascendant's brought his gloved hands above his head and clapped once. The noise reverberated off the arena walls, and the globe that encircled us disintegrated. We stood before him in the arena unprotected.

Then he peeled off his gloves, and underneath the gloves I saw something that changed everything. He held up his hands. My heart sunk. On the backside of his hands, running down his forearms, were lightning scars. Days ago I had worried about finding my Ascendant equal, and now I had.

"Impossible," I said. "You can't be."

"Encountered," he said. "Icarus never told you? Well, the gloves are useful. They hide the truth, but I don't need to hide from any of you. I'm among friends. And family. Aren't I, Icarus?"

Icarus took a few steps toward the Lord Ascendant. My mind did a backflip. They looked so similar. The same height and build, the same facial features, although one held a constant sneer while the other had compassion in his eyes.

"My father raised you better than this. There's still time," said Icarus.

"What do you know of time, other than it has passed you by? You don't know any better than your father."

"You were good once," said Icarus, "and you could be good again."

"They know each other," I said to Adèle. "He's Encountered, like us."

"No, he was never like us," she said.

It was an Encountered secret, one that had not been shared with me. I could only guess at their relationship now—friends, cousins, brothers?

"Are you so blind?" Icarus continued. "We could return to the Earth and give them our power. The people would love you more than you could imagine."

"After all this time, you think I desire love? No, Icarus. Our power has returned, and I will not share it with you or these low-born Earthers."

The Lord Ascendant raised his hands and a red dome covered the arena. The Firsters cheered no longer. Many ran to the exits, but an electric shock knocked them back.

"To me," Icarus said. "His powers are greater than I imagined. Prepare for anything."

"Anything is hard to prepare for," Sunjay said. "Could you be more specific?"

The Lord Ascendant clapped his hands again. A puff of red mist hid him from our sight. Then I heard a loud pop. He reappeared on the other side of the arena.

"Get your guard up," my dad said, but there was no time. I heard another loud pop behind me. Suddenly the Lord Ascendant in our midst. Red lighting exploded from his hands. Before we could react, he blasted Adèle toward Sawyer, then reappeared on the other side of the arena, blasting the rest of us. We dove out of the way, but we needed a shield, which was Adèle's strength—Adèle, who was floating helplessly toward Sawyer. *Not if I can help it.*

I created another mid-air portal and Adèle fell into it, returned to us as quickly as she had left. She raised a shield.

"This won't work," my dad said. "They want to split us up. We'll split them up instead. Sunjay and Tully, focus on the android. We'll keep the Lord Ascendant busy."

Adèle held her shield. The Lord Ascendant spewed lightning from his hands, and then from his mouth.

"Yikes, mouth lightning," Sunjay said. "I'd rather fight Sawyer. Wait, did I really just say that? Well, I mean it. He's about to get my best. Let's do this."

The android awaits us on the other side of the arena. Sunjay went left and I went right. Sawyer reacted in a microsecond, stunning Sunjay once and leaving me alone to face my android foe. As usual.

"That was his best?" Sawyer asked. "Now you will get mine. There are no more human limits on my power. The Ascendant have freed me."

"You're not free," I said, "and you're not that fast."

Sawyer smirked at me. Then he leaped toward Sunjay on the arena floor. Big problem. Sunjay couldn't jump through a portal because he was stunned, and I couldn't blast Sawyer with fire before he reached Sunjay. The only thing I could do was open a portal for Sawyer. I decided to make the exit portal in front of me. It was time to finish this fight.

As usual, he anticipated my move. He launched an incinerator shot into the portal. Bigger problem. If I left the portal open, the shot would hit me. If I closed it, the shot would hit Sunjay. One of us was about to get incinerated. It was checkmate.

I had closed a portal on a friend once before. That choice still tore me apart. It haunted me and led me to this point, millions of miles from home. I would not do that again. I left the portal open and took a deep breath. I watched as the flames of the incinerator shot reached me. I could feel the heat on my skin. My tunic burst into flames. About that time something slammed into me. Sawyer. He had followed his incinerator shot into the portal. The impact and blast knocked us across the arena. I rolled in the dust to put out the flames on my clothes.

My powers must be growing, I thought. *I'm not a pile of dust.*

Only my injured shoulder seemed to be on fire. I rotated my arm, trying to loosen it up, but pain shot through my fingers. Dirty, slightly toasted, and spitting dust, I hopped to my feet.

The Android did the same, but the incinerator shot did more damage to him than me. His skin was gone. He was a gold-plated skeleton with cold blue eyes—and a broken black staff that he tossed aside.

Behind us the other battle raged. I could picture the whole scene: the Lord Ascendant popping up in clouds of red smoke, my dad dodging stun shots, incinerator blasts, Adèle protecting him, Icarus flying side to side, quick like a hummingbird, too quick for the Lord Ascendant's teleportation attacks. It was an even match, and I realized, as I looked at my golden foe, that the outcome of our fight would decide the battle. The Android must have realized this long before. There was nothing more to say.

We fought hand to hand. To the Firsters in the stands we were a blur too fast to see. Punches, kicks, blocks, and holds. Every punch he threw I turned away. Every grapple and choke he tried I avoided. He could overpower me if he could only catch me. It was an even match except that the sweat beaded on my forehead and flew off the tips of my hair. I would eventually tire out, and he would not, so I started to take more risks, to counterpunch when he threw a punch. He saw the change in tactics and grabbed my bad arm in his crushing grip, twisting it until I thought my bones would snap, but I flipped in that direction and grabbed his arm. Immediately his arm felt soft in my grip, like a tube of cookie dough. I squeezed. He wriggled away from me, his forearm bent and glowing. My left arm hung limp at my side, shooting pains in my fingertips. I rubbed my shoulder, which felt out of socket.

"Did I find some weakness?" he asked, smiling.

"Did I?" I replied. Sawyer's forearm was melted, his hand limp at his side, just like mine.

He came at me again, kicking and throwing punches, even head-butts in my direction. I dodged and blocked as best I could, but Sawyer grabbed my bad arm again and tried to get me in an arm bar. He wrapped his legs around my head and pulled on my arm. My arm went from injured to snapped; my mind clouded over, like I was going to faint again.

No.

The pain blinded me and left me desperate. My arm had no strength left but Sawyer kept tugging, like he was trying to rip me to pieces. Then came a moment of slack. Someone re-entered the fight.

"That was *not* my best!" Sunjay said. He grabbed Sawyer's head and twisted it sideways. There was a loud crack. Unfortunately the android's head stayed on his shoulders, but his neck looked bent. Sunjay was thrown through the air, and Sawyer pressed the attack again.

No.

I would not let him do this. My arm was dead but my hand…I could feel it moving, reaching out, searching for some way to end this struggle. Finally it found his neck. I realized that while my arm burned with pain, my hand blazed much hotter. I reached higher, and suddenly my hand found his face. He let go of my arm and tried to escape my grip. He kicked and punched. His jaws snapped at my fingers like a rabid dog, but Sunjay had damaged his neck. He could not shake away from my grip. I could feel the metal beneath my hand growing white-hot.

What had been hard metal turned to liquid in my fingers, until I felt hot wet sand beneath my hand. Moment by moment, I was melting him down. His arm shot up in one last effort to stop me, but it only made me remember my good hand. I brought it around and blasted him with fire. The blast threw me backwards, and when I pushed myself back to my feet, all I saw in the sand in front of me was a sizzling mound of melted metal that used to be Lincoln Sawyer.

For the last year I had lived with the image of his eyes burned into my mind. He was my sparring partner, my confidant, my adversary, my secret friend; he chased me on land, in space, through my dreams; he battled me on board the *Adversity*, in zero gravity, and finally on Europa; he would battle me no more. For a moment I felt alone in the universe and felt the sheer relief of vanquishing an enemy, once and for all.

"Stars, you melted his face," said Sunjay, shaking off the stun. He was in no condition to fight. Neither of us were, but fighting was our only option.

With Sawyer gone, I looked into the royal box. Trackman had stayed to watch my death at the hands of his android, and he had stayed too long. He and Tabitha were on their way out through an escape hatch in the royal box. He jumped in, but I opened a portal beneath her feet. She fell in and landed beside us in the arena. She looked shocked.

"Whatever you do," I told Sunjay, "do not let go of her."

"Tully, no! I have to go with him!" she yelled. Sunjay held on to her, confused at what was happening.

In the distance the newel rumbled to life. Everyone in the arena stared at the great black shadows beneath the ice of the newel. The Ascendant ships began to work their way up from the Undercity. They erupted from the newel top of the newel and into the night sky, bound for Earth. The Exodus had begun.

They were beyond our reach, but the Lord Ascendant had not yet joined them. The fight raged on. I strapped my broken arm against my tunic and headed toward the final battle.

A SEA OF FALLING DAGGERS

Across the arena my dad and Icarus battled the Lord Ascendant with black staffs. Adèle shielded them from the Lord Ascendant's vicious attacks when she could. I charged toward the fray, opening a portal behind the Lord Ascendant. I blasted him with red fire but he vanished into a cloud of mist and the shot almost hit my dad.

"Duck!" my dad yelled. My dad launched an incinerator shot over my head, which the Lord Ascendant deflected into the crowded stands. I didn't even know he was behind me, and before I could spin around he was gone again, popping up beside Adèle, who shielded herself until Icarus could distract him. Then he appeared beside me, throwing deadly punches. He was as fast as I was, and if he landed a punch, I would not have survived. Suddenly he stopped his attack and withdrew to the middle of the arena. He looked at what remained of Lincoln Sawyer.

"An inferior machine made by an inferior race," he said. "Still, I am surprised that you defeated him."

More ships rumbled up the newel into the black sky, their black silhouettes like marbles rolling across the face of Jupiter. We watched them through the glowing red shield that trapped us. The Lord Ascendant smiled and put on his black gloves.

"My Dear Firsters," he said to the terrified crowd, "I hope that you have enjoyed today's show. I am sorry that it will have to be cut short.

The ships are leaving, but do not fear. You have been chosen to stay behind."

The crowd murmured in confusion.

"Today I am making you the masters of Rathmore, or whatever is left of it."

At that, an earthquake shook the arena, knocking us off our feet. Something monstrous was ascending from the Undercity. The newel ruptured and splintered. The entire Fifth Step swayed back and forth, but it did not break. Out of the top of the newel we saw a ship five times the size of the *Lion's Mane*. It ripped right through the newel and headed on a collision course with the dome. That didn't look good.

The Lord Ascendant clapped his hands together and the red force field around the stadium disappeared. It wasn't immediately clear to me what any of this meant, but my dad seemed to know. He launched himself into the air toward the Lord Ascendant, who saw him coming.

"Dad!" I screamed. The Lord Ascendant launched a fireball at my dad but it never reached him. I dove through a portal and met the fireball head on. The pain smoldered on my skin, but I advanced through it nonetheless. The Lord Ascendant vanished, and before I could recover I felt his presence behind me. He placed his hand on my chest. My heart seemed to stop beating. I lost my breath. Then my heart and breath came back to me in one painful gasp. Something felt icy and broken inside me.

"A gift from me to you," he said, "for however long you live."

Then he disappeared into a red mist just as my dad arrived to fight him.

"No," I gasped. "He can't escape."

"He's done worse than that," my dad said, looking upward.

Between that icy feeling, the burns, and the broken arm, I sunk to the ground, exhausted. My dad yelled for Icarus and Adéle. The three of them stood beside me and stared at the sky.

And then she was holding me, hugging me, kissing my forehead. Tabitha Tirelli. She was Tabitha as I remembered her. Tabitha the true. Tabitha the friend. Tabitha I loved. There was a rip in the fabric of time where all of the madness stopped and the universe fell into complete harmony, and she was there with me, far from the Rathmore Chaos.

I've thought back on that moment many times since then, and it's always the same, not polluted by the madness that preceded or followed it: I could not hear the dome shattering above our heads; I felt nothing but her breath on my neck and one word on her lips. "Always. Always. Always." It was our moment and no one else in the universe could steal it, see it, share it. I wondered how many moments like that come in a lifetime. I would be happy with just that one. The Lord Ascendant escaped, the dome shattered, but we were no longer apart.

Sound and feeling returned. A tinkling noise. Cries nearby. Above us, the dome of Rathmore crumbled into a thousand icy daggers, headed straight for us.

"Adèle, protect us!" my dad said. "Shield the arena."

"No, seal the dome," yelled Icarus. "Without the dome we will suffocate and freeze."

"I can't do that from here," she said to Icarus, and they understood what must be done. Icarus grabbed her around the waist.

"Stop the ice," he told me. "We'll seal the dome."

"You'll be cut to shreds," I said.

"We are Ascendant. We always rise," he said, his blue eyes shining. They launched into the air on their way toward a sea of falling daggers.

My friends, my father looked toward me and waited to see what I would do. I couldn't look up. I looked at the one portal I had left open and pictured an exit point on the next step, and then another and another, all the way to the submarine that awaited us in the ocean below. The portal held for a moment and then flickered. My broken arm throbbed, and the burns on my face and hands felt like needle pricks. My chest was worse.

"I can't save them all," I whispered to Tabitha. "I can't even hold a portal open right now."

"I have faith," she said.

"We can complete our mission though. We came to save you."

"You did," she said. "We'll save them, too."

"And if I can't stop this, if it kills us, if we die…"

"…Then we die together, like it should be."

Far above us, Icarus and Adèle flitted their way toward the dome. The Firsters cheered as they passed through the ice until they disappeared out of sight. I watched them go with a prayer on my lips as the crowd grew silent. Tabitha tugged my sleeve.

"Tully, look around you."

Hope.

The Firsters no longer looked to the sky. They looked toward me and lifted their palms to the sky. The Ascendant salute. They needed something from me. I would show them mercy, even if it killed me.

I focused on the task. Only a river of fire would stop the falling ice. *How much power do I have left, Mom? I can't have enough to stop that.* Tabitha helped me unstrap my broken arm, and I brought it over my head using my good hand. Everyone backed away as my hands grew hotter. The hotter my hands became, the colder my chest grew. *If I die like this will you be proud, Mom? If I try and don't succeed?* I closed my eyes and pictured all the Firsters in the arena, and the ice falling toward us all. Each one had a name. *Mom, someone named every one of them. Just like you named me.* Whatever they deserved, I would give them mercy. I pictured the boy in the stands, reaching out toward me to save him.

Everything, everything, everything, I thought. *Hope is everything, Mom. I know now. I know.* The burst of energy from my hands knocked me to my knees. It was like holding a boulder above my head. The strain was terrible, and just when I wanted to give up, it intensified. A roar of flames. A stabbing pain in my chest. A flash of red light. I could hold it no longer. Then all at once the flames stopped, and by the time my body fell to the arena floor, I was unconscious.

DREAM

A lush garden appeared before me, shrouded in red mist, with a stone bench at its center—the place where I first spoke to the Sacred. It seemed like a long time ago, and I did not see any figure now, but I heard a voice.

"Why are you here now?" it asked.

"I did the best I could," I said. "I fought, but I did not hate."

"Then it is not time for us to meet again," said the voice. "Not yet."

"When?" I asked.

"Not when, but where," it said. "Icarus will tell you before he passes into the mist. Go to him now."

Why is the sand so hard and wet? I thought as I awoke, realizing that I lay in a pool of boiling water. The sand around me had become so hot that it turned to glass, and I dragged myself out of the shallow pool. Several people helped me the rest of the way and laid me down.

To my right there was a chunk of sharp ice lodged in the ground. In fact, all around me were splinters of ice. I did not stop them all.

In the stands around us the Ascendant treated their injured. The placed the critical patients in the arena, and an Ascendant doctor cared for them. He was a Fourther, but he must have stayed or been left behind. Maybe he had known of the Lord Ascendant's plan to leave the lower Steps on Europa. He ran toward me, pushed everyone else aside, and produced a gray cartridge from his pocket. He latched the cartridge onto my broken arm, and I felt a needle prick. The cartridge emptied of its gray contents and I felt something under my skin moving. He grabbed my head in his hands.

"This will hurt," he said. "Breathe." It felt like ants were crawling under my skin, stinging me all over. I tried to breathe, wanted to scream. My arm shifted, straightened with a pop, and then ached. The same sensation crawled up to my shoulder. I put my head back down and it landed in someone's lap.

"You did it, Tully. You did all that you could." Tabitha stroked my hair.

"I tried," I said. "We couldn't stop him. At least we have you. At least we survived."

"No one could have done more," she said.

On my left I felt a hand grasp mine. Icarus. There was a weakness in his eyes; he blinked heavily. Beside him lay Adèle, unconscious.

"It is not your fault," he said.

"I failed you," I said, looking up. "I couldn't stop the ice or the Lord Ascendant. But you fixed the dome."

A glowing shield replaced the clear dome.

"Adèle did that," he said. "Her work will last forever. She will be happy to know this. I must tell her soon."

"But you made it through the ice," I said. "What happened?"

"It is not your fault. We began to return and saw, we saw a great fire melting the falling ice, and…what you did was right—"

I understood immediately, and the weight of the thought almost crushed me. I looked at his body, burned and broken.

"No," I said, "I burned you both."

"You saved so many," he whispered. "Look around you. Look at them. They are beautiful. Beautiful and free and alive."

The Firsters gathered in small groups, weeping with joy and sadness. Icarus grimaced in pain for a moment, and when he opened his eyes again, he squeezed my hand.

"Adèle?" I asked.

"She left us already," he whispered. His breath was uneven, and his eyes were too heavy to stay open. "I am going to her now. I can feel it. My time is at an end, my little brother, but yours will continue."

"You have to guide your people," I said, "like you guided me."

"There will be others to do that. Now you must listen. The Lord Ascendant froze something inside you. He left a wound that will not heal, an ice that will not thaw. It will spread."

There was truth in his words. I could still feel where he had placed each finger on my chest.

"Return to the boy in the Outlands," he continued. "The Sacred told me. Here on my last day the Sacred spoke to me at last. What a glorious thing. What a glorious thing was life."

"Everyone dies," I told him, "but only a few truly live. You said that."

His tattoos fluttered and his tunic flickered between all the colors of the Seven Steps. He gripped my hand to his chest.

"Yes, I said this, but now only one thing remains. One word. Now, love, Tully. I can see it now—see it in its glory, see him standing beside the throne. Love. Was I a faithful servant? Then it all mattered after all and where is the sting? Where is the sting? All is glory. Love. All is love. Love..."

With that, Icarus released my hand. Tabitha knelt beside us. I placed Icarus's hands on his chest. His tattoos fluttered and turned from feathers into scales. They hissed furiously. He became the tattoo artist again that I had met on the Third Step, but the snakes swirled and morphed into other forms that I did not know. Other disguises from other times. Finally they settled in a way that I knew him best—wings, feathers that looked soft and real, and those feathers rose from his skin.

One of the feathers brushed against my cheek on its way up into the bright sky above us. Then they gathered together to form the shape of a winged creature, who looked down on us from high above. The image hovered over us, then spread its wings and ascended into the sky. The arena, still packed with hundreds of thousands of Ascendant, fell to their knees. That is how the spirit of Icarus left Rathmore.

I could not mourn for him or Adèle after seeing that: I mourned for the rest of us, for our loss. The Firsters looked at me again, and I looked to my dad. Icarus had given me a mission, but first his people needed help.

Tabitha helped me to my feet, which felt steadier than I expected. My dad walked toward me from across the arena with a black staff still in his hands. He knelt beside me and tousled my hair. He wiped away tears from his eyes and then mine.

"I'm going to be okay, Dad," I said.

"You're more than okay," he said. "You always were, but you're hurt. We have to get you home."

Home. Where is that anymore?

"Somewhere else," I said. "There's something I have to do."

We left the stadium, walking around shards of melting ice, down the Steps with Tabitha supporting me, and a thousand Ascendant lining the streets in silence, this time reaching out to touch me.

Bernard and his followers met us along the way. A great number of Firsters followed him, those that had joined his peace march. He wanted to know where Adèle and Icarus were. None of us had the heart to tell him. "Go to the stadium," my dad said.

"It is what I feared," he said. "I am the last." Bernard led them on. They would need him. They had seen the dome smashed and magically repaired, and many saw an angel ascend into the sky.

Who knows what they thought about it all? I didn't care. I knew that Tabitha was at my side. We found the submarine pulled up to the shore, with Buckshot and Janice there to help us aboard.

"Boy, you look like you've been ridden hard and put away wet," said Buckshot. "Me and Carpool got this sub ship-shape. Time to rock and roll. And Tabitha!" He gave her a big bear hug.

When Buckshot went to hug me, he realized how bad things had been. Bewildered, he shook his head and said a thousand times, "I shoulda been with you, kids, I shoulda been up there…" I told him where we needed to go. He agreed. I crumpled up into a ball in the back and fell asleep. The Sacred was nowhere to be seen.

HOPE AND DISTANCE

The muffled voices of two girls reached my ears. I had fallen into such a deep sleep that my body would not respond to my requests to wake up. I gave up and listened to those two voices as they put together the pieces of the Ascendant puzzle.

"...if that's not true, then what really happened?" Tabitha asked. There was a rustling of papers.

"It says here that the Ascendant wanted to go into space with the Nameless Ones. Yeah, that's the only name I can find for the aliens. But some big fight broke out between the Ascendant and the aliens. It's not very clear but it says here, 'So, in the course of time, we had our revenge. We overthrew the Nameless Ones and took their treasures, their ships, their empire. And thence came we to establish Europa.'"

"Propaganda overdrive," said Tabitha. "You learned more about the Ascendant from those scrolls than I did in months."

"I doubt that," said Janice. "You lived with them. It's like a different knowledge."

"Like the truth," said Tabitha. "The Lord Ascendant lied to them and told them that they were victims. But they keep overcoming crazy obstacles because they're exceptional. He likes that word. Really they are exceptional in some ways. Their art, music, theater is all so amazing."

"That play was pretty cool," Sunjay said, "but you like them after all that they've done?"

"No," said Janice, "Tabitha appreciates some things about them, that's all."

I finally pulled myself out of a stupor and lurched toward the front of the cabin. Everything outside me was bruised. Everything inside felt frozen. With each movement I made, the icy hand of the Lord Ascendant scraped across my chest. I shivered, but when I saw Tabitha, I tried to look strong. She and Janice leaned over some old scraps of paper.

"Hey, Spaceboy," said Tabitha, "twelve hours of sleep don't come cheap."

"Oh, classic tabism," I said. "Please explain."

"You missed all this talk about ancient scrolls. Bernard gave them to Janice for safekeeping. They contain the true history of Rathmore. She started translating a little."

"The myth of Europa makes sense now," Janice told me. "I can't believe we didn't figure it out."

"Yeah," I said. "Trackman explained it to me."

"And," said Janice, "you missed all of Tabitha's adventures. She did some acting, but even more spying. Trackman and the Lord Ascendant trusted her, so she learned all about the Ascendant plans for world domination."

Tabitha looked at me with a hurt in her eyes. She felt terrible about what happened with Trackman, but I was starting to understand why she did it. She couldn't have helped me, so she maintained her cover.

My dad cleared his throat and we turned toward him. He was in the pilot's seat.

"First things first," he said. "We get Tully to the cave to be healed."

"Yeah, but after that—"

"We broadcast everything we know back to Earth. Between what we saw and what Tabitha knows, the Alliance can prepare for the attack. They can organize, fight back, and spread the truth."

They must have already discussed this, but it was hard to swallow all at once. We could not stop the Ascendant, but we could disrupt them. In many ways, the mission was a success. We accomplished more than we planned. At the same time, the Earth was in peril. There was momentary relief, but no celebration.

A light popped on in the submarine. We were near Typhon's lair.

When the submarine surfaced in the underwater dock, Typhon stood there with a black staff aimed at us. He looked imposing the first time I met him. Now he looked small and defenseless.

"I got this," I said. I hoisted myself out of the top of the submarine and onto the landing. He wasted no time.

"Boy thief!" he screamed. "Stealer of submarines! Breaker of laws! I'll be your justice giving!" Out of the black staff streamed an incinerator shot, but I caught it with my good hand and tossed it into the water, where it sizzled. I limped toward him. Typhon dropped the staff while everyone else gathered behind me.

"You—you—you really are him, the Red Thief, here before me standing," he said, throwing himself at my feet.

"Oh, now you believe me," I said. "Where is Jason?"

"No, take me, not him! It's not his fault having. Blame me."

"Call for him. I need his help." Typhon stalled but then whistled. Jason entered and ran toward me as if he would hug me. Then he stopped short.

"You are changed," he said. "You have been through shadow and flame."

I thought back on it. *If the shadow was my "crazy nothing moment" and the flame was the arena, then, yeah, pretty much.*

"Oh, you found her! That is good, like the Misty Man said." Jason took Tabitha's hand. There was something both ancient and youthful about him. He had the face of a boy but the wrinkles of old age around his soft purple eyes. "And did you find Icarus? Is he real and good, too?"

"He was," I said, my voice cracking. "Jason, we came back to thank you, and to ask a favor."

"I know," he said. "The Misty Man told me. The cave is this way. Just you and this girl should come. Bring your space suits, he says."

"We will be back," I said. "We won't be long."

"Take your time," said Buckshot. "I'm sure Sunjay and Janice can find something to argue about to keep us entertained."

Jason took us by the hand and escorted us through the maze of passages to his bedroom. His action figures were lined up in neat rows on his shelf. The last time I was there felt like a lifetime ago.

On one wall was the tube that led to the underwater harbor. On the other wall there was a new tube.

"This was a present from the Misty Man," he said. "He told me you could slide down with the green-eyed girl. You'll find what you need."

"You are sweet," said Tabitha. "You remind me of my little brothers back home."

"The Misty Man was right," said Jason. "You are pretty like my mom was."

If I can, I'm taking this little guy back to Earth, I thought. I picked up his favorite action figure.

"Will you come play with me when you are done?" he asked me.

"It is hard to say," I told Jason, "but will you do me a favor? Show this to my big friend Buckshot. Tell him that you like cowboys. Maybe you can play with him while we are gone."

Jason smiled and pointed toward the tube. Tabitha snapped on her helmet and went first. I followed her. The tube twisted side to side as we descended, the air getting colder for a while, but then as we approached the end, warm and humid. A familiar shade of red.

I landed on a grassy floor covered in red mist and surrounded by exotic fruit trees. No need for helmets here. The tropical odor made me dizzy. We were on an island, and around us was an underwater lake with powder-blue water.

My arm throbbed with pain from the landing, and Tabitha helped me to my feet.

"It's the garden of the Sacred," I said. "I thought this place only existed in my dreams."

"Stars, strange universe, you have dire long sleeves," said Tabitha. I turned toward her and laughed for the first time in days. "Oh, you never get my Tabisms, do you? The universe always has something weird and wacky waiting up its sleeve—"

"—and it's got really long sleeves. I get it."

"Finally," she said, staring into me with her deep green eyes. I thought she was talking about her Tabism, but she wasn't. "Finally. Finally. Finally."

Out of her pocket she took her end of the mood scarf. I did the same. She took the two pieces of fabric in her hands and started to tie a knot between them. Before she could finish, I reached toward the two ends. The scarf shimmered in her hands for a moment and then became whole, like it had never been ripped in half.

Tabitha wrapped the scarf around her neck and it glowed a deep green. The effect on her eyes, seeing her with the scarf again, melted my troubles away.

"This is the new old times," she told me. "Remember how we used to play *Cave-In!* at your house?"

I nodded.

"Now we are living it, but the levels are a lot harder than I expected."

"And the monsters are a lot worse," I said.

"That's okay," she said. "You were always best with the controller. I've got dire good instincts. We'll be fine."

We sat down in the lush green grass with our backs against a tree holding hands. Small purple flowers fell around us. Across the lake, an underwater archway pulsed with red light. It looked like a tunnel to another cave.

"I think that's for you," she said.

"How do you know?"

"Because you always get the obvious signs," she said.

She interlaced her fingers through mine. I wanted to stay in the garden with her for hours and talk about video games and theater and whatever other silly things we could dream up, but dreams and visions were leading me elsewhere. The tunnel pulsated with red light, calling me toward itself and away from Tabitha. I wasn't ready yet.

"What are you going to do when we get back?" I asked her.

"We worked it out while you slept," she said. "The Ascendant need a voice. They chose me. So I'll go to them and explain what happened— that you kidnapped me. Then I will 'escape' from your dad. I can keep playing the spy. It's what I've been doing this whole time."

"I don't like that idea," I said.

"Me neither," she said, crinkling her nose. "I'd rather hang out with you than with the Ascendant, but it's the right role for me. Actress turned spy."

"You're the best actress turned spy that I know."

"Oscar worthy," she said.

"So the Ascendant still think you are theirs. For a while I thought you were theirs, too. But I'm worried about something."

"What?"

"That they changed you, and they'll change you more."

It had concerned me ever since Second Contact. Finally it slipped out. Tabitha stiffened a bit, then let out a sigh.

"Me, too," she said. "They did change me. They treated me like a queen. They put me on stage and made me a star. A billion people know my name now. But what good is that? Every night I went back to that tower alone. I lived through a hundred dark nights there, Tully. I slept on the balcony and watched the sky with tears in my eyes. I looked for a sign that I wasn't alone, but nothing and nobody came. I gave up hope for a while. Finally hope came back for me. Whatever happens, I'm never giving up hope again."

I knew exactly what she meant. We had both lost hope, but hope has a way of finding you if you keep looking for it. Hope was my one word, and it was Tabitha's, too.

I can't tell you how long we sat there looking at each other. I memorized every line of her face, every freckle, every fleck in her perfect green eyes. We kissed. Her fingers traced the lightning scars on the backs of my hands. Finally, the cave pulsed with red light again, and she gave me a playful shove.

"Don't worry," she said, grabbing a piece of fruit from a tree. "I'll wait."

In the end I snapped on my helmet, dove into the water, and swam toward the tunnel, leaving behind my friends, my family, the battle for Earth, and Tabitha. As I swam, the water growing brighter and warmer by the second, I remembered something important—my mom gave me my one word. She started this battle against the Ascendant by herself, and she hoped that I would finish it. Hope. In the coming years, I would learn just how far that one word would take me away from home.

Epilogue: Adrift

Red, red, red, red, red. The water warmed my skin, but I could still feel the Lord Ascendant's icy fingers on my chest. His words rumbled in my ears. *I have a gift for you.* What did he mean?

The farther I swam into the underwater tunnel, the more I drifted into a vision. I saw the great black Ascendant fleet arriving at the Earth; saw the ships, one by one, descending upon the capitols of the world.

My dad was right, I thought. *They will rule.*

I saw Sunjay and my dad fighting black staffs in a jungle, Trackman at the Statue of Liberty, Tabitha in a news studio, Queen Envy dressed in white, and then I searched for myself. I was nowhere to be found.

What will become of me? I asked.

"What will you make of yourself?" a voice answered.

Am I going to make it home?

"One must leave before one may truly return."

The visions whirled in circles. The same images and words, swirling backwards and forwards, in high speed and slow. Finally, they stopped.

The back of my helmet bumped against something and I realized that I had been drifting. Another cave. There was a small island in the middle, and on it sat a familiar figure. The Misty Man, Jason had called him. I knew no better name.

"Is all of that stuff going to happen?" My voice sounded gruff, like I had not spoken in days. I took off my helmet and shook the hair out of my eyes. What a headache.

"Who says it has not already come to pass?" he asked me.

Oh, boy, riddles are coming. I shook my head. Then my chest went cold again. I lost my breath and went down on one knee.

"I wish that Icarus could have healed you," the Misty Man said, "but deep wounds take time. His time had passed."

"Then let's get started," I said. "I have to make it back to Earth."

"Back? There is no back, Tully. Only forward."

I didn't like the sound of that. I didn't want a speech. I wanted him to heal me so I could get...back. I turned around and looked at the underwater tunnel. It was still there, but I could feel something different. I couldn't put a finger on it.

"Fix me," I said. "Tabitha's waiting."

"Oh, she waited," he said. "She waited an hour, a day, but you did not return."

"What are you talking about?"

"Time," he said. "That's the way of it, Tully. Always forward, never back."

"Stop speaking in riddles," I said, turning toward the tunnel. "I'd rather live with this icy feeling than listen to this."

"You'll die if you do," he said. "You hear but you do not understand. These are not riddles. You drifted through the water for days before you reached me. Tully, she left. Now she has work to do, and so do you and I."

"What work?"

"Come and see," he said, and the mist fell away to reveal his true form.

...Thus ends *The Rathmore Chaos,* but a final act remains...

✷✷✷

Dear Earther,

    This story will continue, though it is hard to say exactly when or how. We can be sure of a few things: Tabitha must return to the Ascendant. Janice must decipher the true history of this "alien" race. Someone must fight for freedom on Earth. And, of course, Little Bacon must define things. He wrote a glossary for you on the next page, if you have not read it.

    But what about Tully, who went into space to rescue a friend though he himself did not return? In time we will see where hope takes him, somewhere far beyond the Outlands. Until you meet him again, may the Universe rise up to meet you.

    Sincerely,

    -A

Little Bacon's Glossary of Terms

Atlantis – a mythological city that was destroyed by a terrible upheaval, maybe a volcano or a tsunami.

Bioluminescence – literally, "life light"; a creature capable of producing light. These exist on Earth as well as Europa.

Cave-in! - Tully's favorite video game; requires the player to escape a system of caves inhabited by monsters. The main character has only a portal gun, which can create portals between two places. You see why he likes it so much?

Chaos – disorder, mayhem, upheaval, disarray, dire confusion. From the Greek: "vast chasm, void."

Chosen of the Sacred – a mythological character of the Ascendant; mentioned briefly here; one who will reclaim the Earth for the Ascendant.

Constant acceleration – a proposed method for traveling in the solar system; a ship with such a drive will accelerate constantly until the halfway point in its trip, at which point it will decelerate. No such technology exists yet, because no one has invented an engine that can accelerate like that.

Black staff – an Ascendant weapon that has three known settings:
STUN – this freezes an opponent for several minutes or possibly hours.
TOSS – catch, toss, or throw any object or opponent.
INCINERATE – burn and turn to dust.

Europa (moon) – is the sixth-closest moon of the planet Jupiter, and the smallest of its four Galilean satellites, but still the sixth-largest moon in the Solar System. Europa was discovered in 1610 by Galileo Galilei. Progressively better observations of Europa have occurred over the centuries by Earth-bound telescopes, and by space probe flybys starting in the 1970s. Europa has more water than Earth, and it is one of the most promising places to look for life in the solar system. There is a mission planned to explore Europa in the 2020's or 2030's.

Europa (myth) – a historically accurate retelling appears in this book, although the Ascendant have an extended version that speaks of the Chosen of the Sacred.

Holoclassing – method of distance learning; a student may wear holo-glasses that project an image of him/her into the classroom, thus giving both student and teacher the illusion of being in the same room rather than many miles away.

Hypertube – a series of underground tunnels that use pods to shoot people between cities, under and over mountain and oceans, at 700 miles per hour.

Jupiter – king of planets; a gas giant with enormous gravity; its gravity pulls on Europa so hard that it causes enormous friction on the planet, which produces heat, which produces geysers like the ones that Tully encounters.

Ketea Maximus – great sea beast; slain by Tully before he arrives upon at the Rathmore Chaos.

Livewall – a large interactive television, like an oversized tablet, that was used for many years until it was replaced by holographic technologies; there is one in Tully's house as well as the bar at the general store in Anchorage, Alaska.

Mix tape – an audiotape of recorded songs; often used as a gift between friends or potential love interests; Sunjay makes a mix tape for Lady Gaga.

Newel – the middle post in a spiral staircase; the Grand Newel is an example, although it is roughly two miles high.

Outlander – a citizen of Europa who lives outside the Rathmore Chaos; an agricultural style of life.

The Sacred / the Harper Device – a mysterious object capable of producing dreams, giving humans powers, possibly telling the future; how can something with so many definitions truly be defined?

Turbofizz – a popular carbonated beverage with twice the caffeine of coffee. It can be served hot or cold. Simply turn a dial on the can to select the desired temperature. The drink comes out blue if it's cold or brown if it's hot. TurboFizz causes cancer and heart palpitations in laboratory animals. Try a bottle today.

Upthruster – about the size of a surfboard, a hoverboard that can take its rider forty feet high; top speed is forty miles an hour; invented by Dr. Chet Chan, Janice Chan's uncle.

Character List

IN POWER ON EUROPA
The LORD ASCENDANT, ruler of The Ascendant, self-proclaimed Chosen of the Sacred; GALLANT TRACKMAN, former Space Alliance employee and Ascendant Archspy; AKAKIOS, commander of the black staffs on the Rathmore Chaos; BLACK STAFFS, the name given to the warriors under the Lord Ascendant's command; GOLIATH, a black staff of great strength and size.

THE FRIENDS OF THE ENCOUNTERED
The ENCOUNTERED, survivors of the Sixth Step, those who have touched the Sacred and survived; ICARUS; the commander of the Encountered and leader of a peaceful rebellion; ADELE, his second in command and wife; BERNARD, the last of the Encountered, the protector of Europa; STEPHEN, who died for speaking against the Lord Ascendant.

ON EARTH
DR. NILES CHAKRAVORTY, father of SUNJAY, famed Space Alliance engineer and researcher; QUEEN ENVY, famous diva; most recent pop star to record music in space; AUNT SELMA – sister to

STELLA HARPER, COMMANDER MIKE HARPER'S WIFE; survivalist, aunt to TULLY.

OTHER CHARACTERS, WHOSE IMPORTANCE MAY ONE DAY BE FULLY KNOWN

TYPHON – a fisherman, father of JASON. Their names may be familiar to those who know Greek mythology.

FIRSTERS, SECONDERS, ET AL. – how the citizens of Rathmore are known based on where they were born.

THE MISTY MAN – the embodiment of the Sacred; named by JASON, the fisherman's son; having only been seen by TULLY and JASON.

EKPHRASIS – a tattoo artist who hides secrets beneath his tattoos of writhing snakes.

ASSASSIN SIGMA – a shadow figure tasked with killing Tully Harper.

AWAY TEAM BETA – an elite team of black staffs sent to capture Tully on Earth.

TULLY HARPER – aka The Red Thief; friend of the Harper Device.

THE NAMELESS ONES – aliens; their history was long ago erased by the Ascendant.

AFTERWORD

If anything here seems novel or meaningful, I must thank the Creator God Whose wisdom shaped the Heavens and the Earth. I don't pretend to understand His purposes, but each day I look at His craftsmanship and marvel.

ABOUT THE AUTHOR

Adam Holt makes his home in Space City (Houston, Texas). He left a perfectly good teaching job to write young adult fiction. He enjoys traveling, surfing, reading, and the crunchy boom of a rocket launch. He coaches volleyball in his spare time.

Adam loves to talk to fans about writing, publishing, life, and the universe in general. Find him on instagram, facebook, twitter or in a local coffee shop or book store.

LOCAL AUTHOR

Holt, Adam.
The Rathmore chaos/
Central LOCAL_AUTH
08/15

.

Made in the USA
San Bernardino, CA
28 March 2015